THE ARBOR HOUSE CELEBRITY BOOK OF HORROR STORIES

OTHER BOOKS EDITED BY MARTIN H. GREENBERG AND CHARLES G. WAUGH

The Seven Deadly Sins of Science Fiction
(with Isaac Asimov)

Tantalizing Locked Room Mysteries
(with Isaac Asimov)

Fantastic Creatures
(with Isaac Asimov)

Mysterious Visions
(with Joseph Olander)

THE ARBOR HOUSE CELEBRITY BOOK OF HORROR STORIES

Edited by Charles G. Waugh
and Martin H. Greenberg

ARBOR HOUSE
New York

Library of Congress Catalog Card Number: 81-71667

ISBN: 0-87795-400-3

Hardcover edition: 0-87795-373-2

Manufactured in the United States of America

10 9 8 7 6 5 4 3 2 1

This book is printed on acid free paper. The paper in this book meets the guidelines for permanence and durability of the Committee on Production Guidelines for Book Longevity of the Council on Library Resources.

Permissions

The following pages constitute an extension of the copyright page.

CONTENTS

PREFACE

The organizational concept of this book is a simple one. We asked a number of notable people to choose the most frightening story they had ever read—actually, we asked them to choose several stories because we were concerned with three potential problems: *quality,* since one person's fright can sometimes be another's belly laugh (fortunately, the selections were, we believe, of very high quality, so this worry proved unfounded) *duplication,* which as you can see from reading the notes accompanying the stories, did indeed occur; and *length,* which forced us to select carefully, since some of the choices were short novels of over one hundred pages. We specifically asked our contributors *not* to select stories that scared the wits out of them when they were very young unless they felt certain that the story would still work for an adult readership. Again, we think they did a fine job.

After all, one of your editors has still not gotten over the death of Bambi's mother!

The basis for inviting contributors was also a simple one: we chose people who were famous for their contributions to horror fiction and/or film, like Stephen King, Ray Bradbury and Vincent Price; or people who we knew to be familar with this literature, such as Walker Percy and Joyce Carol Oates. We also asked them to write brief notes on their selections, and these are included along with their comments on favorite stories *not* in this volume.

The field of horror and the supernatural has a long and noble history, and is presently going through a tremendous revival in this country and elsewhere, although there is a considerable amount of *schlock* being produced these days, particularly for the screen. We are happy with the results of the book you are holding, and trust that our selectors and ourselves have brought a number of horrific gems to your attention.

ISAAC ASIMOV

When I was a lad, back in medieval times, I found myself fearfully attracted to stories that scared me. Don't ask me why—I hate being scared, but I didn't mind, as long as I knew in my heart that I was safe.

And then I found a book of ghost stories by M. R. James. He lived from 1862 to 1936, was a British scholar who had administrative posts at Eton and Cambridge, wrote scholarly books on the Bible and on antiquarian subjects and (to amuse himself, I suppose) wrote ghost stories, which were originally published in the first decade of this century.

He wrote in a scholarly fashion, and with a consummately realistic style that built up the mood slowly, from a perfect naturalism to the beginnings of unease to a gradual deepening mood of fear and suspense until you were groveling in terror (at least I was.)

And of all his stories, the one that worked best with me and clung to me clammily for years was "Oh, Whistle, and I'll Come to You, My Lad." There's no gore in the story, no violence, no purple prose, just the skillful and gradual evocation of fear. It should be read alone in a house at night, by the light of a fireplace or candle that casts shifting shadows. Failing that, in these weak piping times of steady light, an ordinary electric light will have to do.

OH, WHISTLE, AND I'LL COME TO YOU, MY LAD

M. R. JAMES

"I suppose you will be getting away pretty soon, now full term is over, professor," said a person not in the story to the professor of ontography, soon after they had sat down next to each other at a feast in the hospitable hall of St. James's College.

The professor was young, neat, and precise in speech.

"Yes," he said; "my friends have been making me take up golf this term, and I mean to go to the east coast—in point of fact to Burnstow—(I daresay you know it) for a week or ten days, to improve my game. I hope to get off tomorrow."

"Oh, Parkins," said his neighbor on the other side, "if you are going to Burnstow, I wish you would look at the site of the Templars' preceptory, and let me know if you think it would be any good to have a dig there in the summer."

It was, as you might suppose, a person of antiquarian pursuits who said this, but, since he merely appears in this prologue, there is no need to give his entitlements.

"Certainly," said Parkins, the professor: "if you will describe to me whereabouts the site is, I will do my best to give you an idea of the lie of the land when I get back; or I could write to you about it, if you would tell me where you are likely to be."

"Don't trouble to do that, thanks. It's only that I'm thinking of taking my family in that direction in the Long, and it occurred to me that, as very few of the English preceptories have ever been properly planned, I might have an opportunity of doing something useful on off-days."

The professor rather sniffed at the idea that planning out a preceptory could be described as useful. His neighbor continued: "The site—I doubt if there is anything showing above ground—must be down quite close to the beach now. The sea has encroached tremendously, as you know, all along that bit of coast. I should think, from the map, that it must be about three-quarters of a mile from the Globe Inn, at the north end of the town. Where are you going to stay?"

"Well, *at* the Globe Inn, as a matter of fact," said Parkins; "I have engaged a room there. I couldn't get in anywhere else; most of the lodging houses are shut up in winter, it seems; and, as it is, they tell me that the only room of any size I can have is really a double-bedded one, and that they haven't a corner in which to store the other bed, and so on. But I must have a fairly large room, for I am taking some books down, and mean to do a bit of work; and though I don't quite fancy having an empty bed —not to speak of two—in what I may call for the time being my study, I suppose I can manage to rough it for the short time I shall be there."

"Do you call having an extra bed in your room roughing it, Parkins?" said a bluff person opposite. "Look here, I shall come down and occupy it for a bit; it'll be company for you."

The professor quivered, but managed to laugh in a courteous manner.

"By all means, Rogers; there's nothing I should like better. But I'm afraid you would find it rather dull; you don't play golf, do you?"

"No, thank heaven!" said rude Mr. Rogers.

"Well, you see, when I'm not writing I shall most likely be out on the links, and that, as I say, would be rather dull for you, I'm afraid."

"Oh, I don't know! There's certain to be somebody I know in the place; but, of course, if you don't want me, speak the word, Parkins; I shan't be offended. Truth, as you always tell us, is never offensive."

Parkins was, indeed, scrupulously polite and strictly truthful. It is to be feared that Mr. Rogers sometimes practiced upon his knowledge of these characteristics. In Parkins's breast there was a conflict now raging, which for a moment or two did not allow him to answer. That interval being over, he said: "Well, if you want the exact truth, Rogers, I was considering whether the room I speak of would really be large enough to accommodate us both comfortably; and also whether (mind, I shouldn't have said this if you hadn't pressed me) you would not constitute something in the nature of a hindrance to my work."

Rogers laughed loudly.

"Well done, Parkins!" he said. "It's all right, I promise not to interrupt your work; don't you disturb yourself about that. No, I won't come if you don't want me; but I thought I should do so nicely to keep the ghosts off." Here he might have been seen to wink and to nudge his next neighbor. Parkins might also have been seen to become pink. "I beg pardon, Parkins," Rogers continued; "I oughtn't to have said that. I forgot you didn't like levity on these topics."

"Well," Parkins said, "as you have mentioned the matter, I freely own that I do *not* like careless talk about what you call ghosts. A man in my position," he went on, raising his voice a little, "cannot, I find, be too careful about appearing to sanction the current beliefs on such subjects. As you know, Rogers, or as you ought to know; for I think I have never concealed my views—"

"No, you certainly have not, old man," put in Rogers sotto voce.

"—I hold that any semblance, any appearance of concession to the view that such things might exist is equivalent to a renunciation of all that I hold most sacred. But I'm afraid I have not succeeded in securing your attention."

"Your *undivided* attention, was what Dr. Blimber actually *said,*" Rogers interrupted, with every appearance of an earnest desire for accuracy. "But I beg your pardon, Parkins: I'm stopping you."

"No, not at all," said Parkins. "I don't remember Blimber; perhaps he was before my time. But I needn't go on. I'm sure you know what I mean."

"Yes, yes," said Rogers, rather hastily—"just so. We'll go into it fully at Burnstow, or somewhere."

In repeating the above dialogue I have tried to give the impression which it made on me, that Parkins was something of an old woman—rather henlike, perhaps, in his little ways; totally destitute, alas! of the sense of humor, but at the same time dauntless and sincere in his convictions, and a man deserving of the greatest respect. Whether or not the reader has gathered so much, that was the character which Parkins had.

On the following day Parkins did, as he had hoped, succeed in getting away from his college, and in arriving at Burnstow. He was made welcome at the Globe Inn, was safely installed in the large double-bedded room of which we have heard, and was able before retiring to rest to arrange his materials for work in apple-pie order upon a commodious table which occupied the outer end of the room, and was surrounded on three sides by windows looking out seaward; that is to say, the central window looked straight out to sea, and those on the left and right commanded prospects along the shore to the north and south respectively. On the south you saw the village of Burnstow. On the north no houses were to be seen, but only the beach and the low cliff backing it. Immediately in front was a strip —not considerable—of rough grass, dotted with old anchors, capstans and so forth; then a broad path; then the beach. Whatever may have been the original distance between the Globe Inn and the sea, not more than sixty yards now separated them.

The rest of the population of the inn was, of course, a golfing one, and included few elements that call for a special description. The most conspicuous figure was, perhaps, that of an *ancien militaire,* secretary of a London club, and possessed of a voice of incredible strength, and of views of a pronouncedly Protestant type. These were apt to find utterance after his attendance upon the ministrations of the vicar, an estimable man with inclinations towards a picturesque ritual, which he gallantly kept down as far as he could out of deference to East Anglian tradition.

Professor Parkins, one of whose principal characteristics was pluck, spent the greater part of the day following his arrival at Burnstow in what he had called improving his game, in company with this Colonel Wilson: and during the afternoon—whether the process of improvement were to blame or not, I am not sure—the colonel's demeanor assumed a coloring so lurid that even Parkins jibbed at the thought of walking home with him from the links. He determined, after a short and furtive look at that bristling mustache and those incarnadined features, that it would be wiser to allow the influences of tea and tobacco to do what they could with the colonel before the dinner hour should render a meeting inevitable.

"I might walk home tonight along the beach," he reflected—"yes, and take a look—there will be light enough for that—at the ruins of which Disney was talking. I don't exactly know where they are, by the way; but I expect I can hardly help stumbling on them."

This he accomplished, I may say, in the most literal sense, for in picking his way from the links to the shingle beach his foot caught, partly in a gorse root and partly in a biggish stone, and over he went. When he got up and surveyed his surroundings, he found himself in a patch of somewhat broken ground covered with small depressions and mounds. These latter, when he came to examine them, proved to be simply masses of flints embedded in mortar and grown over with turf. He must, he quite rightly concluded, be on the site of the preceptory he had promised to look at. It seemed not unlikely to reward the spade of the explorer; enough of the foundations was probably left at no great depth to throw a good deal of light on the general plan. He remembered vaguely that the Templars, to whom this site had belonged, were in the habit of building round churches, and he thought a particular series of the humps or mounds near him did appear to be arranged in something of a circular form. Few people can resist the temptation to try a little amateur research in a department quite outside their own, if only for the satisfaction of showing how successful they would have been had they only taken it up seriously. Our professor, however, if he felt something of this mean desire, was also truly anxious to oblige Mr. Disney. So he paced with care the circular area he had noticed, and wrote down its rough dimensions in his pocketbook. Then he proceeded to examine an oblong eminence which lay east of the center of the circle, and seemed to his thinking likely to be the base of a platform or altar. At one end of it, the northern, a patch of the turf was gone—removed by some boy or other creature *ferae naturae.* It might, he thought, be as well to probe the soil here for evidences of masonry, and he took out his knife and began scraping away the earth. And now followed another little discovery: a portion of soil fell inward as he scraped, and disclosed a small cavity. He lighted one match after another to help him to see of what nature the hole was, but the wind was too strong for them all. By tapping and scratching the sides with his knife, however, he was able to make out that it must be an artificial hole in masonry. It was rectangular, and the sides, top and bottom, if not actually plastered, were smooth and regular. Of course it was empty. No! As he withdrew the knife he heard a metallic clink, and when he introduced his hand it met with a cylindrical object lying on the floor of the hole. Naturally enough, he picked it up, and when he brought it into the light, now fast fading, he could see that it, too, was of man's making—a metal tube about four inches long, and evidently of some considerable age.

By the time Parkins had made sure that there was nothing else in this odd receptacle, it was too late and too dark for him to think of undertaking any further search. What he had done had proved so unexpectedly interesting that he determined to sacrifice a little more of the daylight on the morrow to archaeology. The object which he now had safe in his pocket was bound to be of some slight value at least, he felt sure.

Bleak and solemn was the view on which he took a last look before starting homeward. A faint yellow light in the west showed the links, on which a few figures moving towards the clubhouse were still visible, the squat martello tower, the lights of Aldsey village, the pale ribbon of sands intersected at intervals by black wooden groinings, the dim and murmuring sea. The wind was bitter from the north, but was at his back when he set out for the Globe. He quickly rattled and clashed through the shingle and gained the sand, upon which, but for the groinings which had to be got over every few yards, the going was both good and quiet. One last look behind, to measure the distance he had made since leaving the ruined Templars' church, showed him a prospect of company on his walk, in the shape of a rather indistinct personage, who seemed to be making great efforts to catch up with him, but made little, if any, progress. I mean that there was an appearance of running about his movements, but that the distance between him and Parkins did not seem materially to lessen. So, at least, Parkins thought, and decided that he almost certainly did not know him, and that it would be absurd to wait until he came up. For all that, company, he began to think, would really be very welcome on that lonely shore, if only you could choose your companion. In his unenlightened days he had read of meetings in such places which even now would hardly bear thinking of. He went on thinking of them, however, until he reached home, and particularly of one which catches most people's fancy at some time of their childhood. "Now I saw in my dream that Christian had gone but a very little way when he saw a foul fiend coming over the field to meet him." "What should I do now," he thought, "if I looked back and caught sight of a black figure sharply defined against the yellow sky, and saw that it had horns and wings? I wonder whether I should stand or run for it. Luckily, the gentleman behind is not of that kind, and he seems to be about as far off now as when I saw him first. Well, at this rate, he won't get his dinner as soon as I shall; and, dear me! it's within a quarter of an hour of the time now. I must run!"

Parkins had, in fact, very little time for dressing. When he met the colonel at dinner, peace—or as much of her as that gentleman could manage—reigned once more in the military bosom; nor was she put to flight in the hours of bridge that followed dinner, for Parkins was a more than respectable player. When, therefore, he retired towards twelve o'clock, he felt that he had spent his evening in quite a satisfactory way, and that, even for so long as a fortnight or three weeks, life at the Globe would be supportable under similar conditions—"especially," thought he, "if I go on improving my game."

As he went along the passages he met the boots of the Globe, who stopped and said: "Beg your pardon, sir, but as I was a-brushing your coat just now there was something fell out of the pocket. I put it on your chest of drawers, sir, in your room, sir—a piece of a pipe or something of that, sir. Thank you, sir. You'll find it on your chest of drawers, sir—yes, sir. Good night, sir."

The speech served to remind Parkins of his little discovery of that afternoon. It was with some considerable curiosity that he turned it over by the light of his candles. It was of bronze, he now saw, and was shaped very much after the manner of the modern dog whistle; in fact it was—yes, certainly it was—actually no more nor less than a whistle. He put it to his lips, but it was quite full of a fine, caked-up sand or earth, which would not yield to knocking, but must be loosened with a knife. Tidy as ever in his habits, Parkins cleared out the earth onto a piece of paper, and took the latter to the window to empty it out. The night was clear and bright, as he saw when he had opened the casement, and he stopped for an instant to look at the sea and not a belated wanderer stationed on the shore in front of the inn. Then he shut the window, a little surprised at the late hours people kept at Burnstow, and took his whistle to the light again. Why, surely there were marks on it, and not merely marks, but letters! A very little rubbing rendered the deeply cut inscription quite legible, but the professor had to confess, after some earnest thought, that the meaning of it was as obscure to him as the writing on the wall to Belshazzar. There were legends both on the front and on the back of the whistle. The one read thus:

FLA

FUR BIS

FLE

The other:

QUIS EST ISTE QUI VENIT

"I ought to be able to make it out," he thought; "but I suppose I am a little rusty in my Latin. When I come to think of it, I don't believe I even know the word for a whistle. The long one does seem simple enough. It ought to mean: Who is this who is coming? Well the best way to find out is evidently to whistle for him."

He blew tentatively and stopped suddenly, startled and yet pleased at the note he had elicited. It had a quality of infinite distance in it, and, soft as it was, he somehow felt it must be audible for miles round. It was a sound, too, that seemed to have the power (which many scents possess) of forming pictures in the brain. He saw quite clearly for a moment a vision of a wide, dark expanse at night, with a fresh wind blowing, and in the midst a lonely figure—how employed, he could not tell. Perhaps he would have seen more had not the picture been broken by the sudden surge of a gust of wind against his casement, so sudden that it made him look up, just in time to see the white glint of a seabird's wing somewhere outside the dark panes.

The sound of the whistle had so fascinated him that he could not help trying it once more, this time more boldly. The note was little, if at all, louder than before, and repetition broke the illusion—no picture followed, as he had half-hoped it might. "But what is this? Goodness! what force the wind can get up in a few minutes! What a tremendous gust! There! I knew that window fastening was no use! Ah! I thought so—both candles out. It is enough to tear the room to pieces."

The first thing was to get the window shut. While you might count twenty, Parkins was struggling with the small casement and felt almost as if he were pushing back a sturdy burglar, so strong was the pressure. It slackened all at once, and the window banged to and latched itself. Now to relight the candles and see what damage, if any, had been done. No, nothing seemed amiss; no glass even was broken in the casement. But the noise had evidently roused at least one member of the household: the colonel was to be heard stumping in his stockinged feet on the floor above, and growling.

Quickly as it had risen, the wind did not fall at once. On it went, moaning and rushing past the house, at times rising to a cry so desolate that, as Parkins disinterestedly said, it might have made fanciful people feel quite uncomfortable; even the unimaginative, he thought after a quarter of an hour, might be happier without it.

Whether it was the wind, or the excitement of golf or of the researches in the preceptory that kept Parkins awake, he was not sure. Awake he remained, in any case, long enough to fancy (as I am afraid I often do myself under such conditions) that he was the victim of all manner of fatal disorders: he would lie counting the beats of his heart, convinced that it was going to stop work every moment, and would entertain grave suspicions of his lungs, brain, liver, etc.—suspicions which he was sure would be dispelled by the return of daylight, but which until then refused to be put aside. He found a little vicarious comfort in the idea that someone else was in the same boat. A near neighbor (in the darkness it was not easy to tell his direction) was tossing and rustling in his bed, too.

The next stage was that Parkins shut his eyes and determined to give sleep every chance. Here again overexcitement asserted itself in another form—that of making pictures. *Experto crede,* pictures do come to the closed eyes of one trying to sleep, and are often so little to his taste that he must open his eyes and disperse them.

Parkins's experience on this occasion was a very distressing one. He found that the picture which presented itself to him was continuous. When he opened his eyes, of course, it went; but when he shut them once more it framed itself afresh, and acted itself out again, neither quicker nor slower than before. What he saw was this: a long stretch of shore—shingle-edged by sand, and intersected at short intervals with black groins running down to the water—a scene, in fact, so like that of his afternoon's walk that, in the absence of any landmark, it could not be distinguished therefrom. The light was obscure, conveying an impression of gathering storm, late winter evening and slight cold rain. On this bleak stage at first no actor was visible. Then, in the distance, a bobbing black object appeared; a moment more, and it was a man running, jumping, clambering over the groins, and every few seconds looking eagerly back. The nearer he came the more obvious it was that he was not only anxious, but even terribly frightened, though his face was not to be distinguished. He was, moreover, almost at the end of his strength. On he came; each successive obstacle seemed to cause him more difficulty than the last. "Will he get over this next one?" thought Parkins; "it seems a little higher than the others." Yes; half-climbing, half-throwing himself, he did get over, and fell all in a heap on the other side (the side nearest to the spectator). There, as if really unable to get up again, he remained crouching under the groin, looking up in an attitude of painful anxiety.

So far no cause whatever for the fear of the runner had been shown; but now there began to be seen, far up the shore, a little flicker of something light colored moving to and fro with great swiftness and irregularity. Rapidly growing larger, it, too, declared itself as a figure in pale, fluttering draperies, ill defined. There was something about its motion which made Parkins very unwilling to see it at close quarters. It would stop, raise arms, bow itself toward the sand, then run stooping across the beach to the water's edge and back again; and then, rising upright, once more continue its course forward at a speed that was startling and terrifying. The moment came when the pursuer was hovering about from left to right only a few yards beyond the groin where the runner lay in hiding. After two or three ineffectual castings hither and thither it came to a stop, stood upright, with arms raised high, and then darted straight forward toward the groin.

It was at this point that Parkins always failed in his resolution to keep his eyes shut. With many misgivings as to incipient failure of eyesight, overworked brain, excessive smoking and so on, he finally resigned himself to light his candle, get out a book and pass the night waking, rather than be tormented by this persistent panorama, which he saw clearly enough could only be a morbid reflection of his walk and his thoughts on that very day.

The scraping of the match on box and the glare of light must have startled some creatures of the night—rats or what not—which he heard scurry across the floor from the side of his bed with much rustling. Dear, dear! the match is out! Fool that it is! But the second one burned better, and a candle and book were duly procured, over which Parkins pored till sleep of a wholesome kind came upon him, and that in no long space. For about the first time in his orderly and prudent life he forgot to blow out the candle, and when he was called next morning at eight there was still a flicker in the socket and a sad mess of guttered grease on the top of the little table.

After breakfast he was in his room, putting the finishing touches to his golfing costume—fortune had again allotted the colonel to him for a partner—when one of the maids came in.

"Oh, if you please," she said, "would you like any extra blankets on your bed, sir?"

"Ah! thank you," said Parkins. "Yes, I think I should like one. It seems likely to turn rather colder."

In a very short time the maid was back with the blanket.

"Which bed should I put it on, sir?" she asked.

"What? Why, that one—the one I slept in last night," he said, pointing to it.

"Oh yes! I beg your pardon, sir, but you seemed to have tried both of 'em; leastways, we had to make 'em both up this morning."

"Really? How very absurd!" said Parkins. "I certainly never touched the other, except to lay some things on it. Did it actually seem to have been slept in?"

"Oh yés, sir!" said the maid. "Why, all the things was crumpled and throwed about all ways, if you'll excuse me, sir—quite as if anyone 'adn't passed but a very poor night, sir."

"Dear me," said Parkins. "Well, I may have disordered it more than I thought when I unpacked my things. I'm very sorry to have given you the extra trouble, I'm sure. I expect a friend of mine soon, by the way—a gentleman from Cambridge—to come and occupy it for a night or two. That will be all right, I suppose, won't it?"

"Oh yes, to be sure, sir. Thank you, sir. It's no trouble, sir, I'm sure," said the maid, and departed to giggle with her colleagues.

Parkins set forth, with a stern determination to improve his game.

I am glad to be able to report that he succeeded so far in this enterprise that the colonel, who had been rather repining at the prospect of a second day's play in his company, became quite chatty as the morning advanced; and his voice boomed out over the flats, as certain also of our own minor poets have said, "like some great bourdon in a minster tower."

"Extraordinary wind, that, we had last night," he said. "In my old home we should have said someone had been whistling for it."

"Should you, indeed!" said Parkins. "Is there a superstition of that kind still current in your part of the country?"

"I don't know about superstition," said the colonel. "They believe in it all over Denmark and Norway, as well as on the Yorkshire coast; and my experience is, mind you, that there's generally something at the bottom of what these countryfolk hold to, and have held to for generations. But it's your drive" (or whatever it might have been: the golfing reader will have to imagine appropriate digressions at the proper intervals).

When conversation was resumed, Parkins said, with a slight hesitancy: "Apropos of what you were saying just now, colonel, I think I ought to tell you that my own views on such subjects are very strong. I am, in fact, a convinced disbeliever in what is called the supernatural."

"What!" said the colonel, "do you mean to tell me you don't believe in second sight, or ghosts or anything of that kind?"

"In nothing whatever of that kind," returned Parkins firmly.

"Well," said the colonel, "but it appears to me at that rate, sir, that you must be little better than a Sadducee."

Parkins was on the point of answering that, in his opinion, the Sadducees were the most sensible persons he had ever read of in the Old Testament; but, feeling some doubt as to whether such mention of them was to be found in that work, he preferred to laugh the accusation off.

"Perhaps I am," he said; "but—Here, give me my cleek, boy!—Excuse me one moment, colonel." A short interval. "Now, as to whistling for the wind, let me give you my theory about it. The laws which govern winds are really not at all perfectly known—to fisherfolk and such, of course, not known at all. A man or woman of eccentric habits, perhaps, or a stranger, is seen repeatedly on the beach at some unusual hour, and is heard whistling. Soon afterwards a violent wind rises; a man who could read the sky perfectly or who possessed a barometer could have foretold that it would. The simple people of a fishing village have no barometers, and only a few rough rules for prophesying weather. What more natural than that the eccentric personage I postulated should be regarded as having raised the wind, or that he or she should clutch eagerly at the reputation of being able to do so? Now, take last night's wind: as it happens, I myself was whistling. I blew a whistle twice, and the wind seemed to come absolutely in answer to my call. If anyone had seen me—"

The audience had been a little restive under this harangue, and Parkins had, I fear, fallen somewhat into the tone of a lecturer; but at the last sentence the colonel stopped.

"Whistling, were you?" he said. "And what sort of whistle did you use? Play this stroke first." Interval.

"About that whistle you were asking, colonel. It's rather a curious one. I have it in my—No; I see I've left it in my room. As a matter of fact, I found it yesterday."

And then Parkins narrated the manner of his discovery of the whistle, upon hearing which the colonel grunted, and opined that, in Parkins's place, he should himself be careful about using a thing that had belonged to a set of Papists, of whom, speaking generally, it might be affirmed that you never knew what they might not have been up to. From this topic he diverged to the enormities of the vicar, who had given notice on the previous Sunday that Friday would be the Feast of St. Thomas the Apostle, and that there would be service at eleven o'clock in the church. This and other similar proceedings constituted in the colonel's view a strong presumption that the vicar was a concealed Papist, if not a Jesuit; and Parkins, who could not very readily follow the colonel in this region, did not disagree with him. In fact, they got on so well together in the morning that there was no talk on either side of their separating after lunch.

Both continued to play well during the afternoon, or at least, well enough to make them forget everything else until the light began to fail them. Not until then did Parkins remember that he had meant to do some more investigating at the preceptory; but it was of no great importance, he reflected. One day was as good as another; he might as well go home with the colonel.

As they turned the corner of the house, the colonel was almost knocked down by a boy who rushed into him at the very top of his speed, and then, instead of running away, remained hanging onto him and panting. The first words of the warrior were naturally those of reproof and objurgation, but he very quickly discerned that the boy was almost speechless with fright. Inquiries were useless at first. When the boy got his breath he began to howl, and still clung to the colonel's legs. He was at last detached, but continued to howl.

"What in the world *is* the matter with you? What have you been up to? What have you seen?" said the two men.

"Ow, I seen it wive at me out of the winder," wailed the boy, "and I don't like it."

"What window?" said the irritated colonel. "Come pull yourself together, my boy."

"The front winder it was, at the 'otel," said the boy.

At this point Parkins was in favor of sending the boy home, but the colonel refused; he wanted to get to the bottom of it, he said; it was most dangerous to give a boy such a fright as this one had had, and if it turned out that people had been playing jokes, they should suffer for it in some way. And by a series of questions he made out this story: The boy had been playing about on the grass in front of the Globe with some others; then they had gone home to their teas, and he was just going, when he happened to look up at the front winder and see it a-wiving at him. *It* seemed to be a figure of some sort, in white as far as he knew—couldn't see its face; but it wived at him, and it warn't a right thing—not to say not a right person. Was there a light in the room? No, he didn't think to look if there was a light. Which was the window? Was it the top one or the second one? The seckind one it was—the big winder what got two little uns at the sides.

"Very well, my boy," said the colonel, after a few more questions. "You run away home now. I expect it was some person trying to give you a start. Another time, like a brave English boy, you just throw a stone—well, no, not that exactly, but you go and speak to the waiter, or to Mr. Simpson, the landlord, and—yes—and say that I advised you to do so."

The boy's face expressed some of the doubt he felt as to the likelihood of Mr. Simpson's lending a favorable ear to his complaint, but the colonel did not appear to perceive this, and went on:

"And here's a sixpence—no, I see it's a shilling—and you be off home, and don't think any more about it."

The youth hurried off with agitated thanks, and the colonel and Parkins went round to the front of the Globe and reconnoitered. There was only one window answering to the description they had been hearing.

"Well, that's curious," said Parkins; "it's evidently my window the lad was talking about. Will you come up for a moment, Colonel Wilson? We ought to be able to see if anyone has been taking liberties in my room."

They were soon in the passage, and Parkins made as if to open the door. Then he stopped and felt in his pockets.

"This is more serious than I thought," was his next remark. "I remember now that before I started this morning I locked the door. It is locked now, and, what is more, here is the key." And he held it up. "Now," he went on, "if the servants are in the habit of going into one's room during the day when one is away, I can only say that—well, that I don't approve of it at all." Conscious of a somewhat weak climax, he busied himself in opening the door (which was indeed locked) and in lighting candles. "No," he said, "nothing seems disturbed."

"Except your bed," put in the colonel.

"Excuse me, that isn't my bed," said Parkins. "I don't use that one. But it does look as if someone had been playing tricks with it."

It certainly did: the clothes were bundled up and twisted together in a most tortuous confusion. Parkins pondered.

"That must be it," he said at last. "I disordered the clothes last night in unpacking, and they haven't made it since. Perhaps they came in to make it, and that boy saw them through the window; and then they were called away and locked the door after them. Yes, I think that must be it."

"Well, ring and ask," said the colonel, and this appealed to Parkins as practical.

The maid appeared, and, to make a long story short, deposed that she had made the bed in the morning when the gentleman was in the room, and hadn't been there since. No, she hadn't no other key. Mr. Simpson, he kep' the keys; he'd be able to tell the gentleman if anyone had been up.

This was a puzzle. Investigation showed that nothing of value had been taken, and Parkins remembered the disposition of the small objects on tables and so forth well enough to be pretty sure that no pranks had been played with them. Mr. and Mrs. Simpson furthermore agreed that neither of them had given the duplicate key of the room to any person whatever during the day. Nor could Parkins, fair-minded man as he was, detect anything in the demeanor of master, mistress or maid that indicated guilt. He was much more inclined to think that the boy had been imposing on the colonel.

The latter was unwontedly silent and pensive at dinner and throughout the evening. When he bade good night to Parkins, he murmured in a gruff undertone:

"You know where I am if you want me during the night."

"Why, yes, thank you, Colonel Wilson, I think I do; but there isn't much prospect of my disturbing you, I hope. By the way," he added, "did I show you that old whistle I spoke of? I think not. Well, here it is."

The colonel turned it over gingerly in the light of the candle.

"Can you make anything of the inscription?" asked Parkins, as he took it back.

"No, not in this light. What do you mean to do with it?"

"Oh, well, when I get back to Cambridge I shall submit it to some of the archaeologists there, and see what they think of it; and very likely, if they consider it worth having, I may present it to one of the museums."

"Hmm," said the colonel. "Well, you may be right. All I know is that, if it were mine, I should chuck it straight into the sea. It's no use talking, I'm well aware, but I expect that with you it's a case of live and learn. I hope so, I'm sure, and I wish you a good night."

He turned away, leaving Parkins in act to speak at the bottom of the stair, and soon each was in his own bedroom.

By some unfortunate accident, there were neither blinds nor curtains to the windows of the professor's room. The previous night he had thought little of this, but tonight there seemed every prospect of a bright moon rising to shine directly on his bed, and probably wake him later on. When he noticed this he was a good deal annoyed, but, with an ingenuity which I can only envy, he succeeded in rigging up, with the help of a railway rug, some safety pins, and a stick and umbrella, a screen which, if it only held together, would completely keep the moonlight off his bed. And shortly afterwards he was comfortably in that bed. When he had read a somewhat solid work long enough to produce a decided wish for sleep, he cast a drowsy glance round the room, blew out the candle and fell back upon the pillow.

He must have slept soundly for an hour or more, when a sudden clatter shook him up in a most unwelcome manner. In a moment he realized what had happened: his carefully constructed screen had given way, and a very bright frosty moon was shining directly on his face. This was highly annoying. Could he possibly get up and reconstruct the screen? or could he manage to sleep if he did not?

For some minutes he lay and pondered over the possibilities; then he turned over sharply, and with all his eyes open lay breathlessly listening. There had been a movement, he was sure, in the empty bed on the opposite side of the room. Tomorrow he would have it moved, for there must be rats or something playing about in it. It was quiet now. No! the commotion began again. There was a rustling and shaking: surely more than any rat could cause.

I can figure to myself something of the professor's bewilderment and horror, for I have in a dream thirty years back seen the same thing happen; but the reader will hardly, perhaps, imagine how dreadful it was to him to see a figure suddenly sit up in what he had known was an empty bed. He was out of his own bed in one bound, and made a dash towards the window, where lay his only weapon, the stick with which he had propped his screen. This was, as it turned out, the worst thing he could have done, because the personage in the empty bed, with a sudden smooth motion, slipped from the bed and took up a position, with outspread arms, between the two beds, and in front of the door. Parkins watched it in a horrid perplexity. Somehow, the idea of getting past it and escaping through the door was intolerable to him; he could not have borne—he didn't know why—to touch it; and as for its touching him, he would sooner dash himself through the window than have that happen. It stood for the moment in a band of dark shadow, and he had not seen what its face was like. Now it began to move, in a stooping posture, and all at once the spectator realized, with some horror and some relief, that it must be blind, for it seemed to feel about it with its muffled arms in a groping and random fashion. Turning half-away from him, it became suddenly conscious of the bed he had just left, and darted towards it, and bent and felt over the pillows in a way which made Parkins shudder as he had never in his life thought it possible. In a very few moments it seemed to know that the bed was empty, and then, moving forward into the area of light and facing the window, it showed for the first time what manner of thing it was.

Parkins, who very much dislikes being questioned about it, did once describe something of it in my hearing, and I gathered that what he chiefly remembers about it is a horrible, an intensely horrible, face *of crumpled linen.* What expression he read upon it he could not or would not tell, but that the fear of it went nigh to maddening him is certain.

But he was not at leisure to watch it for long. With formidable quickness it moved into the middle of the room, and, as it groped and waved, one corner of its draperies swept across Parkins's face. He could not, though he knew how perilous a sound was—he could not keep back a cry of disgust, and this gave the searcher an instant clue. It leaped towards him upon the instant, and the next moment he was halfway through the window backwards, uttering cry upon cry at the utmost pitch of his voice, and the linen face was thrust close into his own. At this, almost the last possible second, deliverance came, as you will have guessed: the colonel burst the door open, and was just in time to see the dreadful group at the window. When he reached the figures only one was left. Parkins sank forward into the room in a faint, and before him on the floor lay a tumbled heap of bedclothes.

Colonel Wilson asked no questions, but busied himself in keeping everyone else out of the room and in getting Parkins back to his bed; and himself, wrapped in a rug, occupied the other bed for the rest of the night. Early on the next day Rogers arrived, more welcome than he would have been a day before, and the three of them held a very long consultation in the professor's room. At the end of it the colonel left the hotel door carrying a small object between his finger and thumb, which he cast as far into the sea as a very brawny arm could send it. Later on the smoke of a burning ascended from the back premises of the Globe.

Exactly what explanation was patched up for the staff and visitors at the hotel I must confess I do not recollect. The professor was somehow cleared of the ready suspicion of delirium tremens, and the hotel of the reputation of a troubled house.

There is not much question as to what would have happened to Parkins if the colonel had not intervened when he did. He would either have fallen out of the window or else lost his wits. But it is not so evident what more the creature that came in answer to the whistle could have done than frighten. There seemed to be absolutely nothing material about it save the bedclothes of which it had made itself a body. The colonel, who remembered a not very dissimilar occurrence in India, was of opinion that if Parkins had closed with it, it could really have done very little, and that its one power was that of frightening. The whole thing, he said, served to confirm his opinion of the Church of Rome.

There is really nothing more to tell, but, as you may imagine, the professor's views on certain points are less clear-cut than they used to be. His nerves, too, have suffered: he cannot even now see a surplice hanging on a door quite unmoved, and the spectacle of a scarecrow in a field late on a winter afternoon has cost him more than one sleepless night.

ROBERT BLOCH

Robert Bloch suggested the following three chillers:

1. *"Pickman's Model," by H. P. Lovecraft. I was only ten when I discovered this story, little dreaming that six years later its author would discover me and urge that I try my hand at similar fiction. When I first read "Pickman's Model" I happened to be taking a train trip through the north side of Chicago, and as I finished the ghoulish tale I glanced up and found that by some macabre coincidence the train was passing a cemetery. Right then and there I made a resolution never to allow myself to be buried—a resolution which, I'm happy to say, I've managed to keep to this day.*

2. *"Lukundoo," by Edward Lucas White. I found this title story in a volume picked up in a secondhand bookstore for a fast read. Truth to tell, it didn't take me very long to peruse "Lukundoo," but for a long time after I found myself anxiously examining any wart, blister or minor elevation of my flesh. My hackles had already been raised from the moment I finished this disturbing account of an ailment far worse than terminal acne.*

3. *"The Glass Eye," by John Kier Cross. Many years ago I came across this tale in a collection titled* The Other Passenger. *It offers neither ghosts nor gore, but what frightened me on first reading—and still frightens me today—is the warning which echoes unspoken but unforgettable, that*

things are not always what they seem. *Sometimes reality is the greatest horror of all.*

All right, that's the lot. You may know of them but if by any chance a title is unfamiliar, I envy you your first reading.

And so do your editors!

LUKUNDOO

EDWARD LUCAS WHITE

"It stands to reason," said Twombly, "that a man must accept the evidence of his own eyes, and when eyes and ears agree, there can be no doubt. He has to believe what he has both seen and heard."

"Not always," put in Singleton, softly.

Every man turned toward Singleton. Twombly was standing on the hearthrug, his back to the grate, his legs spread out, with his habitual air of dominating the room. Singleton, as usual, was as much as possible effaced in a corner. But when Singleton spoke he said something. We faced him in that flattering spontaneity of expectant silence which invites utterance.

"I was thinking," he said, after an interval, "of something I both saw and heard in Africa."

Now, if there was one thing we had found impossible, it had been to elicit from Singleton anything definite about his African experiences. As with the Alpinist in the story, who could tell only that he went up and came down, the sum of Singleton's revelations had been that he went there and came away. His words now riveted our attention at once. Twombly faded from the hearthrug, but not one of us could ever recall having seen him go. The room readjusted itself, focused on Singleton, and there was some hasty and furtive lighting of fresh cigars. Singleton lit one also, but it went out immediately, and he never relit it.

I

We were in the Great Forest, exploring for Pygmies. Van Rieten had a theory that the dwarfs found by Stanley and others were a mere crossbreed between ordinary Negroes and the real Pygmies. He hoped to discover a race of men three feet tall at most, or shorter. We had found no trace of any such beings.

Natives were few, game scarce; food, except game, there was none; and the deepest, dankest, drippingest forest all about. We were the only novelty in the country, no native we met had even seen a white man before, most had never heard of white men. All of a sudden, late one afternoon, there came into our camp an Englishman, and pretty well used up he was, too. We had heard no rumor of him; he had not only heard of us but had made an amazing five-day march to reach us. His guide and two bearers were nearly as done up as he. Even though he was in tatters and had five days' beard on, you could see he was naturally dapper and neat and the sort of man to shave daily. He was small, but wiry. His face was the sort of British face from which emotion has been so carefully banished that a foreigner is apt to think the wearer of the face incapable of any sort of feeling; the kind of face which, if it has any expression at all, expresses principally the resolution to go through the world decorously, without intruding upon or annoying anyone.

His name was Etcham. He introduced himself modestly, and ate with us so deliberately that we should never have suspected, if our bearers had not had it from his bearers, that he had had but three meals in the five days, and those small. After we had lit up he told us why he had come.

"My chief is ve'y seedy," he said between puffs. "He is bound to go out if he keeps this way. I thought perhaps . . ."

He spoke quietly in a soft, even tone, but I could see little beads of sweat oozing out on his upper lip under his stubby mustache, and there was a tingle of repressed emotion in his tone, a veiled eagerness in his eye, a palpitating inward solicitude in his demeanor that moved me at once. Van Rieten had no sentiment in him; if he was moved he did not show it. But he listened. I was surprised at that. He was just the man to refuse at once. But he listened to Etcham's halting, difficult hints. He even asked questions.

"Who is your chief?"

"Stone," Etcham lisped.

That electrified both of us.

"Ralph Stone?" we ejaculated together.

Etcham nodded.

For some minutes Van Rieten and I were silent. Van Rieten had never seen him, but I had been a classmate of Stone's, and Van Rieten and I had discussed him over many a campfire. We had heard of him two years before, south of Luebo in the Balunda country, which had been ringing with his theatrical strife against a Balunda witch doctor, ending in the sorcerer's complete discomfiture and the abasement of his tribe before Stone. They had even broken the fetish man's whistle and given Stone the pieces. It had been like the triumph of Elijah over the prophets of Baal, only more real to the Balunda.

We had thought of Stone as far off, if still in Africa at all, and here he turned up ahead of us and probably forestalling our quest.

II

Etcham's naming of Stone brought back to us all his tantalizing story, his fascinating parents, their tragic death; the brilliance of his college days; the dazzle of his millions; the promise of his young manhood; his wide notoriety, so nearly real fame; his romantic elopement with the meteoric authoress whose sudden cascade of fiction had made her so great a name so young, whose beauty and charm were so much heralded; the frightful scandal of the breach-of-promise suit that followed; his bride's devotion through it all; their sudden quarrel after it was all over; their divorce; the too much advertised announcement of his approaching marriage to the plaintiff in the breach-of-promise suit; his precipitate remarriage to his divorced bride; their second quarrel and second divorce; his departure from his native land; his advent in the dark continent. The sense of all this rushed over me and I believe Van Rieten felt it, too, as he sat silent.

Then he asked:

"Where is Werner?"

"Dead," said Etcham. "He died before I joined Stone."

"You were not with Stone above Luebo?"

"No," said Etcham, "I joined him at Stanley Falls."

"Who is with him?" Van Rieten asked.

"Only his Zanzibar servants and the bearers," Etcham replied.

"What sort of bearers?" Van Rieten demanded.

"Mang-Battu men," Etcham responded simply.

Now that impressed both Van Rieten and myself greatly. It bore out Stone's reputation as a notable leader of men. For up to that time no one had been able to use Mang-Battu as bearers outside of their own country, or to hold them for long or difficult expeditions.

"Were you long among the Mang-Battu?" was Van Rieten's next question.

"Some weeks," said Etcham. "Stone was interested in them and made up a fair-sized vocabulary of their words and phrases. He had a theory that they are an offshoot of the Balunda and he found much confirmation in their customs."

"What do you live on?" Van Rieten inquired.

"Game, mostly," Etcham lisped.

"How long has Stone been laid up?" Van Rieten next asked.

"More than a month," Etcham answered.

"And you have been hunting for the camp?" Van Rieten exclaimed.

Etcham's face, burned and flayed as it was, showed a flush.

"I missed some easy shots," he admitted ruefully. "I've not felt ve'y fit myself."

"What's the matter with your chief?" Van Rieten inquired.

"Something like carbuncles," Etcham replied.

"He ought to get over a carbuncle or two," Van Rieten declared.

"They are not carbuncles," Etcham explained. "Nor one or two. He has had dozens, sometimes five at once. If they had been carbuncles he would have been dead long ago. But in some ways they are not so bad, though in others they are worse."

"How do you mean?" Van Rieten queried.

"Well," Etcham hesitated, "they do not seem to inflame so deep nor so wide as carbuncles, nor to be so painful, nor to cause so much fever. But then they seem to be part of a disease that affects his mind. He let me help him dress the first, but the others he has hidden most carefully, from me and from the men. He keeps his tent when they puff up, and will not let me change the dressings or be with him at all."

"Have you plenty of dressings?" Van Rieten asked.

"We have some," said Etcham doubtfully. "But he won't use them; he washes out the dressings and uses them over and over."

"How is he treating the swellings?" Van Rieten inquired.

"He slices them off clear down to flesh level, with his razor."

"What?" Van Rieten shouted.

Etcham made no answer but looked him steadily in the eyes.

"I beg pardon," Van Rieten hastened to say. "You startled me. They can't be carbuncles. He'd have been dead long ago."

"I thought I had said they are not carbuncles," Etcham lisped.

"But the man must be crazy!" Van Rieten exclaimed.

"Just so," said Etcham. "He is beyond my advice or control."

"How many has he treated that way?" Van Rieten demanded.

"Two, to my knowledge," Etcham said.

"Two?" Van Rieten queried.

Etcham flushed again.

"I saw him," he confessed, "through a crack in the hut. I felt impelled to keep a watch on him, as if he was not responsible."

"I should think not," Van Rieten agreed. "And you saw him do that twice?"

"I conjecture," said Etcham, "that he did the like with all the rest."

"How many has he had?" Van Rieten asked.

"Dozens," Etcham lisped.

"Does he eat?" Van Rieten inquired.

"Like a wolf," said Etcham. "More than any two bearers."

"Can he walk?" Van Rieten asked.

"He crawls a bit, groaning," said Etcham simply.

"Little fever, you say," Van Rieten ruminated.

"Enough and too much," Etcham declared.

"Has he been delirious?" Van Rieten asked.

"Only twice," Etcham replied; "once when the first swelling broke, and once later. He would not let anyone come near him then. But we could hear him talking, talking steadily, and it scared the natives."

"Was he talking their patter in delirium?" Van Rieten demanded.

"No," said Etcham, "but he was talking some similar lingo. Hamed Burghash said he was talking Balunda. I know too little Balunda. I do not learn languages readily. Stone learned more Mang-Battu in a week than I could have learned in a year. But I seemed to hear words like Mang-Battu words. Anyhow, the Mang-Battu bearers were scared."

"Scared?" Van Rieten repeated, questioningly.

"So were the Zanzibar men, even Hamed Burghash, and so was I," said Etcham, "only for a different reason. He talked in two voices."

"In two voices," Van Rieten reflected.

"Yes," said Etcham, more excitedly than he had yet spoken. "In two voices, like a conversation. One was his own, one a small, thin, bleaty voice like nothing I ever heard. I seemed to make out, among the sounds the deep voice made, something like Mang-Battu words I knew, as *nedru, metababa* and *nedo,* their terms for 'head,' 'shoulder,' 'thigh,' and perhaps *kudra* and *nekere* ('speak' and 'whistle'); and among the noises of the shrill voice *matomipa, angunzi* and *kamomami* ('kill,' 'death' and 'hate'). Hamed Burghash said he also heard those words. He knew Mang-Battu far better than I."

"What did the bearers say?" Van Rieten asked.

"They said, *'Lukundoo, Lukundoo!'* " Etcham replied. "I did not know that word; Hamed Burghash said it was Mang-Battu for 'leopard.' "

"It's Mang-Battu for 'witchcraft,' " said Van Rieten.

"I don't wonder they thought so," said Etcham. "It was enough to make one believe in sorcery to listen to those two voices."

"One voice answering the other?" Van Rieten asked perfunctorily.

Etcham's face went gray under his tan.

"Sometimes both at once," he answered huskily.

"Both at once!" Van Rieten ejaculated.

"It sounded that way to the men, too," said Etcham. "And that was not all."

He stopped and looked helplessly at us for a moment.

"Could a man talk and whistle at the same time?" he asked.

"How do you mean?" Van Rieten queried.

"We could hear Stone talking away, his big, deep-chested baritone rumbling along, and through it all we could hear a high, shrill whistle, the oddest, wheezy sound. You know, no matter how shrilly a grown man may whistle, the note has a different quality from the whistle of a boy or a woman or a little girl. They sound more treble, somehow. Well, if you can imagine the smallest girl who could whistle keeping it up tunelessly right along, that whistle was like that, only even more piercing, and it sounded right through Stone's bass tones."

"And you didn't go to him?" Van Rieten cried.

"He is not given to threats," Etcham disclaimed. "But he had threatened, not volubly, nor like a sick man, but quietly and firmly, that if any man of us (he lumped me in with the men) came near him while he was in his trouble, that man should die. And it was not so much his words as his manner. It was like a monarch commanding respected privacy for a deathbed. One simply could not transgress."

"I see," said Van Rieten shortly.

"He's ve'y seedy," Etcham repeated helplessly. "I thought perhaps. . . ."

His absorbing affection for Stone, his real love for him, shone out through his envelope of conventional training. Worship of Stone was plainly his master passion.

Like many competent men, Van Rieten had a streak of hard selfishness in him. It came to the surface then. He said we carried our lives in our hands from day to day just as genuinely as Stone; that he did not forget the ties of blood and calling between any two explorers, but that there was no sense in imperiling one party for a very problematical benefit to a man probably beyond any help; that it was enough of a task to hunt for one party; that if two were united, providing food would be more than doubly difficult; that the risk of starvation was too great. Deflecting our march seven full days' journey (he complimented Etcham on his marching powers) might ruin our expedition entirely.

III

Van Rieten had logic on his side and he had a way with him. Etcham sat there apologetic and deferential, like a fourth-form schoolboy before a headmaster. Van Rieten wound up.

"I am after Pygmies, at the risk of my life. After Pygmies I go."

"Perhaps, then, these will interest you," said Etcham, very quietly.

He took two objects out of the side pocket of his blouse, and handed them to Van Rieten. They were round, bigger than big plums, and smaller than small peaches, about the right size to enclose in an average hand. They were black, and at first I did not see what they were.

"Pygmies!" Van Rieten exclaimed. "Pygmies, indeed! Why, they wouldn't be two feet high! Do you mean to claim that these are adult heads?"

"I claim nothing," Etcham answered evenly. "You can see for yourself."

Van Rieten passed one of the heads to me. The sun was just setting and I examined it closely. A dried head it was, perfectly preserved, and the flesh as hard as Argentine jerked beef. A bit of a vertebra stuck out where the muscles of the vanished neck had shriveled into folds. The puny chin was sharp on a projecting jaw, the minute teeth white and even between the retracted lips, the tiny nose was flat, the little forehead retreating, there were inconsiderable clumps of stunted wool on the Lilliputian cranium. There was nothing babyish, childish or youthful about the head; rather it was mature to senility.

"Where did these come from?" Van Rieten inquired.

"I do not know," Etcham replied precisely. "I found them among Stone's effects while rummaging for medicines or drugs or anything that could help me to help him. I do not know where he got them. But I'll swear he did not have them when we entered this district."

"Are you sure?" Van Rieten queried, his eyes big and fixed on Etcham's.

"Ve'y sure," lisped Etcham.

"But how could he have come by them without your knowledge?" Van Rieten demurred.

"Sometimes we were apart ten days at a time hunting," said Etcham. "Stone is not a talking man. He gave me no account of his doings, and Hamed Burghash keeps a still tongue and a tight hold on the men."

"You have examined these heads?" Van Rieten asked.

"Minutely," said Etcham.

Van Rieten took out his notebook. He was a methodical chap. He tore out a leaf, folded it and divided it equally into three pieces. He gave one to me and one to Etcham.

"Just for a test of my impressions," he said, "I want each of us to write separately just what he is most reminded of by these heads. Then I want to compare the writings."

I handed Etcham a pencil and he wrote. Then he handed the pencil back to me and I wrote.

"Read the three," said Van Rieten, handing me his piece.

Van Rieten had written:

"An old Balunda witch doctor."

Etcham had written:

"An old Mang-Battu fetish man."

I had written:

"An old Katongo magician."

"There!" Van Rieten exclaimed. "Look at that! There is nothing Wagabi or Batwa or Wambuttu or Wabotu about these heads. Nor anything Pygmy either."

"I thought as much," said Etcham.

"And you say he did not have them before?"

"To a certainty he did not," Etcham asserted.

"It is worth following up," said Van Rieten. "I'll go with you. And first of all, I'll do my best to save Stone."

He put out his hand and Etcham clasped it silently. He was grateful all over.

IV

Nothing but Etcham's fever of solicitude could have taken him in five days over the track. It took him eight days to retrace with full knowledge of it and our party to help. We could not have done it in seven, and Etcham urged us on, in a repressed fury of anxiety, no mere fever of duty to his chief, but a real ardor of devotion, a glow of personal adoration for Stone which blazed under his dry conventional exterior and showed in spite of him.

We found Stone well cared for. Etcham had seen to a good, high thorn *zareeba* round the camp, the huts were well built and thatched, and Stone's was as good as their resources would permit. Hamed Burghash was not named after two Seyyids for nothing. He had in him the making of a sultan. He had kept the Mang-Battu together, not a man had slipped off, and he had kept them in order. Also he was a deft nurse and a faithful servant.

The two other Zanzibaris had done some creditable hunting. Though all were hungry, the camp was far from starvation.

Stone was on a canvas cot and there was a sort of collapsible camp-stool-table, like a Turkish taboret, by the cot. It had a water bottle and some vials on it and Stone's watch, also his razor in its case.

Stone was clean and not emaciated, but he was far gone; not unconscious, but in a daze; past commanding or resisting anyone. He did not seem to see us enter or to know we were there. I should have recognized him anywhere. His boyish dash and grace had vanished utterly, of course. But his head was even more leonine; his hair was still abundant, yellow and wavy; the close, crisped blond beard he had grown during his illness did not alter him. He was big and big-chested yet. His eyes were dull and he mumbled and babbled mere meaningless syllables, not words.

Etcham helped Van Rieten to uncover him and look him over. He was in good muscle for a man so long bedridden. There were no scars on him except about his knees, shoulders and chest. On each knee and above it he had a full score of roundish cicatrices, and a dozen or more on each shoulder, all in front. Two or three were open wounds and four or five barely healed. He had no fresh swellings, except two, one on each side, on his pectoral muscles, the one on the left being higher up and farther out than the other. They did not look like boils or carbuncles, but as if something blunt and hard were being pushed up through the fairly healthy flesh and skin, not much inflamed.

"I should not lance those," said Van Rieten, and Etcham assented.

They made Stone as comfortable as they could, and just before sunset we looked in at him again. He was lying on his back, and his chest showed big and massive yet, but he lay as if in a stupor. We left Etcham with him and went into the next hut, which Etcham had resigned to us. The jungle noises were no different there than anywhere else for months past, and I was soon fast asleep.

V

Sometime in the pitch dark I found myself awake and listening. I could hear two voices, one Stone's, the other sibilant and wheezy. I knew Stone's voice after all the years that had passed since I heard it last. The other was like nothing I remembered. It had less volume than the wail of a newborn baby, yet there was an insistent carrying power to it, like the shrilling of an insect. As I listened I heard Van Rieten breathing near me in the dark; then he heard me and realized that I was listening, too. Like Etcham I knew little Balunda, but I could make out a word or two. The voices alternated, with intervals of silence between.

Then suddenly both sounded at once and fast. Stone's baritone basso, full as if he were in perfect health, and that incredibly stridulous falsetto, both jabbering at once like the voices of two people quarreling and trying to talk each other down.

"I can't stand this," said Van Rieten. "Let's have a look at him."

He had one of those cylindrical electric night-candles. He fumbled about for it, touched the button and beckoned me to come with him. Outside the hut he motioned me to stand still, and instinctively turned off the light, as if seeing made listening difficult.

Except for a faint glow from the embers of the bearers' fire we were in complete darkness, little starlight struggled through the trees, the river made but a faint murmur. We could hear the two voices together and then suddenly the creaking voice changed into a razor-edged, slicing whistle, indescribably cutting, continuing right through Stone's grumbling torrent of croaking words.

"Good God!" exclaimed Van Rieten.

Abruptly he turned on the light.

We found Etcham utterly asleep, exhausted by his long anxiety and the exertions of his phenomenal march, and relaxed completely now that the load was in a sense shifted from his shoulders to Van Rieten's. Even the light on his face did not wake him.

The whistle had ceased and the two voices now sounded together. Both came from Stone's cot, where the concentrated white ray showed him lying just as we had left him, except that he had tossed his arms above his head and had torn the coverings and bandages from his chest.

The swelling on his right breast had broken. Van Rieten aimed the center line of the light at it and we saw it plainly. From his flesh, grown out of it, there protruded a head, such a head as the dried specimens Etcham had shown us, as if it were a miniature of the head of a Balunda fetish man. It was black, shining black as the blackest African skin; it rolled the whites of its wicked, wee eyes and showed its microscopic teeth between lips repulsively negroid in their red fullness, even in so diminutive a face. It had crisp, fuzzy wool on its minikin skull, it turned malignantly from side to side and chittered incessantly in that inconceivable falsetto. Stone babbled brokenly against its patter.

Van Rieten turned from Stone and waked Etcham, with some difficulty. When he was awake and saw it all, Etcham stared and said not one word.

"You saw him slice off two swellings?" Van Rieten asked.

Etcham nodded, chokingly.

"Did he bleed much?" Van Rieten demanded.

"Ve'y little," Etcham replied.

"You hold his arms," said Van Rieten to Etcham.

He took up Stone's razor and handed me the light. Stone showed no sign of seeing the light or of knowing we were there. But the little head mewled and screeched at us.

Van Rieten's hand was steady, and the sweep of the razor even and true. Stone bled amazingly little and Van Rieten dressed the wound as if it had been a bruise or scrape.

Stone had stopped talking the instant the excrescent head was severed. Van Rieten did all that could be done for Stone and then fairly grabbed the light from me. Snatching up a gun he scanned the ground by the cot and brought the butt down once and twice, viciously.

We went back to our hut, but I doubt if I slept.

VI

Next day, near noon, in broad daylight, we heard the two voices from Stone's hut. We found Etcham dropped asleep by his charge. The swelling on the left had broken, and just such another head was there miauling and spluttering. Etcham woke up and the three of us stood there and glared. Stone interjected hoarse vocables into the tinkling gurgle of the portent's utterance.

Van Rieten stepped forward, took up Stone's razor and knelt down by the cot. The atomy of a head squealed a wheezy snarl at him.

Then suddenly Stone spoke English.

"Who are you with my razor?"

Van Rieten started back and stood up.

Stone's eyes were clear now and bright, they roved about the hut.

"The end," he said; "I recognize the end. I seem to see Etcham, as if in life. But Singleton! Ah, Singleton! Ghosts of my boyhood come to watch me pass! And you, strange specter with the black beard and my razor! Aroint ye all!"

"I'm no ghost, Stone," I managed to say. "I'm alive. So are Etcham and Van Rieten. We are here to help you."

"Van Rieten!" he exclaimed. "My work passes on to a better man. Luck go with you, Van Rieten."

Van Rieten went nearer to him.

"Just hold still a moment, old man," he said soothingly. "It will be only one twinge."

"I've held still for many such twinges," Stone answered quite distinctly. "Let me be. Let me die in my own way. The hydra was nothing to this. You can cut off ten, a hundred, a thousand heads, but the curse you cannot cut off, or take off. What's soaked into the bone won't come out of the flesh, any more than what's bred there. Don't hack me any more. Promise!"

His voice had all the old commanding tone of his boyhood and it swayed Van Rieten as it always had swayed everybody.

"I promise," said Van Rieten.

Almost as he said the word Stone's eyes filmed again.

Then we three sat about Stone and watched that hideous, gibbering prodigy grow up out of Stone's flesh, till two horrid, spindling little black arms disengaged themselves. The infinitesimal nails were perfect to the barely perceptible moon at the quick, the pink spot on the palm was horridly natural. These arms gesticulated and the right plucked toward Stone's blond beard.

"I can't stand this," Van Rieten exclaimed and took up the razor again.

Instantly Stone's eyes opened, hard and glittering.

"Van Rieten break his word?" he enunciated slowly. "Never!"

"But we must help you," Van Rieten gasped.

"I am past all help and all hurting," said Stone. "This is my hour. This curse is not put on me; it grew out of me, like this horror here. Even now I go."

His eyes closed and we stood helpless, the adherent figure spouting shrill sentences.

In a moment Stone spoke again.

"You speak all tongues?" he asked quickly.

And the mergent minikin replied in sudden English:

"Yea, verily, all that you speak," putting out its microscopic tongue, writhing its lips and wagging its head from side to side. We could see the thready ribs on its exiguous flanks heave as if the thing breathed.

"Has she forgiven me?" Stone asked in a muffled strangle.

"Not while the moss hangs from the cypresses," the head squeaked. "Not while the stars shine on Lake Pontchartrain will she forgive."

And then Stone, all with one motion, wrenched himself over on his side. The next instant he was dead.

When Singleton's voice ceased the room was hushed for a space. We could hear each other breathing. Twombly, the tactless, broke the silence.

"I presume," he said, "you cut off the little minikin and brought it home in alcohol."

Singleton turned on him a stern countenance.

"We buried Stone," he said, "unmutilated as he died."

"But," said the unconscionable Twombly, "the whole thing is incredible."

Singleton stiffened.

"I did not expect you to believe it," he said; "I began by saying that although I heard and saw it, when I look back on it I cannot credit it myself."

LAWRENCE BLOCK

Fiction is usually only vicariously frightening for me; i.e., I fear for the characters. Although a daughter of mine read Stephen King's "Salem's Lot" *and had to sleep with a night-light for the next month, I've never had that strong a response.*

But there's one story I can recall very vividly that makes not a character, but the reader himself the target of terror, and that's "Don't Look Behind You," by Fredric Brown. I read the story, and virtually all of Brown's work, in 1957–58, when I was just starting to write crime fiction and was reading tons of it. It seemed to me, and still seems to me, that nobody came up with so many consistently superior story ideas as Brown, or was a more engaging writer. Because I was reading analytically, or trying to, I never lost sight of the fact that "Don't Look Behind You" was a story—but that's its strength; and it was nonetheless frightening when read that way.

I can also recall an Anthony Boucher story that gave me a chill before *I read it. A friend simply described it and that was enough. The story tells how this ordinary sort of chap gets up one morning, gets dressed for work, and en route stops at this house and murders a whole family while they sleep, then continues on his way to the office!*

Editors' Note: Much as we'd like to refer you to it, we can't help with the title, either.

DON'T LOOK BEHIND YOU

FREDRIC BROWN

Just sit back and relax, now. Try to enjoy this; it's going to be the last story you ever read, or nearly the last. After you finish it you can sit there and stall awhile, you can find excuses to hang around your house, or your room, or your office, wherever you're reading this; but sooner or later you're going to have to get up and go out. That's where I'm waiting for you: outside. Or maybe closer than that. Maybe in this room.

You think that's a joke of course. You think this is just a story in a book, and that I don't really mean you. Keep right on thinking so. But be fair; admit that I'm giving you fair warning.

Harley bet me I couldn't do it. He bet me a diamond he's told me about, a diamond as big as his head. So you see why I've got to kill you. And why I've got to tell you how and why and all about it first. That's part of the bet. It's just the kind of idea Harley would have.

I'll tell you about Harley first. He's tall and handsome, and suave and cosmopolitan. He looks something like Ronald Colman, only he's taller. He dresses like a million dollars, but it wouldn't matter if he didn't; I mean that he'd look distinguished in overalls. There's a sort of magic about Harley, a mocking magic in the way he looks at you; it makes you think of palaces and far-off countries and bright music.

It was in Springfield, Ohio, that he met Justin Dean. Justin was a funny-looking little runt who was just a printer. He worked for the Atlas

Printing & Engraving Company. He was a very ordinary little guy, just about as different as possible from Harley; you couldn't pick two men more different. He was only thirty-five, but he was mostly bald already, and he had to wear thick glasses because he'd worn out his eyes doing fine printing and engraving. He was a good printer and engraver; I'll say that for him.

I never asked Harley how he happened to come to Springfield, but the day he got there, after he'd checked in at the Castle Hotel, he stopped in at Atlas to have some calling cards made. It happened that Justin Dean was alone in the shop at the time, and he took Harley's order for the cards; Harley wanted engraved ones, the best. Harley always wants the best of everything.

Harley probably didn't even notice Justin; there was no reason why he should have. But Justin noticed Harley all right, and in him he saw everything that he himself would like to be, and never would be, because most of the things Harley has, you have to be born with.

And Justin made the plates for the cards himself and printed them himself, and he did a wonderful job—something he thought would be worthy of a man like Harley Prentice. That was the name engraved on the card, just that and nothing else, as all really important people have their cards engraved.

He did fine-line work on it, freehand cursive style, and used all the skill he had. It wasn't wasted, because the next day when Harley called to get the cards he held one and stared at it for a while, and then he looked at Justin, seeing him for the first time. He asked, "Who did this?"

And little Justin told him proudly who had done it, and Harley smiled at him and told him it was the work of an artist, and he asked Justin to have dinner with him that evening after work, in the Blue Room of the Castle Hotel.

That's how Harley and Justin got together, but Harley was careful. He waited until he'd known Justin awhile before he asked him whether or not he could make plates for five and ten dollar bills. Harley had the contacts; he could market the bills in quantity with men who specialized in passing them, and—most important—he knew where he could get paper with the silk threads in it, paper that wasn't quite the genuine thing, but was close enough to pass inspection by anyone but an expert.

So Justin quit his job at Atlas and he and Harley went to New York, and they set up a little printing shop as a blind, on Amsterdam Avenue south of Sherman Square, and they worked at the bills. Justin worked hard, harder than he had ever worked in his life, because besides working on the plates for the bills, he helped meet expenses by handling what legitimate printing work came into the shop.

He worked day and night for almost a year, making plate after plate, and each one was a little better than the last, and finally he had plates that Harley said were good enough. That night they had dinner at the Waldorf-Astoria to celebrate and after dinner they went the rounds of the best nightclubs, and it cost Harley a small fortune, but that didn't matter because they were going to get rich.

They drank champagne, and it was the first time Justin ever drank champagne and he got disgustingly drunk and must have made quite a fool of himself. Harley told him about it afterwards, but Harley wasn't mad at him. He took him back to his room at the hotel and put him to bed, and Justin was pretty sick for a couple of days. But that didn't matter, either, becaue they were going to get rich.

Then Justin started printing bills from the plates, and they got rich. After that, Justin didn't have to work so hard, either, because he turned down most jobs that came into the print shop, told them he was behind schedule and couldn't handle any more. He took just a little work, to keep up a front. And behind the front, he made five and ten dollar bills, and he and Harley got rich.

He got to know other people whom Harley knew. He met Bull Mallon, who handled the distribution end. Bull Mallon was built like a bull, that was why they called him that. He had a face that never smiled or changed expression at all except when he was holding burning matches to the soles of Justin's bare feet. But that wasn't then; that was later, when he wanted Justin to tell him where the plates were.

And he got to know Captain John Willys of the Police Department, who was a friend of Harley's, to whom Harley gave quite a bit of the money they made, but that didn't matter either, because there was plenty left and they all got rich. He met a friend of Harley's who was a big star of the stage, and one who owned a big New York newspaper. He got to know other people equally important, but in less respectable ways.

Harley, Justin knew, had a hand in lots of other enterprises besides the little mint on Amsterdam Avenue. Some of these ventures took him out of town, usually over weekends. And the weekend that Harley was murdered Justin never found out what really happened, except that Harley went away and didn't come back. Oh, he knew that he was murdered, all right, because the police found his body—with three bullet holes in his chest—in the most expensive suite of the best hotel in Albany. Even for a place to be found dead in Harley Prentice had chosen the best.

All Justin ever knew about it was that a long distance call came to him at the hotel where he was staying, the night that Harley was murdered—it must have been a matter of minutes, in fact, before the time the newspapers said Harley was killed.

It was Harley's voice on the phone, and his voice was debonair and unexcited as ever. But he said, "Justin? Get to the shop and get rid of the plates, the paper, everything. Right away. I'll explain when I see you." He waited only until Justin said, "Sure, Harley," and then he said, "Attaboy" and hung up.

Justin hurried around to the printing shop and got the plates and the paper and a few thousand dollars worth of counterfeit bills that were on hand. He made the paper and bills into one bundle and the copper plates into another, smaller one, and he left the shop with no evidence that it had ever been a mint in miniature.

He was very careful and very clever in disposing of both bundles. He got rid of the big one first by checking in at a big hotel, not one he or Harley ever stayed at, under a false name, just to have a chance to put the big bundle in the incinerator there. It was paper and it would burn. And he made sure there was a fire in the incinerator before he dropped it down the chute.

The plates were different. They wouldn't burn, he knew, so he took a trip to Staten Island and back on the ferry and, somewhere out in the middle of the bay, he dropped the bundle over the side into the water.

Then, having done what Hartley had told him to do, and having done it well and thoroughly, he went back to the hotel—his own hotel, not the one where he had dumped the paper and the bills—and went to sleep.

In the morning he read in the newspapers that Harley had been killed, and he was stunned. It didn't seem possible. He couldn't believe it; it was a joke someone was playing on him. Harley would come back to him, he knew. And he was right; Harley did, but that was later, in the swamp.

But anyway, Justin had to know, so he took the very next train for Albany. He must have been on the train when the police went to his hotel, and at the hotel they must have learned he'd asked at the desk about trains for Albany, because they were waiting for him when he got off the train there.

They took him to a station and they kept him there a long long time, days and days, asking him questions. They found out, after a while, that he couldn't have killed Harley because he'd been in New York City at the time Harley was killed in Albany but they knew, also, that he and Harley had been operating the little mint, and they thought that might be a lead to who killed Harley, and they were interested in the counterfeiting, too, maybe even more than in the murder. They asked Justin Dean questions, over and over and over, and he couldn't answer them, so he didn't. They kept him awake for days at a time, asking him questions over and over. Most of all they wanted to know where the plates were. He wished he could tell them that the plates were safe where nobody could ever get them again, but he couldn't tell them that without admitting that he and Harley had been counterfeiting, so he couldn't tell them.

They located the Amsterdam shop, but they didn't find any evidence there, and they really had no evidence to hold Justin on at all, but he didn't know that, and it never occurred to him to get a lawyer.

He kept wanting to see Harley, and they wouldn't let him; then, when they learned he really didn't believe Harley could be dead, they made him look at a dead man they said was Harley, and he guessed it was, although Harley looked different dead. He didn't look magnificent, dead. And Justin believed, then, but still didn't believe. And after that he just went silent and wouldn't say a word, even when they kept him awake for days and days with a bright light in his eyes, and kept slapping him to keep him awake. They didn't use clubs or rubber hoses, but they slapped him a million times and wouldn't let him sleep. And after a while he lost track of things and couldn't have answered their questions even if he'd wanted to.

For a while after that, he was in a bed in a white room, and all he remembers about that are nightmares he had, and calling for Harley and an awful confusion as to whether Harley was dead or not, and then things came back to him gradually and he knew he didn't want to stay in the white room; he wanted to get out so he could hunt for Harley. And if Harley was dead, he wanted to kill whoever had killed Harley, because Harley would have done the same for him.

So he began pretending, and acting, very cleverly, the way the doctors and nurses seemed to want him to act, and after a while they gave him his clothes and let him go.

He was becoming cleverer now. He thought, What would Harley tell me to do? And he knew they'd try to follow him because they'd think he might lead them to the plates, which they didn't know were at the bottom of the bay, and he gave them the slip before he left Albany, and he went first to Boston, and from there by boat to New York, instead of going direct.

He went first to the print shop, and went in the back way after watching the alley for a long time to be sure the place wasn't guarded. It was a mess;

they must have searched it very thoroughly for the plates.

Harley wasn't there, of course. Justin left and from a phone booth in a drugstore, he telephoned their hotel and asked for Harley and was told Harley no longer lived there; and to be clever and not let them guess who he was, he asked for Justin Dean, and they said Justin Dean didn't live there anymore either.

Then he moved to a different drugstore and from there he decided to call up some friends of Harley's, and he phoned Bull Mallon first and because Bull was a friend, he told him who he was and asked if he knew where Harley was.

Bull Mallon didn't pay any attention to that; he sounded excited, a little, and he asked, "Did the cops get the plates, Dean?" and Justin said they didn't, that he wouldn't tell them, and he asked again about Harley.

Bull asked, "Are you nuts, or kidding?" And Justin just asked him again, and Bull's voice changed and he said, "Where are you?" and Justin told him. Bull said, "Harley's here. He's staying under cover, but it's all right if you know, Dean. You wait right there at the drugstore, and we'll come and get you."

They came and got Justin, Bull Mallon and two other men in a car, and they told him Harley was hiding out way deep in New Jersey and that they were going to drive there now. So he went along and sat in the back seat between two men he didn't know, while Bull Mallon drove.

It was late afternoon then, when they picked him up, and Bull drove all evening and most of the night and he drove fast, so he must have gone farther than New Jersey, at least into Virginia or maybe farther, into the Carolinas.

The sky was getting faintly gray with first dawn when they stopped at a rustic cabin that looked like it had been used as a hunting lodge. It was miles from anywhere, there wasn't even a road leading to it, just a trail that was level enough for the car to be able to make it.

They took Justin into the cabin and tied him to a chair, and they told him Harley wasn't there, but Harley had told them that Justin would tell them where the plates were, and he couldn't leave until he did tell.

Justin didn't believe them; he knew then that they'd tricked him about Harley, but it didn't matter, as far as the plates were concerned. It didn't matter if he told them what he'd done with the plates, because they couldn't get them again, and they wouldn't tell the police. So he told them, quite willingly.

But they didn't believe him. They said he'd hidden the plates and was lying. They tortured him to make him tell. They beat him, and they cut him with knives, and they held burning matches and lighted cigars to the soles of his feet, and they pushed needles under his fingernails. Then they'd rest and ask him questions and if he could talk, he'd tell them the truth, and after a while they'd start to torture him again.

It went on for days and weeks—Justin doesn't know how long, but it was a long time. Once they went away for several days and left him tied up with nothing to eat or drink. They came back and started in all over again. And all the time he hoped Harley would come to help him, but Harley didn't come, not then.

After a while what was happening in the cabin ended, or anyway he didn't know any more about it. They must have thought he was dead; maybe they were right, or anyway not far from wrong.

The next thing he knows was the swamp. He was lying in shallow water at the edge of deeper water. His face was out of the water; it woke him when he turned a little and his face went under. They must have thought him dead and thrown him into the water, but he had floated into the shallow part before he had drowned, and a last flicker of consciousness had turned him over on his back with his face out.

I don't remember much about Justin in the swamp; it was a long time, but I just remember flashes of it. I couldn't move at first; I just lay there in the shallow water with my face out. It got dark and it got cold, I remember, and finally my arms would move a little and I got farther out of the water, lying in the mud with only my feet in the water. I slept or was unconscious again and when I woke up it was getting gray dawn, and that was when Harley came. I think I'd been calling him, and he must have heard.

He stood there, dressed as immaculately and perfectly as ever, right in the swamp, and he was laughing at me for being so weak and lying there like a log, half in the dirty water and half in the mud, and I got up and nothing hurt anymore.

We shook hands and he said, "Come on, Justin, let's get you out of here," and I was so glad he'd come that I cried a little. He laughed at me for that and said I should lean on him and he'd help me walk, but I wouldn't do that, because I was coated with mud and filth of the swamp and he was so clean and perfect in a white linen suit, like an ad in a magazine. And all the way out of that swamp, all the days and nights we spent there, he never even got mud on his trouser cuffs, nor his hair mussed.

I told him just to lead the way, and he did, walking just ahead of me, sometimes turning around, laughing and talking to me and cheering me up. Sometimes I'd fall but I wouldn't let him come back and help me. But he'd wait patiently until I could get up. Sometimes I'd crawl instead when I couldn't stand up anymore. Sometimes I'd have to swim streams that he'd leap lightly across.

And it was day and night and day and night, and sometimes I'd sleep, and things would crawl across me. And some of them I caught and ate, or maybe I dreamed that. I remember other things, in that swamp, like an organ that played a lot of the time, and sometimes angels in the air and devils in the water, but those were delirium, I guess.

Harley would say, "A little farther, Justin; we'll make it. And we'll get back at them, at all of them."

And we made it. We came to dry fields, cultivated fields with waist-high corn, but there weren't ears on the corn for me to eat. And then there was a stream, a clear stream that wasn't stinking water like the swamp, and Harley told me to wash myself and my clothes and I did, although I wanted to hurry on to where I could get food.

I still looked pretty bad; my clothes were clean of mud and filth but they were mere rags and wet, because I couldn't wait for them to dry, and I had a ragged beard and I was barefoot.

But we went on and came to a little farm building, just a two-room shack, and there was a smell of fresh bread just out of an oven, and I ran the last few yards to knock on the door. A woman, an ugly woman, opened the door and when she saw me she slammed it again before I could say a word.

Strength came to me from somewhere, maybe from Harley, although I can't remember him being there just then. There was a pile of kindling logs beside the door. I picked one of them up as though it were no heavier than a broomstick, and I broke down the door and killed the woman. She screamed a lot, but I killed her. Then I ate the hot fresh bread.

I watched from the window as I ate, and saw a man running across the field toward the house. I found a knife, and I killed him as he came in at the door. It was much better, killing with the knife; I liked it that way.

I ate more bread, and kept watching from all the windows, but no one else came. Then my stomach hurt from the hot bread I'd eaten and I had to lie down, doubled up, and when the hurting quit, I slept.

Harley woke me up, and it was dark. He said, "Let's get going; you should be far away from here before it's daylight."

I knew he was right, but I didn't hurry away. I was becoming, as you see, very clever now. I knew there were things to do first. I found matches and a lamp, and lighted the lamp. Then I hunted through the shack for everything I could use. I found clothes of the man, and they fitted me not too badly except that I had to turn up the cuffs of the trousers and the shirt. His shoes were big, but that was good because my feet were so swollen.

I found a razor and shaved; it took a long time because my hand wasn't steady, but I was very careful and didn't cut myself much.

I had to hunt hardest for their money, but I found it finally. It was sixty dollars.

And I took the knife, after I had sharpened it. It isn't fancy; just a bone-handled carving knife, but it's good steel. I'll show it to you, pretty soon now. It's had a lot of use.

Then we left and it was Harley who told me to stay away from the roads, and find railroad tracks. That was easy because we heard a train whistle far off in the night and knew which direction the tracks lay. From then on, with Harley helping, it's been easy.

You won't need the details from here. I mean, about the brakeman, and about the tramp we found asleep in the empty reefer, and about the near thing I had with the police in Richmond. I learned from that; I learned I mustn't talk to Harley when anybody else was around to hear. He hides himself from them; he's got a trick and they don't know he's there, and they think I'm funny in the head if I talk to him. But in Richmond I bought better clothes and got a haircut and a man I killed in an alley had forty dollars on him, so I had money again. I've done a lot of traveling since then. If you stop to think you'll know where I am right now.

I'm looking for Bull Mallon and the two men who helped him. Their names are Harry and Carl. I'm going to kill them when I find them. Harley keeps telling me that those fellows are big time and that I'm not ready for them yet. But I can be looking while I'm getting ready so I keep moving around. Sometimes I stay in one place long enough to hold a job as a printer for a while. I've learned a lot of things. I can hold a job and people don't think I'm too strange; they don't get scared when I look at them like they sometimes did a few months ago. And I've learned not to talk to Harley except in our own room and then only very quietly so people in the next room won't think I'm talking to myself.

And I've kept in practice with the knife. I've killed lots of people with it, mostly on the streets at night. Sometimes because they look like they might have money on them, but mostly just for practice and because I've come to like doing it. I'm really good with the knife by now. You'll hardly feel it.

But Harley tells me that kind of killing is easy and that it's something else to kill a person who's on guard, as Bull and Harry and Carl will be.

And that's the conversation that led to the bet I mentioned. I told Harley that I'd bet him that, right now, I could warn a man I was going to use the knife on him and even tell him why and approximately when, and that I could still kill him. And he bet me that I couldn't and he's going to lose that bet.

He's going to lose it because I'm warning you right now and you're not going to believe me. I'm betting that you're going to believe that this is just another story in a book. That you won't believe that this is the *only* copy of this book that contains this story and that this story is true. Even when I tell you how it was done, I don't think you'll really believe me.

You see I'm putting it over on Harley, winning the bet, by putting it over on you. He never thought, and you won't realize, how easy it is for a good printer, who's been a counterfeiter too, to counterfeit one story in a book. Nothing like as hard as counterfeiting a five dollar bill.

I had to pick a book of short stories and I picked this one because I happened to notice that the last story in the book was titled "Don't Look Behind You" and that was going to be a good title for this. You'll see what I mean in a few minutes.

I'm lucky that the printing shop I'm working for now does book work and had a type face that matches the rest of this book. I had a little trouble matching the paper exactly, but I finally did and I've got it ready while I'm writing this. I'm writing this directly on a Linotype, late at night in the shop where I'm working days. I even have the boss's permission, told him I was going to set up and print a story that a friend of mine had written, as a surprise for him, and that I'd melt the type metal back as soon as I'd printed one good copy.

When I finish writing this I'll make up the type in pages to match the rest of the book and I'll print it on the matching paper I have ready. I'll cut the new pages to fit and bind them in; you won't be able to tell the difference, even if a faint suspicion may cause you to look at it. Don't forget I made five and ten dollar bills you couldn't have told from the original, and this is kindergarten stuff compared to that job. And I've done enough bookbinding that I'll be able to take the last story out of the book and bind this one in instead of it and you won't be able to tell the difference no matter how closely you look. I'm going to do a perfect job of it if it takes me all night.

And tomorrow I'll go to some bookstore, or maybe a newsstand or even a drugstore that sells books and has other copies of this book, ordinary copies, and I'll plant this one there. I'll find myself a good place to watch from, and I'll be watching when you buy it.

The rest I can't tell you yet because it depends a lot on circumstances, whether you went right home with the book or what you did. I won't know till I follow you and keep watch till you read it—and I see that you're reading the last story in the book.

If you're home while you're reading this, maybe I'm in the house with you right now. Maybe I'm in this very room, hidden, waiting for you to finish the story. Maybe I'm watching through a window. Or maybe I'm sitting near you on the streetcar or train, if you're reading it there. Maybe I'm on the fire escape outside your hotel room. But wherever you're reading it, I'm near you, watching and waiting for you to finish. You can count on that.

You're pretty near the end now. You'll be finished in seconds and you'll close the book, still not believing. Or, if you haven't read the stories in order, maybe you'll turn back to start another story. If you do, you'll never finish it.

But don't look around; you'll be happier if you don't know, if you don't see the knife coming. When I kill people from behind they don't seem to mind so much.

Go on, just a few seconds or minutes, thinking this is just another story. Don't look behind you. Don't believe this—*until you feel the knife.*

RAY BRADBURY

Here are my choices: "The Monkey's Paw," by W. W. Jacobs; "The Cask of Amontillado," by Edgar Allan Poe, and "The Outsider," by H. P. Lovecraft.

The memories that go with them? As follows: I was fifteen, in the tenth grade in high school, when my teacher and inspirer for the rest of my life, Jennet Johnson, read "The Monkey's Paw" aloud to our short story writing class. Her reading was such, and the story was such, that I had permanent hackles for a month. I knew that a kindred spirit was at hand, and as the year went by, showed her more and more of my "strange" stories and science fiction. Her response: "I don't quite know what you're doing, but you have talent. Continue." The dear lady died two years ago, at ninety-two, after half-a-lifetime of friendship shared with her young half-Martian friend from Waukegan.

Poe and the Amontillado? My Aunt Neva, the crazy aunt in our family, which means the one with imagination, designed dresses and costumes for the Chicago Opera and the World's Fair there in 1933, at which time she also read Poe aloud to me. "The Cask" was one of the first, when I was ten. It marked me indelibly and I went on, a few years later, to enter and stay in a prolonged period of Poe imitation, which only a good dose of Hemingway and Steinbeck could cure me of.

I still think "The Cask of Amontillado" is one of the best stories ever written by any author in any genre.

I read "The Outsider" when I got my huge collected Lovecraft from Arkham House, in 1939, when I was a member of the Los Angeles Science Fantasy Society. The ending knocked me off my heels, caught me by surprise. I was never a Lovecraft fanatic, but this story was superb. There ensued no period of Lovecraft imitation in my life—I was too old for that, and I saw that his style would weigh me down. I escaped his gravity, even as I did that of Henry James, on a more sophisticated level, a few years later. Love at a distance was best in the case of both of these authors.

THE MONKEY'S PAW

W. W. JACOBS

Without, the night was cold and wet, but in the small parlor of Lakesnam Villa the blinds were drawn and the fire burned brightly. Father and son were at chess, the former, who possessed ideas about the game involving radical changes, putting his king into such sharp and unnecessary perils that it even provoked comment from the white-haired old lady knitting placidly by the fire.

"Hark at the wind," said Mr. White, who, having seen a fatal mistake after it was too late, was amiably desirous of preventing his son from seeing it.

"I'm listening," said the latter, grimly surveying the board as he stretched out his hand. "Check."

"I should hardly think that he'd come tonight," said his father, with his hand poised over the board.

"Mate," replied the son.

"That's the worst of living so far out," bawled Mr. White, with sudden and unlooked-for violence; "of all the beastly, slushy, out-of-the-way places to live in, this is the worst. Pathway's a bog, and the road's a torrent. I don't know what people are thinking about. I suppose because only two houses on the road are let, they think it doesn't matter."

"Never mind, dear," said his wife soothingly; "perhaps you'll win the next one."

Mr. White looked up sharply, just in time to intercept a knowing glance between mother and son. The words died away on his lips, and he hid a guilty grin in his thin gray beard.

"There he is," said Herbert White, as the gate banged to loudly and heavy footsteps came toward the door.

The old man rose with hospitable haste, and opening the door, was heard condoling with the new arrival. The new arrival also condoled with himself, so that Mrs. White said, "Tut, tut!" and coughed gently as her husband entered the room, followed by a tall burly man, beady of eye and rubicund of visage.

"Sergeant Major Morris," he said, introducing him.

The sergeant major shook hands and, taking the proffered seat by the fire, watched contentedly while his host got out whisky and tumblers and stood a small copper kettle on the fire.

At the third glass his eyes got brighter, and he began to talk, the little family circle regarding with eager interest this visitor from distant parts, as he squared his broad shoulders in the chair and spoke of strange scenes and doughty deeds, of wars and plagues and strange peoples.

"Twenty-one years of it," said Mr. White, nodding at his wife and son. "When he went away he was a slip of a youth in the warehouse. Now look at him."

"He don't look to have taken much harm," said Mrs. White politely.

"I'd like to go to India myself," said the old man, "just to look round a bit, you know."

"Better where you are," said the sergeant major, shaking his head. He put down the empty glass and, sighing softly, shook it again.

"I should like to see those old temples and fakirs and jugglers," said the old man. "What was that you started telling me the other day about a monkey's paw or something, Morris?"

"Nothing," said the soldier hastily. "Leastways, nothing worth hearing."

"Monkey's paw?" said Mrs. White curiously.

"Well, it's just a bit of what you might call magic, perhaps," said the sergeant major offhandedly.

His three listeners leaned forward eagerly. The visitor absentmindedly put his empty glass to his lips and then set it down again. His host filled it for him.

"To look at," said the sergeant major, fumbling in his pocket, "it's just an ordinary little paw, dried to a mummy."

He took something out of his pocket and proffered it. Mrs. White drew back with a grimace, but her son, taking it, examined it curiously.

"And what is there special about it?" inquired Mr. White, as he took it from his son and, having examined it, placed it upon the table.

"It had a spell put on it by an old fakir," said the sergeant major, "a very holy man. He wanted to show that fate ruled people's lives, and that those who interfered with it did so to their sorrow. He put a spell on it so that three separate men could have three wishes from it."

His manner was so impressive that his hearers were conscious that their light laughter jarred somewhat.

"Well, why don't you have three, sir?" said Herbert White cleverly.

The soldier regarded him in the way that middle age is wont to regard presumptuous youth. "I have," he said quietly, and his blotchy face whitened.

"And did you really have the three wishes granted?" asked Mrs. White.

"I did," said the sergeant major, and his glass tapped against his strong teeth.

"And has anybody else wished?" inquired the old lady.

"The first man had his three wishes, yes," was the reply. "I don't know what the first two were, but the third was for death. That's how I got the paw."

His tones were so grave that a hush fell upon the group.

"If you've had your three wishes, it's no good to you now, then, Morris," said the old man at last. "What do you keep it for?"

The soldier shook his head. "Fancy, I suppose," he said slowly. "I did have some idea of selling it, but I don't think I will. It has caused enough mischief already. Besides, people won't buy. They think it's a fairy tale, some of them, and those who do think anything of it want to try it first and pay me afterward."

"If you could have another three wishes," said the old man, eyeing him keenly, "would you have them?"

"I don't know," said the other. "I don't know."

He took the paw and, dangling it between his front finger and thumb, suddenly threw it upon the fire. White, with a slight cry, stooped down and snatched it off.

"Better let it burn," said the soldier solemnly.

"If you don't want it, Morris," said the old man, "give it to me."

"I won't," said his friend doggedly. "I threw it on the fire. If you keep it, don't blame me for what happens. Pitch it on the fire again, like a sensible man."

The other shook his head and examined his new possession closely. "How do you do it?" he inquired.

"Hold it up in your right hand and wish aloud," said the sergeant major, "but I warn you of the consequences."

"Sounds like the *Arabian Nights,*" said Mrs. White, as she rose and began to set the supper. "Don't you think you might wish for four pairs of hands for me?"

Her husband drew the talisman from his pocket and then all three burst into laughter as the sergeant major, with a look of alarm on his face, caught him by the arm.

"If you must wish," he said gruffly, "wish for something sensible."

Mr. White dropped it back into his pocket, and placing chairs, motioned his friend to the table. In the business of supper the talisman was partly forgotten, and afterward the three sat listening in an enthralled fashion to a second installment of the soldier's adventures in India.

"If the tale about the monkey's paw is not more truthful than those he has been telling us," said Herbert, as the door closed behind their guest, just in time for him to catch the last train, "we shan't make much out of it."

"Did you give him anything for it, father?" inquired Mrs. White, regarding her husband closely.

"A trifle," said he, coloring slightly. "He didn't want it, but I made him take it. And he pressed me again to throw it away."

"Likely," said Herbert, with pretended horror. "Why, we're going to be rich, and famous and happy. Wish to be an emperor, father, to begin with; then you can't be henpecked."

He darted round the table, pursued by the maligned Mrs. White armed with an antimacassar.

Mr. White took the paw from his pocket and eyed it dubiously. "I don't know what to wish for, and that's a fact," he said slowly. "It seems to me I've got all I want."

"If you only cleared the house, you'd be quite happy, wouldn't you?" said Herbert, with his hand on his shoulder. "Well, wish for two hundred pounds, then; that'll just do it."

His father, smiling shamefacedly at his own credulity, held up the talisman, as his son, with a solemn face somewhat marred by a wink at his mother, sat down at the piano and struck a few impressive chords.

"I wish for two hundred pounds," said the old man distinctly.

A fine crash from the piano greeted the words, interrupted by a shuddering cry from the old man. His wife and son ran toward him.

"It moved," he cried, with a glance of disgust at the object as it lay on the floor. "As I wished it twisted in my hands like a snake."

"Well, I don't see the money," said his son, as he picked it up and placed it on the table, "and I bet I never shall."

"It must have been your fancy, father," said his wife, regarding him anxiously.

He shook his head. "Never mind, though; there's no harm done, but it gave me a shock all the same."

They sat down by the fire again while the two men finished their pipes. Outside, the wind was higher than ever, and the old man started nervously at the sound of a door banging upstairs. A silence unusual and depressing settled upon all three, which lasted until the old couple rose to retire for the night.

"I expect you'll find the cash tied up in a big bag in the middle of your bed," said Herbert, as he bade them good night, "and something horrible squatting up on top of the wardrobe watching you as you pocket your ill-gotten gains."

II

In the brightness of the wintry sun next morning as it streamed over the breakfast table, Herbert laughed at his fears. There was an air of prosaic wholesomeness about the room which it had lacked on the previous night, and the dirty, shriveled little paw was pitched on the sideboard with a carelessness which betokened no great belief in its virtues.

"I suppose all old soldiers are the same," said Mrs. White. "The idea of our listening to such nonsense! How could wishes be granted in these days? And if they could, how could two hundred pounds hurt you, father?"

"Might drop on his head from the sky," said the frivolous Herbert.

"Morris said the things happened so naturally," said his father, "that you might if you so wished attribute it to coincidence."

"Well, don't break into the money before I come back," said Herbert, as he rose from the table. "I'm afraid it'll turn you into a mean, avaricious man, and we shall have to disown you."

His mother laughed, and following him to the door, watched him down the road, and returning to the breakfast table, was very happy at the expense of her husband's credulity. All of which did not prevent her from scurrying to the door at the postman's knock, nor prevent her from referring somewhat shortly to retired sergeant majors of bibulous habits when she found that the post brought a tailor's bill.

"Herbert will have some more of his funny remarks, I expect, when he comes home," she said, as they sat at dinner.

"I daresay," said Mr. White, pouring himself out some beer; "but for all that, the thing moved in my hand; that I'll swear to."

"You thought it did," said the old lady soothingly.

"I say it did," replied the other. "There was no thought about it; I had just—What's the matter?"

His wife made no reply. She was watching the mysterious movements of a man outside, who, peering in an undecided fashion at the house, appeared to be trying to make up his mind to enter. In mental connection with the two hundred pounds, she noticed that the stranger was well dressed and wore a silk hat of glossy newness. Three times he paused at the gate, and then walked on again. The fourth time he stood with his hand upon it, and then with sudden resolution flung it open and walked up the path. Mrs. White at the same moment placed her hands behind her, and hurriedly unfastening the strings of her apron, put that useful article of apparel beneath the cushion of her chair.

She brought the stranger, who seemed ill at ease, into the room. He gazed furtively at Mrs. White, and listened in a preoccupied fashion as the old lady apologized for the appearance of the room, and her husband's coat, a garment which he usually reserved for the garden. She then waited as patiently as her sex would permit for him to broach his business, but he was at first strangely silent.

"I—was asked to call," he said at last, and stooped and picked a piece of cotton from his trousers. "I come from Maw and Meggins."

The old lady started. "Is anything the matter?" she asked breathlessly. "Has anything happened to Herbert? What is it? What is it?"

Her husband interposed. "There, there, mother," he said hastily. "Sit down, and don't jump to conclusions. You've not brought bad news, I'm sure, sir," and he eyed the other wistfully.

"I'm sorry—" began the visitor.

"Is he hurt?" demanded the mother.

The visitor bowed in assent. "Badly hurt," he said quietly, "but he is not in any pain."

"Oh, thank God!" said the old woman, clasping her hands. "Thank God for that! Thank—"

She broke off suddenly as the sinister meaning of the assurance dawned upon her and she saw the awful confirmation of her fears in the other's averted face. She caught her breath, and turning to her slower-witted husband, laid her trembling old hand upon his. There was a long silence.

"He was caught in the machinery," said the visitor at length, in a low voice.

"Caught in the machinery," repeated Mr. White, in a dazed fashion, "yes."

He sat staring blankly out at the window and, taking his wife's hand between his own, pressed it as he had been wont to do in their old courting days nearly forty years before.

"He was the only one left us," he said, turning gently to the visitor. "It is hard."

The other coughed and, rising, walked slowly to the window. "The firm wished me to convey their sincere sympathy with you in your great loss," he said, without looking round. "I beg that you will understand I am only their servant and merely obeying orders."

There was no reply; the old woman's face was white, her eyes staring and her breath inaudible; on the husband's face was a look such as his friend the sergeant might have carried into his his first action.

"I was to say that Maw and Meggins disclaim all responsibility," continued the other. "They admit no liability at all, but in consideration of your son's services they wish to present you with a certain sum as compensation."

Mr. White dropped his wife's hand, and rising to his feet, gazed with a look of horror at his visitor. His dry lips shaped the words, "How much?"

"Two hundred pounds," was the answer.

Unconscious of his wife's shriek, the old man smiled faintly, put out his hands like a sightless man and dropped, a senseless heap, to the floor.

III

In the huge new cemetery, some two miles distant, the old people buried their dead and came back to a house steeped in shadow and silence. It was all over so quickly that at first they could hardly realize it, and remained in a state of expectation as though of something else to happen—something else which was to lighten this load, too heavy for old hearts to bear. But the days passed, and expectation gave place to resignation—the hopeless resignation of the old, sometimes miscalled apathy. Sometimes they hardly exchanged a word, for now they had nothing to talk about, and their days were long to weariness.

It was about a week after that that the old man, waking suddenly in the night, stretched out his hand and found himself alone. The room was in darkness, and the sound of subdued weeping came from the window. He raised himself in bed and listened.

"Come back," he said tenderly. "You will be cold."

"It is colder for my son," said the old woman, and wept afresh.

The sound of her sobs died away on his ears. The bed was warm, and his eyes heavy with sleep. He dozed fitfully, and then slept until a sudden wild cry from his wife awoke him with a start.

"The monkey's paw!" she cried wildly. "The monkey's paw!"

He started up in alarm. "Where? Where is it? What's the matter?"

She came stumbling across the room toward him. "I want it," she said quietly. "You've not destroyed it?"

"It's in the parlor, on the bracket," he replied, marveling. "Why?"

She cried and laughed together and, bending over, kissed his cheek.

"I only just thought of it," she said hysterically. "Why didn't I think of it before? Why didn't you think of it?"

"Think of what?" he questioned.

"The other two wishes," she replied rapidly. "We've only had one."

"Was not that enough?" he demanded fiercely.

"No," she cried triumphantly; "We'll have one more. Go down and get it quickly, and wish our boy alive again."

The man sat up in bed and flung the bedclothes from his quaking limbs. "Good God, you are mad!" he cried, aghast.

"Get it," she panted; "get it quickly, and wish—Oh, my boy, my boy!"

Her husband struck a match and lit the candle. "Get back to bed," he said unsteadily. "You don't know what you are saying."

"We had the first wish granted," said the old woman feverishly; "why not the second?"

"A coincidence," stammered the old man.

"Go and get it and wish," cried the old woman, and dragged him toward the door.

He went down in the darkness, and felt his way to the parlor, and then to the mantelpiece. The talisman was in its place, and a horrible fear that the unspoken wish might bring his mutilated son before him ere he could escape from the room seized upon him, and he caught his breath as he found that he had lost the direction of the door. His brow cold with sweat, he felt his way round the table, and groped along the wall until he found himself in the small passage with the unwholesome thing in his hand.

Even his wife's face seemed changed as he entered the room. It was white and expectant, and to his fears seemed to have an unusual look upon it. He was afraid of her.

"Wish!" she cried, in a strong voice.

"It is foolish and wicked," he faltered.

"Wish!" repeated his wife.

He raised his hand. "I wish my son alive again."

The talisman fell to the floor, and he regarded it shudderingly. Then he sank trembling into a chair as the old woman, with burning eyes, walked to the window and raised the blind.

He sat until he was chilled with the cold, glancing occasionally at the figure of the old woman peering through the window. The candle end, which had burned below the rim of the china candlestick, was throwing pulsating shadows on the ceiling and walls, until, with a flicker larger than the rest, it expired. The old man, with an unspeakable sense of relief at the failure of the talisman, crept back to his bed, and a minute or two afterward the old woman came silently and apathetically beside him.

Neither spoke, but both lay silently listening to the ticking of the clock. A stair creaked, and a squeaky mouse scurried noisily through the wall. The darkness was oppressive, and after lying for some time screwing up his courage, the husband took the box of matches and, striking one, went downstairs for a candle.

At the foot of the stairs the match went out, and he paused to strike another, and at the same moment a knock, so quiet and stealthy as to be scarcely audible, sounded on the front door.

The matches fell from his hand. He stood motionless, his breath suspended until the knock was repeated. Then he turned and fled swiftly back to his room, and closed the door behind him. A third knock sounded through the house.

"*What's that?*" cried the old woman, starting up.

"A rat," said the old man, in shaking tones—"a rat. It passed me on the stairs."

His wife sat up in bed, listening. A loud knock resounded through the house.

"It's Herbert!" she screamed. "It's Herbert!"

She ran to the door, but her husband was before her and, catching her by the arm, held her tightly.

"What are you going to do?" he whispered hoarsely.

"It's my boy; it's Herbert!" she cried, struggling mechanically. "I forgot it was two miles away. What are you holding me for? Let go. I must open the door."

"For God's sake don't let it in," cried the old man, trembling.

"You're afraid of your own son," she cried, struggling. "Let me go. I'm coming. Herbert; I'm coming."

There was another knock, and another. The old woman with a sudden wrench broke free and ran from the room. Her husband followed to the landing, and called after her appealingly as she hurried downstairs. He heard the chain rattle back and the bottom bolt drawn slowly and stiffly from the socket. Then the old woman's voice, strained and panting.

"The bolt," she cried loudly. "Come down. I can't reach it."

But her husband was on his hands and knees groping wildly on the floor in search of the paw. If he could only find it before the thing outside got in. A perfect fusillade of knocks reverberated through the house, and he heard the scraping of a chair as his wife put it down in the passage against the door. He heard the creaking of the bolt as it came slowly back, and at the same moment, he found the monkey's paw, and frantically breathed his third and last wish.

The knocking ceased suddenly, although the echoes of it were still in the house. He heard the chair drawn back and the door opened. A cold wind rushed up the staircase, and a long loud wail of disappointment and misery from his wife gave him courage to run down to her side, and then to the gate beyond. The street lamp flickering opposite shone on a quiet and deserted road.

HELEN GURLEY BROWN

This story chilled me enormously! Maybe it's because I am compulsive, like the heroine, and if I ever quit compulsing with editing and exercising and dieting and a few other things, I can easily see myself in a garden clipping roses just like Samantha. She brought her horrible demise on herself, of course, but still I find her touching and sympathetic. Gardner McKay has a beautiful, understated way with terror and horror . . . the story so moved me I still *want somehow to locate that poor woman and cut her out of the brambles. She* haunts *me.*

INTO THE ROSE GARDEN

GARDNER MCKAY

There was something about them, the roses. They looked, how would you say it, defensive? No. Brambly. Ugly.

Conversation slows. Day hangs. Standstill. The Atlantic Ocean, seen out the window across the dunes shimmering white, is stopped, cooking.

A bug whines in the dining room.

"Who in hell would want to wall off an area for those things, anyway? If they were real roses—maybe—but those? Jesus, will I ever cease to be amazed?"

"They've got a craggy grace, Sam," Amalia says.

"They go. Out-out-out."

"Samantha knows what she's up to, Amalia. This house hasn't come to grips with the fact that it's been waiting a hundred years for her to coordinate it with wicker and chrome." David is the only person allowed to call her Samantha. David is her husband.

"Bravo!"

She never looked like a Sam to him. Which is why, of course, the name suited her so perfectly, she explained to him long ago. If she looked like a Sam, she'd be called Lisa. But she is a small, decorated person and not at all a Sam and he liked to say the name Samantha. He keeps only one photograph of her, taken before she'd cut her hair close, when it had hung to her shoulders, and when he would have to look for that place just under her ear if he wanted to kiss it.

Chewing. The conversation stops. The dining room, held back in 1910, is bordered everywhere by dark, varnished wood. It is only cool when there is a sea breeze and it is hot when the breeze backs around and comes over the land, and the breeze has backed around. The screens are rusted black or rusted through.

"Screens," Sam says, and David knows it means she will measure the windows and order aluminum screens, probably Monday.

"The blue shutters are perfect." The Martins are down to Westcove for the weekend, seeing the new house before Sam transforms it. They come each summer, always to a different house, and Sam has done this to houses for the past fourteen summers. Fourteen summer towns, fourteen summer houses.

David comes out by train each weekend, carrying cushions or something he's been told to pick up in the city during the week. But the house is Sam's occupation, not his.

The trick was always to find the right house, that house which could be bought run-down during the winter, transformed over the summer, and listed for sale before Labor Day, furnished and decorated, at a thirty to fifty percent profit.

And so here was this shingled "treasure," given up for sale by a widow who had outlived her husband for forty years and had now gone to live at the Imperial Convalescent Home near Long Island City, to play cards there and to wait it out.

Last night, when David had brought the Martins out from the city, he had seen that Sam had painted the shutters and the front door light blue.

"I knew they'd be going."

"I really hated those gray shutters a lot," Sam said.

"What color is that?"

"Periwinkle blue."

He rarely argued. He visited each weekend, drank, slept, watched each house change, and left. It seemed to be a good marriage.

Sam knew which effects to spend money on. The best paint was certainly never to be used. Repairs to pipes had to look good. Curtains didn't need to close, but a yard of fabric had to hang on either side of a window, accenting. What she did to a house she called lipsticking.

After lunch, after everyone had tried to play canasta, after another drink, they all took naps except David, who went to look at the roses.

Walled by brick, they were in their own place behind the house, entered only through a brick archway with a broken ornate iron gate, which swung without touching the wall and could not keep anything in or out.

Wild as cats, the stalks grew from everywhere. Down from the walls, bowed strands longer than fishing rods barely swayed in the heat. Up from the ground and over to the walls and then back, grown into themselves, into tiny leaf clusters, into rashes of thorns, and the roses themselves, white and penny sized. David wouldn't have known they were roses unless Sam had complained about them and she was right; they were small trees.

He walked in two or three steps and felt the sleeve of his short-sleeved shirt catch on an overhanging stem. Once, maybe, when they had been tended, a person was meant to walk in, see the roses, turn around, and walk out: a rose garden.

The heat was extreme. The bricks he could see through the stalks had once been painted white and what was still white reflected the sun and what was red held the sun. And it had all been set in a depression behind the house without a view of anything.

The next day—Sunday—early, Sam was already in her swatch room, a small room she chose in each house to become her control center while the house was under transformation. Here hung swatches of fabric, sketches, bills, estimates, and on the walls were painted smears of paint and on a drawing table, which stood center rear, there were tile samples, removed doorknobs to be sold and a telephone. There was importance to her control centers.

David, though he had not yet read the Sunday *Times,* had gone out into the rose garden and found that it was already warming up even though the day was still cool. He cut several hanging tips that curled out into the air—just enough of them to fill a cream pitcher which he put on the table in front of the bay window, under the shade of the lamp.

But the only mention of roses made later, at the crab salad and chilled Riesling lunch, was by Sam, who had just measured the brick walls around the rose garden and said that the area would be cleared and made into a badminton court.

No one played badminton and David knew that you couldn't play between close brick walls, but he didn't say that because he knew it didn't matter. What mattered was how it would look with white cotton service lines, and a white net strung across the center, one wall to the other. What mattered was how much it would add to the resale price. What mattered was how large it would look in the house photographs for the New York listing agency. There didn't even have to be rackets.

"Bravo badminton!" Martin said.

"Brilliant!" Amalia said.

Late that night, coming downstairs for hot chocolate, David studied the roses in the cream pitcher. Sometimes he looked carefully at things that had not been shown to him.

He turned on the shaded lamp just above them and leaned over them with both his elbows on the table, staring into them, waiting for the pot of milk on the stove to heat. They were small roses, color-bled, but still definitely roses, their perfect scent faintly certifying them as roses, and the ugly clusters of thorns, small as cats' teeth.

He had never cared for flowers indoors or out, but he had never looked at roses. The attainable miracle of nature, they grew menacing stalks yet came to fragile tips. Each stem had hundreds of thorns, overbred, without a place to hold them, but the flowers! He stared at them under the lamp. He thought them white before but they weren't, they were barely pink. He looked into one, fine and small, each shield turning in on itself inside. He brought his crossword pencil out of his robe and separated the center shields and they yielded softly, softly like other yieldings in his past, and he saw that at its center, the rose became a truer pink, a ballet pink, and he put his pencil away.

They won't live long, he thought, maybe they don't like to stand around a house, dying in a cream pitcher. And while he was thinking about the intriguing respect for roses, he heard the hissing in the kitchen and smelled the flame-black milk.

Monday morning, after Sam had driven the others to the station, after she had measured the screens and left her order at Paul's Hardware, and still before the day had grown hot, she faced the rose garden, holding a new pair of Wiss nine-inch shears and wearing a gardening skirt, a cotton blouse, denim gauntlets, and a good sun hat. She cut where she stood. Branches fell as she snipped and she began to cut her way back and forth, wall to wall. The rose branches had spread everywhere and now fell everywhere, long straight arms falling across uncut straight arms underneath. Her skirt was cool and protected her knees but it caught again and again on thorns no bigger than stingers.

She stopped and looked at her watch. Only ten minutes had gone and she was sweating. She looked back at the glass of iced tea she had left by the iron gate under the brick archway. It stood fuming in the sun, making its own hard shadow. She started back to it but there were too many loose stems to catch her.

She cut again, at random, easily, with the power the good shears gave her, cutting overhead, sometimes cutting at her waist level, back and forth from the wall on one side to the wall on the other, leaving a high bed of cut and fallen barbed coils, hardly woven, higher than her waist. Down from the sides of the walls the rose branches came, falling higher by the walls than in the middle. She cut whatever she could reach and the minutes passed into an hour and now she stood in the farthest corner, close to the brick wall. She was working in the shade, but the sun was just gleaming over the top of the wall above where she stood.

It all lay before her now in a great sprung bed, four feet in the middle and rising to the walls on all sides. It was time for iced tea. She could no longer see the glass through the wild coils. Flying bugs stood on the air, looking for the stalks that had been there overhead a few minutes before. A brilliant July day had begun and if there was an ocean breeze, she could not feel it behind the house, between the walls of the rose garden.

She stood in the corner, leaning against the wall still cool from the night, still in the shade. The walls were new to her. They were of the brick she liked best. Where they weren't white, they were orange red and porous, easily worn. She imagined it all again, without brambles, as a badminton court. How much prettier it would look.

It was time to go. The cut stalks in the middle were higher than her waist but the way along the walls was higher. It was good to be this hot, good to sweat. The sides along the walls were rampant and still with downed stems, which ran the length of the rose garden. The middle was a trampoline of lighter arms hardly touching one another and of tiny nearly white flowers, cut dead but not yet showing it.

It did look impenetrable, but still pleasantly challenging. Cutting them had felt good. Now she would call a contractor to haul them away in truckloads, to dig the roots out and surface the floor.

She leaned in the corner thinking. Then she made several cuts straight ahead to cut a path out. She cut both ends of a stem and lifted it away. Another stem clung to it, holding it back. She freed it and threw it aside. That was one. She cut another and did the same but a stem sprung back. She cut it and lifted it free and threw it aside. She advanced a foot.

Cutting in, she had not made a path but had cut across, one side to the other, letting stalks fall behind her. Now they were there, great easy springs of brambles formed into a solid mattress wide as the rose garden.

If she could step on the main stalks and stay up and above it all she could get across in a dozen steps, maybe more.

Balancing herself with the new shears, she took the first high step onto the top of the brambles, taking them down with her weight, but not down to the ground. They carried her springing to her second step, springing to her third, forward on the main stalks above the ground, free of thorns, springing to her fourth step, then missing her fifth. She jammed her leg through between the cut stems feeling the scratches up to her thigh and fell forward and lay face down, rocking.

Now lying on the stalks and stems, flattened forward, she reached out but there was nothing to take hold of. Pulling against nothing, she could not pull her leg back through. She did not have the weight to bow the stalks to the ground and so she lay, hung there above the ground, flat, spread, springing slightly. She was afloat.

She had let go of the shears when she had fallen and they had slipped through the surface and were down and out of sight. She felt scratched on her arms and legs but she was comfortable, as long as she didn't move.

She rested. Sweat ran from her eyebrows to the tip of her nose and dropped. Plant bugs landed on her and took off, uninterested. She raised her head and saw a long red pen mark along her arm. This was ridiculous.

With the sudden writhing motion of a swimming crayfish, she flipped herself, working her body in and out, flipped herself again and again and entangled herself so well that in less than a minute she could not move without tearing her skin. She lay there panting, not quite still, swaying slightly, and began to think in terms of time.

A cry for help. What would that do from a walled area behind a house, back from the road, with the onshore breeze blowing the words inland? If there were cars driving by, they were cars of swimmers and they turned in toward the ocean on a road between the dunes.

Whenever she moved she jounced small flowers over near the walls. It was all connected of woven spring fibers that easily held her weight. She tried again to touch the ground with her foot

It was probably noon. She looked across at her watch without moving her arm: not noon, eleven-ten. She was dry in her throat, dry on the roof of her mouth, and her face was wet. It was good to be this hot, this wet, this dry. It cleaned you out. She really liked the brick walls. They'd be perfect. Why had they been built so high? Maybe to keep the sand out? Maybe.

If she craned her neck up she could see between the coils to her iced tea, sweating in the sun. The ice had melted.

There was the constant murmur of insects. The day stopped. Noon. It was too hot. It was too still. She tried again. The thorns held her and hurt her everywhere. Someone would come to deliver something. Carpets were due. The plumber.

Five more hours of sun. Then it would be behind the wall and there would be three hours of light after that. This was a good lesson. She had really painted herself into a corner this time, hadn't she?

She let her head drop to look at the ground nearly three feet below her, looking at the strength and age of the roses, more trunks than stalks. She wondered if they lived from underground water.

The first cool breath of evening came long after the sun had gone behind the wall. The bricks held the heat, cooling slowly. Just at dark she felt a mosquito land on her arm. Another. Another. One stung her. It was a signal. They all stung her. She writhed her hips trying to pull her legs up to her, trying to get on her back, without caring about the cuts or the pain from the thorns and when she couldn't move anymore, she felt dozens of new scratches and in the gloom felt the mosquitoes landing again, one at a time, on her arms and legs, walking among the gentlest parts of her skin, inside her elbows and behind her knees. She felt them between her thighs.

Sometime that night she could not tell the difference between the thorns and the mosquitoes and when she felt them on her back she realized that she had ripped the back from her blouse and that it was gone.

She began screaming Tuesday morning, when she knew the swimmers would be driving by. She had not fallen asleep and the mosquitoes had not left until dawn. She would scream and rest. Scream and rest. She stopped when she heard seagulls answering her.

Late that afternoon, long after the sun had gone behind the wall, just at dark, she knew that the first mosquito would come, and it did. She watched it on her elbow inject her, taking blood, again and again, until it couldn't fly and walked around fat and easy to kill. They were all easy to kill. But she couldn't kill them.

That night she saw the moonlight shining on the ocean through the rugged ornateness of the broken iron gate. She felt it so close she could have taken a salt bath in it and healed her sores. But of course she couldn't see the ocean from where she lay, it was a trick of the moon.

The dryness in her throat now went down her windpipe and into her lungs. She slept and woke after the moon had set and felt dew on her arms. She licked her shoulders.

Wednesday morning with the first dismal heat of the sun over the wall, already hot when it touched her back, she tried to call out but couldn't. Her throat was clear and dry and the only sound she could make was a rasping growl. Soon each breath was hot; soon the walls of the rose garden had turned it into a sun oven for another day.

That night, even though it was cool, her back stayed hot and she felt the mosquitoes by the hundreds clustered at each open blister and when she slept or screamed she listened to their conversation and in the night heard music, a concert of bass violins running in an odd rhythm with the conversation of the mosquitoes, which seemed to be dinner music played in a noisy restaurant. She felt her arms and legs and back wet with blood moving away from her body.

Thursday morning just as the sun gleamed over the wall, she screamed at it, screaming to hold it back.

Sometime that day she felt a bird standing on her back, a bluejay shrieking at another bluejay who was trying to land. Later she felt the bluejay pecking into the sores on her back. But she could not move.

Neddy Price from Eastcove, twenty-three, tall, stands at the front door Friday afternoon wearing damp swimming shorts and a terry-cloth hat and pauses between knocks to see if anyone will come. His car has stalled and he holds an empty gallon bottle he wants to fill with water. He's sure somebody's home because he's seen a car in the garage and so he walks barefoot around to the back door and calls through the screen. He peers through it and sees the sink and slips in and fills his bottle in the cool, shadowed kitchen, its floor cold on the bottoms of his feet. He opens the refrigerator and takes three gulps of grapefruit juice and slips back out the screen door.

Now he turns, looking back away from the house and sees the walls of the rose garden. He sees the ornate iron gate and the roses just inside and decides to walk over and get himself a couple of roses. After all, his girl friend, Paula Cabiri, is waiting in the hot car and Neddy has never in his life seen a rose garden full of so many incredibly red roses.

C. TERRY CLINE, JR.

C. Terry Cline's comments on his alternate choices were so interesting that we thought we would share them with you, along with his thoughts on his first choice, Stephen King's "The Mangler."

"A Voice in the Night," by William Hope Hodgson—Lordy how that kept me blinking in the dark when I read it. It is the rue of any author that he should be repelled and attracted to the acid taste of fear, but how else can he replicate it, unless he has endured the taut abdomen and copper scent of terror? This story haunted me for years. It still does. Just as I was subduing the nightmares, Rod Serling used the story for a very successful segment on his TV series, "The Twilight Zone." Our fears today are more than primordial movements beyond the flicker of a campfire. The beasts are vanquished and no sabertooth is likely to rend our flesh. The fungi of today may be the product of government bureaucrats (a malignant growth unto themselves, perhaps), and we are constantly threatened by unknown by-products of the atomic age. But Mr. Hodgson's story has social relevance that is timeless. His story speaks of those wretched souls who suffer the worst of all maladies—social ostracism. We are all vulnerable. We fear the leper because we fear we may be forced to join his isolated colony. "A Voice in the Night" sets atremble a basic chord, a primitive pang, and I warn you—it will keep you awake more nights than you'll care to remember. . . .

Jerome Bixby's "It's a Good Life" has a simple psychological dread to offer—the child who, spawned by us as parents, goes on to control and terrify us. That fear is the genesis of many tales, including my own novel, Damon. *I suspect that fear of our children is universal. It has to do with the normal parental loss of dominance, Oedipus complexes notwithstanding. But, mostly, I think the fear is a fear that we will suffer the same fate we delivered to our own parents. Children are, after all, God's best ploy to punish us for what we've done to our fathers and mothers. Life begins when you get married. It escalates and assumes value with progeny. And we all fear the chance that we will have to present a facade, a transparent visage of our own good life. . . .*

I know about manglers. They lurk in wait for their pound of flesh, humming at 115 cycles and 120 volts. They roar as lawn mowers, chain saws, purr as blenders and hiss as pressure cookers. My automobile tried to blind me with an exploding battery. Razors have lunged for flesh. Using an electric knife to carve the Thanksgiving turkey, temporarily distracted, the beast severed one curtain, snatched at the sleeve of my son's shirt and, when hurled to the floor, pursued us into a corner snapping at the stomping foot. Long before Mr. King wrote of it, I knew—it's out there.

THE MANGLER

STEPHEN KING

Officer Hunton got to the laundry just as the ambulance was leaving—slowly, with no siren or flashing lights. Ominous. Inside, the office was stuffed with milling, silent people, some of them weeping. The plant itself was empty; the big automatic washers at the far end had not even been shut down. It made Hunton very wary. The crowd should be at the scene of the accident, not in the office. It was the way things worked—the human animal had a built-in urge to view the remains. A very bad one, then. Hunton felt his stomach tighten as it always did when the accident was very bad. Fourteen years of cleaning human litter from highways and streets and the sidewalks at the bases of very tall buildings had not been able to erase that little hitch in the belly, as if something evil had clotted there.

A man in a white shirt saw Hunton and walked toward him reluctantly. He was a buffalo of a man with head thrust forward between shoulders, nose and cheeks vein-broken either from high blood pressure or too many conversations with the brown bottle. He was trying to frame words, but after two tries Hunton cut him off briskly: "Are you the owner? Mr. Gartley?"

"No . . . no. I'm Stanner. The foreman. God, this—"

Hunton got out his notebook. "Please show me the scene of the accident, Mr. Stanner, and tell me what happened."

Stanner seemed to grow even more white; the blotches on his nose and cheeks stood out like birthmarks. "D-do I have to?"

Hunton raised his eyebrows. "I'm afraid you do. The call I got said it was serious."

"Serious—" Stanner seemed to be battling with his gorge; for a moment his Adam's apple went up and down like a monkey on a stick. "Mrs. Frawley is dead. Jesus, I wish Bill Gartley *was* here."

"What happened?"

Stanner said, "You better come over here."

He led Hunton past a row of hand presses, a shirt-folding unit, and then stopped by a laundry-marking machine. He passed a shaky hand across his forehead. "You'll have to go over by yourself, officer. I can't look at it again. It makes me . . . I can't. I'm sorry."

Hunton walked around the marking machine with a mild feeling of contempt for the man. They run a loose shop, cut corners, run live steam through home-welded pipes, they work with dangerous cleaning chemicals without the proper protection, and finally, someone gets hurt. Or gets dead. Then they can't look. They can't—

Hunton saw it.

The machine was still running. No one had shut it off. The machine he later came to know intimately: the Hadley-Watson Model-6 Speed Ironer and Folder. A long and clumsy name. The people who worked here in the steam and the wet had a better name for it. The mangler.

Hunton took a long, frozen look, and then he performed a first in his fourteen years as a law-enforcement officer: he turned around, put a convulsive hand to his mouth, and threw up.

"You didn't eat much," Jackson said.

The women were inside, doing dishes and talking babies while John Hunton and Mark Jackson sat in lawn chairs near the aromatic barbecue. Hunton smiled slightly at the understatement. He had eaten nothing.

"There was a bad one today," he said. "The worst."

"Car crash?"

"No. Industrial."

"Messy?"

Hunton did not reply immediately, but his face made an involuntary, writhing grimace. He got a beer out of the cooler between them, opened it and emptied half of it. "I suppose you college profs don't know anything about industrial laundries?"

Jackson chuckled. "This one does. I spent a summer working in one as an undergraduate."

"Then you know the machine they call the speed ironer?"

Jackson nodded. "Sure. They run damp flatwork through them, mostly sheets and linen. A big, long machine."

"That's it," Hunton said. "A woman named Adelle Frawley got caught in it at the Blue Ribbon Laundry crosstown. It sucked her right in."

Jackson looked suddenly ill. "But . . . that can't happen, Johnny. There's a safety bar. If one of the women feeding the machine accidentally gets a hand under it, the bar snaps up and stops the machine. At least that's how I remember it."

Hunton nodded. "It's a state law. But it happened."

Hunton closed his eyes and in the darkness he could see the Hadley-Watson speed ironer again, as it had been that afternoon. It formed a long, rectangular box in shape, thirty feet by six. At the feeder end, a moving canvas belt moved under the safety bar, up at a slight angle, and then down. The belt carried the damp-dried, wrinkled sheets in continuous cycle over and under sixteen huge revolving cylinders that made up the main body of the machine. Over eight and under eight, pressed between them like thin ham between layers of superheated bread. Steam heat in the cylinders could be adjusted up to three hundred degrees for maximum drying. The pressure on the sheets that rode the moving canvas belt was set at eight hundred pounds per square foot to get out every wrinkle.

And Mrs. Frawley, somehow, had been caught and dragged in. The steel, asbestos-jacketed pressing cylinders had been as red as barn paint, and the rising steam from the machine had carried the sickening stench of hot blood. Bits of her white blouse and blue slacks, even ripped segments of her bra and panties, had been torn free and ejected from the machine's far end thirty feet down, the bigger sections of cloth folded with grotesque and bloodstained neatness by the automatic folder. But not even that was the worst.

"It tried to fold everything," he said to Jackson, tasting bile in his throat. "But a person isn't a sheet, Mark. What I saw . . . what was left of her . . ." Like Stanner, the hapless foreman, he could not finish. "They took her out in a basket," he said softly.

Jackson whistled. "Who's going to get it in the neck? The laundry or the state inspectors?"

"Don't know yet," Hunton said. The malign image still hung behind his eyes, the image of the mangler wheezing and thumping and hissing, blood dripping down the green sides of the long cabinet in runnels, the burning *stink* of her . . . "It depends on who okayed that goddamn safety bar and under what circumstances."

"If it's the management, can they wiggle out of it?"

Hunton smiled without humor. "The woman died, Mark. If Gartley and Stanner were cutting corners on the speed ironer's maintenance, they'll go to jail. No matter who they know on the City Council."

"Do you think they were cutting corners?"

Hunton thought of the Blue Ribbon Laundry, badly lighted, floors wet and slippery, some of the machines incredibly ancient and creaking. "I think it's likely," he said quietly.

They got up to go in the house together. "Tell me how it comes out, Johnny," Jackson said. "I'm interested."

Hunton was wrong about the mangler; it was clean as a whistle.

Six state inspectors went over it before the inquest, piece by piece. The net result was absolutely nothing. The inquest verdict was death by misadventure.

Hunton, dumbfounded, cornered Roger Martin, one of the inspectors, after the hearing. Martin was a tall drink of water with glasses as thick as the bottoms of shot glasses. He fidgeted with a ball-point pen under Hunton's questions.

"Nothing? Absolutely nothing doing with the machine?"

"Nothing," Martin said. "Of course, the safety bar was the guts of the matter. It's in perfect working order. You heard that Mrs. Gillian testify. Mrs. Frawley must have pushed her hand too far. No one saw that; they were watching their own work. She started screaming. Her hand was gone already, and the machine was taking her arm. They tried to pull her out instead of shutting it down—pure panic. Another woman, Mrs. Keene, said she *did* try to shut it off, but it's a fair assumption that she hit the start button rather than the stop in the confusion. By then it was too late."

"Then the safety bar malfunctioned," Hunton said flatly. "Unless she put her hand over it rather than under?"

"You can't. There's a stainless-steel facing above the safety bar. And the bar itself didn't malfunction. It's circuited into the machine itself. If the safety bar goes on the blink, the machine shuts down."

"Then how did it happen, for Christ's sake?"

"We don't know. My colleagues and I are of the opinion that the only way the speed ironer could have killed Mrs. Frawley was for her to have fallen into it from above. And she had both feet on the floor when it happened. A dozen witnesses can testify to that."

"You're describing an impossible accident," Hunton said.

"No. Only one we don't understand." He paused, hesitated, and then said: "I will tell you one thing, Hunton, since you seem to have taken this case to heart. If you mention it to anyone else, I'll deny I said it. But I didn't like that machine. It seemed . . . almost to be mocking us. I've inspected over a dozen speed ironers in the last five years on a regular basis. Some of them are in such bad shape that I wouldn't leave a dog unleashed around them—the state law is lamentably lax. But they were only machines for all that. But this one . . . it's a spook. I don't know why, but it is. I think if I'd found one thing, even a technicality, that was off whack, I would have ordered it shut down. Crazy, huh?"

"I felt the same way," Hunton said.

"Let me tell you about something that happened two years ago in Milton," the inspector said. He took off his glasses and began to polish them slowly on his vest. "Fella had parked an old icebox out in his backyard. The woman who called us said her dog had been caught in it and suffocated. We got the state policeman in the area to inform him it had to go to the town dump. Nice enough fella, sorry about the dog. He loaded it into his pickup and took it to the dump the next morning. That afternoon a woman in the neighborhood reported her son missing."

"God," Hunton said.

"The icebox was at the dump and the kid was in it, dead. A smart kid, according to his mother. She said he'd no more play in an empty icebox than he would take a ride with a strange man. Well, he did. We wrote it off. Case closed?"

"I guess," Hunton said.

"No." The dump caretaker went out next day to take the door off the thing. City Ordinance No. 58 on the maintenance of public dumping places." Martin looked at him expressionlessly. "He found six dead birds inside. Gulls, sparrows, a robin. And he said the door closed on his arm while he was brushing them out. Gave him a hell of a lump. That mangler at the Blue Ribbon strikes me like that, Hunton. I don't like it."

They looked at each other wordlessly in the empty inquest chamber, some six city blocks from where the Hadley-Watson Model-6 Speed Ironer and Folder sat in the busy laundry, steaming and fuming over its sheets.

The case was driven out of his mind in the space of a week by the press of more prosaic police work. It was only brought back when he and his wife dropped over to Mark Jackson's house for an evening of bid whist and beer.

Jackson greeted him with: "Have you ever wondered if that laundry machine you told me about is haunted, Johnny?"

Hunton blinked, at a loss. "What?"

"The speed ironer at the Blue Ribbon Laundry, I guess you didn't catch the squeal this time."

"What squeal?" Hunton asked, interested.

Jackson passed him the evening paper and pointed to an item at the bottom of page two. The story said that a steam line had let go on the large speed ironer at the Blue Ribbon Laundry, burning three of the six women working at the feeder end. The accident had occurred at 3:45 P.M. and was attributed to a rise in steam pressure from the laundry's boiler. One of the women, Mrs. Annette Gillian, had been held at City Receiving Hospital with second-degree burns.

"Funny coincidence," he said, but the memory of Inspector Martin's words in the empty inquest chamber suddenly recurred: *It's a spook* . . . And the story about the dog and the boy and the birds caught in the discarded refrigerator.

He played cards very badly that night.

Mrs. Gillian was propped up in bed reading *Screen Secrets* when Hunton came into the four-bed hospital room. A large bandage blanketed one arm and the side of her neck. The room's other occupant, a young woman with a pallid face, was sleeping.

Mrs. Gillian blinked at the blue uniform and then smiled tentatively. "If it was for Mrs. Cherinikov, you'll have to come back later. They just gave her medication."

"No, it's for you, Mrs. Gillian." Her smile faded a little. "I'm here unofficially—which means I'm curious about the accident at the laundry. John Hunton." He held out his hand.

It was the right move. Mrs. Gillian's smile became brilliant and she took his grip awkwardly with her unburned hand. "Anything I can tell you, Mr. Hunton. God, I thought my Andy was in trouble at school again."

"What happened?"

"We was running sheets and the ironer just blew up—or it seemed that way. I was thinking about going home an' getting off my dogs when there's this great big bang, like a bomb. Steam is everywhere and this hissing noise . . . awful." Her smile trembled on the verge of extinction. "It was like the ironer was breathing. Like a dragon, it was. And Alberta—that's Alberta Keene—shouted that something was exploding and everyone was running and screaming and Ginny Jason started yelling she was burned. I started to run away and I fell down. I didn't know I got it worst until then. God forbid it was no worse than it was. That live steam is three hundred degrees."

"The paper said a steam line let go. What does that mean?"

"The overhead pipe comes down into this kinda flexible line that feeds the machine. George—Mr. Stanner—said there must have been a surge from the boiler or something. The line split wide open."

Hunton could think of nothing else to ask. He was making ready to leave when she said reflectively: "We never used to have these things on that machine. Only lately. The steam line breaking. That awful, awful accident with Mrs. Frawley, God rest her. And little things. Like the day Essie got her dress caught in one of the drive chains. That could have been dangerous if she hadn't ripped it right out. Bolts and things fall off. Oh, Herb Diment—he's the laundry repairman—has had an awful time with it. Sheets get caught in the folder. George says that's because they're using too much bleach in the washers, but it never used to happen. Now the girls hate to work on it. Essie even says there are still little bits of Adelle Frawley caught in it and it's sacrilege or something. Like it had a curse. It's been that way ever since Sherry cut her hand on one of the clamps."

"Sherry?" Hunton asked.

"Sherry Ouelette. Pretty little thing, just out of high school. Good worker. But clumsy sometimes. You know how young girls are."

"She cut her hand on something?"

"Nothing strange about *that.* There are clamps to tighten down the feeder belt, see. Sherry was adjusting them so we could do a heavier load and probably dreaming about some boy. She cut her finger and bled all over everything." Mrs. Gillian looked puzzled. "It wasn't until after that the bolts started falling off. Adelle was . . . you know . . . about a week later. As if the machine had tasted blood and found it liked it. Don't women get funny ideas sometimes, Officer Hinton?"

"Hunton," he said absently, looking over her head and into space.

Ironically, he had met Mark Jackson in a washateria in the block that separated their houses, and it was there that the cop and the English professor still had their most interesting conversations.

Now they sat side by side in bland plastic chairs, their clothes going round and round behind the glass portholes of the coin-op washers. Jackson's paperback copy of Milton's collected works lay neglected beside him while he listened to Hunton tell Mrs. Gillian's story.

When Hunton had finished, Jackson said, "I asked you once if you thought the mangler might be haunted. I was only half-joking. I'll ask you again now."

"No," Hunton said uneasily. "Don't be stupid."

Jackson watched the turning clothes reflectively. "Haunted is a bad word. Let's say possessed. There are almost as many spells for casting demons in as there are for casting them out. Frazer's *Golden Bough* is replete with them. Druidic and Aztec lore contain others. Even older ones, back to Egypt. Almost all of them can be reduced to startlingly common denominators. The most common, of course, is the blood of a virgin." He looked at Hunton. "Mrs. Gillian said the trouble started after this Sherry Ouelette accidentally cut herself."

"Oh, come on," Hunton said.

"You have to admit she sounds just the type," Jackson said.

"I'll run right over to her house," Hunton said with a small smile. "I can see it. "Miss Ouelette, I'm Officer John Hunton. I'm investigating an ironer with a bad case of demon possession and would like to know if you're a virgin.' Do you think I'd get a chance to say good-bye to Sandra and the kids before they carted me off to the booby hatch?"

"I'd be willing to bet you'll end up saying something just like that," Jackson said without smiling. "I'm serious, Johnny. That machine scares the hell out of me and I've never seen it."

"For the sake of conversation," Hunton said, "what are some of the other so-called common denominators?"

Jackson shrugged. "Hard to say without study. Most Anglo-Saxon hex formulas specify graveyard dirt or the eye of a toad. European spells often mention the hand of glory, which can be interpreted as the actual hand of a dead man or one of the hallucinogenics used in connection with the witches' Sabbath—usually belladonna or a psilocybin derivative. There could be others."

"And you think all those things got into the Blue Ribbon ironer? Christ, Mark, I'll be there isn't any belladonna within a five-hundred-mile radius. Or do you think someone whacked off their Uncle Fred's hand and dropped it in the folder?"

"If seven hundred monkeys typed for seven hundred years—"

"One of them would turn out the works of Shakespeare," Hunton finished sourly. "Go to hell. Your turn to go across to the drugstore and get some dimes for the dryers."

It was very funny how George Stanner lost his arm in the mangler.

Seven o'clock Monday morning the laundry was deserted except for Stanner and Herb Diment, the maintenance man. They were performing the twice-yearly function of greasing the mangler's bearings before the laundry's regular day began at seven-thirty. Diment was at the far end, greasing the four secondaries and thinking of how unpleasant this machine made him feel lately, when the mangler suddenly roared into life.

He had been holding up four of the canvas exit belts to get at the motor beneath and suddenly the belts were running in his hands, ripping the flesh off his palms, dragging him along.

He pulled free with a convulsive jerk seconds before the belts would have carried his hands into the folder.

"What the Christ, George!" he yelled. "Shut the frigging thing *off!*"

George Stanner began to scream.

It was a high, wailing, blood-maddened sound that filled the laundry, echoing off the steel faces of the washers, the grinning mouths of the steam presses, the vacant eyes of the industrial dryers. Stanner drew in a great, whooping gasp of air and screamed again: *"Oh God of Christ I'm caught I'M CAUGHT—"*

The rollers began to produce rising steam. The folder gnashed and thumped. Bearings and motors seemed to cry out with a hidden life of their own.

Diment raced to the other end of the machine.

The first roller was already going a sinister red. Diment made a moaning, gobbling noise in his throat. The mangler howled and thumped and hissed.

A deaf observer might have thought at first that Stanner was merely bent over the machine at an odd angle. Then even a deaf man would have seen the pallid, eye-bulging rictus of his face, mouth twisted open in a continuous scream. The arm was disappearing under the safety bar and beneath the first roller; the fabric of his shirt had torn away at the shoulder seam and his upper arm bulged grotesquely as the blood was pushed steadily backward.

"Turn it off!" Stanner screamed. There was a snap as his elbow broke.

Diment thumbed the off button.

The mangler continued to hum and growl and turn.

Unbelieving, he slammed the button again and again—nothing. The skin of Stanner's arm had grown shiny and taut. Soon it would split with the pressure the roll was putting on it; and still he was conscious and screaming. Diment had a nightmare cartoon image of a man flattened by a steamroller, leaving only a shadow.

"Fuses—" Stanner screeched. His head was being pulled down, down, as he was dragged forward.

Diment whirled and ran to the boiler room, Stanner's screams chasing him like lunatic ghosts. The mixed stench of blood and steam rose in the air.

On the left wall were three heavy gray boxes containing all the fuses for the laundry's electricity. Diment yanked them open and began to pull the long, cylindrical fuses like a crazy man, throwing them back over his shoulders. The overhead lights went out; then the air compressor; then the boiler itself, with a huge dying whine.

And still the mangler turned. Stanner's screams had been reduced to bubbly moans.

Diment's eye happened on the fire ax in its glassed-in box. He grabbed it with a small, gagging whimper and ran back. Stanner's arm was gone almost to the shoulder. Within seconds his bent and straining neck would be snapped against the safety bar.

"I can't," Diment blubbered, holding the ax. "Jesus, George, I can't, I can't, I—"

The machine was an abattoir now. The folder spat out pieces of shirt sleeve, scraps of flesh, a finger. Stanner gave a huge, whooping scream and Diment swung the ax up and brought it down in the laundry's shadowy lightlessness. Twice. Again.

Stanner fell away, unconscious and blue, blood jetting from the stump just below the shoulder. The mangler sucked what was left into itself . . . and shut down.

Weeping, Diment pulled his belt out of its loops and began to make a tourniquet.

Hunton was talking on the phone with Roger Martin, the inspector. Jackson watched him while he patiently rolled a ball back and forth for three-year-old Patty Hunton to chase.

"He pulled *all* the fuses?" Hunton was asking. "And the off button just didn't function, huh? . . . Has the ironer been shut down? . . . Good. Great. Huh? . . . No, not official." Hunton frowned, then looked sideways at Jackson. "Are you still reminded of that refrigerator, Roger? . . . Yes. Me too. Goodbye."

He hung up and looked at Jackson. "Let's go see the girl, Mark."

She had her own apartment (the hesitant yet proprietary way she showed them in after Hunton had flashed his buzzer made him suspect that she hadn't had it long), and she sat uncomfortably across from them in the carefully decorated, postage-stamp living room.

"I'm Officer Hunton and this is my associate, Mr. Jackson. It's about the accident at the laundry." He felt hugely uncomfortable with this dark, shyly pretty girl.

"Awful," Sherry Ouelette murmured. "It's the only place I've ever worked. Mr. Gartley is my uncle. I liked it because it let me have this place and my own friends. But now . . . it's so *spooky.*"

"The State Board of Safety has shut the ironer down pending a full investigation," Hunton said. "Did you know that?"

"Sure." She sighed restlessly. "I don't know what I'm going to do—"

"Miss Ouelette," Jackson interrupted, "you had an accident with the ironer, didn't you? Cut your hand on a clamp, I believe?"

"Yes, I cut my finger." Suddenly her face clouded. "That was the first thing." She looked at them woefully. "Sometimes I feel like the girls don't like me so much anymore . . . as if I were to blame."

"I have to ask you a hard question," Jackson said slowly. "A question you won't like. It seems absurdly personal and off the subject, but I can only tell you it is not. Your answers won't ever be marked down in a file or record."

She looked frightened. "D-did I do something?"

Jackson smiled and shook his head; she melted. *Thank God for Mark,* Hunton thought.

"I'll add this, though: the answer may help you keep your nice little flat here, get your job back, and make things at the laundry the way they were before."

"I'd answer anything to have that," she said.

"Sherry, are you a virgin?"

She looked utterly flabbergasted, utterly shocked, as if a priest had given communion and then slapped her. Then she lifted her head, made a gesture at her neat efficiency apartment, as if asking them how they could believe it might be a place of assignation.

"I'm saving myself for my husband," she said simply.

Hunton and Jackson looked calmly at each other, and in that tick of a second, Hunton knew that it was all true: a devil had taken over the inanimate steel and cogs and gears of the mangler and had turned it into something with its own life.

"Thank you," Jackson said quietly.

"What now?" Hunton asked bleakly as they rode back. "Find a priest to exorcise it?"

Jackson snorted. "You'd go a far piece to find one that wouldn't hand you a few tracts to read while he phoned the booby hatch. It has to be our play, Johnny."

"Can we do it?"

"Maybe. The problem is this: we know something is in the mangler. We don't know *what.*" Hunton felt cold, as if touched by a fleshless finger. "There are a great many demons. Is the one we're dealing with in the circle of Bubastis or Pan? Baal? Or the Christian deity we call Satan? We don't know. If the demon had been deliberately cast, we would have a better chance. But this seems to be a case of random possession."

Jackson ran his fingers through his hair. "The blood of a virgin, yes. But that narrows it down hardly at all. We have to be sure, very sure."

"Why?" Hunton asked bluntly. "Why not just get a bunch of exorcism formulas together and try them out?"

Jackson's face went cold. "This isn't cops 'n' robbers, Johnny. For Christ's sake, don't think it is. The rite of exorcism is horribly dangerous. It's like controlled nuclear fission, in a way. We could make a mistake and destroy ourselves. The demon is caught in that piece of machinery. But give it a chance and—"

"It could get out?"

"It would love to get out," Jackson said grimly. "And it likes to kill."

When Jackson came over the following evening, Hunton had sent his wife and daughter to a movie. They had the living room to themselves, and for this Hunton was relieved. He could still barely believe what he had become involved in.

"I canceled my classes," Jackson said, "and spent the day with some of the most god-awful books you can imagine. This afternoon I fed over thirty recipes for calling demons into the tech computer. I've got a number of common elements. Surprisingly few."

He showed Hunton the list: blood of a virgin, graveyard dirt, hand of glory, bat's blood, night moss, horse's hoof, eye of toad.

There were others, all marked secondary.

"Horse's hoof," Hunton said thoughtfully. "Funny—"

"Very common. In fact—"

"Could these things—any of them—be interpreted loosely?" Hunton interrupted.

"If lichens picked at night could be substituted for night moss, for instance?"

"Yes."

"It's very likely," Jackson said. "Magical formulas are often ambiguous and elastic. The black arts have always allowed plenty of room for creativity."

"Substitute Jell-O for horse's hoof," Hunton said. "Very popular in bag lunches. I noticed a little container of it sitting under the ironer's sheet platform on the day the Frawley woman died. Gelatin is made from horses' hooves."

Jackson nodded. "Anything else?"

"Bat's blood . . . well, it's a big place. Lots of unlighted nooks and crannies. Bats seem likely, although I doubt if the management would admit to it. One could conceivably have been trapped in the mangler."

Jackson tipped his head back and knuckled bloodshot eyes. "It fits . . . it all fits."

"It does?"

"Yes. We can safely rule out the hand of glory, I think. Certainly no one dropped a hand into the ironer *before* Mrs. Frawley's death, and belladonna is definitely not indigenous to the area."

"Graveyard dirt?"

"What do you think?"

"It would have to be a hell of a coincidence," Hunton said. "Nearest cemetery is Pleasant Hill, and that's five miles from the Blue Ribbon."

"Okay," Jackson said. "I got the computer operator—who thought I was getting ready for Halloween—to run a positive breakdown of all the primary and secondary elements on the list. Every possible combination. I threw out some two dozen which were completely meaningless. The others fall into fairly clear-cut categories. The elements we've isolated are in one of those."

"What is it?"

Jackson grinned. "An easy one. The mythos centers in South America with branches in the Caribbean. Related to voodoo. The literature I've got looks on the deities as strictly bush league, compared to some of the real heavies, like Saddath or He-Who-Cannot-Be-Named. The thing in that machine is going to slink away like the neighborhood bully."

"How do we do it?"

"Holy water and a smidgen of the Holy Eucharist ought to do it. And we can read some of the Leviticus to it. Strictly Christian white magic."

"You're sure it's not worse?"

"Don't see how it can be," Jackson said pensively. "I don't mind telling you I was worried about that hand of glory. That's very black juju. Strong magic."

"Holy water wouldn't stop it?"

"A demon called up in conjunction with the hand of glory could eat a stack of Bibles for breakfast. We would be in bad trouble messing with something like that at all. Better to pull the goddamn thing apart."

"Well, are you completely sure—"

"No, but fairly sure. It all fits too well."

"When?"

"The sooner, the better," Jackson said. "How do we get in? Break a window?"

Hunton smiled, reached into his pocket, and dangled a key in front of Jackson's nose.

"Where'd you get that? Gartley?"

"No," Hunton said. "From a state inspector named Martin."

"He know what we're doing?"

"I think he suspects. He told me a funny story a couple of weeks ago."

"About the mangler?"

"No," Hunton said. "About a refrigerator. Come on."

Adelle Frawley was dead; sewed together by a patient undertaker, she lay in her coffin. Yet something of her spirit perhaps remained in the machine, and if it did, it cried out. She would have known, could have warned them. She had been prone to indigestion, and for this common ailment she had taken a common stomach tablet called E-Z Gel, purchasable over the counter of any drugstore for seventy-nine cents. The side panel holds a printed warning: people with glaucoma must not take E-Z Gel, because the active ingredients causes an aggravation of that condition. Unfortunately, Adelle Frawley did not have that condition. She might have remembered the day, shortly before Sherry Ouelette cut her hand, that she had dropped a full box of E-Z Gel tablets into the mangler by accident. But she was dead, unaware that the active ingredient which soothed her heartburn was a chemical derivative of belladonna, known quaintly in some European countries as the hand of glory.

There was a sudden ghastly burping noise in the spectral silence of the Blue Ribbon Laundry—a bat fluttered madly for its hole in the insulation above the dryers where it had roosted, wrapping wings around its blind face.

It was a noise almost like a chuckle.

The mangler began to run with a sudden, lurching grind—belts hurrying through the darkness, cogs meeting and meshing and grinding, heavy pulverizing rollers rotating on and on.

It was ready for them.

When Hunton pulled into the parking lot it was shortly after midnight and the moon was hidden behind a raft of moving clouds. He jammed on the brakes and switched off the lights in the same motion; Jackson's forehead almost slammed against the padded dash.

He switched off the ignition and the steady thump-hiss-thump became louder. "It's the mangler," he said slowly. "It's the mangler. Running by itself. In the middle of the night."

They sat for a moment in silence; feeling the fear crawl up their legs.

Hunton said, "All right. Let's do it."

They got out and walked to the building, the sound of the mangler growing louder. As Hunton put the key into the lock of the service door, he thought that the machine *did* sound alive—as if it were breathing in great hot gasps and speaking to itself in hissing, sardonic whispers.

"All of a sudden I'm glad I'm with a cop," Jackson said. He shifted the brown bag he held from one arm to the other. Inside was a small jelly jar filled with holy water wrapped in waxed paper, and a Gideon Bible.

They stepped inside and Hunton snapped up the light switches by the door. The fluorescents flickered into cold life. At the same instant the mangler shut off.

A membrane of steam hung over its rollers. It waited for them in its new ominous silence.

"God, it's an ugly thing," Jackson whispered.

"Come on," Hunton said. "Before we lose our nerve."

They walked over to it. The safety bar was in its down position over the belt which fed the machine.

Hunton put out a hand. "Close enough, Mark. Give me the stuff and tell me what to do."

"But—"

"No argument."

Jackson handed him the bag and Hunton put it on the sheet table in front of the machine. He gave Jackson the Bible.

"I'm going to read," Jackson said. "When I point at you, sprinkle the holy water on the machine with your fingers. You say: in the name of the Father, and of the Son, and of the Holy Ghost, get thee from this place, thou unclean. Got it?"

"Yes."

"The second time I point, break the wafer and repeat the incantation again."

"How will we know if it's working?"

"You'll know. The thing is apt to break every window in the place getting out. If it doesn't work the first time, we keep doing it until it does."

"I'm scared green," Hunton said.

"As a matter of fact, so am I."

"If we're wrong about the hand of glory—"

"We're not," Jackson said. "Here we go."

He began. His voice filled the empty laundry with spectral echoes. "Turnest not thou aside to idols, nor make molten gods of yourself. I am the Lord thy God . . ." The words fell like stones into a silence that had suddenly become filled with a creeping, tomblike cold. The mangler remained still and silent under the fluorescents, and to Hunton it still seemed to grin.

". . . and the land will vomit you out for having defiled it, as it vomited out nations before you." Jackson looked up, his face strained, and pointed.

Hunton sprinkled holy water across the feeder belt.

There was a sudden, gnashing scream of tortured metal. Smoke rose from the canvas belts where the holy water had touched and took on writhing, red-tinged shapes. The mangler suddenly jerked into life.

"We've got it!" Jackson cried above the rising clamor. "It's on the run!"

He began to read again, his voice rising over the sound of the machinery. He pointed to Hunton again, and Hunton sprinkled some of the host. As he did so he was suddenly swept with a bone-freezing terror, a sudden vivid feeling that it had gone wrong, that the machine had called their bluff—and was the stronger.

Jackson's voice was still rising, approaching climax.

Sparks began to jump across the arc between the main motor and the secondary; the smell of ozone filled the air, like the copper smell of hot blood. Now the main motor was smoking; the mangler was running at an insane, blurred speed: a finger touched to the central belt would have caused the whole body to be hauled in and turned to a bloody rag in the space of five seconds. The concrete beneath their feet trembled and thrummed.

A main bearing blew with a searing flash of purple light, filling the chill air with the smell of thunderstorms, and still the mangler ran, faster and faster, belts and rollers and cogs moving at a speed that made them seem to blend and merge, change, melt, transmute—

Hunton, who had been standing almost hypnotized, suddenly took a step backward. "Get away!" he screamed over the blaring racket.

"We've almost got it!" Jackson yelled back. "Why—"

There was a sudden indescribable ripping noise and a fissure in the concrete floor suddenly raced toward them and past, widening. Chips of ancient cement flew up in a starburst.

Jackson looked at the mangler and screamed.

It was trying to pull itself out of the concrete, like a dinosaur trying to escape a tar pit. And it wasn't precisely an ironer anymore. It was still changing, melting. The 550-volt cable fell, spitting blue fire, into the rollers and was chewed away. For a moment two fireballs glared at them like lambent eyes, eyes filled with a great and cold hunger.

Another fault line tore open. The mangler leaned toward them, within an ace of being free of the concrete moorings that held it. It leered at them; the safety bar had slammed up and what Hunton saw was a gaping, hungry mouth filled with steam.

They turned to run and another fissure opened at their feet. Behind them, a great screaming roar as the thing came free. Hunton leaped over, but Jackson stumbled and fell sprawling.

Hunton turned to help and a huge, amorphous shadow fell over him, blocking the fluorescents.

It stood over Jackson, who lay on his back, staring up in a silent rictus of terror—the perfect sacrifice. Hunton had only a confused impression of something black and moving that bulked to a tremendous height above them both, something with glaring electric eyes the size of footballs, an open mouth with a moving canvas tongue.

He ran; Jackson's dying scream followed him.

When Roger Martin finally got out of bed to answer the doorbell, he was still only a third awake; but when Hunton reeled in, shock slapped him fully into the world with a rough hand.

Hunton's eyes bulged madly from his head, and his hands were claws as he scratched at the front of Martin's robe. There was a small oozing cut on his cheek and his face was splashed with dirty gray specks of powdered cement.

His hair had gone dead white.

"Help me . . . for Jesus' sake, help me. Mark is dead. Jackson is dead."

"Slow down," Martin said. "Come in the living room."

Hunton followed him, making a thick whining noise in his throat, like a dog.

Martin poured him a two-ounce knock of Jim Beam and Hunton held the glass in both hands, downing the raw liquor in a choked gulp. The glass fell unheeded to the carpet and his hands, like wandering ghosts, sought Martin's lapels again.

"The mangler killed Mark Jackson. It . . . it . . . oh God, it might get out! We can't let it get out! We can't . . . we . . . oh—" He began to scream, a crazy, whooping sound that rose and fell in jagged cycles.

Martin tried to hand him another drink but Hunton knocked it aside. "We have to burn it," he said. "Burn it before it can get out. Oh, what if it gets out? Oh Jesus, what if—" His eyes suddenly flickered, glazed, rolled up to show the whites, and he fell to the carpet in a stonelike faint.

Mrs. Martin was in the doorway, clutching her robe to her throat. "Who is he, Rog? Is he crazy? I thought—" She shuddered.

"I don't think he's crazy." She was suddenly frightened by the sick shadow of fear on her husband's face. "God, I hope he came quick enough."

He turned to the telephone, picked up the receiver, froze.

There was a faint, swelling noise from the east of the house, the way that Hunton had come. A steady, grinding clatter, growing louder. The living-room window stood half-open and now Martin caught a dark smell on the breeze. An odor of ozone . . . or blood.

He stood with his hand on the useless telephone as it grew louder, louder, gnashing and fuming, something in the streets that was hot and steaming. The blood stench filled the room.

His hand dropped from the telephone.

It was already out.

RONA JAFFE

I *don't know whether or not the author meant this to be a horror story, but to me it is a classic example of the kind of horror story in which quite ordinary people find their lives being invaded by something sinister, emerging from something as ordinary as they are—in this case a radio. They didn't go out looking for adventure or trouble; it came to them. And then they started finding out things they didn't want to know about their neighbors, and this made them look at their (also very ordinary) neighbors in a different way, and eventually at themselves in a new way.*

We are living in more sophisticated times since this story was first written—and I first read it—and television brings domestic horror stories into our homes every evening on the news. We are no longer shocked by the perfidy behind the smile. Yet we hear the news by choice, *and are prepared for it. It is not supernatural; it does not creep up on us. I guess what makes "The Enormous Radio" particularly intriguing to me is that I want to know people's secrets, but I also know there are risks in knowing them because it can shake your complacency terribly.*

THE ENORMOUS RADIO

JOHN CHEEVER

Jim and Irene Westcott were the kind of people who seem to strike that satisfactory average of income, endeavor and respectability that is reached by the statistical reports in college alumni bulletins. They were the parents of two young children, they had been married nine years, they lived on the twelfth floor of an apartment house in the East Seventies between Fifth and Madison avenues, they went to the theater on an average of 10.3 times a year, and they hoped someday to live in Westchester. Irene Westcott was a pleasant, rather plain girl with soft brown hair and a wide, fine forehead upon which nothing at all had been written, and in the cold weather she wore a coat of fitch skins dyed to resemble mink. You could not say that Jim Westcott, at thirty-seven, looked younger than he was, but you could at least say of him that he seemed to feel younger. He wore his graying hair cut very short, he dressed in the kind of clothes his class had worn at Andover, and his manner was earnest, vehement and intentionally naive. The Westcotts differed from their friends, their classmates and their neighbors only in an interest they shared in serious music. They went to a great many concerts—although they seldom mentioned this to anyone—and they spent a good deal of time listening to music on the radio.

Their radio was an old instrument, sensitive, unpredictable, and beyond repair. Neither of them understood the mechanics of radio—or of any of the other appliances that surrounded them—and when the instrument faltered, Jim would strike the side of the cabinet with his hand. This sometimes helped. One Sunday afternoon, in the middle of a Schubert quartet, the music faded away altogether. Jim struck the cabinet repeatedly, but there was no response; the Schubert was lost to them forever. He promised to buy Irene a new radio, and on Monday when he came home from work he told her that he had got one. He refused to describe it, and said it would be a surprise for her when it came.

The radio was delivered at the kitchen door the following afternoon, and with the assistance of her maid and the handyman Irene uncrated it and brought it into the living room. She was struck at once with the physical ugliness of the large gumwood cabinet. Irene was proud of her living room, she had chosen its furnishings and colors as carefully as she chose her clothes, and now it seemed to her that the new radio stood among her intimate possessions like an aggressive intruder. She was confounded by the number of dials and switches on the instrument panel, and she studied them thoroughly before she put the plug into a wall socket and turned the radio on. The dials flooded with a malevolent green light, and in the distance she heard the music of a piano quintet. The quintet was in the distance for only an instant; it bore down upon her with a speed greater than light and filled the apartment with the noise of music amplified so mightily that it knocked a china ornament from a table to the floor. She rushed to the instrument and reduced the volume. The violent forces that were snared in the ugly gumwood cabinet made her uneasy. Her children came home from school then, and she took them to the park. It was not until later in the afternoon that she was able to return to the radio.

The maid had given the children their suppers and was supervising their baths when Irene turned on the radio, reduced the volume and sat down to listen to a Mozart quintet that she knew and enjoyed. The music came through clearly. The new instrument had a much purer tone, she thought, than the old one. She decided that tone was most important and that she could conceal the cabinet behind a sofa. But as soon as she had made her peace with the radio, the interference began. A crackling sound like the noise of a burning powder fuse began to accompany the singing of the strings. Beyond the music, there was a rustling that reminded Irene unpleasantly of the sea, and as the quintet progressed, these noises were joined by many others. She tried all the dials and switches but nothing dimmed the interference, and she sat down, disappointed and bewildered, and tried to trace the flight of the melody. The elevator shaft in her building ran beside the living-room wall, and it was the noise of the elevator that gave her a clue to the character of the static. The rattling of the elevator cables and the opening and closing of the elevator doors were reproduced in her loudspeaker, and, realizing that the radio was sensitive to electrical currents of all sorts, she began to discern through the Mozart the ringing of telephone bells, the dialing of phones and the lamentation of a vacuum cleaner. By listening more carefully, she was able to distinguish doorbells, elevator bells, electric razors and Waring mixers, whose sounds had been picked up from the apartments that surrounded hers and transmitted through her loudspeaker. The powerful and ugly instrument, with its mistaken sensitivity to discord, was more than she could hope to master, so she turned the thing off and went into the nursery to see her children.

When Jim Westcott came home that night, he went to the radio confidently and worked the controls. He had the same sort of experience Irene had had. A man was speaking on the station Jim had chosen, and his voice swung instantly from the distance into a force so powerful that it shook the apartment. Jim turned the volume control and reduced the voice. Then, a minute or two later, the interference began. The ringing of telephones and doorbells set in, joined by the rasp of the elevator doors and the whir of cooking appliances. The character of the noise had changed since Irene had tried the radio earlier; the last of the electric razors was being unplugged, the vacuum cleaners had all been returned to their closets and the static reflected that change in pace that overtakes the city after the sun goes down. He fiddled with the knobs but couldn't get rid of the noises, so he turned the radio off and told Irene that in the morning he'd call the people who had sold it to him and give them hell.

The following afternoon, when Irene returned to the apartment from a luncheon date, the maid told her that a man had come and fixed the radio. Irene went into the living room before she took off her hat and her furs and tried the instrument. From the loudspeaker came a recording of the "Missouri Waltz." It reminded her of the thin, scratchy music from an old-fashioned phonograph that she sometimes heard across the lake where she spent her summers. She waited until the waltz had finished, expecting an explanation of the recording, but there was none. The music was followed by silence, and then the plaintive and scratchy record was repeated. She turned the dial and got a satisfactory burst of Caucasian music—the thump of bare feet in the dust and the rattle of coin jewelry—but in the background she could hear the ringing of bells and a confusion of voices. Her children came home from school then, and she turned off the radio and went to the nursery.

When Jim came home that night, he was tired, and he took a bath and changed his clothes. Then he joined Irene in the living room. He had just turned on the radio when the maid announced dinner, so he left it on, and he and Irene went to the table.

Jim was too tired to make even a pretense of sociability, and there was nothing about the dinner to hold Irene's interest, so her attention wandered from the food to the deposits of silver polish on the candlesticks and from there to the music in the other room. She listened for a few moments to a Chopin prelude and then was surprised to hear a man's voice break in. "For Christ's sake, Kathy," he said, "do you always have to play the piano when I get home?" The music stopped abruptly. "It's the only chance I have," the woman said. "I'm at the office all day." "So am I," the man said. He added something obscene about an upright piano, and slammed a door. The passionate and melancholy music began again.

"Did you hear that?" Irene asked.

"What?" Jim was eating his dessert.

"The radio. A man said something while the music was still going on —something dirty."

"It's probably a play."

"I don't think it *is* a play," Irene said.

They left the table and took their coffee into the living room. Irene asked Jim to try another station. He turned the knob. "Have you seen my garters?" a man asked. "Button me up," a woman said. "Have you seen my garters?" the man said again. "Just button me up and I'll find your garters," the woman said. Jim shifted to another station. "I wish you wouldn't leave apple cores in the ashtrays," a man said. "I hate the smell."

"This is strange," Jim said.

"Isn't it?" Irene said.

Jim turned the knob again. " 'On the coast of Coromandel where the early pumpkins blow,' " a woman with a pronounced English accent said, " 'in the middle of the woods lived the Yonghy-Bonghy-Bò. Two old chairs, and half a candle, one old jug without a handle . . .' "

"My God!" Irene cried. "That's the Sweeneys' nurse."

" 'These were all his worldly goods,' " the British voice continued.

"Turn that thing off," Irene said. "Maybe they can hear *us.*" Jim switched the radio off. "That was Miss Armstrong, the Sweeneys' nurse," Irene said. "She must be reading to the little girl. They live in 17-B. I've talked with Miss Armstrong in the park. I know her voice very well. We must be getting other people's apartments."

"That's impossible," Jim said.

"Well, that was the Sweeneys' nurse," Irene said hotly. "I know her voice. I know it very well. I'm wondering if they can hear us."

Jim turned the switch. First from a distance and then nearer, nearer, as if borne on the wind, came the pure accents of the Sweeneys' nurse again: " ' "Lady Jingly! Lady Jingly!" ' " she said, " ' "Sitting where the pumpkins blow, will you come and be my wife," said the Yonghy-Bonghy-Bò . . .' "

Jim went over to the radio and said, "Hello" loudly into the speaker.

" ' "I am tired of living singly," ' " the nurse went on, " ' "on this coast so wild and shingly, I'm a-weary of my life; if you'll come and be my wife, quite serene would be my life . . ." ' "

"I guess she can't hear us," Irene said. "Try something else."

Jim turned to another station, and the living room was filled with the uproar of a cocktail party that had overshot its mark. Someone was playing the piano and singing the "Whiffenpoof Song," and the voices that surrounded the piano were vehement and happy. "Eat some more sandwiches," a woman shrieked. There were screams of laughter and a dish of some sort crashed to the floor.

"Those must be the Hutchinsons, in 15-B," Irene said. "I knew they were giving a party this afternoon. I saw her in the liquor store. Isn't this too divine? Try something else. See if you can get those people in 18-C."

The Westcotts overheard that evening a monologue on salmon fishing in Canada, a bridge game, running comments on home movies of what had apparently been a fortnight at Sea Island and a bitter family quarrel about an overdraft at the bank. They turned off their radio at midnight and went to bed, weak with laughter. Sometime in the night their son began to call for a glass of water and Irene got one and took it to his room. It was very early. All the lights in the neighborhood were extinguished, and from the boy's window she could see the empty street. She went into the living room and tried the radio. There was a faint coughing, a moan, and then a man spoke. "Are you all right, darling?" he asked. "Yes," a woman said wearily. "Yes, I'm all right, I guess," and then she added with great feeling, "But, you know, Charlie, I don't feel like myself anymore. Sometimes there are about fifteen or twenty minutes in the week when I feel like myself. I don't like to go to another doctor, because the doctor's bills are so awful already, but I just don't feel like myself, Charlie. I just never feel like myself." They were not young, Irene thought. She guessed from the timbre of their voices that they were middle-aged. The restrained melancholy of the dialogue and the draft from the bedroom window made her shiver, and she went back to bed.

The following morning, Irene cooked breakfast for the family—the maid didn't come up from her room in the basement until ten—braided her daughter's hair and waited at the door until her children and her husband had been carried away in the elevator. Then she went into the living room and tried the radio. "I don't want to go to school," a child screamed. "I hate school. I won't go to school. I hate school." "You will go to school," an enraged woman said. "We paid eight hundred dollars to get you into that school and you'll go if it kills you." The next number on the dial produced the worn record of the "Missouri Waltz." Irene shifted the control and invaded the privacy of several breakfast tables. She overheard demonstrations of indigestion, carnal love, abysmal vanity, faith and despair. Irene's life was nearly as simple and sheltered as it appeared to be, and the forthright and sometimes brutal language that came from the loudspeaker that morning astonished and troubled her. She continued to listen until her maid came in. Then she turned off the radio quickly, since this insight, she realized, was a furtive one.

Irene had a luncheon date with a friend that day, and she left her apartment at a little after twelve. There were a number of women in the elevator when it stopped at her floor. She stared at their handsome and impassive faces, their furs and the cloth flowers in their hats. Which one of them had been to Sea Island, she wondered. Which one had overdrawn her bank account? The elevator stopped at the tenth floor and a woman with a pair of Skye terriers joined them. Her hair was rigged high on her head and she wore a mink cape. She was humming the "Missouri Waltz."

Irene had two martinis at lunch, and she looked searchingly at her friend and wondered what her secrets were. They had intended to go shopping after lunch, but Irene excused herself and went home. She told the maid that she was not to be disturbed; then she went into the living room, closed the doors and switched on the radio. She heard, in the course of the afternoon, the halting conversation of a woman entertaining her aunt, the hysterical conclusion of a luncheon party, and a hostess briefing her maid about some cocktail guests. "Don't give the best scotch to anyone who hasn't white hair," the hostess said. "See if you can get rid of that liver paste before you pass those hot things, and could you lend me five dollars? I want to tip the elevator man."

As the afternoon waned, the conversations increased in intensity. From where Irene sat, she could see the open sky above Central Park. There were hundreds of clouds in the sky, as though the south wind had broken the winter into pieces and were blowing it north, and on her radio she could hear the arrival of cocktail guests and the return of children and businessmen from their schools and offices. "I found a good-sized diamond on the bathroom floor this morning," a woman said. "It must have fallen out of that bracelet Mrs. Dunston was wearing last night." "We'll sell it," a man said. "Take it down to the jeweler on Madison Avenue and sell it. Mrs. Dunston won't know the difference, and we could use a couple of hundred bucks . . ." " 'Oranges and lemons, say the bells of St. Clement's,' " the Sweeneys' nurse sang. " 'Half-pence and farthings, say the bells of St. Martin's. When will you pay me? say the bells at old Bailey . . .' " "It's not a hat," a woman cried, and at her back roared a cocktail party. "It's not a hat, it's a love affair. That's what Walter Florell said. He said it's not a hat, it's a love affair," and then, in a lower voice, the same woman added, "Talk to somebody, for Christ's sake, honey, talk to somebody. If she catches you standing here not talking to anybody, she'll take us off her invitation list, and I love these parties."

The Westcotts were going out for dinner that night, and when Jim came home, Irene was dressing. She seemed sad and vague, and he brought her a drink. They were dining with friends in the neighborhood, and they walked to where they were going. The sky was broad and filled with light. It was one of those splendid spring evenings that excite memory and desire, and the air that touched their hands and faces felt very soft. A Salvation Army band was on the corner playing "Jesus Is Sweeter." Irene drew on her husband's arm and held him there for a minute, to hear the music. "They're really such nice people, aren't they?" she said. "They have such nice faces. Actually, they're so much nicer than a lot of the people we know." She took a bill from her purse and walked over and dropped it into the tambourine. There was in her face, when she returned to her husband, a look of radiant melancholy that he was not familiar with. And her conduct at the dinner party that night seemed strange to him, too. She interrupted her hostess rudely and stared at the people across the table from her with an intensity for which she would have punished her children.

It was still mild when they walked home from the party, and Irene looked up at the spring stars. " 'How far that little candle throws its beams,' " she exclaimed. " 'So shines a good deed in a naughty world.' " She waited that night until Jim had fallen asleep, and then went into the living room and turned on the radio.

Jim came home about six the next night. Emma, the maid, let him in, and he had taken off his hat and was taking off his coat when Irene ran into the hall. Her face was shining with tears and her hair was disordered. "Go up to 16-C, Jim!" she screamed. "Don't take off your coat. Go up to 16-C. Mr. Osborn's beating his wife. They've been quarreling since four o'clock, and now he's hitting her. Go up there and stop him."

From the radio in the living room, Jim heard screams, obscenities and thuds. "You know you don't have to listen to this sort of thing," he said. He strode into the living room and turned the switch. "It's indecent," he said. "It's like looking in windows. You know you don't have to listen to this sort of thing. You can turn it off."

"Oh, it's so horrible, it's so dreadful," Irene was sobbing. "I've been listening all day, and it's so depressing."

"Well, if it's so depressing, why do you listen to it? I bought this damned radio to give you some pleasure," he said. "I paid a great deal of money for it. I thought it might make you happy. I wanted to make you happy."

"Don't, don't, don't, don't quarrel with me," she moaned, and laid her head on his shoulder. "All the others have been quarreling all day. Everybody's been quarreling. They're all worried about money. Mrs. Hutchinson's mother is dying of cancer in Florida and they don't have enough money to send her to the Mayo Clinic. At least, Mr. Hutchinson says they don't have enough money. And some woman in this building is having an affair with the superintendent—with that hideous superintendent. It's too disgusting. And Mrs. Melville has heart trouble and Mr. Hendricks is going to lose his job in April and Mrs. Hendricks is horrid about the whole thing and that girl who plays the 'Missouri Waltz' is a whore, a common whore, and the elevator man has tuberculosis and Mr. Osborn has been beating Mrs. Osborn." She wailed, she trembled with grief and checked the stream of tears down her face with the heel of her palm.

"Well, why do you have to listen?" Jim asked again. "Why do you have to listen to this stuff if it makes you so miserable?"

"Oh, don't, don't, don't," she cried. "Life is too terrible, too sordid and awful. But we've never been like that, have we, darling? Have we? I mean we've always been good and decent and loving to one another, haven't we? And we have two children, two beautiful children. Our lives aren't sordid, are they, darling? Are they?" She flung her arms around his neck and drew his face down to hers. "We're happy, aren't we, darling? We are happy, aren't we?"

"Of course we're happy," he said tiredly. He began to surrender his resentment. "Of course we're happy. I'll have that damned radio fixed or taken away tomorrow." He stroked her soft hair. "My poor girl," he said.

"You love me, don't you?" she asked. "And we're not hypercritical or worried about money or dishonest, are we?"

"No, darling," he said.

A man came in the morning and fixed the radio. Irene turned it on cautiously and was happy to hear a California-wine commercial and a recording of Beethoven's Ninth Symphony, including Schiller's "Ode to Joy." She kept the radio on all day and nothing untoward came from the speaker.

A Spanish suite was being played when Jim came home. "Is everything all right?" he asked. His face was pale, she thought. They had some cocktails and went in to dinner to the "Anvil Chorus" from *Il Trovatore*. This was followed by Debussy's *La Mer*.

"I paid the bill for the radio today," Jim said. "It cost four hundred dollars. I hope you'll get some enjoyment out of it."

"Oh, I'm sure I will," Irene said.

"Four hundred dollars is a good deal more than I can afford," he went on. "I wanted to get something that you'd enjoy. It's the last extravagance we'll be able to indulge in this year. I see that you haven't paid your clothing bills yet. I saw them on your dressing table." He looked directly at her. "Why did you tell me you'd paid them? Why did you lie to me?"

"I just didn't want you to worry, Jim," she said. She drank some water. "I'll be able to pay my bills out of this month's allowance. There were the slipcovers last month, and that party."

"You've got to learn to handle the money I give you a little more intelligently, Irene," he said. "You've got to understand that we won't have as much money this year as we had last. I had a very sobering talk with Mitchell today. No one is buying anything. We're spending all our time promoting new issues, and you know how long that takes. I'm not getting any younger, you know. I'm thirty-seven. My hair will be gray next year. I haven't done as well as I'd hoped to do. And I don't suppose things will get any better."

"Yes, dear," she said.

"We've got to start cutting down," Jim said. "We've got to think of the children. To be perfectly frank with you, I worry about money a great deal. I'm not at all sure of the future. No one is. If anything should happen to me, there's the insurance, but that wouldn't go very far today. I've worked awfully hard to give you and the children a comfortable life," he said bitterly. "I don't like to see all of my energies, all of my youth, wasted in fur coats and radios and slipcovers and—"

"Please, Jim," she said. "Please. They'll hear us."

"*Who'll* hear us? Emma can't hear us."

"The radio."

"Oh, I'm sick!" he shouted. "I'm sick to death of your apprehensiveness. The radio can't hear us. Nobody can hear us. And what if they can hear us? Who cares?"

Irene got up from the table and went into the living room. Jim went to the door and shouted at her from there. "Why are you so Christly all of a sudden? What's turned you overnight into a convent girl? You stole your mother's jewelry before they probated her will. You never gave your sister a cent of that money that was intended for her—not even when she needed it. You made Grace Howland's life miserable, and where was all your piety and your virtue when you went to that abortionist? I'll never forget how cool you were. You packed your bag and went off to have that child murdered as if you were going to Nassau. If you'd had any reasons, if you'd any good reasons—"

Irene stood for a minute before the hideous cabinet, disgraced and sickened, but she held her hand on the switch before she extinguished the music and the voices, hoping that the instrument might speak to her kindly, that she might hear the Sweeneys' nurse. Jim continued to shout at her from the door. The voice on the radio was suave and noncommittal. "An early-morning railroad disaster in Tokyo," the loudspeaker said, "killed twenty-nine people. A fire in a Catholic hospital near Buffalo for the care of blind children was extinguished early this morning by nuns. The temperature is forty-seven. The humidity is eighty-nine."

pigtails trailing, blond. She went laughing, and the sun was on her small twelve-year-old shoulders. I thought of the water settling quiet, of the lifeguard leaping into it, of Tally's mother screaming, and of how Tally never came out. . . .

The lifeguard tried to persuade her to come out, but she did not. He came back with only bits of waterweed in his big-knuckled fingers, and Tally was gone. She would not sit across from me at school any longer, or chase indoor balls on the brick streets on summer nights. She had gone too far out, and the lake would not let her return.

And now in the lonely autumn when the sky was huge and the water was huge and the beach was so very long, I had come down for the last time, alone.

I called her name again and again. Tally, oh, Tally!

The wind blew so very softly over my ears, the way wind blows over the mouths of seashells to set them whispering. The water rose, embraced my chest, then my knees, up and down, one way and another, sucking under my heels.

"Tally! Come back, Tally!"

I was only twelve. But I know how much I loved her. It was that love that comes before all significance of body and morals. It was that love that is no more bad than wind and sea and sand lying side by side forever. It was made of all the warm long days together at the beach, and the humming quiet days of droning education at the school. All the long autumn days of the years past when I had carried her books home from school.

Tally!

I called her name for the last time. I shivered. I felt water on my face and did not know how it got there. The waves had not splashed that high.

Turning, I retreated to the sand and stood there for half an hour, hoping for one glimpse, one sign, one little bit of Tally to remember. Then, I knelt and built a sand castle, shaping it fine, building it as Tally and I had often built so many of them. But this time, I only built half of it. Then I got up.

"Tally, if you hear me, come in and build the rest."

I walked off toward that faraway speck that was mama. The water came in, blended the sand castle circle by circle, mashing it down little by little into the original smoothness.

Silently, I walked along the shore.

Far away, a merry-go-round jangled faintly, but it was only the wind.

The next day, I went away on the train.

A train has a poor memory; it soon puts all behind it. It forgets the cornlands of Illinois, the rivers of childhood, the bridges, the lakes, the valleys, the cottages, the hurts and the joys. It spreads them out behind and they drop back of a horizon.

I lengthened my bones, put flesh on them, changed my young mind for an older one, threw away clothes as they no longer fitted, shifted from grammar to high school, to college. And then there was a young woman in Sacramento. I knew her for a time, and we were married. By the time I was twenty-two, I had almost forgotten what the East was like.

Margaret suggested that our delayed honeymoon be taken back in that direction.

Like a memory, a train works both ways. A train can bring rushing back all those things you left behind so many years before.

Lake Bluff, population ten thousand, came up over the sky. Margaret looked so handsome in her fine new clothes. She watched me as I felt my old world gather me back into its living. She held my arm as the train slid into Bluff Station and our baggage was escorted out.

So many years, and the things they do to people's faces and bodies. When we walked through the town together I saw no one I recognized. There were faces with echoes in them. Echoes of hikes on ravine trails. Faces with small laughter in them from closed grammar schools and swinging on metal-linked swings and going up and down on teeter-totters. But I didn't speak. I walked and looked and filled up inside with all those memories, like leaves stacked for autumn burning.

We stayed on two weeks in all, revisiting all the places together. The days were happy. I thought I loved Margaret well. At least I thought I did.

It was on one of the last days that we walked down by the shore. It was not quite as late in the year as that day so many years before, but the first evidences of desertion were coming upon the beach. People were thinning out, several of the hot-dog stands had been shuttered and nailed, and the wind, as always, waited there to sing for us.

I almost saw mama sitting on the sand as she used to sit. I had that feeling again of wanting to be alone. But I could not force myself to speak of this to Margaret. I only held on to her and waited.

It got late in the day. Most of the children had gone home and only a few men and women remained basking in the windy sun.

The lifeguard boat pulled up on the shore. The lifeguard stepped out of it, slowly, with something in his arms.

I froze there. I held my breath and I felt small, only twelve years old, very little, very infinitesimal and afraid. The wind howled. I could not see Margaret. I could see only the beach, the lifeguard slowly emerging from the boat with a gray sack in his hands, not very heavy, and his face almost as gray and lined.

"Stay here, Margaret," I said. I don't know why I said it.

"But, why?"

"Just stay here, that's all . . ."

I walked slowly down the sand to where the lifeguard stood. He looked at me.

"What is it?" I asked.

The lifeguard kept looking at me for a long time and he couldn't speak. He put the gray sack on the sand, and water whispered wet up around it and went back.

"What is it?" I insisted.

"Strange," said the lifeguard, quietly.

I waited.

"Strange," he said, softly. "Strangest thing I ever saw. She's been dead a long time."

I repeated his words.

He nodded. "Ten years, I'd say. There haven't been any children drowned here this year. There were twelve children drowned here since 1933, but we found all of them before a few hours had passed. All except one, I remember. This body here, why it must be ten years in the water. It's not—pleasant."

I stared at the gray sack in his arms. "Open it," I said. I don't know why I said it. The wind was louder.

He fumbled with the sack.

"Hurry, man, open it!" I cried.

"I better not do that," he said. Then perhaps he saw the way my face must have looked. "She was such a *little* girl. . . . "

He opened it only part way. That was enough.

The beach was deserted. There was only the sky and the wind and the water and the autumn coming on lonely. I looked down at her there.

I said something over and over. A name. The lifeguard looked at me. "Where did you find her?" I asked.

"Down the beach, that way, in the shallow water. It's a long, long time for her, isn't it?"

I shook my head.

"Yes, it is. Oh God, yes it is."

I thought: people grow. I have grown. But she has not changed. She is still small. She is still young. Death does not permit growth or change. She still has golden hair. She will be forever young and I will love her forever, oh God, I will love her forever.

The lifeguard tied up the sack again.

Down the beach, a few moments later, I walked by myself. I stopped, and looked down at something. This is where the lifeguard found her, I said to myself.

There, at the water's edge, lay a sand castle, only half-built. Just like Tally and I used to build them. She half and I half.

I looked at it. I knelt beside the sand castle and saw the small prints of feet coming in from the lake and going back out to the lake again and not returning.

Then—I knew.

"I'll help you finish it," I said.

I did. I built the rest of it up very slowly, then I arose and turned away and walked off, so as not to watch it crumble in the waves, as all things crumble.

I walked back up the beach to where a strange woman named Margaret was waiting for me, smiling. . . .

GARSON KANIN

Editor's Note:

Most people normally associate Mark Twain with humor and sardonic philosophy. However, he had a dark side, and a strong sense of pessimism and even despair runs through his work. A considerable proportion of his huge output was in the science-fiction/fantasy areas, the best known being *A Connecticut Yankee in King Arthur's Court* (1889). We were particularly pleased that Garson Kanin chose "Cannibalism in the Cars," a story that brilliantly combines biting humor with real terror.

CANNIBALISM IN THE CARS

MARK TWAIN

I visited St. Louis lately, and on my way West, after changing cars at Terre Haute, Indiana, a mild, benevolent-looking gentleman of about forty-five, or maybe fifty, came in at one of the way stations and sat down beside me. We talked together pleasantly on various subjects for an hour, perhaps, and I found him exceedingly intelligent and entertaining. When he learned that I was from Washington, he immediately began to ask questions about various public men, and about congressional affairs; and I saw very shortly that I was conversing with a man who was perfectly familiar with the ins and outs of political life at the capital, even to the ways and manners, and customs of procedure of senators and representatives in the chambers of the national legislature. Presently two men halted near us for a single moment, and one said to the other: "Harris, if you'll do that for me, I'll never forget you, my boy."

My new comrade's eye lighted pleasantly. The words had touched upon a happy memory, I thought. Then his face settled into thoughtfulness—almost into gloom. He turned to me and said, "Let me tell you a story; let me give you a secret chapter of my life—a chapter that has never been referred to by me since its events transpired. Listen patiently, and promise that you will not interrupt me."

I said I would not, and he related the following strange adventure, speaking sometimes with animation, sometimes with melancholy, but always with feeling and earnestness.

On the nineteenth of December, 1853, I started from St. Louis on the evening train bound for Chicago. There were only twenty-four passengers, all told. There were no ladies and no children. We were in excellent spirits, and pleasant acquaintanceships were soon formed. The journey bade fair to be a happy one; and no individual in the party, I think, had even the vaguest presentiment of the horrors we were soon to undergo.

At 11:00 P.M. it began to snow hard. Shortly after leaving the small village of Welden, we entered upon that tremendous prairie solitude that stretches its leagues on leagues of houseless dreariness far away toward the Jubilee Settlements. The winds, unobstructed by trees or hills, or even vagrant rocks, whistled fiercely across the level desert, driving the falling snow before it like spray from the crested waves of a stormy sea. The snow was deepening fast; and we knew, by the diminished speed of the train, that the engine was plowing through it with steadily increasing difficulty. Indeed, it almost came to a dead halt sometimes, in the midst of great drifts that piled themselves like colossal graves across the track. Conversation began to flag. Cheerfulness gave place to grave concern. The possibility of being imprisoned in the snow, on the bleak prairie, fifty miles from any house, presented itself to every mind, and extended its depressing influence over every spirit.

At two o'clock in the morning I was aroused out of an uneasy slumber by the ceasing of all motion about me. The appalling truth flashed upon me instantly—we were captives in a snowdrift! "All hands to the rescue!" Every man sprang to obey. Out into the wild night, the pitchy darkness, the billowy snow, the driving storm, every soul leaped, with the consciousness that a moment lost now might bring destruction to us all. Shovels, hands, boards—anything, everything that could displace snow, was brought into instant requisition. It was a weird picture, that small company of frantic men fighting the banking snows, half in the blackest shadow and half in the angry light of the locomotive's reflector.

One short hour sufficed to prove the utter uselessness of our efforts. The storm barricaded the track with a dozen drifts while we dug one away. And worse than this, it was discovered that the last grand charge the engine had made upon the enemy had broken the fore-and-aft shaft of the driving wheel! With a free track before us we should still have been helpless. We entered the car wearied with labor, and very sorrowful. We gathered about the stoves, and gravely canvassed our situation. We had no provisions whatever—in this lay our chief distress. We could not freeze, for there was a good supply of wood in the tender. This was our only comfort. The discussion ended at last in accepting the disheartening decision of the conductor, *viz.*, that it would be death for any man to attempt to travel fifty miles on foot through snow like that. We could not send for help, and even if we could it would not come. We must submit, and await, as patiently as we might, succor or starvation! I think the stoutest heart there felt a momentary chill when those words were uttered.

Within the hour conversation subsided to a low murmur here and there about the car, caught fitfully between the rising and falling of the blast; the lamps grew dim; and the majority of the castaways settled themselves among the flickering shadows to think—to forget the present, if they could—to sleep, if they might.

The eternal night—it surely seemed eternal to us—wore its lagging hours away at last, and the cold gray dawn broke in the east. As the light grew stronger the passengers began to stir and give signs of life, one after another, and each in turn pushed his slouched hat up from his forehead, stretched his stiffened limbs and glanced out of the windows upon the cheerless prospect. It was cheerless, indeed!—not a living thing visible anywhere, not a human habitation; nothing but a vast white desert; uplifted sheets of snow drifting hither and thither before the wind—a world of eddying flakes shutting out the firmament above.

All day we moped about the cars, saying little, thinking much. Another lingering dreary night—and hunger.

Another dawning—another day of silence, sadness, wasting hunger, hopeless watching for succor that could not come. A night of restless slumber, filled with dreams of feasting—wakings distressed with the gnawings of hunger.

The fourth day came and went—and the fifth! Five days of dreadful imprisonment! A savage hunger looked out at every eye. There was in it a sign of awful import—the foreshadowing of a something that was vaguely shaping itself in every heart—a something which no tongue dared yet to frame into words.

The sixth day passed—the seventh dawned upon as gaunt and haggard and hopeless a company of men as ever stood in the shadow of death. It must out now! That thing which had been growing up in every heart was ready to leap from every lip at last! Nature had been taxed to the utmost—she must yield. Richard H. Gaston of Minnesota, tall, cadaverous, and pale, rose up. All knew what was coming. All prepared—every emotion, every semblance of excitement was smothered—only a calm, thoughtful seriousness appeared in the eyes that were lately so wild.

"Gentlemen: It cannot be delayed longer! The time is at hand! We must determine which of us shall die to furnish food for the rest!"

Mr. John J. Williams of Illinois rose and said: "Gentlemen—I nominate the Reverend James Sawyer of Tennessee."

Mr. Wm. R. Adams of Indiana said: "I nominate Mr. Daniel Slote of New York."

Mr. Charles J. Langdon: "I nominate Mr. Samuel A. Bowen of St. Louis."

Mr. Slote: "Gentlemen—I desire to decline in favor of Mr. John A. Van Nostrand, Jr., of New Jersey."

Mr. Gaston: "If there be no objection, the gentleman's desire will be acceded to."

Mr. Van Nostrand objecting, the resignation of Mr. Slote was rejected. The resignations of Messrs. Sawyer and Bowen were also offered, and refused upon the same grounds.

Mr. A. L. Bascom of Ohio: "I move that the nominations now close, and that the House proceed to an election by ballot."

Mr. Sawyer: "Gentlemen—I protest earnestly against these proceedings. They are, in every way, irregular and unbecoming. I must beg to move that they be dropped at once, and that we elect a chairman of the meeting and proper officers to assist him, and then we can go on with the business before us understandingly."

Mr. Bell of Iowa: "Gentlemen—I object. This is no time to stand upon forms and ceremonious observances. For more than seven days we have been without food. Every moment we lose in idle discussion increases our distress. I am satisfied with the nominations that have been made—every gentleman present is, I believe—and I, for one, do not see why we should not proceed at once to elect one or more of them. I wish to offer a resolution—"

Mr. Gaston: "It would be objected to, and have to lie over one day under the rules, thus bringing about the very delay you wish to avoid. The gentleman from New Jersey—"

Mr. Van Nostrand: "Gentlemen—I am a stranger among you; I have not sought the distinction that has been conferred upon me, and I feel a delicacy—"

Mr. Morgan of Alabama (interrupting): "I move the previous question."

The motion was carried, and further debate shut off, of course. The motion to elect officers was passed, and under it Mr. Gaston was chosen chairman, Mr. Blake, secretary, Messrs. Holcomb, Dyer and Baldwin a committee on nominations, and Mr. R. M. Howland, purveyor, to assist the committee in making selections.

A recess of half an hour was then taken, and some little caucusing followed. At the sound of the gavel the meeting reassembled, and the committee reported in favor of Messrs. George Ferguson of Kentucky, Lucien Herrman of Louisiana and W. Messick of Colorado as candidates. The report was accepted.

Mr. Rogers of Missouri: "Mr. President—The report being properly before the House now, I move to amend it by substituting for the name of Mr. Herrman that of Mr. Lucius Harris of St. Louis, who is well and honorably known to us all. I do not wish to be understood as casting the least reflection upon the high character and standing of the gentleman from Louisiana—far from it. I respect and esteem him as much as any gentleman here present possibly can; but none of us can be blind to the fact that he had lost more flesh during the week that we have lain here than any among us—none of us can be blind to the fact that the committee has been derelict in its duty, either through negligence or a graver fault, in thus offering for our suffrages a gentleman who, however pure his own motives may be, has really less nutriment in him—"

The Chair: "The gentleman from Missouri will take his seat. The Chair cannot allow the integrity of the committee to be questioned save by the regular course, under the rules. What action will the House take upon the gentleman's motion?"

Mr. Halliday of Virginia: "I move to further amend the report by substituting Mr. Harvey Davis of Oregon for Mr. Messick. It may be urged by gentlemen that the hardships and privations of a frontier life have rendered Mr. Davis tough; but, gentlemen, is this a time to cavil at toughness? Is this a time to be fastidious concerning trifles? Is this a time to dispute about matters of paltry significance? No, gentlemen, bulk is what we desire—substance, weight, bulk—these are the supreme requisites now—not talent, not genius, not education. I insist upon my motion."

Mr. Morgan (excitedly): "Mr. Chairman—I do most strenuously object to this amendment. The gentleman from Oregon is old, and furthermore is bulky only in bone—not in flesh. I ask the gentleman from Virginia if it is soup we want instead of solid sustenance? if he would delude us with shadows? if he would mock our suffering with an Oregonian specter? I ask him if he can look upon the anxious faces around him, if he can gaze into our sad eyes, if he can listen to the beating of our expectant hearts, and still thrust this famine-stricken fraud upon us? I ask him if he can think of our desolate state, of our past sorrows, of our dark future, and still unpityingly foist upon us this wreck, this ruin, this tottering swindle, this gnarled and blighted and sapless vagabond from Oregon's inhospitable shores? Never! [Applause.]"

The amendment was put to vote, after a fiery debate, and lost. Mr. Harris was substituted on the first amendment. The balloting then began. Five ballots were held without a choice. On the sixth, Mr. Harris was elected, all voting for him but himself. It was then moved that his election should be ratified by acclamation, which was lost, in consequence of his again voting against himself.

Mr. Radway moved that the House now take up the remaining candidates, and go into an election for breakfast. This was carried.

On the first ballot there was a tie, half the members favoring one candidate on account of his youth, and half favoring the other on account of his superior size. The president gave the casting vote for the latter, Mr. Messick. This decision created considerable dissatisfaction among the friends of Mr. Ferguson, the defeated candidate, and there was some talk of demanding a new ballot; but in the midst of it a motion to adjourn was carried, and the meeting broke up at once.

The preparations for supper diverted the attention of the Ferguson faction from the discussion of their grievance for a long time, and then, when they would have taken it up again, the happy announcement that Mr. Harris was ready drove all thought of it to the winds.

We improvised tables by propping up the backs of car seats, and sat down with hearts full of gratitude to the finest supper that had blessed our vision for seven torturing days. How changed we were from what we had been a few short hours before! Hopeless, sad-eyed misery, hunger, feverish anxiety, desperation, then; thankfulness, serenity, joy too deep for utterance now. That I know was the cheeriest hour of my eventful life. The winds howled, and blew the snow wildly about our prison house, but they were powerless to distress us anymore. I liked Harris. He might have been better done, perhaps, but I am free to say that no man ever agreed with me better than Harris, or afforded me so large a degree of satisfaction. Messick was very well, though rather high-flavored, but for genuine nutritiousness and delicacy of fiber, give me Harris. Messick had his good points—I will not attempt to deny it, nor do I wish to do it—but he was no more fitted for breakfast than a mummy would be, sir—not a bit. Lean?—why, bless me!—and tough? Ah, he was very tough! You could not imagine it—you could never imagine anything like it.

"Do you mean to tell me that—"

"Do not interrupt me, please. After breakfast we elected a man by the name of Walker, from Detroit, for supper. He was very good. I wrote his wife so afterward. He was worthy of all praise. I shall always remember Walker. He was a little rare, but very good. And then the next morning we had Morgan of Alabama for breakfast. He was one of the finest men I ever sat down to—handsome, educated, refined, spoke several languages fluently—a perfect gentleman—he was a perfect gentleman, and singularly juicy. For supper we had that Oregon patriarch, and he *was* a fraud, there is no question about it—old, scraggy, tough, nobody can picture the reality. I finally said, 'Gentlemen, you can do as you like, but *I* will wait for another election.' And Grimes of Illinois said, 'Gentlemen, *I* will wait also. When you elect a man that has *something* to recommend him, I shall be glad to join you again.' It soon became evident that there was general dissatisfaction with Davis of Oregon, and so, to preserve the good will that had prevailed so pleasantly since we had had Harris, an election was called, and the result of it was that Baker of Georgia was chosen. He was splendid! Well, well—after that we had Doolittle, and Hawkins, and McElroy (there was some complaint about McElroy, because he was uncommonly short and thin), and Penrod, and two Smiths, and Bailey (Bailey had a wooden leg, which was clear loss, but he was otherwise good), and an Indian boy, and an organ-grinder and a gentleman by the name of Buckminster—a poor stick of a vagabond that wasn't any good for company and no account for breakfast. We were glad we got him elected before relief came."

"And so the blessed relief *did* come at last?"

"Yes, it came one bright, sunny morning, just after election. John Murphy was the choice, and there never was a better, I am willing to testify; but John Murphy came home with us, in the train that came to succor us, and lived to marry the widow Harris—"

"Relict of—"

"Relict of our first choice. He married her, and is happy and respected and prosperous yet. Ah, it was like a novel, sir—it was like a romance. This is my stopping-place, sir; I must bid you goodbye. Any time that you can make it convenient to tarry a day or two with me, I shall be glad to have you. I like you, sir; I have conceived an affection for you. I could like you as well as I liked Harris himself, sir. Good day, sir, and a pleasant journey."

He was gone. I never felt so stunned, so distressed, so bewildered in my life. But in my soul I was glad he was gone. With all his gentleness of manner and his soft voice, I shuddered whenever he turned his hungry eye upon me; and when I heard that I had achieved his perilous affection, and that I stood almost with the late Harris in his esteem, my heart fairly stood still!

I was bewildered beyond description. I did not doubt his word; I could not question a single item in a statement so stamped with the earnestness of truth as his; but its dreadful details overpowered me, and threw my thoughts into hopeless confusion. I saw the conductor looking at me. I said, "Who is that man?"

"He was a member of congress once, and a good one. But he got caught in a snowdrift in the cars, and like to have been starved to death. He got so frostbitten and frozen up generally, and used up for want of something to eat, that he was sick and out of his head two or three months afterward. He is all right now, only he is a monomaniac, and when he gets on that old subject he never stops till he has eat up that whole carload of people he talks about. He would have finished the crowd by this time, only he had to get out here. He has got their names as past as *ABC.* When he gets them all eat up but himself, he always says: "Then the hour for the unusual election for breakfast having arrived, and there being no opposition, I was duly elected, after which, there being no objections offered, I resigned. Thus I am here.' "

I felt inexpressibly relieved to know that I had only been listening to the harmless vagaries of a madman instead of the genuine experiences of a bloodthirsty cannibal.

STEPHEN KING

Mr. King selected the following stories:

"The Color Out of Space." While all of H. P. Lovecraft worked for me as a kid, there are only two or three which continue to work for me as an adult. One of them is "Pickman's Model," another is "The Rats in the Walls," but it seems to me that the best of them is "The Colour Out of Space." I can remember being frozen even in July by the terror of those colors in the well and the way they turned everything on that isolated farm gray and sterile.

"Sweets to the Sweet," by Robert Bloch. Bloch was the first horror writer whose work was easily available to me in paperback editions while I was growing up. Consequently, he was the first horror writer whose works I owned. Belmont Books issued his two classic Arkham House collections, Pleasant Dreams *and* The Opener of the Way *in about four paperback editions. Many of those stories stand out clearly in my memory, but I thought then and think now that "Sweets to the Sweet" had one of the most chilling snap endings I had ever read.*

"The Companion" by Ramsey Campbell. This was the first Campbell story I ever read. It was one of a collection of originals put out as Frights. Frights *was edited by Kirby McCauley, my agent, before he was my agent —I trust that takes care of any conflict of interest. I have never fully understood what's going on in "The Companion"; all I know is that it*

produces a sense of growing dreamlike menace, capped by one of the most frightening final moments in short horror fiction. I can't remember ever reading a finer example of the genre.

And neither can we.

THE COMPANION

RAMSEY CAMPBELL

When Stone reached the fairground, having been misdirected twice, he thought it looked more like a gigantic amusement arcade. A couple of paper cups tumbled and rattled on the shore beneath the promenade, and the cold insinuating October wind scooped the Mersey across the slabs of red rock that formed the beach and over the tires and broken bottles. Beneath the stubby white mock turrets of the long fairground facade were tucked souvenir shops and fish and chips; among them, in the fairground entrances, scraps of paper whirled.

Stone almost walked away. This wasn't his best holiday. One fairground in Wales had been closed, and this one certainly wasn't what he'd expected. The guidebook had made it sound like a genuine fairground, sideshows you must stride among not looking in case their barkers lured you in, the sudden shock of waterfalls cascading down what looked like painted cardboard, the familiar sensations which were almost always there and for which welcome surged through him: the shots and bells and wooden concussions of sideshows, the girls' shrieks overhead, the slippery armor and juicy crunch of toffee-apples, the illuminations springing alight against a darkening sky. But at least, he thought, he had chosen his time well. Few people were about, and if he went in now he might have the funfair almost to himself.

As he approached an entrance, he saw his mother eating fish and chips from a paper tray in the shop. No, rubbish. Besides, she would never have eaten standing up in public—"like a horse," as she used to say. As he passed the shop she hurried onto the promenade, face averted from him and the wind. He picked at the image gingerly, anxious not to awaken its implications. Of course, it had been the way she ate, with little snatching motions of her fork and mouth. He pushed the incident to the side of his mind in the hope that it would fall away, and hurried through the entrance.

Noise and color collided with him. Beneath the iron girders of a roof like that of a railway station the sirens and simulated whistling jets and groaning metal and gnashing gears fused with their echoes in a single, roaring, almost indistinguishable mass of sound, while panels of illuminated plastic, bright pink, pale green, sour orange and yellow, spun and changed and fluttered on Stone's eyes. He retreated a step. Then, since none of the sensations diminished and he would have had to turn and run to reduce them, he strode forward.

Once he'd adjusted to its excesses the fairground looked and felt dusty. The machines—a great disk rimmed with seats that lifted roofward and tilted on its axis as it spun, dangling a lone couple over its gears; an Ouroboros of seats that undulated brutally and trapped its passengers beneath a canvas canopy; a kind of roundabout whose independently rotating seats were given sudden violent jerks and spun helplessly—seemed grimy, as if just removed from a cupboard where they'd been left for years. With so few people in sight it seemed almost that the machines, frustrated by inaction, were operating themselves. For a moment Stone had the impression of being shut in a dusty room where the toys, as in childhood tales, had come to life.

He shrugged vaguely and turned to leave. He wondered whether he had time to drive to the fairground at Southport; it was a good few miles across the Mersey. His holiday was dwindling rapidly. He wondered how they were managing at the tax office this year in his absence. Slower as usual, no doubt.

Then he saw the roundabout. It was like a toy forgotten by another child and left here, or handed down the generations. Beneath its ornate scrolled canopy the horses rode on poles toward their reflections in a ring of mirrors. The horses were white wood or wood painted white, their bodies dappled with purple, red and green, and some of their sketched faces, too. From the hub, above a large notice MADE IN AMSTERDAM, an organ piped to itself. On the hub Stone saw carved fish, mermen, zephyrs, a head and shoulders smoking a pipe in a frame, a landscape of hills and lake and unfurling perched hawk. "Oh, yes," Stone said.

He clambered onto the platform. He felt a hint of embarrassment and glanced about, but nobody was watching. "Can you pay me?" said the head in the frame. "My boy's gone for a minute."

The man's hair was the color of the smoke from his pipe, and his lips puckered on the stem and smiled. "It's a good roundabout," Stone said.

"You know about them, do you?"

"Well, a little." The man looked disappointed; Stone hurried on. "I know a good deal about fairgrounds. They're my holiday, you see, every year. Each year I cover a different area. I may write a book." At least the idea had occasionally tempted him; but he hadn't taken notes, and he had ten years to retirement, for which the book had suggested itself as an activity.

"You go alone every year?"

"It has its merits. Less expensive, for one thing. I'm saving. Before I retire I intend to see Disneyland and Vienna." He thought of the Big Wheel, Harry Lime, the earth falling away beneath. "I'll get on," he said.

He patted the unyielding shoulders of the horse beneath him. He remembered a childhood friend who'd had a rocking horse in his bedroom. Stone had ridden it a few times, more and more wildly as the time to go home approached; his friend's bedroom was brighter and better lit than his, and as he clung to the wooden shoulders he was clutching the friendly room, too. Funny thinking of that now, he thought. Because I haven't been on a real roundabout for years, I suppose.

The roundabout shifted and the horse rose, bearing him, and sank. As they moved forward, slowly gathering momentum, Stone saw a crowd surging through one of the entrances and spreading through the funfair. He grimaced: it had been his fairground for a while, they needn't have arrived just as he was enjoying his roundabout.

The crowd swung away. A jangle of pinball machines sailed by. Amid the dodgems a giant with a barrel body spun, limp arms flapping, a red electric cigar thrust in its blankly grinning face and throbbing like an arrested balloon of slow thick laughter. A tinny voice read Bingo numbers, buzzing indistinctly. The roundabout was rotating faster; the fairground flashed on Stone's eyes like the images of a thaumatrope. Perhaps it was because he hadn't eaten for a while, saving himself for the toffee-apples, but he was becoming dizzy. It felt like the whirling, blurring shot of the fair in *Saturday Night and Sunday Morning,* a fair he hadn't liked because it was too grim. Give him *Strangers on a Train, The Third Man, Some*

Came Running, even the fairground murder in *Horrors of the Black Museum.* He shook his head to try to control his pouring thoughts.

A howling wind mixed with screams whipped by. It was looped on a tape inside the Ghost Train. The roundabout completed a quickening turn, and Stone's eyes fixed for a moment on the crowd standing beneath the beckoning green corpse. They were staring at him. No, he realized the next time they came round, they were staring at the roundabout. He was just something that kept reappearing as they watched. At the back of the crowd, staring and poking around inside his nostrils, stood Stone's father.

Stone gripped the horse's neck as he began to fall. The man had already been incorporated into the retreating crowd. Why was his mind so traitorous today? It wouldn't be so bad if the comparisons it was making weren't so repulsive. Why, he'd never met a man or woman since his parents to compare with them. Admired people, yes, but not in the same way. Not since the two polished boxes had been lowered into holes and hidden. Noise and color spun about him and inside him. Why wasn't he allowing himself to think about his parents' death? He knew why he was blocking, and that should be his salvation. At the age of ten he'd suffered death and hell every night.

The memories tumbled over him as he clung to the wood in the whirlpool. His father had denied him a night-light and his mother had nodded, saying "Yes, I think it's time." He'd lain in bed, terrified to move in case he betrayed his presence to the darkness, mouthing "Please God don't let it" over and over. He lay so that he could see the faint gray rectangle of the window between the parted curtains in the far distance, but even that light seemed to be receding. He knew that death and hell would be like this. Sometimes, as he began to blur with sleep and the room grew larger and the shapes dark against the darkness awoke, he couldn't tell that he hadn't already died.

He sat back as the horse slowed and he began to slip forward across its neck. What then? Well, of course he'd seen through the self-perpetuating trap of religious guilt, of hell, of not daring not to believe in it because then it would get you. For a while he'd been vaguely uneasy in dark places, but not sufficiently so to track down the feeling and conquer it. After a while it had dissipated, along with his parents' overt disapproval of his atheism. Yes, he thought as his memories and the roundabout slowed, I was happiest then, lying in bed hearing them, no, feeling them and the house around me. Then, when he was thirty, a telephone call had summoned him to the hole in the road. There had been a moment of sheer vertiginous terror at the sight of the car like a black beetle thrust nose first

clothes. If nothing else, Stone thought, it's instructive to watch my mind working. Now let's get on.

Then he noticed that the almost invisible light was flickering. Either that, which was possible although he couldn't determine the source of the light, or the clothes were shifting; very gradually but nonetheless definitely, as if something hidden by them on the seat of the chair were lifting them to peer out, perhaps preparatory to emerging. Stone leaned toward the chair. Let's see what it is, let's get it over with. But the light was far too dim and the chair too distant. Probably he would be unable to see it even when it emerged, the way the light had been allowed to run down, unless he left the car and went closer.

He had one hand on the side of the car when he realized that if the car moved off while he was out of it he would be left to grope his way through the darkness. He slumped back and at that moment glimpsed a violent movement among the clothes near the seat of the chair. He glanced toward it. Before his eyes could focus, the dim gray light was extinguished.

Stone sat for a moment, all of him concentrating on the silence, the blind darkness. Then he began to kick frantically at the nose of the car. The car shook a little with his attack, then jerked forward.

When the car nosed its way around the next curve, slowing as if sniffing the track ahead, and the clacking and rumbling had ceased, Stone heard a muted thud and creak of wood. It came from in front of him. The sort of thing you hear in a house at night, he thought. Soon be out now.

Without warning a face came speeding toward him out of the darkness a few feet ahead. It jerked forward as he did. Of course it would, he thought with a grimace, sinking back and watching his face recede briefly in the mirror. He realized that he and the car were surrounded by a faint light which extended as far as the wooden frame of the mirror. Must be the end of the ride. They can't get any more obvious than that. Effective in its way, I suppose.

He watched himself in the mirror as the car followed the curve past. The light had fallen behind, but his silhouette loomed on it. Suddenly he frowned. His silhouette was moving independent of the movement of the car. It was beginning to swing out of the limits of the mirror. Then he remembered the wardrobe which had stood at the foot of the bed in his childhood, and understood. The mirror was set into a door, which was opening.

Stone pressed himself against the opposite side of the car, which had slowed almost to a halt. No no, he thought, it mustn't. Don't. He heard a grinding of gears beneath him. Unmeshed metal shrieked. He threw his body forward against the nose of the car. In the darkness to his left he heard the creak of the door and a soft thud. The car moved a little, then caught the gears and ground forward.

As the light went out behind him, Stone felt a weight fall beside him on the seat.

He cried out. Or tried to, for as he gulped in air it seemed to draw darkness into his lungs, darkness that swelled and poured into his heart and brain. There was a moment at which he knew nothing, as if he'd become darkness and silence and the memory of suffering. Then the car was rattling on, the darkness was sweeping over him and by, and the nose of the car banged open the doors and plunged out into the night.

As the car swung into the length of track outside the Ghost Train, Stone caught sight of the gap between the stalls where he had thought he'd seen the stall-holders. A welling moonlight showed him that between the stalls stood a pile of sacks, nodding and gesticulating in the wind. Then the seat beside him emerged from the shadow, and he looked down.

Next to him on the seat was a shrunken hooded figure. It wore a faded jacket and trousers striped and patched in various colors, indistinguishable in the receding moonlight. The head almost reached his shoulder. Its arms hung slack at its sides, and its feet drummed laxly on the metal beneath the seat. Shrinking back, Stone reached for the front of the car to pull himself up, and the figure's head fell back.

Stone closed his eyes. When he opened them he saw within the hood an oval of white cloth upon which—black crosses for eyes and nose, a barred crescent for a mouth—a grinning face was stitched.

As he had suddenly realized that the car hadn't halted nor even slowed before plunging down the incline back into the Ghost Train, Stone did not immediately notice that the figure had taken his hand.

IRA LEVIN

Ira Levin had a wonderful first choice—however. . . .

The scariest short story I've ever read, bar none, is one whose author and title I can't recall. How's that for frustration? Maybe you know it, maybe someone else will suggest it. It was written by a woman, I believe, and I must have read it about twenty years ago. I can't even recall whether it was in a magazine or a book.

The story dealt with a woman recently released from a mental institution. She was staying with her married sister's family, and for some plausible reason was left to take care of an infant for a few hours. Deciding to be helpful, she gave the baby a bath, and while he was happily splashing, began doing a few other household chores. The body of the story simply described the woman getting involved in one chore after another, confident that she was proving how helpful and fully recovered she was, while the reader agonized, but agonized, *over the baby forgotten in the bath. Wow!*

We tried and tried, but we could not turn up the story. Mr. Levin was kind enough to send us this equally terrific second choice.

PREY

RICHARD MATHESON

Amelia arrived at her apartment at six-forteen. Hanging her coat in the hall closet, she carried the small package into the living room and sat on the sofa. She nudged off her shoes while she unwrapped the package on her lap. The wooden box resembled a casket. Amelia raised its lid and smiled. It was the ugliest doll she'd ever seen. Seven inches long and carved from wood, it had a skeletal body and an oversized head. Its expression was maniacally fierce, its pointed teeth completely bared, its glaring eyes protuberant. It clutched an eight-inch spear in its right hand. A length of fine, gold chain was wrapped around its body from the shoulders to the knees. A tiny scroll was wedged between the doll and the inside wall of its box. Amelia picked it up and unrolled it. There was handwriting on it. *This is He Who Kills,* it began. *He is a deadly hunter.* Amelia smiled as she read the rest of the words. Arthur would be pleased.

The thought of Arthur made her turn to look at the telephone on the table beside her. After a while, she sighed and set the wooden box on the sofa. Lifting the telephone to her lap, she picked up the receiver and dialed a number.

Her mother answered.

"Hello, mom," Amelia said.

"Haven't you left yet?" her mother asked.

Amelia steeled herself. "Mom, I know it's Friday night—" she started.

She couldn't finish. There was silence on the line. Amelia closed her eyes. Mom, please, she thought. She swallowed. "There's this man," she said. "His name is Arthur Breslow. He's a high school teacher."

"You aren't coming," her mother said.

Amelia shivered. "It's his birthday," she said. She opened her eyes and looked at the doll. "I sort of promised him we'd . . . spend the evening together."

Her mother was silent. There aren't any good movies playing tonight, anyway, Amelia's mind continued. "We could go tomorrow night," she said.

Her mother was silent.

"Mom?"

"Now even Friday night's too much for you."

"Mom, I see you two, three nights a week."

"To *visit,*" said her mother. "When you have your own room here."

"Mom, *let's not start on that again,*" Amelia said. I'm not a child, she thought. Stop treating me as though I were a child!

"How long have you been seeing him?" her mother asked.

"A month or so."

"Without telling me," her mother said.

"I had every intention of telling you." Amelia's head was starting to throb. I will *not* get a headache, she told herself. She looked at the doll. It seemed to be glaring at her. "He's a nice man, mom," she said.

Her mother didn't speak. Amelia felt her stomach muscles drawing taut. I won't be able to eat tonight, she thought.

She was conscious suddenly of huddling over the telephone. She forced herself to sit erect. *I'm thirty-three years old,* she thought. Reaching out, she lifted the doll from its box. "You should see what I'm giving him for his birthday," she said. "I found it in a curio shop on Third Avenue. It's a genuine Zuñi fetish doll, extremely rare. Arthur is a buff on anthropology. That's why I got it for him."

There was silence on the line. All right, *don't talk,* Amelia thought. "It's a hunting fetish," she continued, trying hard to sound untroubled. "It's supposed to have the spirit of a Zuñi hunter trapped inside it. There's a golden chain around it to prevent the spirit from"—She couldn't think of the word. She ran a shaking finger over the chain—"escaping, I guess," she said. "His name is He Who Kills. You should see his face." She felt warm tears trickling down her cheeks.

"Have a good time," said her mother, hanging up.

Amelia stared at the receiver, listening to the dial tone. Why is it always like this? she thought. She dropped the receiver onto its cradle and set aside the telephone. The darkening room looked blurred to her. She stood the doll on the coffee-table edge and pushed to her feet. I'll take my bath now, she told herself. I'll meet him and we'll have a lovely time. She walked across the living room. A lovely time, her mind repeated emptily. She knew it wasn't possible. Oh, *mom!* she thought. She clenched her fists in helpless fury as she went into the bedroom.

In the living room, the doll fell off the table edge. It landed head down and the spear point, sticking into the carpet, braced the doll's legs in the air.

The fine, gold chain began to slither downward.

It was almost dark when Amelia came back into the living room. She had taken off her clothes and was wearing her terry-cloth robe. In the bathroom, water was running into the tub.

She sat on the sofa and placed the telephone on her lap. For several minutes, she stared at it. At last, with a heavy sigh, she lifted the receiver and dialed a number.

"Arthur?" she said when he answered.

"Yes?" Amelia knew the tone—pleasant but suspecting. She couldn't speak.

"Your mother," Arthur finally said.

That cold, heavy sinking in her stomach. "It's our night together," she explained. "Every Friday—" She stopped and waited. Arthur didn't speak. "I've mentioned it before," she said.

"I know you've mentioned it," he said.

Amelia rubbed at her temple.

"She's still running your life, isn't she?" he said.

Amelia tensed. "I just don't want to hurt her feelings any more," she said. "My moving out was hard enough on her."

"I don't want to hurt her feelings either," Arthur said. "But how many birthdays a year do I have? We *planned* on this."

"I know." She felt her stomach muscles tightening again.

"Are you really going to let her do this to you?" Arthur asked. "One Friday night out of the whole year?"

Amelia closed her eyes. Her lips moved soundlessly. I just can't hurt her feelings any more, she thought. She swallowed. "She's my mother," she said.

"Very well," he said. "I'm sorry. I was looking forward to it, but—" He paused. "I'm sorry," he said. He hung up quietly.

Amelia sat in silence for a long time, listening to the dial tone. She started when the recorded voice said loudly, "Please hang up." Putting the receiver down, she replaced the telephone on its table. So much for my birthday present, she thought. It would be pointless to give it to Arthur now. She reached out, switching on the table lamp. She'd take the doll back tomorrow.

The doll was not on the coffee table. Looking down, Amelia saw the gold chain lying on the carpet. She eased off the sofa edge onto her knees and picked it up, dropping it into the wooden box. The doll was not beneath the coffee table. Bending over, Amelia felt around underneath the sofa.

She cried out, jerking back her hand. Straightening up, she turned to the lamp and looked at her hand. There was something wedged beneath the index fingernail. She shivered as she plucked it out. It was the head of the doll's spear. She dropped it into the box and put the finger in her mouth. Bending over again, she felt around more cautiously beneath the sofa.

She couldn't find the doll. Standing with a weary groan, she started pulling one end of the sofa from the wall. It was terribly heavy. She recalled the night that she and her mother had shopped for the furniture. She'd wanted to furnish the apartment in Danish modern. Mother had insisted on this heavy, maple sofa; it had been on sale. Amelia grunted as she dragged it from the wall. She was conscious of the water running in the bathroom. She'd better turn it off soon.

She looked at the section of carpet she'd cleared, catching sight of the spear shaft. The doll was not beside it. Amelia picked it up and set it on the coffee table. The doll was caught beneath the sofa, she decided; when she'd moved the sofa, she had moved the doll as well.

She thought she heard a sound behind her—fragile, skittering. Amelia turned. The sound had stopped. She felt a chill move up the backs of her legs. "It's He Who Kills," she said with a smile. "He's taken off his chain and gone—"

She broke off suddenly. There had definitely been a noise inside the kitchen; a metallic, rasping sound. Amelia swallowed nervously. What's going on? she thought. She walked across the living room and reached into the kitchen, switching on the light. She peered inside. Everything looked normal. Her gaze moved falteringly across the stove, the pan of water on it, the table and chair, the drawers and cabinet doors all shut, the electric clock, the small refrigerator with the cookbook lying on top of it, the picture on the wall, the knife rack fastened to the cabinet side—

—its small knife missing.

Amelia stared at the knife rack. Don't be silly, she told herself. She'd put the knife in the drawer, that's all. Stepping into the kitchen, she pulled out the silverware drawer. The knife was not inside it.

Another sound made her look down quickly at the floor. She gasped in shock. For several moments, she could not react; then, stepping to the doorway, she looked into the living room, her heartbeat thudding. Had it been imagination? She was sure she'd seen a movement.

"Oh, come on," she said. She made a disparaging sound. She hadn't seen a thing.

Across the room, the lamp went out.

Amelia jumped so startledly, she rammed her right elbow against the doorjamb. Crying out, she clutched the elbow with her left hand, eyes closed momentarily, her face a mask of pain.

She opened her eyes and looked into the darkened living room. "Come on," she told herself in aggravation. Three sounds plus a burned-out bulb did not add up to anything as idiotic as—

She willed away the thought. She had to turn the water off. Leaving the kitchen, she started for the hall. She rubbed her elbow, grimacing.

There was another sound. Amelia froze. Something was coming across the carpet toward her. She looked down dumbly. No, she thought.

She saw it then—a rapid movement near the floor. There was a glint of metal, instantly, a stabbing pain in her right calf. Amelia gasped. She kicked out blindly. Pain again. She felt warm blood running down her skin. She turned and lunged into the hall. The throw rug slipped beneath her and she fell against the wall, hot pain lancing through her right ankle. She clutched at the wall to keep from falling, then went sprawling on her side. She thrashed around with a sob of fear.

More movement, dark on dark. Pain in her left calf, then her right again. Amelia cried out. Something brushed along her thigh. She scrabbled back, then lurched up blindly, almost falling again. She fought for balance, reaching out convulsively. The heel of her left hand rammed against the wall, supporting her. She twisted around and rushed into the darkened bedroom. Slamming the door, she fell against it, panting. Something banged against it on the other side, something small and near the floor.

Amelia listened, trying not to breathe so loudly. She pulled carefully at the knob to make sure the latch had caught. When there were no further sounds outside the door, she backed toward the bed. She started as she bumped against the mattress edge. Slumping down, she grabbed at the extension phone and pulled it to her lap. Whom could she call? The police? They'd think her mad. Mother? She was too far off.

She was dialing Arthur's number by the light from the bathroom when the doorknob started turning. Suddenly, her fingers couldn't move. She stared across the darkened room. The door latch clicked. The telephone slipped off her lap. She heard it thudding onto the carpet as the door swung open. Something dropped from the outside knob.

Amelia jerked back, pulling up her legs. A shadowy form was scurrying across the carpet toward the bed. She gaped at it. It isn't true, she thought. She stiffened at the tugging on her bedspread. *It was climbing up to get her.* No, she thought; *it isn't true.* She couldn't move. She stared at the edge of the mattress.

Something that looked like a tiny head appeared. Amelia twisted around with a cry of shock, flung herself across the bed and jumped to the floor. Plunging into the bathroom, she spun around and slammed the door, gasping at the pain in her ankle. She had barely thumbed in the button on the doorknob when something banged against the bottom of the door. Amelia heard a noise like the scratching of a rat. Then it was still.

She turned and leaned across the tub. The level of the water was almost to the overflow drain. As she twisted shut the faucets, she saw drops of blood falling into the water. Straightening up, she turned to the medicine-cabinet mirror above the sink.

She caught her breath in horror as she saw the gash across her neck. She pressed a shaking hand against it. Abruptly, she became aware of pain in her legs and looked down. She'd been slashed along the calves of both legs. Blood was running down her ankles, dripping off the edges of her feet. Amelia started crying. Blood ran between the fingers of the hand against her neck. It trickled down her wrist. She looked at her reflection through a glaze of tears.

Something in her face aroused her, a wretchedness, a look of terrified surrender. *No,* she thought. She reached out for the medicine-cabinet door. Opening it, she pulled out iodine, gauze and tape. She dropped the cover of the toilet seat and sank down gingerly. It was a struggle to remove the stopper of the iodine bottle. She had to rap it hard against the sink three times before it opened.

The burning of the antiseptic on her calves made her gasp. Amelia clenched her teeth as she wrapped gauze around her right leg.

A sound made her twist toward the door. She saw the knife blade being jabbed beneath it. It's trying to stab my feet, she thought; it thinks I'm standing there. She felt unreal to be considering its thoughts. *This is He Who Kills;* the scroll flashed suddenly across her mind. *He is a deadly hunter.* Amelia stared at the poking knife blade. God, she thought.

Hastily, she bandaged both her legs, then stood and, looking into the mirror, cleaned the blood from her neck, with a washrag. She swabbed some iodine along the edges of the gash, hissing at the fiery pain.

She whirled at the new sound, heartbeat leaping. Stepping to the door, she leaned down, listening hard. There was a faint, metallic noise inside the knob.

The doll was trying to unlock it.

Amelia backed off slowly, staring at the knob. She tried to visualize the doll. Was it hanging from the knob by one arm, using the other to probe inside the knob lock with the knife? The vision was insane. She felt an icy prickling on the back of her neck. *I mustn't let it in,* she thought.

A hoarse cry pulled her lips back as the doorknob button popped out. Reaching out impulsively, she dragged a bath towel off its rack. The doorknob turned, the latch clicked free. The door began to open.

Suddenly the doll came darting in. It moved so quickly that its figure blurred before Amelia's eyes. She swung the towel down hard, as though it were a huge bug rushing at her. The doll was knocked against the wall. Amelia heaved the towel on top of it and lurched across the floor, gasping at the pain in her ankle. Flinging open the door, she lunged into the bedroom.

She was almost to the hall door when her ankle gave. She pitched across the carpet with a cry of shock. There was a noise behind her. Twisting around, she saw the doll come through the bathroom doorway like a jumping spider. She saw the knife blade glinting in the light. Then the doll was in the shadows, coming at her fast. Amelia scrabbled back. She glanced over her shoulder, saw the closet and backed into its darkness, clawing for the doorknob.

Pain again, an icy slashing at her foot. Amelia screamed and heaved back. Reaching up, she yanked a topcoat down. It fell across the doll. She jerked down everything in reach. The doll was buried underneath a mound of blouses, skirts and dresses. Amelia pitched across the moving pile of clothes. She forced herself to stand and limped into the hall as quickly as she could. The sound of thrashing underneath the clothes faded from her hearing. She hobbled to the door. Unlocking it, she pulled the knob.

The door was held. Amelia reached up quickly to the bolt. It had been shot. She tried to pull it free. It wouldn't budge. She clawed at it with sudden terror. It was twisted out of shape. "No," she muttered. *She was trapped.* "Oh, God." She started pounding on the door. "Please help me! *Help* me!"

Sound in the bedroom. Amelia whirled and lurched across the living room. She dropped to her knees beside the sofa, feeling for the telephone, but her fingers trembled so much that she couldn't dial the numbers. She began to sob, then twisted around with a strangled cry. The doll was rushing at her from the hallway.

Amelia grabbed an ashtray from the coffee table and hurled it at the doll. She threw a vase, a wooden box, a figurine. She couldn't hit the doll. It reached her, started jabbing at her legs. Amelia reared up blindly and fell across the coffee table. Rolling to her knees, she stood again. She staggered toward the hall, shoving over furniture to stop the doll. She toppled a chair, a table. Picking up a lamp, she hurled it at the floor. She backed into the hall and, spinning, rushed into the closet, slammed the door shut.

She held the knob with rigid fingers. Waves of hot breath pulsed against her face. She cried out as the knife was jabbed beneath the door, its sharp point sticking into one of her toes. She shuffled back, shifting her grip on the knob. Her robe hung open. She could feel a trickle of blood between her breasts. Her legs felt numb with pain. She closed her eyes. Please, someone help, she thought.

She stiffened as the doorknob started turning in her grasp. Her flesh went cold. It couldn't be stronger than she: it *couldn't* be. Amelia tightened her grip. *Please,* she thought. The side of her head bumped against the front edge of her suitcase on the shelf.

The thought exploded in her mind. Holding the knob with her right hand, she reached up, fumbling, with her left. The suitcase clasps were open. With a sudden wrench, she turned the doorknob, shoving at the door as hard as possible. It rushed away from her. She heard it bang against the wall. The doll thumped down.

Amelia reached up, hauling down her suitcase. Yanking open the lid, she fell to her knees in the closet doorway, holding the suitcase like an open book. She braced herself, eyes wide, teeth clenched together. She felt the doll's weight as it banged against the suitcase bottom. Instantly, she slammed the lid and threw the suitcase flat. Falling across it, she held it shut until her shaking hands could fasten the clasps. The sound of them clicking into place made her sob with relief. She shoved away the suitcase. It slid across the hall and bumped against the wall. Amelia struggled to her feet, trying not to listen to the frenzied kicking and scratching inside the suitcase.

She switched on the hall light and tried to open the bolt. It was hopelessly wedged. She turned and limped across the living room, glancing at her legs. The bandages were hanging loose. Both legs were streaked with caking blood, some of the gashes still bleeding. She felt at her throat. The cut was still wet. Amelia pressed her shaking lips together. She'd get to a doctor soon now.

Removing the ice pick from its kitchen drawer, she returned to the hall. A cutting sound made her look toward the suitcase. She caught her breath. The knife blade was protruding from the suitcase wall, moving up and down with a sawing motion. Amelia stared at it. She felt as though her body had been turned to stone.

She limped to the suitcase and knelt beside it, looking, with revulsion, at the sawing blade. It was smeared with blood. She tried to pinch it with the fingers of her left hand, pull it out. The blade was twisted, jerked down, and she cried out, snatching back her hand. There was a deep slice in her thumb. Blood ran down across her palm. Amelia pressed the finger to her robe. She felt as though her mind were going blank.

Pushing to her feet, she limped back to the door and started prying at the bolt. She couldn't get it loose. Her thumb began to ache. She pushed the ice pick underneath the bolt socket and tried to force it off the wall. The ice pick point broke off. Amelia slipped and almost fell. She pushed up, whimpering. There was no time, no time. She looked around in desperation.

The window! She could throw the suitcase out! She visualized it tumbling through the darkness. Hastily, she dropped the ice pick, turning toward the suitcase.

She froze. The doll had forced its head and shoulders through the rent in the suitcase wall. Amelia watched it struggling to get out. She felt paralyzed. The twisting doll was staring at her. No, she thought, it isn't true. The doll jerked free its legs and jumped to the floor.

Amelia jerked around and ran into the living room. Her right foot landed on a shard of broken crockery. She felt it cutting deep into her heel and lost her balance. Landing on her side, she thrashed around. The doll came leaping at her. She could see the knife blade glint. She kicked out wildly, knocking back the doll. Lunging to her feet, she reeled into the kitchen, whirled, and started pushing shut the door.

Something kept it from closing. Amelia thought she heard a screaming in her mind. Looking down, she saw the knife and a tiny wooden hand.

The doll's arm was wedged between the door and the jamb! Amelia shoved against the door with all her might, aghast at the strength with which the door was pushed the other way. There was a cracking noise. A fierce smile pulled her lips back and she pushed berserkly at the door. The screaming in her mind grew louder, drowning out the sound of splintering wood.

The knife blade sagged. Amelia dropped to her knees and tugged at it. She pulled the knife into the kitchen, seeing the wooden hand and wrist fall from the handle of the knife. With a gagging noise, she struggled to her feet and dropped the knife into the sink. The door slammed hard against her side; the doll rushed in.

Amelia jerked away from it. Picking up the chair, she slung it toward the doll. It jumped aside, then ran around the fallen chair. Amelia snatched the pan of water off the stove and hurled it down. The pan clanged loudly off the floor, spraying water on the doll.

She stared at the doll. It wasn't coming after her. It was trying to climb the sink, leaping up and clutching at the counter side with one hand. It wants the knife, she thought. It has to have its weapon.

She knew abruptly what to do. Stepping over to the stove, she pulled down the broiler door and twisted the knob on all the way. She heard the puffing detonation of the gas as she turned to grab the doll.

She cried out as the doll began to kick and twist, its maddened thrashing flinging her from one side of the kitchen to the other. The screaming filled her mind again and suddenly she knew it was the spirit in the doll that screamed. She slid and crashed against the table, wrenched herself around and, dropping to her knees before the stove, flung the doll inside. She slammed the door and fell against it.

The door was almost driven out. Amelia pressed her shoulder, then her back against it, turning to brace her legs against the wall. She tried to ignore the pounding scrabble of the doll inside the broiler. She watched the red blood pulsing from her heel. The smell of burning wood began to reach her and she closed her eyes. The door was getting hot. She shifted carefully. The kicking and pounding filled her ears. The screaming flooded through her mind. She knew her back would get burned, but she didn't dare to move. The smell of burning wood grew worse. Her foot ached terribly.

Amelia looked up at the electric clock on the wall. It was four minutes to seven. She watched the red second hand revolving slowly. A minute passed. The screaming in her mind was fading now. She shifted uncomfortably, gritting her teeth against the burning heat on her back.

Another minute passed. The kicking and the pounding stopped. The screaming faded more and more. The smell of burning wood had filled the kitchen. There was a pall of gray smoke in the air. That they'll see, Amelia thought. Now that it's over, they'll come and help. That's the way it always is.

She started to ease herself away from the broiler door, ready to throw her weight back against it if she had to. She turned around and got on her knees. The reek of charred wood made her nauseated. She had to know, though. Reaching out, she pulled down the door.

Something dark and stifling rushed across her and she heard the screaming in her mind once more as hotness flooded over her and into her. It was a scream of victory now.

Amelia stood and turned off the broiler. She took a pair of ice tongs from its drawer and lifted out the blackened twist of wood. She dropped it into the sink and ran water over it until the smoke had stopped. Then she went into the bedroom, picked up the telephone and depressed its cradle. After a moment, she released the cradle and dialed her mother's number.

"This is Amelia, mom," she said. "I'm sorry I acted the way I did. I want us to spend the evening together. It's a little late, though. Can you come by my place and we'll go from here?" She listened. "Good," she said. "I'll wait for you."

Hanging up, she walked into the kitchen, where she slid the longest carving knife from its place in the rack. She went to the front door and pushed back its bolt, which now moved freely. She carried the knife into the living room, took off her bathrobe and danced a dance of hunting, of the joy of hunting, of the joy of the impending kill.

Then she sat down, cross-legged, in the corner. He Who Kills sat, cross-legged, in the corner, in the darkness, waiting for the prey to come.

WILLIAM F. NOLAN

A *roundabout route is required to get us to the story I've selected. . . .*

We begin with Ramsey Campbell. Ramsey and I met at the Fifth World Fantasy Convention in Rhode Island, in October of 1979. A jolly fellow indeed. Immediate rapport. Subsequently, in the company of our mutual agent Kirby McCauley and our mutual friend Dennis Etchison, we spent a night on the town in New York. Fine dinner. Fine evening.

I found Ramsey to be a spirited, fun-loving gentleman. During our New York visit he told me to watch for a book he was editing back in England, New Terrors 1, *due in 1980.*

I obtained the book, published by Pan, and upon finishing the third story in the volume, "Sun City" by Lisa Tuttle, I was stunned to discover that I was still capable of actually being chilled *by a horror tale. I had considered myself far too sophisticated, far too much the veteran writer/reader of horror, to experience genuine fear at words on a printed page—but "Sun City" proved me wrong. From the moody opening sentence to the horrifying last one, this story is a guaranteed shocker.*

SUN CITY

LISA TUTTLE

It was 3:00 A.M., the dead, silent middle of the night. Except for the humming of the soft-drink machine in one corner, and the irregular, rumbling cough of the ice machine hidden in an alcove just beyond it, the lobby was quiet. There weren't likely to be any more check-ins until after dawn—all the weary cross-country drivers would be settled elsewhere by now, or grimly determined to push on without a rest.

Clerking the 11:00 P.M. to 7:00 A.M. shift was a dull, lonely job, but usually Nora Theale didn't mind it. She preferred working at night, and the solitude didn't bother her. But tonight, for the third night in a row, she was jumpy. It was an irrational nervousness, and it annoyed Nora that she couldn't pin it down. There was always the possibility of robbery, of course, but the Posada del Norte hadn't been hit in the year she had worked there, and Nora didn't think the motel made a very enticing target.

Seeking a cause for her unease, Nora often glanced around the empty lobby and through the glass doors at the parking lot and the highway beyond. She never saw anything out of place—except a shadow which might have been cast by someone moving swiftly through the bluish light of the parking lot. But it was gone in an instant, and she couldn't be sure she had seen it.

Nora picked up the evening paper and tried to concentrate. She read about plans to build a huge fence along the border, to keep illegal aliens out. It was an idea she liked—the constant flow back and forth between Mexico and the United States was one of the things she hated most about El Paso—but she didn't imagine it would work. After a few more minutes of scanning state and national news, Nora tossed the paper into the garbage can. She didn't want to read about El Paso; El Paso bored and depressed and disturbed her. She couldn't wait to leave it.

Casting another uneasy glance around the unchanged lobby, Nora leaned over to the file cabinet and pulled open the drawer where she kept her books. She picked out a mystery by Josephine Tey and settled down to it, determined to win over her nerves.

She read, undisturbed except for a few twinges of unease, until 6:00 A.M. when she had to let the man with the newspapers in and make the first wake-up call. The day clerk arrived a few minutes after seven, and that meant it was time for Nora to leave. She gathered her things together into a shoulder bag. She had a lot with her because she had spent the past two days in one of the motel's free rooms rather than go home. But the rooms were all booked up for that night, so she had to clear out. Since her husband had moved out, Nora hadn't felt like spending much time in the apartment that was now hers alone. She meant to move, but since she didn't want to stay in El Paso, it seemed more sensible simply to let the lease run out rather than go to the expense and trouble of finding another temporary home. She meant to leave El Paso just as soon as she got a little money together and decided on a place to go.

She didn't like the apartment, but it was large and cheap. Larry had picked it out because it was close to his office, and he liked to ride his bicycle to work. It wasn't anywhere near the motel where Nora worked, but Nora didn't care. She had her car.

She parked it now in the space behind the small, one-story apartment complex. It was a hideous place; Nora winced every time she came home to it. It was made of an ugly pink fake adobe, and had a red-tiled roof. There were some diseased-looking cactuses planted along the concrete walkway, but no grass or trees: water was scarce.

The stench of something long dead and richly rotting struck Nora as she opened the door to her apartment. She stepped back immediately, gagging. Her heart raced; she felt, oddly, afraid. But she recovered in a moment—it was just a smell, after all, and in her apartment. She had to do something about it. Breathing through her mouth, she stepped forward again.

The kitchen was clean, the garbage pail empty, and the refrigerator nearly bare. She found nothing there, or in the bedroom or bathroom, that seemed to be the cause of the odor. In the bedroom, she cautiously breathed in through her nose to test the air. It was clean. She walked slowly back to the living room, but there was nothing there, either. The whiff of foulness had gone as if it had never been.

Nora shrugged, and locked the door. It might have been something outside. If she smelled it again, she'd talk to the landlord about it.

There was nothing in the kitchen she could bear the thought of eating, so, after she had showered and changed, Nora walked down to the Seven-Eleven, three blocks away, and bought a few essentials: milk, eggs, bread, Dr. Pepper and a package of sugared doughnuts.

The sun was already blazing and the dry wind abraded her skin. It would be another hot, dry, windy day—a day like every other day in El Paso. Nora was glad she slept through most of them. She thought about North Carolina, where she had gone to college, reflecting wistfully that up there the leaves would be starting to turn now. As she walked back to her apartment with the bag of groceries in her arms, Nora thought about moving east to North Carolina.

The telephone was ringing as Nora walked in.

"I've been trying to get in touch with you for the past three days!"

It was her husband, Larry.

"I've been out a lot." She began to peel the cellophane wrapping off the doughnuts.

"Do tell. Look, Nora, I've got some papers for you to sign."

"Aw, and I thought maybe you'd called to say 'Happy anniversary.' "

He was silent. One side of Nora's mouth twitched upwards: she'd scored.

Then he sighed. "What do you want, Nora? Am I supposed to think that today means something to you? That you still care? That you want me back?"

"God forbid."

"Then cut the crap, all right? So we didn't make it to our third wedding anniversary—all right, so *legally* we're still married—but what's the big deal?"

"I was joking, Larry. You never could recognize a joke."

"I didn't call to fight with you, Nora. Or to joke. I'd just like you to sign these papers so we can get this whole thing over with. You won't even have to show up in court."

Nora bit into a doughnut and brushed off the spray of sugar that powdered her shirt.

"Nora? When should I bring the papers by?"

She set the half-eaten doughnut down on the counter and reflected. "Um, come this evening, if you want. Not too early, or I'll still be asleep. Say . . . seven-thirty?"

'Seven-thirty.'

"That won't cut into your dinner plans with what's-her-name?"

"Seven-thirty will be fine, Nora. I'll see you then. Just be there." And he hung up before she could get in another dig.

Nora grimaced, then shrugged as she hung up. She finished the doughnut, feeling depressed. Despite herself, she'd started thinking about Larry again, and their marriage which had seemed to go bad before it had properly started. She thought about their brief honeymoon. She remembered Mexico.

It had been Larry's idea to drive down to Mexico—Nora had always thought of Mexico as a poor and dirty place, filled with undesirables who were always sneaking into the United States. But Larry had wanted to go, and Nora had wanted to make Larry happy.

It was their *luna de miel,* moon of honey, Larry said, and the Spanish words sounded almost sweet to her, coming from his mouth. Even Mexico, in his company, had seemed freshly promising, especially after they escaped the dusty borderlands and reached the ocean.

One afternoon they had parked on an empty beach and made love. Larry had fallen asleep, and Nora had left him to walk up the beach and explore.

She walked along in a daze of happiness, her body tingling, climbing over rocks and searching for shells to bring back to her husband. She didn't realize how far she had traveled until she was shocked out of her pleasant haze by a sharp cry, whether human or animal she could not be certain. She heard some indistinct words, then, tossed to her by the wind.

Nora was frightened. She didn't want to know what the sounds meant or where they came from. She wanted to get back to Larry and forget that she had heard anything. She turned around immediately, and began to weave her way back among the white boulders. But she must have mistaken her way, for as she clambered back over a rock she was certain she had just climbed, she saw them below her, posed like some sacrificial tableau.

At the center was a girl, spread out on a low, flat rock. The victim. Crouching over her, doing something, was a young man. Another young man stared at them greedily. Nora gazed at the girl's face, which was contorted in pain. She heard her whimper. It was only then that she realized, with a cold flash of dread, what she was seeing. The girl was being raped.

Nora was frozen with fear and indecision, and then the girl opened her eyes, and gazed straight up at Nora. Her brown eyes were eloquent with agony. Was there a glimmer of hope there at the sight of Nora? Nora couldn't be sure. She stared into those eyes for what seemed like a very long time, trying desperately to think of what to do. She wanted to help this girl, to chase away the men. But there were *two* men, and she, Nora, had no particular strengths. They would probably be pleased to have two victims. And at any time one of them might look up and see her watching.

Trying to make no noise, Nora slipped backwards off the rock. The scene vanished from her sight; the pleading brown eyes could no longer accuse her. Nora began to run as best she could over the uneven ground. She hoped she was running in the right direction, and that she would soon come upon Larry. Larry would help her—she would tell him what she had seen, and he would know what to do. He might be able to frighten away the men, or, speaking Spanish, he could at least tell the police what she had seen. She would be safe with Larry.

The minutes passed and Nora still, blindly, ran. She couldn't see their car, and knew the horrifying possibility that she was running in the wrong direction—but she didn't dare go back. A cramp in her side and ragged pains when she drew breath forced her to walk: she felt the moment when she might have been of some help, when she could have reached Larry in time, drain inexorably away. She never knew how long she had walked and run before she finally caught sight of their car, but, even allowing for her panic, Nora judged it had been at the very least a half an hour. She felt as if she had been running desperately all day. And she was too late. Much too late. By now, they would have finished with the girl. They might have killed her, they might have let her go. In either case, Nora and Larry would be too late to help her.

"There you are! Where'd you go? I was worried," Larry said, slipping off the hood of the car and coming to embrace her. He sounded not worried but lazily contented.

It was too late. She did not tell him, after all, what she had witnessed. She never told him.

Nora became deathly ill that night in a clean, American-style hotel near Acapulco. Two days later, still shaking and unable to keep anything in her stomach, Nora flew back to her mother and the family doctor in Dallas, leaving Larry to drive back by himself.

It was the stench that woke her. Nora lurched out of sleep, sitting up on the bed, gagging and clutching the sheet to her mouth, trying not to breathe in the smell. It was the smell of something dead.

Groggy with sleep, she needed another moment to realize something much more frightening than the smell: there was someone else in the room.

A tall figure stood, motionless, not far from the foot of her bed. The immediate fear Nora felt at the sight was quickly pushed out of the way by a coldly rational, self-preserving consciousness. In the dim light Nora could not tell much about the intruder except that that he was oddly dressed in some sort of cloak, and that his features were masked by some sort of head mask. The most important thing she noticed was that he did not block her path to the door, and if she moved quickly . . .

Nora bolted, running through the apartment like a rabbit, and bursting out through the front door into the courtyard.

It was late afternoon, the sun low in the sky but not yet gone. One of her neighbors, a Mexican, was grilling hamburgers on a little hibachi. He stared at her sudden appearance, then grinned. Nora realized she was wearing only an old T-shirt of Larry's and a pair of brightly colored bikini pants, and she scowled at the man.

"Somebody broke into my apartment," she said sharply, cutting into his grin.

"Want to use our phone? Call the police?"

Nora thought of Larry and felt a sudden fierce hatred of him: he had left her to this, abandoned her to the mercy of burglars, potential rapists and the leers of this Mexican.

"No, thanks," she said, her tone still harsh. "But I think he's still inside. Do you think you could . . ."

"You want me to see if he still there? Sure, sure, I'll check. You don't have to worry." He sprang forward. Nora hated his eagerness to help, but she needed him right now.

There was no one in her apartment. The back door was still locked, and the screens on all the windows were undisturbed.

Nora didn't ask her neighbor to check behind every piece of furniture after he had looked into the closets: she was feeling the loathing she always felt for hysterical, overemotional reactions. Only this time the loathing was directed at herself.

Although one part of her persisted in believing she had seen an intruder, reason told her she had been mistaken. She had been tricked by a nightmare into running for help like a terrified child.

She was rude to the man who had helped her, dismissing him as sharply as if he were an erring servant. She didn't want to see the smug, masculine concern on his face; didn't want him around knowing he must be chuckling inwardly at a typical hysterical female.

Nora intended to forget about it, as she had forgotten other embarrassing incidents, other disturbing dreams, but she was not allowed.

She had a hard time falling asleep the next day. Children were playing in the parking lot, and her doze was broken time and again by their shouts, meaningless fragments of talk, and the clamor of a bicycle bell.

When, at last, she did sleep in the afternoon, it was to dream that she and Larry were having one of their interminable, pointless, low-voiced arguments. She woke from the frustrating dream with the impression that someone had come into the room and, certain it was Larry and ready to resume the argument in real life, she opened her eyes.

Before she could speak his name, the stench struck her like a blow—that too familiar, dead smell—and she saw the tall, weirdly draped figure again.

Nora sat up quickly, trying not to breathe in, and the effort made her dizzy. The figure did not move. There was more light in the room this time, and she could see him clearly.

The strange cloak ended in blackened tatters that hung over his hands and feet, and the hood had ragged holes torn for eyes and mouth—with a rush of horror, Nora realized what she was seeing. The figure was dressed in a human skin. The gutted shell of some other human being flapped grotesquely against his own.

Nora's mouth dropped open, and she breathed in the smell of the rotting skin, and, for one horrible moment, she feared she was about to vomit, that she would be immobilized, sick and at the monster's mercy.

Fear tightened her throat and gut, and she managed to stumble out of the room and down the hall.

She didn't go outside. She remembered, as she reached the front door, that she had seen that figure before. That it was only a nightmarish hallucination. Only a dream. She could scarcely accept it, but she knew it was true. Only a dream. Her fingers clutched the cool metal doorknob, but she did not turn it. She leaned against the door, feeling her stomach muscles contract spasmodically, aware of the weakness in her legs and the bitter taste in her mouth.

She tried to think of something calming, but could not chase the visions from her mind: knives, blood, putrefaction. What someone who had been skinned must look like. And what was he, beneath that rotten skin? What could that ghastly disguise hide?

When at last she bullied and cajoled herself into returning to the bedroom, the thing, of course, was gone. Not even the cadaverine smell remained.

Nightmare or hallucination, whatever it was, it came again on the third day. She was ready for it—had lain rigidly awake for hours in the sunlit room knowing he would come—but the stench and the sight was scarcely any easier to endure the third time. No matter how much she told herself she was dreaming, no matter how hard she tried to believe that what she saw (and smelled?) was mere hallucination, Nora had not the cold-bloodedness to remain on her bed until it vanished.

Once again she ran from the room in fear, hating herself for such irrational behavior. And, again, the thing had gone when she calmed herself and returned to look.

On the fourth day Nora stayed at the motel.

If someone else had suggested escaping a nightmare by sleeping somewhere else, Nora would have been scornful. But she justified her action to herself: this dream was different. There was the smell, for one thing. Perhaps there was some real source to the smell, and it was triggering the nightmare. In that case, a change of air should cure her.

The room she moved into when she got off work that morning was like all the other rooms in the Posada del Norte. It was clean and uninspired, the decor hovering between the merely bland and the aggressively ugly. The carpet was a stubby, mottled gold; the bedspread and chair cushions were dark orange. The walls were covered in white, textured vinyl with a mural painted above the bed. The murals differed from room to room—in this room, it was a picture of a stepped Aztec pyramid, rendered in shades of orange and brown.

Nora turned on the air conditioning, and a blast of air came out in a frozen rush. She took a few toilet articles into the bathroom, but left everything else packed in the overnight bag which she had dropped on to a chair. She had no desire to "settle in" or to intrude herself on the bland anonymity of the room.

She turned on the television and lay back on the bed to observe the meaningless interactions of the guests on a morning talk show. She had nothing better to do. After the network show was a talk show of the local variety, with a plain, overly made-up hostess who smiled, blinked and nodded a lot. Her guests were a red-faced, middle-aged man who talked about the problems caused by illegal aliens; and a woman who discussed the ancient beauties of Mexico. Nora turned off the set halfway through her slide show featuring pyramids and other monuments in Mexico.

The television silent, she heard the sound of people moving in next door. There seemed to be a lot of them, and they were noisy. A radio clicked on, bringing in music and commercials from Mexico. There was a lot of laughter from the room, and Nora caught an occasional Spanish-sounding word.

Nora swore, not softly. Why couldn't they party on their own side of the border? And who ever carried on in such a way at ten o'clock in the morning? But she hesitated to pound on the wall: that would only draw attention to herself, and she didn't imagine it would deter them.

Instead, to shield herself, she turned on the television set again. It was game-show time, and the sounds of hysteria, clanging bells and idiotic laughter filled the room. Nora sighed, turned the volume down a bit, and pulled off her clothes. Then, she climbed under the blankets and gazed blankly at the flickering images.

She was tired, but too keyed up to sleep. Her mind kept circling until she deliberately thought about what was bothering her: the man in the skin. What did it mean? Why was it haunting her?

It seemed more a hallucination than an ordinary dream, and that made Nora doubly uneasy. It was too *real.* When she saw, and smelled, the nightmarish figure, she could never quite convince herself she was only dreaming.

And what did the hideous figure itself mean? It must have come crawling out of her subconscious for some reason, thought Nora. But she didn't really think she had just made it up herself—the idea of a man draped in another's skin stirred some deep memory. Somewhere, long before, she had read about, or seen a picture of, a figure who wore the stripped-off skin of another. Was it something from Mexico? Some ancient, pre-Columbian god?

Yet whenever she strained to recall it, the memory moved perversely away.

And why did the dream figure haunt her now? Because she was alone? But that was absurd. Nora shifted uncomfortably in bed. She had no regrets about the separation or the impending divorce; she was glad Larry was gone. They should have had the sense to call it quits years before. She didn't want him back under any circumstances.

And yet—Larry was gone, and old two-skins was haunting her.

Finally, worn out by the useless excavations of her memory, Nora turned off the television and went to sleep.

She woke feeling sick. She didn't need to turn her head or open her eyes to know, but she did. And, of course, he was in the room. He would come to her wherever she fled. The stench came from the rotting skin he wore, not from a neighbor's garbage or something dead between the walls. He didn't look like something hallucinated—he seemed perfectly substantial standing there beside the television set and in front of the draperies.

Staring at him, Nora willed herself to wake up. She willed him to melt and vanish. Nothing happened. She saw the dark gleam of his eyes through ragged eye holes, and she was suddenly more frightened than she had ever been in her life.

She closed her eyes. The blood pounding in her ears was the sound of fear. She would not be able to hear him if he moved closer. Unable to bear the thought of what he might be doing, unseen by her, Nora opened her eyes. He was still there. He did not seem to have moved.

She had to get out, Nora thought. She had to give him the chance to vanish—he always had, before. But she was naked—she couldn't go out as she was, and all her clothes were on the chair beside the window, much too close to him. In a moment, Nora knew, she might start screaming. Already she was shaking—she had to do *something.*

On fear-weakened legs, Nora climbed out of bed and stumbled towards the bathroom. She slammed the door shut behind her, hearing the comforting snick of the lock as she pressed the button in.

Then she stood with palms pressed on the Formica surface surrounding the basin, head hanging down, breathing shallowly in and out, waiting for the fear to leave her. When she had calmed herself, she raised her head and looked in the mirror.

There she was, the same old Nora. Lost her husband, driven out of her apartment by nerves, surrounded by the gray and white sterility of a hotel bathroom. There was no reason for her to be here—not in this building, not in El Paso, not in Texas, not in this *life.* But here she was, going on as if it all had some purpose. And for no better reason than that she didn't know what else to do—she had no notion of how to start over.

Nora caught a glimpse of motion in the mirror, and then the clear reflection of the one who had come for her: the lumpish head with the mask of another's face stretched crudely over his own. She looked calmly into the mirror, right into the reflections of his eyes. They were brown, she realized, very much like a pair of eyes she remembered from Mexico.

Feeling a kind of relief because there was no longer anywhere else to run, Nora turned away from the mirror to face him, to see this man in his dead skin for the first time in a fully lighted room. "She sent you to me," Nora said, and realized she was no longer afraid.

The skin was horrible—a streaky gray with ragged, black edges. But what of the man underneath? She had seen his eyes. Suddenly, as she gazed steadily at the figure, his name came into her mind, as clearly as if he had written it on the mirror for her: Xipe, the Flayed One. She had been right in thinking him some ancient Mexican god, Nora thought. But she knew nothing else about him, nor did she need to know. He was not a dream to be interpreted—he was here, now.

She saw that he carried a curved knife; watched without fear as he tore seams in the skin he wore, and it fell away, a discarded husk.

Revealed without the disfiguring, concealing outer skin, Xipe was a dark young man with a pure, handsome face. Not a Mexican, Nora thought, but an Indian, of noble and ancient blood. He smiled at her. Nora smiled back, realizing now that there had never been any reason to fear him.

He offered her the knife. So easy, his dark eyes promised her. No fear, no question in their brown depths. Shed the old skin, the old life, as I have done, and be reborn.

When she hesitated, he reached out with his empty hand and traced a line along her skin. The touch of his hand seared like ice. Her skin was too tight. Xipe, smooth, clean and new, watched her, offering the ritual blade.

At last she took the knife and made the first incision.

JOYCE CAROL OATES

"The Turn of the Screw" is a Gothic tale with an almost palpable secret. In reading it one becomes a kind of detective and psychologist combined, as well as a half-willing participant in the governess's terrifying experience. Unlike most horror stories that reveal their secrets with a single reading, "The Turn of the Screw" never entirely reveals its secret—but is always on the verge of doing so. An almost unbearable tension is created from the outset; and the story will long linger in the memory, a fairy tale not altogether understood, a wicked parable not entirely grasped.

THE TURN OF THE SCREW

HENRY JAMES

The story had held us, round the fire, sufficiently breathless, but except the obvious remark that it was gruesome, as, on Christmas Eve in an old house, a strange tale should essentially be, I remember no comment uttered till somebody happened to say that it was the only case he had met in which such a visitation had fallen on a child. The case, I may mention, was that of an apparition in just such an old house as had gathered us for the occasion—an appearance, of a dreadful kind, to a little boy sleeping in the room with his mother and waking her up in the terror of it; waking her not to dissipate his dread and soothe him to sleep again, but to encounter also, herself, before she had succeeded in doing so, the same sight that had shaken him. It was this observation that drew from Douglas—not immediately, but later in the evening—a reply that had the interesting consequence to which I call attention. Someone else told a story not particularly effective, which I saw he was not following. This I took for a sign that he had himself something to produce and that we should only have to wait. We waited in fact till two nights later; but that same evening, before we scattered, he brought out what was in his mind.

"I quite agree—in regard to Griffin's ghost, or whatever it was—that its appearing first to the little boy, at so tender an age, adds a particular touch. But it's not the first occurrence of its charming kind that I know to have involved a child. If the child gives the effect another turn of the screw, what do you say to *two* children—?"

"We say, of course," somebody exclaimed, "that they give two turns! Also that we want to hear about them."

I can see Douglas there before the fire, to which he had got up to present his back, looking down at his interlocutor with his hands in his pockets. "Nobody but me, till now, has ever heard. It's quite too horrible." This, naturally, was declared by several voices to give the thing the utmost price, and our friend, with quiet art, prepared his triumph by turning his eyes over the rest of us and going on: "It's beyond everything. Nothing at all that I know touches it."

"For sheer terror?" I remember asking.

He seemed to say it was not so simple as that; to be really at a loss how to qualify it. He passed his hand over his eyes, made a little wincing grimace. "For dreadful—dreadfulness!"

"Oh, how delicious!" cried one of the women.

He took no notice of her; he looked at me, but as if, instead of me, he saw what he spoke of. "For general uncanny ugliness and horror and pain."

"Well then," I said, "just sit right down and begin."

He turned round to the fire, gave a kick to a log, watched it an instant. Then as he faced us again: "I can't begin. I shall have to send to town." There was a unanimous groan at this, and much reproach; after which, in his preoccupied way, he explained. "The story's written. It's in a locked drawer—it has not been out for years. I could write to my man and enclose the key; he could send down the packet as he finds it." It was to me in particular that he appeared to propound this—appeared almost to appeal for aid not to hesitate. He had broken a thickness of ice, the formation of many a winter; had had his reasons for a long silence. The others resented postponement, but it was just his scruples that charmed me. I adjured him to write by the first post and to agree with us for an early hearing; then I asked him if the experience in question had been his own. To this his answer was prompt. "Oh, thank God, no!"

"And is the record yours? You took the thing down?"

"Nothing but the impression. I took that *here*"—he tapped his heart. "I've never lost it."

"Then your manuscript—?"

"Is in old, faded ink, and in the most beautiful hand." He hung fire again. "A woman's. She has been dead these twenty years. She sent me the pages in question before she died." They were all listening now, and of course there was somebody to be arch, or at any rate to draw the inference. But if he put the inference by without a smile it was also without irritation. "She was a most charming person, but she was ten years older than I. She was my sister's governess," he quietly said. "She was the most agreeable woman I've ever known in her position; she would have been worthy of any whatever. It was long ago, and this episode was long before. I was at Trinity, and I found her at home on my coming down the second summer. I was much there that year—it was a beautiful one; and we had, in her off-hours, some strolls and talks in the garden—talks in which she struck me as awfully clever and nice. Oh yes; don't grin: I liked her extremely and am glad to this day to think she liked me too. If she hadn't she wouldn't have told me. She had never told anyone. It wasn't simply that she said so, but that I knew she hadn't. I was sure; I could see. You'll easily judge why when you hear."

"Because the thing had been such a scare?"

He continued to fix me. "You'll easily judge," he repeated: "*you* will."

I fixed him too. "I see. She was in love."

He laughed for the first time. "You *are* acute. Yes, she was in love. That is she had been. That came out—she couldn't tell her story without its coming out. I saw it, and she saw I saw it; but neither of us spoke of it. I remember the time and the place—the corner of the lawn, the shade of the great beeches and the long, hot summer afternoon. It wasn't a scene for a shudder; but oh—!" He quitted the fire and dropped back into his chair.

"You'll receive the packet Thursday morning?" I inquired.

"Probably not till the second post."

"Well then; after dinner—"

"You'll all meet me here?" He looked us round again. "Isn't anybody going?" It was almost the tone of hope.

"Everybody will stay!"

"*I* will—and *I* will!" cried the ladies whose departure had been fixed. Mrs. Griffin, however, expressed the need for a little more light. "Who was it she was in love with?"

"The story will tell," I took upon myself to reply.

"Oh, I can't wait for the story!"

"The story *won't* tell," said Douglas; "not in any literal, vulgar way."

"More's the pity then. That's the only way I ever understand."

"Won't *you* tell, Douglas?" somebody else inquired.

He sprang to his feet again. "Yes—tomorrow. Now I must go to bed. Good night." And, quickly, catching up a candlestick, he left us slightly bewildered. From our end of the great brown hall we heard his step on the stair; whereupon Mrs. Griffin spoke. "Well, if I don't know who she was in love with, I know who *he* was."

"She was ten years older," said her husband.

"*Raison de plus*—at that age! But it's rather nice, his long reticence."

"Forty years!" Griffin put in.

"With this outbreak at last."

"The outbreak," I returned, "will make a tremendous occasion of Thursday night"; and everyone so agreed with me that, in the light of it, we lost all attention for everything else. The last story, however incomplete and like the mere opening of a serial, had been told; we handshook and "candle-stuck," as somebody said, and went to bed.

I knew the next day that a letter containing the key had, by the first post, gone off to his London apartments; but in spite of—or perhaps just on account of—the eventual diffusion of this knowledge we quite let him alone till after dinner, till such an hour of the evening, in fact, as might best accord with the kind of emotion on which our hopes were fixed. Then he became as communicative as we could desire and indeed gave us his best reason for being so. We had it from him again before the fire in the hall, as we had had our mild wonders of the previous night. It appeared that the narrative he had promised to read us really required for a proper intelligence a few words of prologue. Let me say here distinctly, to have done with it, that this narrative, from an exact transcript of my own made much later, is what I shall presently give. Poor Douglas, before his death —when it was in sight—committed to me the manuscript that reached him on the third of these days and that, on the same spot, with immense effect, he began to read to our hushed little circle on the night of the fourth. The departing ladies who had said they would stay didn't, of course, thank heaven, stay: they departed, in consequence of arrangements made, in a rage of curiosity, as they professed, produced by the touches with which he had already worked us up. But that only made his little final auditory more compact and select, kept it, round the hearth, subject to a common thrill.

The first of these touches conveyed that the written statement took up the tale at a point after it had, in a manner, begun. The fact to be in possession of was therefore that his old friend, the youngest of several daughters of a poor country parson, had, at the age of twenty, on taking service for the first time in the schoolroom, come up to London, in trepidation, to answer in person an advertisement that had already placed her in brief correspondence with the advertiser. This person proved, on her presenting herself, for judgment, at a house, in Harley Street, that impressed her as vast and imposing—this prospective patron proved a gentleman, a bachelor in the prime of life, such a figure as had never risen, save in a dream or an old novel, before a fluttered, anxious girl out of a Hampshire vicarage. One could easily fix his type; it never, happily, dies out. He was handsome and bold and pleasant, offhand and gay and kind. He struck her, inevitably, as gallant and splendid, but what took her most of all and gave her the courage she afterward showed was that he put the whole thing to her as a kind of favor, an obligation he should gratefully incur. She conceived him as rich, but as fearfully extravagant—saw him all in a glow of high fashion, of good looks, of expensive habits, of charming ways with women. He had for his town residence a big house filled with the spoils of travel and the trophies of the chase; but it was to his country home, an old family place in Essex, that he wished her immediately to proceed.

He had been left, by the death of their parents in India, guardian to a small nephew and a small niece, children of a younger, a military brother, whom he had lost two years before. These children were, by the strangest of chances for a man in his position—a lone man without the right sort of experience or a grain of patience—very heavily on his hands. It had all been a great worry and, on his own part doubtless, a series of blunders, but he immensely pitied the poor chicks and had done all he could; had in particular sent them down to his other house, the proper place for them being of course the country, and kept them there, from the first, with the best people he could find to look after them, parting even with his own servants to wait on them and going down himself, whenever he might, to see how they were doing. The awkward thing was that they had practically no other relations and that his own affairs took up all his time. He had put them in possession of Bly, which was healthy and secure, and had placed at the head of their little establishment—but below stairs only—an excellent woman, Mrs. Grose, whom he was sure his visitor would like and who had formerly been maid to his mother. She was now housekeeper and was also acting for the time as superintendent to the little girl, of whom, without children of her own, she was, by good luck, extremely fond. There were plenty of people to help, but of course the young lady who should go down as governess would be in supreme authority. She would also have, in holidays, to look after the small boy, who had been for a term at school—young as he was to be sent, but what else could be done?—and who, as the holidays were about to begin, would be back from one day to the other. There had been for the two children at first a young lady whom they had had the misfortune to lose. She had done for them quite beautifully—she was a most respectable person—till her death, the great awkwardness of which had, precisely, left no alternative but the school for little Miles. Mrs. Grose, since then, in the way of manners and things, had done as she could for Flora; and there were, further, a cook, a housemaid, a dairywoman, an old pony, an old groom and an old gardener, all likewise thoroughly respectable.

So far had Douglas presented his picture when someone put a question. "And what did the former governess die of?—of so much respectability?"

Our friend's answer was prompt. "That will come out. I don't anticipate."

"Excuse me—I thought that was just what you *are* doing."

"In her successor's place," I suggested, "I should have wished to learn if the office brought with it—"

"Necessary danger to life?" Douglas completed my thought. "She did wish to learn, and she did learn. You shall hear tomorrow what she learned. Meanwhile, of course, the prospect struck her as slightly grim. She was young, untried, nervous: it was a vision of serious duties and little company, of really great loneliness. She hesitated—took a couple of days to consult and consider. But the salary offered much exceeded her modest measure, and on a second interview she faced the music, she engaged." And Douglas, with this, made a pause that, for the benefit of the company, moved me to throw in—

"The moral of which was of course the seduction exercised by the splendid young man. She succumbed to it."

He got up and, as he had done the night before, went to the fire, gave a stir to a log with his foot, then stood a moment with his back to us. "She saw him only twice."

"Yes, but that's just the beauty of her passion."

A little to my surprise, on this, Douglas turned round to me. "It *was* the beauty of it. There were others," he went on, "who hadn't succumbed. He told her frankly all his difficulty—that for several applicants the conditions had been prohibitive. They were, somehow, simply afraid. It sounded dull—it sounded strange; and all the more so because of his main condition."

"Which was—?"

"That she should never trouble him—but never, never: neither appeal nor complain nor write about anything; only meet all questions herself, receive all moneys from his solicitor, take the whole thing over and let him alone. She promised to do this, and she mentioned to me that when, for a moment, disburdened, delighted, he held her hand, thanking her for the sacrifice, she already felt rewarded."

"But was that all her reward?" one of the ladies asked.

"She never saw him again."

"Oh!" said the lady; which, as our friend immediately left us again, was the only other word of importance contributed to the subject till, the next night, by the corner of the hearth, in the best chair, he opened the faded red cover of a thin old-fashioned gilt-edged album. The whole thing took indeed more nights than one, but on the first occasion the same lady put another question. "What is your title?"

"I haven't one."

"Oh, *I* have!" I said. But Douglas, without heeding me, had begun to read with a fine clearness that was like a rendering to the ear of the beauty of his author's hand.

I

I remember the whole beginning as a succession of flights and drops, a little seesaw of the right throbs and the wrong. After rising, in town, to meet his appeal, I had at all events a couple of very bad days—found myself doubtful again, felt indeed sure I had made a mistake. In this state of mind I spent the long hours of bumping, swinging coach that carried me to the stopping-place at which I was to be met by a vehicle from the house. This convenience, I was told, had been ordered, and I found, towards the close of the June afternoon, a commodious fly in waiting for me. Driving at that hour, on a lovely day, through a country to which the summer sweetness seemed to offer me a friendly welcome, my fortitude mounted afresh and, as we turned into the avenue, encountered a reprieve that was probably but a proof of the point to which it had sunk. I suppose I had expected, or had dreaded, something so melancholy that what greeted me was a good surprise. I remember as a most pleasant impression the broad, clear front, its open windows and fresh curtains and the pair of maids looking out; I remember the lawn and the bright flowers and the crunch of my wheels on the gravel and the clustered treetops over which the rooks circled and cawed in the golden sky. The scene had a greatness that made it a different affair from my own scant home, and there immediately appeared at the door, with a little girl in her hand, a civil person who dropped me as decent a curtsy as if I had been the mistress or a distinguished visitor. I had received in Harley Street a narrower notion of the place, and that, as I recalled it, made me think the proprietor still more of a gentleman, suggested that what I was to enjoy might be something beyond his promise.

I had no drop again till the next day, for I was carried triumphantly through the following hours by my introduction to the younger of my pupils. The little girl who accompanied Mrs. Grose appeared to me on the spot a creature so charming as to make it a great fortune to have to do with her. She was the most beautiful child I had ever seen, and I afterwards wondered that my employer had not told me more of her. I slept little that night—I was too much excited; and this astonished me too, I recollect, remained with me, adding to my sense of the liberality with which I was treated. The large, impressive room, one of the best in the house, the great state bed, as I almost felt it, the full, figured draperies, the long glasses in which, for the first time, I could see myself from head to foot, all struck me—like the extraordinary charm of my small charge—as so many things thrown in. It was thrown in as well, from the first moment, that I should get on with Mrs. Grose in a relation over which, on my way, in the coach, I fear I had rather brooded. The only thing indeed that in this early outlook might have made me shrink again was the clear circumstance of her being so glad to see me. I perceived within half an hour that she was so glad—stout, simple, plain, clean, wholesome woman—as to be positively on her guard against showing it too much. I wondered even then a little why she should wish not to show it and that, with reflection, with suspicion, might of course have made me uneasy.

But it was a comfort that there could be no uneasiness in a connection with anything so beatific as the radiant image of my little girl, the vision of whose angelic beauty had probably more than anything else to do with the restlessness that, before morning, made me several times rise and wander about my room to take in the whole picture and prospect; to watch, from my open window, the faint summer dawn, to look at such portions of the rest of the house as I could catch, and to listen, while, in the fading dusk, the first birds began to twitter, for the possible recurrence of a sound or two, less natural and not without, but within, that I had fancied I heard. There had been a moment when I believed I recognized, faint and far, the cry of a child; there had been another when I found myself just consciously starting as at the passage, before my door, of a light footstep. But these fancies were not marked enough not to be thrown off, and it is only in the light, or the gloom, I should rather say, of other and subsequent matters that they now come back to me. To watch, teach, "form" little Flora would too evidently be the making of a happy and useful life. It had been agreed between us downstairs that after this first occasion I should have her as a matter of course at night, her small white bed being already arranged, to that end, in my room. What I had undertaken was the whole care of her, and she had remained, just this last time, with Mrs. Grose only as an effect of our consideration for my inevitable strangeness and her natural timidity. In spite of this timidity—which the child herself, in the oddest way in the world, had been perfectly frank and brave about, allowing it, without a sign of uncomfortable consciousness, with the deep, sweet serenity indeed of one of Raphael's holy infants, to be discussed, to be imputed to her and to determine us—I felt quite sure she would presently like me. It was part of what I already liked Mrs. Grose herself for, the pleasure I could see her feel in my admiration and wonder as I sat at supper with four tall candles and with my pupil, in a high chair and a bib, brightly facing me, between them, over bread and milk. There were naturally things that in Flora's presence could pass between us only as prodigious and gratified looks, obscure and roundabout allusions.

"And the little boy—does he look like her? Is he too so very remarkable?"

One wouldn't flatter a child. "Oh miss, *most* remarkable. If you think well of this one!"—and she stood there with a plate in her hand, beaming at our companion, who looked from one of us to the other with placid heavenly eyes that contained nothing to check us.

"Yes; if I do—?"

"You *will* be carried away by the little gentleman!"

"Well, that, I think, is what I came for—to be carried away. I'm afraid, however," I remember feeling the impulse to add, "I'm rather easily carried away. I was carried away in London!"

I can still see Mrs. Grose's broad face as she took this in. "In Harley Street?"

"In Harley Street."

"Well, miss, you're not the first—and you won't be the last."

"Oh, I've no pretension," I could laugh, "to being the only one. My other pupil, at any rate, as I understand, comes back tomorrow?"

"Not tomorrow—Friday, miss. He arrives, as you did, by the coach, under care of the guard, and is to be met by the same carriage."

I forthwith expressed that the proper as well as the pleasant and friendly thing would be therefore that on the arrival of the public conveyance I should be in waiting for him with his little sister; an idea in which Mrs. Grose concurred so heartily that I somehow took her manner as a kind of comforting pledge—never falsified, thank heaven!—that we should on every question be quite at one. Oh, she was glad I was there!

What I felt the next day was, I suppose, nothing that could be fairly called a reaction from the cheer of my arrival; it was probably at the most only a slight oppression produced by a fuller measure of the scale, as I walked round them, gazed up at them, took them in, of my new circumstances. They had, as it were, an extent and mass for which I had not been prepared and in the presence of which I found myself, freshly, a little scared as well as a little proud. Lessons, in this agitation, certainly suffered some delay; I reflected that my first duty was, by the gentlest arts I could contrive, to win the child into the sense of knowing me. I spent the day with her out-of-doors; I arranged with her, to her great satisfaction, that it should be she, she only, who might show me the place. She showed it step by step and room by room and secret by secret, with droll, delightful, childish talk about it and with the result, in half an hour, of our becoming immense friends. Young as she was, I was struck, throughout our little tour, with her confidence and courage with the way, in empty chambers and dull corridors, on crooked staircases that made me pause and even on the summit of an old machicolated square tower that made me dizzy, her morning music, her disposition to tell me so many more things than she asked, rang out and led me on. I have not seen Bly since the day I left it, and I daresay that to my older and more informed eyes it would now appear sufficiently contracted. But as my little conductress, with her hair of gold and her frock of blue, danced before me round corners and pattered down passages, I had the view of a castle of romance inhabited by a rosy sprite, such a place as would somehow, for diversion of the young idea, take all color out of storybooks and fairy tales. Wasn't it just a storybook over which I had fallen a-doze and a-dream? No; it was a big, ugly, antique, but convenient house, embodying a few features of a building still older, half-replaced and half-utilized, in which I had the fancy of our being almost as lost as a handful of passengers in a great drifting ship. Well, I was, strangely, at the helm!

II

This came home to me when, two days later, I drove over with Flora to meet, as Mrs. Grose said, the little gentleman; and all the more for an incident that, presenting itself the second evening, had deeply disconcerted me. The first day had been, on the whole, as I have expressed, reassuring; but I was to see it wind up in keen apprehension. The post-bag, that evening—it came late—contained a letter for me, which, however, in the hand of my employer, I found to be composed but of a few words enclosing another, addressed to himself, with a seal still unbroken. "This, I recognize, is from the headmaster, and the headmaster's an awful bore. Read him, please; deal with him; but mind you don't report. Not a word. I'm off!" I broke the seal with a great effort—so great a one that I was a long time coming to it; took the unopened missive at last up to my room and only attacked it just before going to bed. I had better have let it wait till morning, for it gave me a second sleepless night. With no counsel to take, the next day, I was full of distress; and it finally got so the better of me that I determined to open myself at least to Mrs. Grose.

"What does it mean? The child's dismissed his school."

She gave me a look that I remarked at the moment; then, visibly, with a quick blankness, seemed to try to take it back. "But aren't they all—?"

"Sent home—yes. But only for the holidays. Miles may never go back at all."

Consciously, under my attention, she reddened. "They won't take him?"

"They absolutely decline."

At this she raised her eyes, which she had turned from me; I saw them fill with good tears. "What has he done?"

I hesitated; then I judged best simply to hand her my letter—which, however, had the effect of making her, without taking it, simply put her hands behind her. She shook her head sadly. "Such things are not for me, miss."

My counselor couldn't read! I winced at my mistake, which I attenuated as I could, and opened my letter again to repeat it to her; then, faltering in the act and folding it up once more, I put it back in my pocket. "Is he really *bad?*"

The tears were still in her eyes. "Do the gentlemen say so?"

"They go into no particulars. They simply express their regret that it should be impossible to keep him. That can have only one meaning." Mrs. Grose listened with dumb emotion; she forbore to ask me what this meaning might be; so that, presently, to put the thing with some coherence and with the mere aid of her presence to my own mind, I went on: "That he's an injury to the others."

At this, with one of the quick turns of simple folk, she suddenly flamed up. "Master Miles!—*him* an injury?"

There was such a flood of good faith in it that, though I had not yet seen the child, my very fears made me jump to the absurdity of the idea. I found myself, to meet my friend the better, offering it, on the spot, sarcastically. "To his poor little innocent mates!"

"It's too dreadful," cried Mrs. Grose, "to say such cruel things! Why, he's scarce ten years old."

"Yes, yes; it would be incredible."

She was evidently grateful for such a profession. "See him, miss, first. *Then* believe it!" I felt forthwith a new impatience to see him; it was the beginning of a curiosity that, for all the next hours, was to deepen almost to pain. Mrs. Grose was aware, I could judge, of what she had produced in me, and she followed it up with assurance. "You might as well believe it of the little lady. Bless her," she added the next moment—"*look* at her!"

I turned and saw that Flora, whom, ten minutes before, I had established in the schoolroom with a sheet of white paper, a pencil and a copy of nice "round *O*'s," now presented herself to view at the open door. She expressed in her little way an extraordinary detachment from disagreeable duties, looking at me, however, with a great childish light that seemed to offer it as a mere result of the affection she had conceived for my person, which had rendered necessary that she should follow me. I needed nothing more than this to feel the full force of Mrs. Grose's comparison, and, catching my pupil in my arms, covered her with kisses in which there was a sob of atonement.

Nonetheless, the rest of the day, I watched for further occasion to approach my colleague, especially as, towards evening, I began to fancy she rather sought to avoid me. I overtook her, I remember, on the staircase; we went down together, and at the bottom I detained her, holding her there with a hand on her arm. "I take what you said to me at noon as a declaration that *you've* never known him to be bad."

She threw back her head; she had clearly, by this time, and very honestly, adopted an attitude. "Oh, never known him—I don't pretend *that!*"

I was upset again. "Then you *have* known him—?"

"Yes indeed, miss, thank God!"

On reflection I accepted this. "You mean that a boy who never is—?"

"Is no boy for *me!*"

I held her tighter. "You like them with the spirit to be naughty?" Then, keeping pace with her answer, "So do I!" I eagerly brought out. "But not to the degree to contaminate—"

"To contaminate?"—my big word left her at a loss.

I explained it. "To corrupt."

She stared, taking my meaning in; but it produced in her an odd laugh. "Are you afraid he'll corrupt *you?*" She put the question with such a fine bold humor that, with a laugh, a little silly doubtless, to match her own, I gave way for the time to the apprehension of ridicule.

But the next day, as the hour for my drive approached, I cropped up in another place. "What was the lady who was here before?"

"The last governess? She was also young and pretty—almost as young and almost as pretty, miss, even as you."

"Ah, then, I hope her youth and her beauty helped her!" I recollect throwing off. "He seems to like us young and pretty!"

"Oh, he *did,*" Mrs. Grose assented: "it was the way he liked everyone!" She had no sooner spoken indeed than she caught herself up. "I mean that's *his* way—the master's."

I was struck. "But of whom did you speak first?"

She looked blank, but she colored. "Why, of *him.*"

"Of the master?"

"Of who else?"

There was so obviously no one else that the next moment I had lost my impression of her having accidentally said more than she meant; and I merely asked what I wanted to know. "Did *she* see anything in the boy—?"

"That wasn't right? She never told me."

I had a scruple, but I overcame it. "Was she careful—particular?"

Mrs. Grose appeared to try to be conscientious. "About some things—yes."

"But not about all?"

Again she considered. "Well, miss—she's gone. I won't tell tales."

"I quite understand your feeling," I hastened to reply; but I thought it, after an instant, not opposed to this concession to pursue: "Did she die here?"

"No—she went off."

I don't know what there was in this brevity of Mrs. Grose's that struck me as ambiguous. "Went off to die?" Mrs. Grose looked straight out of the window, but I felt that, hypothetically, I had a right to know what young persons engaged for Bly were expected to do. "She was taken ill, you mean, and went home?"

"She was not taken ill, so far as appeared, in this house. She left it, at the end of the year, to go home, as she said, for a short holiday, to which the time she had put in had certainly given her a right. We had then a young woman—a nursemaid who had stayed on and who was a good girl and clever; and *she* took the children altogether for the interval. But our young lady never came back, and at the very moment I was expecting her I heard from the master that she was dead."

"I turned this over. "But of what?"

"He never told me! But please, miss," said Mrs. Grose, "I must get to my work."

III

Her thus turning her back on me was fortunately not, for my just preoccupations, a snub that could check the growth of our mutual esteem. We met, after I had brought home little Miles, more intimately than ever on the ground of my stupefaction, my general emotion: so monstrous was I then ready to pronounce it that such a child as had now been revealed to me should be under an interdict. I was a little late on the scene, and I felt, as he stood wistfully looking out for me before the door of the inn at which the coach had put him down, that I had seen him, on the instant, without and within, in the great glow of freshness, the same positive fragrance of purity, in which I had, from the first moment, seen his little sister. He was incredibly beautiful, and Mrs. Grose had put her finger on it: everything but a sort of passion of tenderness for him was swept away by his presence. What I then and there took him to my heart for was something divine that I have never found to the same degree in any child —his indescribable little air of knowing nothing in the world but love. It would have been impossible to carry a bad name with a greater sweetness of innocence, and by the time I had got back to Bly with him I remained merely bewildered—so far, that is, as I was not outraged—by the sense of the horrible letter locked up in my room, in a drawer. As soon as I could compass a private word with Mrs. Grose I declared to her that it was grotesque.

She promptly understood me. "You mean the cruel charge—?"

"It doesn't live an instant. My dear woman, *look* at him!"

She smiled at my pretension to have discovered his charm. "I assure you, miss, I do nothing else! What will you say, then?" she immediately added.

"In answer to the letter?" I had made up my mind. "Nothing."

"And to his uncle?"

I was incisive. "Nothing."

"And to the boy himself?"

I was wonderful. "Nothing."

She gave with her apron a great wipe to her mouth. "Then I'll stand by you. We'll see it out."

"We'll see it out!" I ardently echoed, giving her my hand to make it a vow.

She held me there a moment, then whisked up her apron again with her detached hand. "Would you mind, miss, if I used the freedom—"

"To kiss me? No!" I took the good creature in my arms and, after we had embraced like sisters, felt still more fortified and indignant.

This, at all events, was for the time: a time so full that, as I recall the way it went, it reminds me of all the art I now need to make it a little distinct. What I look back at with amazement is the situation I accepted. I had undertaken, with my companion, to see it out, and I was under a charm, apparently, that could smooth away the extent and the far and difficult connections of such an effort. I was lifted aloft on a great wave of infatuation and pity. I found it simple, in my ignorance, my confusion and perhaps my conceit, to assume that I could deal with a boy whose education for the world was all on the point of beginning. I am unable even to remember at this day what proposal I framed for the end of his holidays and the resumption of his studies. Lessons with me indeed, that charming summer, we all had a theory that he was to have; but I now feel that, for weeks, the lessons must have been rather my own. I learned something—at first certainly—that had not been one of the teachings of my small, smothered life; learned to be amused, and even amusing, and not to think for the morrow. It was the first time, in a manner, that I had known space and air and freedom, all the music of summer and all the mystery of nature. And then there was consideration—and consideration was sweet. Oh, it was a trap—not designed, but deep—to my imagination, to my delicacy, perhaps to my vanity; to whatever, in me, was most excitable. The best way to picture it all is to say that I was off my guard. They gave me so little trouble—they were of a gentleness so extraordinary. I used to speculate—but even this with a dim disconnectedness—as to how the rough future (for all futures are rough!) would handle them and might bruise them. They had the bloom of health and happiness; and yet, as if I had been in charge of a pair of little grandees, of princes of the blood, for whom everything, to be right, would have to be enclosed and protected, the only form that, in my fancy, the afteryears could take for them was that of a romantic, a really royal extension of the garden and the park. It may be, of course, above all, that what suddenly broke into this gives the previous time a charm of stillness—that hush in which something gathers or crouches. The change was actually like the spring of a beast.

In the first weeks the days were long; they often, at their finest, gave me what I used to call my own hour, the hour when, for my pupils, teatime and bedtime having come and gone, I had, before my final retirement, a small interval alone. Much as I liked my companions, this hour was the thing in the day I liked most; and I liked it best of all when, as the light faded—or rather, I should say, the day lingered and the last calls of the last birds sounded, in a flushed sky, from the old trees—I could take a turn into the grounds and enjoy, almost with a sense of property that amused and flattered me, the beauty and dignity of the place. It was a pleasure at these moments to feel myself tranquil and justified; doubtless, perhaps, also to reflect that by my discretion, my quiet good sense and general high propriety, I was giving pleasure—if he ever thought of it!—to the person to whose pressure I had responded. What I was doing was what he had earnestly hoped and directly asked of me, and that I *could,* after all, do it proved even a greater joy than I had expected. I daresay I fancied myself, in short, a remarkable young woman and took comfort in the faith that this would more publicly appear. Well, I needed to be remarkable to offer a front to the remarkable things that presently gave their first sign.

It was plump, one afternoon, in the middle of my very hour: the children were tucked away and I had come out for my stroll. One of the thoughts that, as I don't in the least shrink now from noting, used to be with me in these wanderings was that it would be as charming as a charming story suddenly to meet someone. Someone would appear there at the turn of a path and would stand before me and smile and approve. I didn't ask more than that—I only asked that he should *know;* and the only way to be sure he knew would be to see it, and the kind light of it, in his handsome face. That was exactly present to me—by which I mean the face was—when, on the first of these occasions, at the end of a long June day, I stopped short on emerging from one of the plantations and coming into view of the house. What arrested me on the spot—and with a shock much greater than any vision had allowed for—was the sense that my imagination had, in a flash, turned real. He did stand there!—but high up, beyond the lawn and at the very top of the tower to which, on that first morning, little Flora had conducted me. This tower was one of a pair—square, incongruous, crenelated structures—that were distinguished, for some reason, though I could see little difference, as the new and the old. They flanked opposite ends of the house and were probably architectural absurdities, redeemed in a measure indeed by not being wholly disengaged nor of a height too pretentious, dating, in their gingerbread antiquity, from a romantic revival that was already a respectable past. I admired them, had fancies about them, for we could all profit in a degree, especially when they loomed through the dusk, by the grandeur of their actual battlements; yet it was not at such an elevation that the figure I had so often invoked seemed most in place.

It produced in me, this figure, in the clear twilight, I remember, two distinct gasps of emotion, which were, sharply, the shock of my first and that of my second surprise. My second was a violent perception of the mistake of my first: the man who met my eyes was not the person I had precipitately supposed. There came to me thus a bewilderment of vision of which, after these years, there is no living view that I can hope to give. An unknown man in a lonely place is a permitted object of fear to a young woman privately bred; and the figure that faced me was—a few more seconds assured me—as little anyone else I knew as it was the image that had been in my mind. I had not seen it in Harley Street—

I had not seen it anywhere. The place, moreover, in the strangest way in the world, had, on the instant, and by the very fact of its appearance, become a solitude. To me at least, making my statement here with a deliberation with which I have never made it, the whole feeling of the moment returns. It was as if, while I took in—what I did take in—all the rest of the scene had been stricken with death. I can hear again, as I write, the intense hush in which the sounds of evening dropped. The rooks stopped cawing in the golden sky and the friendly hour lost, for the minute, all its voice. But there was no other change in nature, unless indeed it were a change that I saw with a stranger sharpness. The gold was still in the sky, the clearness in the air, and the man who looked at me over the battlements was as definite as a picture in a frame. That's how I thought, with extraordinary quickness, of each person that he might have been and that he was not. We were confronted across our distance quite long enough for me to ask myself with intensity who then he was and to feel, as an effect of my inability to say, a wonder that in a few instants more became intense.

The great question, or one of these, is, afterwards, I know, with regard to certain matters, the question of how long they have lasted. Well, this matter of mine, think what you will of it, lasted while I caught at a dozen possibilities, none of which made a difference for the better, that I could see, in there having been in the house—and for how long, above all?—a person of whom I was in ignorance. It lasted while I just bridled a little with the sense that my office demanded that there should be no such ignorance and no such person. It lasted while this visitant, at all events—and there was a touch of the strange freedom, as I remember, in the sign of familiarity of his wearing no hat—seemed to fix me, from his position, with just the question, just the scrutiny through the fading light, that his own presence provoked. We were too far apart to call to each other, but there was a moment at which, at shorter range, some challenge between us, breaking the hush, would have been the right result of our straight mutual stare. He was in one of the angles, the one away from the house, very erect, as it struck me, and with both hands on the ledge. So I saw him as I see the letters I form on this page; then, exactly, after a minute, as if to add to the spectacle, he slowly changed his place—passed, looking at me hard all the while, to the opposite corner of the platform. Yes, I had the sharpest sense that during this transit he never took his eyes from me, and I can see at this moment the way his hand, as he went, passed from one of the crenelations to the next. He stopped at the other corner, but less long, and even as he turned away still markedly fixed me. He turned away; that was all I knew.

IV

It was not that I didn't wait, on this occasion, for more, for I was rooted as deeply as I was shaken. Was there a "secret" at Bly—a mystery of Udolpho or an insane, an unmentionable relative kept in unsuspected confinement? I can't say how long I turned it over, or how long, in a confusion of curiosity and dread, I remained where I had had my collision; I only recall that when I reentered the house darkness had quite closed in. Agitation, in the interval, certainly had held me and driven me, for I must, in circling about the place, have walked three miles; but I was to be, later on, so much more overwhelmed that this mere dawn of alarm was a comparatively human chill. The most singular part of it in fact—singular as the rest had been—was the part I became, in the hall, aware of in meeting Mrs. Grose. This picture comes back to me in the general train—the impression, as I received it on my return, of the wide white paneled space, bright in the lamplight and with its portraits and red carpet, and of the good surprised look of my friend, which immediately told me she had missed me. It came to me straightway, under her contact, that, with plain heartiness, mere relieved anxiety at my appearance, she knew nothing whatever that could bear upon the incident I had there ready for her. I had not suspected in advance that her comfortable face would pull me up, and I somehow measured the importance of what I had seen by my thus finding myself hesitate to mention it. Scarce anything in the whole history seems to me so odd as this fact that my real beginning of fear was one, as I may say, with the instinct of sparing my companion. On the spot, accordingly, in the pleasant hall and with her eyes on me, I, for a reason that I couldn't then have phrased, achieved an inward revolution—offered a vague pretext for my lateness and, with the plea of the beauty of the night and of the heavy dew and wet feet, went as soon as possible to my room.

Here it was another affair; here, for many days after, it was a queer affair enough. There were hours, from day to day—or at least there were moments, snatched even from clear duties—when I had to shut myself up to think. It was not so much yet that I was more nervous than I could bear to be as that I was remarkably afraid of becoming so; for the truth I had now to turn over was, simply and clearly, the truth that I could arrive at no account whatever of the visitor with whom I had been so inexplicably and yet, as it seemed to me, so intimately concerned. It took little time to see that I could sound without forms of inquiry and without exciting remark any domestic complication. The shock I had suffered must have sharpened all my senses; I felt sure, at the end of three days and as the result of mere closer attention, that I had not been practiced upon by the servants nor made the object of any "game." Of whatever it was that I knew nothing was known around me. There was but one sane inference: someone had taken a liberty rather gross. That was what, repeatedly, I dipped into my room and locked the door to say to myself. We had been, collectively, subject to an intrusion; some unscrupulous traveler, curious in old houses, had made his way in unobserved, enjoyed the prospect from the best point of view and then stolen out as he came. If he had given me such a bold hard stare, that was but a part of his indiscretion. The good thing, after all, was that we should surely see no more of him.

This was not so good a thing, I admit, as not to leave me to judge that what, essentially, made nothing else much signify was simply my charming work. My charming work was just my life with Miles and Flora, and through nothing could I so like it as through feeling that I could throw myself into it in trouble. The attraction of my small charges was a constant joy, leading me to wonder afresh at the vanity of my original fears, the distaste I had begun by entertaining for the probable gray prose of my office. There was to be no gray prose, it appeared, and no long grind; so how could work not be charming that presented itself as daily beauty? It was all the romance of the nursery and the poetry of the schoolroom. I don't mean by this, of course, that we studied only fiction and verse; I mean I can express no otherwise the sort of interest my companions inspired. How can I describe that except by saying that instead of growing used to them—and it's a marvel for a governess: I call the sisterhood to witness!—I made constant fresh discoveries. There was one direction, assuredly, in which these discoveries stopped: deep obscurity continued to cover the region of the boy's conduct at school. It had been promptly given me, I have noted, to face that mystery without a pang. Perhaps even it would be nearer the truth to say that—without a word—he himself had cleared it up. He had made the whole charge absurd. My conclusion bloomed there with the real rose-flush of his innocence: he was only too fine and fair for the little horrid, unclean school-world, and he had paid a price for it. I reflected acutely that the sense of such differences, such superiorities of quality, always, on the part of the majority—which could include even stupid, sordid headmasters—turns infallibly to the vindictive.

Both the children had a gentleness (it was their only fault, and it never made Miles a muff) that kept them—how shall I express it?—almost impersonal and certainly quite unpunishable. They were like the cherubs of the anecdote, who had—normally, at any rate—nothing to whack! I remember feeling with Miles in especial as if he had had, as it were, no history. We expect of a small child a scant one, but there was in this beautiful little boy something extraordinarily sensitive, yet extraordinarily happy, that, more than in any creature of his age I have seen, struck me as beginning anew each day. He had never for a second suffered. I took this as a direct disproof of his having really been chastised. If he had been wicked he would have "caught" it, and I should have caught it by the rebound—I should have found the trace. I found nothing at all, and he was therefore an angel. He never spoke of his school, never mentioned a comrade or a master; and I, for my part, was quite too much disgusted to allude to them. Of course I was under the spell, and the wonderful part is that, even at the time, I perfectly knew I was. But I gave myself up to it; it was an antidote to any pain, and I had more pains than one. I was in receipt in these days of disturbing letters from home, where things were not going well. But with my children, what things in the world mattered? That was the question I used to put to my scrappy retirements. I was dazzled by their loveliness.

There was a Sunday—to get on—when it rained with such force and for so many hours that there could be no procession to church; in consequence of which, as the day declined, I had arranged with Mrs. Grose that, should the evening show improvement, we would attend together the late service. The rain happily stopped, and I prepared for our walk, which, through the park and by the good road to the village, would be a matter of twenty minutes. Coming downstairs to meet my colleague in the hall, I remembered a pair of gloves that had required three stitches and that had received them—with a publicity perhaps not edifying—while I sat with the children at their tea, served on Sundays, by exception, in that cold, clean temple of mahogany and brass, the "grown-up" dining room. The gloves had been dropped there, and I turned in to recover them. The day was gray enough, but the afternoon light still lingered, and it enabled me, on crossing the threshold, not only to recognize, on a chair near the wide window, then closed, the articles I wanted, but to become aware of a person on the other side of the window and looking straight in. One step into the room had sufficed; my vision was instantaneous; it was all there. The person looking straight in was the person who had already appeared to me. He appeared thus again with I won't say greater distinctness, for that was impossible, but with a nearness that represented a forward stride in our intercourse and made me, as I met him, catch my breath and turn cold. He was the same—he was the same, and seen, this time, as he had been seen before, from the waist up, the window, though the dining room was on the ground floor, not going down to the terrace on which he stood. His face was close to the glass, yet the effect of this better view was, strangely, only to show me how intense the former had been. He remained but a few seconds—long enough to convince me he also saw and recognized; but it was as if I had been looking at him for years and had known him always. Something, however, happened this time that had not happened before; his stare into my face, through the glass and across the room, was as deep and hard as then, but it quitted me for a moment during which I could still watch it, see it fix successively several other things. On the spot there came to me the added shock of a certitude that it was not for me he had come there. He had come for someone else.

The flash of this knowledge—for it was knowledge in the midst of dread—produced in me the most extraordinary effect, started, as I stood there, a sudden vibration of duty and courage. I say courage because I was beyond all doubt already far gone. I bounded straight out of the door again, reached that of the house, got, in an instant, upon the drive, and, passing along the terrace as fast as I could rush, turned a corner and came full in sight. But it was in sight of nothing now—my visitor had vanished. I stopped, I almost dropped, with the real relief of this; but I took in the whole scene—I gave him time to reappear. I call it time, but how long was it? I can't speak to the purpose today of the duration of these things. That kind of measure must have left me: they couldn't have lasted as they actually appeared to me to last. The terrace and the whole place, the lawn and the garden beyond it, all I could see of the park, were empty with a great emptiness. There were shrubberies and big trees, but I remember the clear assurance I felt that none of them concealed him. He was there or was not there: not there if I didn't see him. I got hold of this; then, instinctively, instead of returning as I had come, went to the window. It was confusedly present to me that I ought to place myself where he had stood. I did so; I applied my face to the pane and looked, as he had looked, into the room. As if, at this moment, to show me exactly what his range had been, Mrs. Grose, as I had done for himself just before, came in from the hall. With this I had the full image of a repetition of what had already occurred. She saw me as I had seen my own visitant; she pulled up short as I had done; I gave her something of the shock that I had received. She turned white, and this made me ask myself if I had blanched as much. She stared, in short, and retreated on just *my* lines, and I knew she had then passed out and come round to me and that I should presently meet her. I remained where I was, and while I waited I thought of more things than one. But there's only one I take space to mention. I wondered why *she* should be scared.

V

Oh, she let me know as soon as, round the corner of the house, she loomed again into view. "What in the name of goodness is the matter—?" She was now flushed and out of breath.

I said nothing till she came quite near. "With me?" I must have made a wonderful face. "Do I show it?"

"You're as white as a sheet. You look awful."

I considered; I could meet on this, without scruple, any innocence. My need to respect the bloom of Mrs. Grose's had dropped, without a rustle, from my shoulders, and if I wavered for the instant it was not with what I kept back. I put out my hand to her and she took it; I held her hard a little, liking to feel her close to me. There was a kind of support in the shy heave of her surprise. "You came for me for church, of course, but I can't go."

"Has anything happened?"

"Yes. You must know now. Did I look very queer?"

"Through this window? Dreadful!"

"Well," I said, "I've been frightened." Mrs. Grose's eyes expressed plainly that *she* had no wish to be, yet also that she knew too well her place not to be ready to share with me any marked inconvenience. Oh, it was quite settled that she *must* share! "Just what you saw from the dining room a minute ago was the effect of that. What *I* saw—just before —was much worse."

Her hand tightened. "What was it?"

"An extraordinary man. Looking in."

"What extraordinary man?"

"I haven't the least idea."

Mrs. Grose gazed round us in vain. "Then where is he gone?"

"I know still less."

"Have you seen him before?"

"Yes—once. On the old tower."

She could only look at me harder. "Do you mean he's a stranger?"

"Oh, very much!"

"Yet you didn't tell me?"

"No—for reasons. But now that you've guessed—"

Mrs. Grose's round eyes encountered this charge. "Ah, I haven't guessed!" she said very simply. "How can I if *you* don't imagine?"

"I don't in the very least."

"You've seen him nowhere but on the tower?"

"And on this spot just now."

Mrs. Grose looked round again. "What was he doing on the tower?"

"Only standing there and looking down at me."

She thought a minute. "Was he a gentleman?"

I found I had no need to think. "No." She gazed in deeper wonder. "No."

"Then nobody about the place? Nobody from the village?"

"Nobody—nobody. I didn't tell you, but I made sure."

She breathed a vague relief: this was, oddly, so much to the good. It only went indeed a little way. "But if he isn't a gentleman—"

"What *is* he? He's a horror."

"A horror?"

"He's—God help me if I know *what* he is!"

Mrs. Grose looked round once more; she fixed her eyes on the duskier distance, then, pulling herself together, turned to me with abrupt inconsequence. "It's time we should be at church."

"Oh, I'm not fit for church!"

"Won't it do you good?"

"It won't do *them—!*" I nodded at the house.

"The children?"

"I can't leave them now."

"You're afraid—?"

I spoke boldly. "I'm afraid of *him.*"

Mrs. Grose's large face showed me, at this, for the first time, the faraway faint glimmer of a consciousness more acute: I somehow made out in it the delayed dawn of an idea I myself had not given her and that was as yet quite obscure to me. It comes back to me that I thought instantly of this as something I could get from her; and I felt it to be connected with the desire she presently showed to know more. "When was it—on the tower?"

"About the middle of the month. At this same hour."

"Almost at dark," said Mrs. Grose.

"Oh no, not nearly. I saw him as I see you."

"Then how did he get in?"

"And how did he get out?" I laughed. "I had no opportunity to ask him! This evening, you see," I pursued, "he has not been able to get in."

"He only peeps?"

"I hope it will be confined to that!" She had now let go my hand; she turned away a little. I waited an instant; then I brought out: "Go to church. Goodbye. I must watch."

Slowly she faced me again. "Do you fear for them?"

We met in another long look. "Don't *you?*" Instead of answering she came nearer to the window and, for a minute, applied her face to the glass. "You see how he could see," I meanwhile went on.

She didn't move. "How long was he here?"

"Till I came out. I came to meet him."

Mrs. Grose at last turned round, and there was still more in her face. "*I* couldn't have come out."

"Neither could I!" I laughed again. "But I did come. I have my duty."

"So have I mine," she replied; after which she added: "What is he like?"

"I've been dying to tell you. But he's like nobody."

"Nobody?" she echoed.

"He has no hat." Then seeing in her face that she already, in this, with a deeper dismay, found a touch of picture, I quickly added stroke to stroke. "He has red hair, very red, close-curling, and a pale face, long in shape, with straight, good features and little, rather queer whiskers that are as red as his hair. His eyebrows are, somehow, darker; they look particularly arched and as if they might move a good deal. His eyes are sharp, strange —awfully; but I only know clearly that they're rather small and very fixed.

His mouth's wide, and his lips are thin, and except for his little whiskers he's quite clean-shaven. He gives me a sort of sense of looking like an actor."

"An actor!" It was impossible to resemble one less, at least, than Mrs. Grose at that moment.

"I've never seen one, but so I suppose them. He's tall, active, erect," I continued, "but never—no, never!—a gentleman."

My companion's face had blanched as I went on; her round eyes started and her mild mouth gaped. "A gentleman?" she gasped, confounded, stupefied: "a gentleman *he?*"

"You know him then?"

She visibly tried to hold herself. "But he *is* handsome?"

I saw the way to help her. "Remarkably!"

"And dressed—?"

"In somebody's clothes. They're smart, but they're not his own."

She broke into a breathless affirmative groan. "They're the master's!"

I caught it up. "You *do* know him?"

She faltered but a second. "Quint!" she cried.

"Quint?"

"Peter Quint—his own man, his valet, when he was here!"

"When the master was?"

Gaping still, but meeting me, she pieced it all together. "He never wore his hat, but he did wear—well, there were waistcoats missed! They were both here—last year. Then the master went, and Quint was alone."

I followed, but halting a little. "Alone?"

"Alone with *us.*" Then, as from a deeper depth, "In charge," she added.

"And what became of him?"

She hung fire so long that I was still more mystified. "He went too," she brought out at last.

"Went where?"

Her expression, at this, became extraordinary. "God knows where! He died."

"Died?" I almost shrieked.

She seemed fairly to square herself, plant herself more firmly to utter the wonder of it. "Yes. Mr. Quint is dead."

VI

It took of course more than that particular passage to place us together in presence of what we had now to live with as we could—my dreadful liability to impressions of the order so vividly exemplified, and my companion's knowledge, henceforth—a knowledge half-consternation and half-compassion—of that liability. There had been, this evening, after the revelation that left me, for an hour, so prostrate—there had been, for either of us, no attendance on any service but a little service of tears and vows, of prayers and promises, a climax to the series of mutual challenges and pledges that had straightway ensued on our retreating together to the schoolroom and shutting ourselves up there to have everything out. The result of our having everything out was simply to reduce our situation to the last rigor of its elements. She herself had seen nothing, not the shadow of a shadow, and nobody in the house but the governess was in the governess's plight; yet she accepted without directly impugning my sanity the truth as I gave it to her, and ended by showing me, on this ground, an awestricken tenderness, an expression of the sense of my more than questionable privilege, of which the very breath has remained with me as that of the sweetest of human charities.

What was settled between us, accordingly, that night, was that we thought we might bear things together; and I was not even sure that, in spite of her exemption, it was she who had the best of the burden. I knew at this hour, I think, as well as I knew later what I was capable of meeting to shelter my pupils; but it took me some time to be wholly sure of what my honest ally was prepared for to keep terms with so compromising a contract. I was queer company enough—quite as queer as the company I received; but as I trace over what we went through I see how much common ground we must have found in the one idea that, by good fortune, *could* steady us. It was the idea, the second movement, that led me straight out, as I may say, of the inner chamber of my dread. I could take the air in the court, at least, and there Mrs. Grose could join me. Perfectly can I recall now the particular way strength came to me before we separated for the night. We had gone over and over every feature of what I had seen.

"He was looking for someone else, you say—someone who was not you?"

"He was looking for little Miles." A portentous clearness now possessed me. "*That's* whom he was looking for."

"But how do you know?"

"I know, I know, I know!" My exaltation grew. "And *you* know, my dear!"

She didn't deny this, but I required, I felt, not even so much telling as that. She resumed in a moment, at any rate: "What if *he* should see him?"

"Little Miles? That's what he wants!"

She looked immensely scared again. "The child?"

"Heaven forbid! The man. He wants to appear to *them.*" That he might was an awful conception, and yet, somehow, I could keep at bay; which, moreover, as we lingered there, was what I succeeded in practically proving. I had an absolute certainty that I should see again what I had already seen, but something within me said that by offering myself bravely as the sole subject of such experience, by accepting, by inviting, by surmounting it all, I should serve as an expiatory victim and guard the tranquility of my companions. The children, in especial, I should thus fence about and absolutely save. I recall one of the last things I said that night to Mrs. Grose.

"It does strike me that my pupils have never mentioned—"

She looked at me hard as I musingly pulled up. "His having been here and the time they were with him?"

"The time they were with him, and his name, his presence, his history, in any way."

"Oh, the little lady doesn't remember. She never heard or knew."

"The circumstances of his death?" I thought with some intensity. "Perhaps not. But Miles would remember—Miles would know."

"Ah, don't try him!" broke from Mrs. Grose.

I returned her the look she had given me. "Don't be afraid." I continued to think. "It *is* rather odd."

"That he has never spoken of him?"

"Never by the least allusion. And you tell me they were 'great friends'?"

"Oh, it wasn't *him!*" Mrs. Grose with emphasis declared. "It was Quint's own fancy. To play with him, I mean—to spoil him." She paused a moment; then she added: "Quint was much too free."

This gave me, straight from my vision of his face—*such* a face!—a sudden sickness of disgust. "Too free with *my* boy?"

"Too free with everyone!"

I forbore, for the moment, to analyze this description further than by the reflection that a part of it applied to several of the members of the household, of the half-dozen maids and men who were still of our small colony. But there was everything, for our apprehension, in the lucky fact that no discomfortable legend, no perturbation of scullions, had ever, within anyone's memory, attached to the kind old place. It had neither bad name nor ill fame, and Mrs. Grose, most apparently, only desired to cling to me and to quake in silence. I even put her, the very last thing of all, to the test. It was when, at midnight, she had her hand on the schoolroom door to take leave. "I have it from you then—for it's of great importance—that he was definitely and admittedly bad?"

"Oh, not admittedly. *I* knew it—but the master didn't."

"And you never told him?"

"Well, he didn't like talebearing—he hated complaints. He was terribly short with anything of that kind, and if people were all right to *him*—"

"He wouldn't be bothered with more?" This squared well enough with my impression of him: he was not a trouble-loving gentleman, nor so very particular perhaps about some of the company *he* kept. All the same, I pressed my interlocutress. "I promise you *I* would have told!"

She felt my discrimination. "I daresay I was wrong. But, really, I was afraid."

"Afraid of what?"

"Of things that man could do. Quint was so clever—he was so deep."

I took this in still more than, probably, I showed. "You weren't afraid of anything else? Not of his effect—?"

"His effect?" she repeated with a face of anguish and waiting while I faltered.

"On innocent little precious lives. They were in your charge."

"No, they were not in mine!" she roundly and distressfully returned. "The master believed in him and placed him here because he was supposed not to be well and the country air so good for him. So he had everything to say. Yes"—she let me have it—"even about *them.*"

"Them—that creature?" I had to smother a kind of howl. "And you could bear it?"

"No. I couldn't—and I can't now!" And the poor woman burst into tears.

A rigid control, from the next day, was, as I have said, to follow them; yet how often and how passionately, for a week, we came back together to the subject! Much as we had discussed it that Sunday night, I was, in the immediate later hours in especial—for it may be imagined whether I slept—still haunted with the shadow of something she had not told me. I myself had kept back nothing, but there was a word Mrs. Grose had kept back. I was sure, moreover, by morning, that this was not from a failure of frankness, but because on every side there were fears. It seems to me indeed, in retrospect, that by the time the morrow's sun was high I had restlessly read into the facts before us almost all the meaning they were to receive from subsequent and more cruel occurrences. What they gave me above all was just the sinister figure of the living man—the dead one would keep awhile!—and of the months he had continuously passed at Bly, which, added up, made a formidable stretch. The limit of this evil time had arrived only when, on the dawn of a winter's morning, Peter Quint was found, by a laborer going to early work, stone dead on the road from the village: a catastrophe explained—superficially at least—by a visible wound to his head; such a wound as might have been produced—and as, on the final evidence, *had* been—by a fatal slip, in the dark and after leaving the public house, on the steepish icy slope, a wrong path altogether, at the bottom of which he lay. The icy slope, the turn mistaken at night and in liquor, accounted for much—practically, in the end and after the inquest and boundless chatter, for everything; but there had been matters in his life—strange passages and perils, secret disorders, vices more than suspected—that would have accounted for a good deal more.

I scarce know how to put my story into words that shall be a credible picture of my state of mind; but I was in these days literally able to find a joy in the extraordinary flight of heroism the occasion demanded of me. I now saw that I had been asked for a service admirable and difficult; and there would be a greatness in letting it be seen—oh, in the right quarter!—that I could succeed where many another girl might have failed. It was an immense help to me—I confess I rather applaud myself as I look back!—that I saw my service so strongly and so simply. I was there to protect and defend the little creatures in the world the most bereaved and the most lovable, the appeal of whose helplessness had suddenly become only too explicit, a deep, constant ache of one's own committed heart. We were cut off, really, together; we were united in our danger. They had nothing but me, and I—well, I had *them.* It was in short a magnificent chance. This chance presented itself to me in an image richly material. I was a screen—I was to stand before them. The more I saw, the less they would. I began to watch them in a stifled suspense, a disguised excitement that might well, had it continued too long, have turned to something like madness. What saved me, as I now see, was that it turned to something else altogether. It didn't last as suspense—it was superseded by horrible proofs. Proofs, I say, yes—from the moment I really took hold.

This moment dated from an afternoon hour that I happened to spend in the grounds with the younger of my pupils alone. We had left Miles indoors, on the red cushion of a deep window seat; he had wished to finish a book, and I had been glad to encourage a purpose so laudable in a young man whose only defect was an occasional excess of the restless. His sister, on the contrary, had been alert to come out, and I strolled with her half an hour, seeking the shade, for the sun was still high and the day exceptionally warm. I was aware afresh, with her, as we went, of how, like her brother, she contrived—it was the charming thing in both children—to let me alone without appearing to drop me and to accompany me without appearing to surround. They were never importunate and yet never listless. My attention to them all really went to seeing them amuse themselves immensely without me: this was a spectacle they seemed actively to prepare and that engaged me as an active admirer. I walked in a world of their invention—they had no occasion whatever to draw upon mine; so that my time was taken only with being, for them, some remarkable person or thing that the game of the moment required and that was merely, thanks to my superior, my exalted stamp, a happy and highly distinguished sinecure. I forget what I was on the present occasion; I only remember that I was something very important and very quiet and that Flora was playing very hard. We were on the edge of the lake, and, as we had lately begun geography, the lake was the Sea of Azof.

Suddenly, in these circumstances, I became aware that, on the other side of the Sea of Azof, we had an interested spectator. The way this knowledge gathered in me was the strangest thing in the world—the strangest, that is, except the very much stranger in which it quickly merged itself. I had sat down with a piece of work—for I was something or other that could sit—on the old stone bench which overlooked the pond; and in this position I began to take in with certitude, and yet without direct vision, the presence, at a distance, of a third person. The old trees, the thick shrubbery, made a great and pleasant shade, but it was all suffused with the brightness of the hot, still hour. There was no ambiguity in anything; none whatever, at least, in the conviction I from one moment to another found myself forming as to what I should see straight before me and across the lake as a consequence of raising my eyes. They were attached at this juncture to the stitching in which I was engaged, and I can feel once more the spasm of my effort not to move them till I should so have steadied myself as to be able to make up my mind what to do. There was an alien object in view—a figure whose right of presence I instantly, passionately questioned. I recollect counting over perfectly the possibilities, reminding myself that nothing was more natural, for instance, than the appearance of one of the men about the place, or even of a messenger, a postman or a tradesman's boy, from the village. That reminder had as little effect on my practical certitude as I was conscious—still even without looking—of its having upon the character and attitude of our visitor. Nothing was more natural than that these things should be the other things that they absolutely were not.

Of the positive identity of the apparition I would assure myself as soon as the small clock of my courage should have ticked out the right second; meanwhile, with an effort that was already sharp enough, I transferred my eyes straight to little Flora, who, at the moment, was about ten yards away. My heart had stood still for an instant with the wonder and terror of the question whether she too would see; and I held my breath while I waited for what a cry from her, what some sudden innocent sign either of interest or of alarm, would tell me. I waited, but nothing came; then, in the first place—and there is something more dire in this, I feel, than in anything I have to relate—I was determined by a sense that, within a minute, all sounds from her had previously dropped; and, in the second, by the circumstance that, also within the minute, she had, in her play, turned her back to the water. This was her attitude when I at last looked at her—looked with the confirmed conviction that we were still, together, under direct personal notice. She had picked up a small flat piece of wood, which happened to have in it a little hole that had evidently suggested to her the idea of sticking in another fragment that might figure as a mast and make the thing a boat. This second morsel, as I watched her, she was very markedly and intently attempting to tighten in its place. My apprehension of what she was doing sustained me so that after some seconds I felt I was ready for more. Then I again shifted my eyes—I faced what I had to face.

VII

I got hold of Mrs. Grose as soon after this as I could; and I can give no intelligible account of how I fought out the interval. Yet I still hear myself cry as I fairly threw myself into her arms: "They *know*—it's too monstrous: they know, they know!"

"And what on earth—?" I felt her incredulity as she held me.

"Why, all that *we* know—and heaven knows what else besides!" Then, as she released me, I made it out to her, made it out perhaps only now with full coherency even to myself. "Two hours ago, in the garden"—I could scarce articulate—"Flora *saw!*"

Mrs. Grose took it as she might have taken a blow in the stomach. "She has told you?" she panted.

"Not a word—that's the horror. She kept it to herself! The child of eight, *that* child!" Unutterable still, for me, was the stupefaction of it.

Mrs. Grose, of course, could only gape the wider. "Then how do you know?"

"I was there—I saw with my eyes: saw that she was perfectly aware."

"Do you mean aware of *him?*"

"No—of *her.*" I was conscious as I spoke that I looked prodigious things, for I got the slow reflection of them in my companion's face. "Another person—this time; but a figure of quite as unmistakable horror and evil: a woman in black, pale and dreadful—with such an air also, and such a face!—on the other side of the lake. I was there with the child—quiet for the hour; and in the midst of it she came."

"Came how—from where?"

"From where they come from! She just appeared and stood there—but not so near."

"And without coming nearer?"

"Oh, for the effect and the feeling, she might have been as close as you!"

My friend, with an odd impulse, fell back a step. "Was she someone you've never seen?"

"Yes. But someone the child has. Someone *you* have." Then, to show how I had thought it all out: "My predecessor—the one who died."

"Miss Jessel?"

"Miss Jessel. You don't believe me?" I pressed.

She turned right and left in her distress. "How can you be sure?"

This drew from me, in the state of my nerves, a flash of impatience. "Then ask Flora—*she's* sure!" But I had no sooner spoken than I caught myself up. "No, for God's sake, *don't!* She'll say she isn't—she'll lie!"

Mrs. Grose was not too bewildered instinctively to protest. "Ah, how *can* you?"

"Because I'm clear. Flora doesn't want me to know."

"It's only then to spare you."

"No, no—there are depths, depths! The more I go over it, the more I see in it, and the more I see in it the more I fear. I don't know what I *don't* see—what I *don't* fear!"

Mrs. Grose tried to keep up with me. "You mean you're afraid of seeing her again?"

"Oh no; that's nothing—now!" Then I explained. "It's of *not* seeing her."

But my companion only looked wan. "I don't understand you."

"Why, it's that the child may keep it up—and that the child assuredly *will*—without my knowing it."

At the image of this possibility Mrs. Grose for a moment collapsed, yet presently to pull herself together again, as if from the positive force of the sense of what, should we yield an inch, there would really be to give way to. "Dear, dear—we must keep our heads! And after all, if she doesn't mind it—!" She even tried a grim joke. "Perhaps she likes it!"

"Likes *such* things—a scrap of an infant!"

"Isn't it just a proof of her blessed innocence?" my friend bravely inquired.

She brought me, for the instant, almost round. "Oh, we must clutch at *that*—we must cling to it! If it isn't a proof of what you say, it's a proof of—God knows what! For the woman's a horror of horrors."

Mrs. Grose, at this, fixed her eyes a minute on the ground; then at last raising them, "Tell me how you know," she said.

"Then you admit it's what she was?" I cried.

"Tell me how you know," my friend simply repeated.

"Know? By seeing her! By the way she looked."

"At you, do you mean—so wickedly?"

"Dear me, no—I could have borne that. She gave me never a glance. She only fixed the child."

Mrs. Grose tried to see it. "Fixed her?"

"Ah, with such awful eyes!"

She stared at mine as if they might really have resembled them. "Do you mean of dislike?"

"God help us, no. Of something much worse."

"Worse than dislike?"—this left her indeed at a loss.

"With a determination—indescribable. With a kind of fury of intention."

I made her turn pale. "Intention?"

"To get hold of her." Mrs. Grose—her eyes just lingering on mine—gave a shudder and walked to the window; and while she stood there looking out I completed my statement. *"That's* what Flora knows."

After a little she turned round. "The person was in black, you say?"

"In mourning—rather poor, almost shabby. But—yes—with extraordinary beauty." I now recognized to what I had at last, stroke by stroke, brought the victim of my confidence, for she quite visibly weighed this. "Oh, handsome—very, very," I insisted; "wonderfully handsome. But infamous."

She slowly came back to me. "Miss Jessel—*was* infamous." She once more took my hand in both her own, holding it as tight as if to fortify me against the increase of alarm I might draw from this disclosure. "They were both infamous," she finally said.

So, for a little, we faced it once more together; and I found absolutely a degree of help in seeing it now so straight. "I appreciate," I said, "the great decency of your not having hitherto spoken; but the time has certainly come to give me the whole thing." She appeared to assent to this, but still only in silence; seeing which I went on: "I must have it now. Of what did she die? Come, there was something between them."

"There was everything."

"In spite of the difference—?"

"Oh, of their rank, their condition"—she brought it woefully out. *"She* was a lady."

I turned it over; I again saw. "Yes—she was a lady."

"And he so dreadfully below," said Mrs. Grose.

I felt that I doubtless needn't press too hard, in such company, on the place of a servant in the scale; but there was nothing to prevent an acceptance of my companion's own measure of my predecessor's abasement. There was a way to deal with that, and I dealt; the more readily for my full vision—on the evidence—of our employer's late clever, good-looking "own" man; impudent, assured, spoiled, depraved. "The fellow was a hound."

Mrs. Grose considered as if it were perhaps a little a case for a sense of shades. "I've never seen one like him. He did what he wished."

"With *her?*"

dow, that the yielding dusk of earliest morning rendered it unnecessary. Without it, the next instant, I saw that there was someone on the stair. I speak of sequences, but I required no lapse of seconds to stiffen myself for a third encounter with Quint. The apparition had reached the landing halfway up and was therefore on the spot nearest the window, where, at sight of me, it stopped short and fixed me exactly as it had fixed me from the tower and from the garden. He knew me as well as I knew him; and so, in the cold, faint twilight, with a glimmer in the high glass and another on the polish of the oak stair below, we faced each other in our common intensity. He was absolutely, on this occasion, a living, detestable, dangerous presence. But that was not the wonder of wonders; I reserve this distinction for quite another circumstance: the circumstance that dread had unmistakably quitted me and that there was nothing in me there that didn't meet and measure him.

I had plenty of anguish after that extraordinary moment, but I had, thank God, no terror. And he knew I had not—I found myself at the end of an instant magnificently aware of this. I felt, in a fierce rigor of confidence, that if I stood my ground a minute I should cease—for the time, at least—to have him to reckon with; and during the minute, accordingly, the thing was as human and hideous as a real interview: hideous just because it *was* human, as human as to have met alone, in the small hours, in a sleeping house, some enemy, some adventurer, some criminal. It was the dead silence of our long gaze at such close quarters that gave the whole horror, huge as it was, its only note of the unnatural. If I had met a murderer in such a place and at such an hour we still at least would have spoken. Something would have passed, in life, between us; if nothing had passed one of us would have moved. The moment was so prolonged that it would have taken but little more to make me doubt if even *I* were in life. I can't express what followed it save by saying that the silence itself—which was indeed in a manner an attestation of my strength—became the element into which I saw the figure disappear; in which I definitely saw it turn, as I might have seen the low wretch to which it had once belonged turn on receipt of an order, and pass, with my eyes on the villainous back that no hunch could have more disfigured, straight down the staircase and into the darkness in which the next bend was lost.

X

I remained awhile at the top of the stair, but with the effect presently of understanding that when my visitor had gone, he had gone: then I returned to my room. The foremost thing I saw there by the light of the candle I had left burning was that Flora's little bed was empty; and on this I caught my breath with all the terror that, five minutes before, I had been able to resist. I dashed at the place in which I had left her lying and over which (for the small silk counterpane and the sheets were disarranged), the white curtains had been deceivingly pulled forward; then my step, to my unutterable relief, produced an answering sound: I perceived an agitation of the window blind, and the child, ducking down, emerged rosily from the other side of it. She stood there in so much of her candor and so little of her nightgown, with her pink bare feet and the golden glow of her curls. She looked intensely grave, and I had never had such a sense of losing an advantage acquired (the thrill of which had just been so prodigious), as on my consciousness that she addressed me with a reproach. "You naughty: where *have* you been?"—instead of challenging her own irregularity I found myself arraigned and explaining. She herself explained, for that matter, with the loveliest, eagerest simplicity. She had known suddenly, as she lay there, that I was out of the room, and had jumped up to see what had become of me. I had dropped, with the joy of her reappearance, back into my chair—feeling then, and then only, a little faint; and she had pattered straight over to me, thrown herself upon my knee, given herself to be held with the flame of the candle full in the wonderful little face that was still flushed with sleep. I remember closing my eyes an instant, yieldingly, consciously, as before the excess of something beautiful that shone out of the blue of her own. "You were looking for me out of the window?" I said. "You thought I might be walking in the grounds?"

"Well, you know, I thought someone was"—she never blanched as she smiled out that at me.

Oh, how I looked at her now! "And did you see anyone?"

"Ah, *no!*" she returned, almost, with the full privilege of childish inconsequence, resentfully, though with a long sweetness in her little drawl of the negative.

At that moment, in the state of my nerves, I absolutely believed she lied; and if I once more closed my eyes it was before the dazzle of the three or four possible ways in which I might take this up. One of these, for a moment, tempted me with such singular intensity that, to withstand it, I must have gripped my little girl with a spasm that, wonderfully, she submitted to without a cry or a sign of fright. Why not break out at her on the spot and have it all over?—give it to her straight in her lovely little lighted face? "You see, you see, you *know* that you do and that you already quite suspect I believe it; therefore why not frankly confess it to me, so that we may at least live with it together and learn perhaps, in the strangeness of our fate, where we are and what it means?" This solicitation dropped, alas, as it came: if I could immediately have succumbed to it I might have spared myself—well, you'll see what. Instead of succumbing I sprang again to my feet, looked at her bed and took a helpless middle way. "Why did you pull the curtain over the place to make me think you were still there?"

Flora luminously considered; after which, with her little divine smile: "Because I don't like to frighten you!"

"But if I had, by your idea, gone out—?"

She absolutely declined to be puzzled; she turned her eyes to the flame of the candle as if the question were as irrelevant, or at any rate as impersonal, as Mrs. Marcet or nine-times-nine. "Oh, but you know," she quite adequately answered, "that you might come back, you dear, and that you *have!*" And after a little, when she had got into bed, I had, for a long time, by almost sitting on her to hold her hand, to prove that I recognized the pertinence of my return.

You may imagine the general complexion, from that moment, of my nights. I repeatedly sat up till I didn't know when; I selected moments when my roommate unmistakably slept, and, stealing out, took noiseless turns in the passage and even pushed as far as to where I had last met Quint. But I never met him there again; and I may as well say at once that I on no other occasion saw him in the house. I just missed, on the staircase, on the other hand, a different adventure. Looking down it from the top I once recognized the presence of a woman seated on one of the lower steps with her back presented to me, her body half-bowed and her head, in an attitude of woe, in her hands. I had been there but an instant, however, when she vanished without looking round at me. I knew, nonetheless, exactly what dreadful face she had to show; and I wondered whether, if instead of being above I had been below, I should have had, for going up, the same nerve I had lately shown Quint. Well, there continued to be plenty of chance for nerve. On the eleventh night after my latest encounter with that gentleman—they were all numbered now—I had an alarm that perilously skirted it and that indeed, from the particular quality of its unexpectedness, proved quite my sharpest shock.

It was precisely the first night during this series that, weary with watching, I had felt that I might again without laxity lay myself down at my old hour. I slept immediately and, as I afterwards knew, till about one o'clock; but when I woke it was to sit straight up, as completely roused as if a hand had shook me. I had left a light burning, but it was now out, and I felt an instant certainty that Flora had extinguished it. This brought me to my feet and straight, in the darkness, to her bed, which I found she had left. A glance at the window enlightened me further, and the striking of a match completed the picture.

The child had again got up—this time blowing out the taper, and had again, for some purpose of observation or response, squeezed in behind the blind and was peering out into the night. That she now saw—as she had not, I had satisfied myself, the previous time—was proved to me by the fact that she was disturbed neither by my reillumination nor by the haste I made to get into slippers and into a wrap. Hidden, protected, absorbed, she evidently rested on the sill—the casement opened forward—and gave herself up. There was a great still moon to help her, and this fact had counted in my quick decision. She was face to face with the apparition we had met at the lake, and could now communicate with it as she had not then been able to do. What I, on my side, had to care for was, without disturbing her, to reach, from the corridor, some other window in the same quarter. I got to the door without her hearing me; I got out of it, closed it and listened, from the other side, for some sound from her. While I stood in the passage I had my eyes on her brother's door, which was but ten steps off and which, indescribably, produced in me a renewal of the strange impulse that I lately spoke of as my temptation. What if I should go straight in and march to *his* window?—what if, by risking to his boyish bewilderment a revelation of my motive, I should throw across the rest of the mystery the long halter of my boldness?

This thought held me sufficiently to make me cross to his threshold and pause again. I preternaturally listened; I figured to myself what might portentously be; I wondered if his bed were also empty and he too were secretly at watch. It was a deep, soundless minute, at the end of which my impulse failed. He was quiet; he might be innocent; the risk was hideous; I turned away. There was a figure in the grounds—a figure prowling for a sight, the visitor with whom Flora was engaged; but it was not the visitor most concerned with my boy. I hesitated afresh, but on other grounds and only a few seconds; then I had made my choice. There were empty rooms at Bly, and it was only a question of choosing the right one. The right one suddenly presented itself to me as the lower one—

though high above the gardens—in the solid corner of the house that I have spoken of as the old tower. This was a large, square chamber, arranged with some state as a bedroom, the extravagant size of which made it so inconvenient that it had not for years, though kept by Mrs. Grose in exemplary order, been occupied. I had often admired it and I knew my way about in it; I had only, after just faltering at the first chill gloom of its disuse, to pass across it and unbolt as quietly as I could one of the shutters. Achieving this transit, I uncovered the glass without a sound and, applying my face to the pane, was able, the darkness without being much less than within, to see that I commanded the right direction. Then I saw something more. The moon made the night extraordinarily penetrable and showed me on the lawn a person, diminished by distance, who stood there motionless and as if fascinated, looking up to where I had appeared—looking, that is, not so much straight at me as at something that was apparently above me. There was clearly another person above me—there was a person on the tower; but the presence on the lawn was not in the least what I had conceived and had confidently hurried to meet. The presence on the lawn—I felt sick as I made it out—was poor little Miles himself.

XI

It was not till late next day that I spoke to Mrs. Grose; the rigor with which I kept my pupils in sight making it often difficult to meet her privately, and the more as we each felt the importance of not provoking—on the part of the servants quite as much as on that of the children—any suspicion of a secret flurry or of a discussion of mysteries. I drew a great security in this particular from her mere smooth aspect. There was nothing in her fresh face to pass on to others my horrible confidences. She believed me, I was sure, absolutely: if she hadn't I don't know what would have become of me, for I couldn't have borne the business alone. But she was a magnificent monument to the blessing of a want of imagination, and if she could see in our little charges nothing but their beauty and amiability, their happiness and cleverness, she had no direct communication with the sources of my trouble. If they had been at all visibly blighted or battered she would doubtless have grown, on tracing it back, haggard enough to match them; as matters stood, however, I could feel her, when she surveyed them with her large white arms folded and the habit of serenity in all her look, thank the Lord's mercy that if they were ruined the pieces would still serve. Flights of fancy gave place, in her mind, to a steady fireside glow, and I had already begun to perceive how, with the development of the conviction that—as time went on without a public accident—our young things could, after all, look out for themselves, she addressed her greatest solicitude to the sad case presented by their instructress. That, for myself, was a sound simplification: I could engage that, to the world, my face should tell no tales, but it would have been, in the conditions, an immense added strain to find myself anxious about hers.

At the hour I now speak of she had joined me, under pressure, on the terrace, where, with the lapse of the season, the afternoon sun was now agreeable; and we sat there together while, before us, at a distance, but within call if we wished, the children strolled to and fro in one of their most manageable moods. They moved slowly, in unison, below us, over the lawn, the boy, as they went, reading aloud from a storybook and passing his arm round his sister to keep her quite in touch. Mrs. Grose watched them with positive placidity; then I caught the suppressed intellectual creak with which she conscientiously turned to take from me a view of the back of the tapestry. I had made her a receptacle of lurid things, but there was an odd recognition of my superiority—my accomplishments and my function—in her patience under my pain. She offered her mind to my disclosures as, had I wished to mix a witch's broth and proposed it with assurance, she would have held out a large clean saucepan. This had become thoroughly her attitude by the time that, in my recital of the events of the night, I reached the point of what Miles had said to me when, after seeing him, at such a monstrous hour, almost on the very spot where he happened now to be, I had gone down to bring him in; choosing then, at the window, with a concentrated need of not alarming the house, rather that method than a signal more resonant. I had left her meanwhile in little doubt of my small hope of representing with success even to her actual sympathy my sense of the real splendor of the little inspiration with which, after I had got him into the house, the boy met my final articulate challenge. As soon as I appeared in the moonlight on the terrace he had come to me as straight as possible; on which I had taken his hand without a word and led him, through the dark spaces, up the staircase where Quint had so hungrily hovered for him, along the lobby where I had listened and trembled, and so to his forsaken room.

Not a sound, on the way, had passed between us, and I had wondered —oh, *how* I had wondered!—if he were groping about in his little mind for something plausible and not too grotesque. It would tax his invention, certainly, and I felt, this time, over his real embarrassment, a curious thrill of triumph. It was a sharp trap for the inscrutable! He couldn't play any longer at innocence; so how the deuce would he get out of it? There beat in me indeed, with the passionate throb of this question, an equal dumb appeal as to how the deuce *I* should. I was confronted at last, as never yet, with all the risk attached even now to sounding my own horrid note. I remember in fact that as we pushed into his little chamber, where the bed had not been slept in at all and the window, uncovered to the moonlight, made the place so clear that there was no need of striking a match—I remember how I suddenly dropped, sank upon the edge of the bed from the force of the idea that he must know how he really, as they say, "had" me. He could do what he liked, with all his cleverness to help him, so long as I should continue to defer to the old tradition of the criminality of those caretakers of the young who minister to superstitions and fears. He "had" me indeed, and in a cleft stick; for who would ever absolve me, who would consent that I should go unhung, if, by the faintest tremor of an overture, I were the first to introduce into our perfect intercourse an element so dire? No, no: it was useless to attempt to convey to Mrs. Grose, just as it is scarcely less so to attempt to suggest here, how, in our short, stiff brush in the dark, he fairly shook me with admiration. I was of course thoroughly kind and merciful; never, never yet had I placed on his little shoulders hands of such tenderness as those with which, while I rested against the bed, I held him there well under fire. I had no alternative but, in form at least, to put it to him.

"You must tell me now—and all the truth. What did you go out for? What were you doing there?"

I can still see his wonderful smile, the whites of his beautiful eyes and the uncovering of his little teeth, shine to me in the dusk. "If I tell you why, will you understand?" My heart, at this, leaped into my mouth. *Would* he tell me why? I found no sound on my lips to press it, and I was aware of replying only with a vague, repeated, grimacing nod. He was gentleness itself, and while I wagged my head at him he stood there more than ever a little fairy prince. It was his brightness indeed that gave me a respite. Would it be so great if he were really going to tell me? "Well," he said at last, "just exactly in order that you should do this."

"Do what?"

"Think me—for a change—*bad!*" I shall never forget the sweetness and gaiety with which he brought out the word, nor how, on top of it, he bent forward and kissed me. It was practically the end of everything. I met his kiss and I had to make, while I folded him for a minute in my arms, the most stupendous effort not to cry. He had given exactly the account of himself that permitted least of my going behind it, and it was only with the effect of confirming my acceptance of it that, as I presently glanced about the room, I could say—"Then you didn't undress at all?"

He fairly glittered in the gloom. "Not at all. I sat up and read."

"And when did you go down?"

"At midnight. When I'm bad I *am* bad!"

"I see, I see—it's charming. But how could you be sure I would know it?"

"Oh, I arranged that with Flora." His answers rang out with a readiness! "She was to get up and look out."

"Which is what she did do." It was I who fell into the trap!

"So she disturbed you, and, to see what she was looking at, you also looked—you saw."

"While you," I concurred, "caught your death in the night air!"

He literally bloomed so from this exploit that he could afford radiantly to assent. "How otherwise should I have been bad enough?" he asked. Then, after another embrace, the incident and our interview closed on my recognition of all the reserves of goodness that, for his joke, he had been able to draw upon.

XII

The particular impression I had received proved in the morning light, I repeat, not quite successfully presentable to Mrs. Grose, though I reinforced it with the mention of still another remark that he had made before we separated. "It all lies in half a dozen words." I said to her, "words that really settle the matter. 'Think, you know, what I *might* do!' He threw that off to show me how good he is. He knows down to the ground what he 'might' do. That's what he gave them a taste of at school."

"Lord, you do change!" cried my friend.

"I don't change—I simply make it out. The four, depend upon it, perpetually meet. If on either of these last nights you had been with either child you would clearly have understood. The more I've watched and waited the more I've felt that if there were nothing else to make it sure it would be made so by the systematic silence of each. *Never,* by a slip of the tongue, have they so much as alluded to either of their old friends, any more than Miles has alluded to his expulsion. Oh yes, we may sit here and look at them, and they may show off to us there to their fill; but even while they pretend to be lost in their fairy tale they're steeped in their vision of the dead restored. He's not reading to her," I declared; "they're talking of *them*—they're talking horrors! I go on, I know, as if I were crazy; and it's a wonder I'm not. What I've seen would have made *you* so; but it has only made me more lucid, made me get hold of still other things."

My lucidity must have seemed awful, but the charming creatures who were victims of it, passing and repassing in their interlocked sweetness, gave my colleague something to hold on by; and I felt how tight she held as, without stirring in the breath of my passion, she covered them still with her eyes. "Of what other things have you got hold?"

"Why, of the very things that have delighted, fascinated and yet, at bottom, as I now so strangely see, mystified and troubled me. Their more than earthly beauty, their absolutely unnatural goodness. It's a game," I went on; "it's a policy and a fraud!"

"On the part of little darlings—?"

"As yet mere lovely babies? Yes, mad as that seems!" The very act of bringing it out really helped me to trace it—follow it all up and piece it all together. "They haven't been good—they've only been absent. It has been easy to live with them, because they're simply leading a life of their own. They're not mine—they're not ours. They're his and they're hers!"

"Quint's and that woman's?"

"Quint's and that woman's. They want to get to them."

Oh, how, at this, poor Mrs. Grose appeared to study them! "But for what?"

"For the love of all the evil that, in those dreadful days, the pair put into them. And to ply them with that evil still, to keep up the work of demons, is what brings the others back."

"Laws!" said my friend under her breath. The exclamation was homely, but it revealed a real acceptance of my further proof of what, in the bad time—for there had been a worse even than this!—must have occurred. There could have been no such justification for me as the plain assent of her experience to whatever depth of depravity I found credible in our brace of scoundrels. It was in obvious submission of memory that she brought out after a moment: "They *were* rascals! But what can they now do?" she pursued.

"Do?" I echoed so loud that Miles and Flora, as they passed at their distance, paused an instant in their walk and looked at us. "Don't they do enough?" I demanded in a lower tone, while the children, having smiled and nodded and kissed hands to us, resumed their exhibition. We were held by it a minute; then I answered: "They can destroy them!" At this my companion did turn, but the inquiry she launched was a silent one, the effect of which was to make me more explicit. "They don't know, as yet, quite how—but they're trying hard. They're seen only across, as it were, and beyond—in strange places and on high places, the top of towers, the roof of houses, the outside of windows, the further edge of pools; but there's a deep design, on either side, to shorten the distance and overcome the obstacle; and the success of the tempters is only a question of time. They've only to keep to their suggestions of danger."

"For the children to come?"

"And perish in the attempt!" Mrs. Grose slowly got up, and I scrupulously added: "Unless, of course, we can prevent!"

Standing there before me while I kept my seat, she visibly turned things over. "Their uncle must do the preventing. He must take them away."

"And who's to make him?"

She had been scanning the distance, but she now dropped on me a foolish face. "You, miss."

"By writing to him that his house is poisoned and his little nephew and niece mad?"

"But if they *are,* miss?"

"And if I am myself, you mean? That's charming news to be sent him by a governess whose prime undertaking was to give him no worry."

Mrs. Grose considered, following the children again. "Yes, he do hate worry. That was the great reason—"

"Why those fiends took him in so long? No doubt, though his indifference must have been awful. As I'm not a fiend, at any rate, I shouldn't take him in."

My companion, after an instant and for all answer, sat down again and grasped my arm. "Make him at any rate come to you."

I stared. "To *me?*" I had a sudden fear of what she might do. " 'Him'?"

"He ought to *be* here—he ought to help."

I quickly rose, and I think I must have shown her a queerer face than ever yet. "You see me asking him for a visit?" No, with her eyes on my face she evidently couldn't. Instead of it even—as a woman reads another—she could see what I myself saw: his derision, his amusement, his contempt for the breakdown of my resignation at being left alone and for the fine machinery I had set in motion to attract his attention to my slighted charms. She didn't know—no one knew—how proud I had been to serve him and to stick to our terms; yet she nonetheless took the measure, I think, of the warning I now gave her. "If you should so lose your head as to appeal to him for me—"

She was really frightened. "Yes, miss?"

"I would leave, on the spot, both him and you."

XIII

It was all very well to join them, but speaking to them proved quite as much as ever an effort beyond my strength—offered, in close quarters, difficulties as insurmountable as before. This situation continued a month, and with new aggravations and particular notes, the note above all, sharper and sharper, of the small ironic consciousness on the part of my pupils. It was not, I am as sure today as I was sure then, my mere infernal imagination: it was absolutely traceable that they were aware of my predicament and that this strange relation made, in a manner, for a long time, the air in which we moved. I don't mean that they had their tongues in their cheeks or did anything vulgar, for that was not one of their dangers: I do mean, on the other hand, that the element of the unnamed and untouched became, between us, greater than any other, and that so much avoidance could not have been so successfully effected without a great deal of tacit arrangement. It was as if, at moments, we were perpetually coming into sight of subjects before which we must stop short, turning suddenly out of alleys that we perceived to be blind, closing with a little bang that made us look at each other—for, like all bangs, it was something louder than we had intended—the doors we had indiscreetly opened. All roads lead to Rome, and there were times when it might have struck us that almost every branch of study or subject of conversation skirted forbidden ground. Forbidden ground was the question of the return of the dead in general and of whatever, in especial, might survive, in memory, of the friends little children had lost. There were days when I could have sworn that one of them had, with a small invisible nudge, said to the other: "She thinks she'll do it this time—but she *won't!*" To "do it" would have been to indulge for instance—and for once in a way—in some direct reference to the lady who had prepared them for my discipline. They had a delightful endless appetite for passages in my own history, to which I had again and again treated them; they were in possession of everything that had ever happened to me, had had, with every circumstance, the story of my smallest adventures and of those of my brothers and sisters and of the cat and the dog at home, as well as many particulars of the eccentric nature of my father, of the furniture and arrangement of our house and of the conversation of the old women of our village. There were things enough, taking one with another, to chatter about, if one went very fast and knew by instinct when to go round. They pulled with an art of their own the strings of my invention and my memory; and nothing else perhaps, when I thought of such occasions afterward, gave me so the suspicion of being watched from under cover. It was in any case over *my* life, *my* past and *my* friends alone that we could take anything like our ease; a state of affairs that led them sometimes without the least pertinence to break out into sociable reminders. I was invited—with no visible connection—to repeat afresh Goody Gosling's celebrated *mot* or to confirm the details already supplied as to the cleverness of the vicarage pony.

It was partly at such junctures as these and partly at quite different ones that, with the turn my matters had now taken, my predicament, as I have called it, grew most sensible. The fact that the days passed for me without another encounter ought, it would have appeared, to have done something towards soothing my nerves. Since the light brush, that second night on the upper landing, of the presence of a woman at the foot of the stair, I had seen nothing, whether in or out of the house, that one had better not have seen. There was many a corner round which I expected to come upon Quint, and many a situation that, in a merely sinister way, would have favored the appearance of Miss Jessel. The summer had turned, the summer had gone; the autumn had dropped upon Bly and had blown out half our lights. The place, with its gray sky and withered garlands, its bared spaces and scattered dead leaves, was like a theater after the performance—all strewn with crumpled playbills. There were exactly states of the air, conditions of sound and of stillness, unspeakable impressions of the *kind* of ministering moment, that brought back to me, long enough to catch it, the feeling of the medium in which, that June evening out-of-doors, I had had my first sight of Quint, and in which, too, at those other instants, I had, after seeing him through the window, looked for him in vain in the circle of shrubbery. I recognized the signs, the portents—I recognized the moment, the spot. But they remained unaccompanied and empty, and I continued unmolested; if unmolested one could call a young woman whose sensibility had, in the most extraordinary fashion, not declined but deepened. I had said in my talk with Mrs. Grose on that horrid scene of Flora's by the lake—and had perplexed her by so saying—that it would from that moment distress me much more to lose my power than to keep it. I had then expressed what was vividly in my mind:

the truth that, whether the children really saw or not—since, that is, it was not yet definitely proved—I greatly preferred, as a safeguard, the fullness of my own exposure. I was ready to know the very worst that was to be known. What I had then had an ugly glimpse of was that my eyes might be sealed just while theirs were most opened. Well, my eyes *were* sealed, it appeared, at present—a consummation for which it seemed blasphemous not to thank God. There was, alas, a difficulty about that: I would have thanked him with all my soul had I not had in a proportionate measure this conviction of the secret of my pupils.

How can I retrace today the strange steps of my obsession? There were times of our being together when I would have been ready to swear that, literally, in my presence, but with my direct sense of it closed, they had visitors who were known and were welcome. Then it was that, had I not been deterred by the very chance that such an injury might prove greater than the injury to be averted, my exaltation would have broken out. "They're here, they're here, you little wretches," I would have cried, "and you can't deny it now!" The little wretches denied it with all the added volume of their sociability and their tenderness, in just the crystal depths of which—like the flash of a fish in a stream—the mockery of their advantage peeped up. The shock, in truth, had sunk into me still deeper than I knew on the night when, looking out to see either Quint or Miss Jessel under the stars, I had beheld the boy over whose rest I watched and who had immediately brought in with him—had straightway, there, turned it on me—the lovely upward look with which, from the battlements above me, the hideous apparition of Quint had played. If it was a question of a scare, my discovery on this occasion had scared me more than any other, and it was in the condition of nerves produced by it that I made my actual inductions. They harassed me so that sometimes, at odd moments, I shut myself up audibly to rehearse—it was at once a fantastic relief and a renewed despair—the manner in which I might come to the point. I approached it from one side and the other while, in my room, I flung myself about, but I always broke down in the monstrous utterance of names. As they died away on my lips I said to myself that I should indeed help them to represent something infamous if, by pronouncing them, I should violate as rare a little case of instinctive delicacy as any schoolroom, probably, had ever known. When I said to myself: "*They* have the manners to be silent, and you, trusted as you are, the baseness to speak!" I felt myself crimson and I covered my face with my hands. After these secret scenes I chattered more than ever, going on volubly enough till one of our prodigious, palpable hushes occurred—I can call them nothing else—the strange, dizzy lift or swim (I try for terms!) into a stillness, a pause of all life, that had nothing to do with the more or less noise that at the moment we might be engaged in making and that I could hear through any deepened exhilaration or quickened recitation or louder strum of the piano. Then it was that the others, the outsiders, were there. Though they were not angels, they "passed," as the French say, causing me, while they stayed, to tremble with the fear of their addressing to their younger victims some yet more infernal message or more vivid image than they had thought good enough for myself.

What it was most impossible to get rid of was the cruel idea that, whatever I had seen, Miles and Flora saw *more*—things terrible and unguessable and that sprang from dreadful passages of intercourse in the past. Such things naturally left on the surface, for the time, a chill which we vociferously denied that we felt; and we had, all three, with repetition, got into such splendid training that we went, each time, almost automatically, to mark the close of the incident, through the very same movements. It was striking of the children, at all events, to kiss me inveterately with a kind of wild irrelevance and never to fail—one or the other—of the precious question that has helped us through many a peril. "When do you think he *will* come? Don't you think we *ought* to write?"—there was nothing like that inquiry, we found by experience, for carrying off an awkwardness. "He" of course was their uncle in Harley Street; and we lived in much profusion of theory that he might at any moment arrive to mingle in our circle. It was impossible to have given less encouragement than he had done to such a doctrine, but if we had not had the doctrine to fall back upon we should have deprived each other of some of our finest exhibitions. He never wrote to them—that may have been selfish, but it was a part of the flattery of his trust of me; for the way in which a man pays his highest tribute to a woman is apt to be but by the more festal celebration of one of the sacred laws of his comfort; and I held that I carried out the spirit of the pledge given not to appeal to him when I let my charges understand that their own letters were but charming literary exercises. They were too beautiful to be posted; I kept them myself; I have them all to this hour. This was a rule indeed which only added to the satiric effect of my being plied with the supposition that he might at any moment be among us. It was exactly as if my charges knew how almost more awkward than anything else that might be for me. There appears to me, moreover, as I look back, no note in all this more extraordinary than the mere fact that, in spite of my tension and of their triumph, I never lost patience with them. Adorable they must in truth have been, I now reflect, that I didn't in these days hate them! Would exasperation, however, if relief had longer been postponed, finally have betrayed me? It little matters, for relief arrived. I call it relief though it was only the relief that a snap brings to a strain or the burst of a thunderstorm to a day of suffocation. It was at least change, and it came with a rush.

XIV

Walking to church a certain Sunday morning, I had little Miles at my side and his sister, in advance of us and at Mrs. Grose's, well in sight. It was a crisp, clear day, the first of its order for some time; the night had brought a touch of frost, and the autumn air, bright and sharp, made the church bells almost gay. It was an odd accident of thought that I should have happened at such a moment to be particularly and very gratefully struck with the obedience of my little charges. Why did they never resent my inexorable, my perpetual society? Something or other had brought nearer home to me that I had all but pinned the boy to my shawl and that, in the way our companions were marshaled before me, I might have appeared to provide against some danger of rebellion. I was like a jailer with an eye to possible surprises and escapes. But all this belonged—I mean their magnificent little surrender—just to the special array of the facts that were most abysmal. Turned out for Sunday by his uncle's tailor, who had had a free hand and a notion of pretty waistcoats and of his grand little air, Miles's whole title to independence, the rights of his sex and situation, were so stamped upon him that if he had suddenly struck for freedom I should have had nothing to say. I was by the strangest of chances wondering how I should meet him when the revolution unmistakably occurred. I call it a revolution because I now see how, with the word he spoke, the curtain rose on the last act of my dreadful drama and the catastrophe was precipitated. "Look here, my dear, you know," he charmingly said, "when in the world, please, am I going back to school?"

Transcribed here the speech sounds harmless enough, particularly as uttered in the sweet, high, casual pipe with which, at all interlocutors, but above all at his eternal governess, he threw off intonations as if he were tossing roses. There was something in them that always made one "catch," and I caught, at any rate, now so effectually that I stopped as short as if one of the trees of the park had fallen across the road. There was something new, on the spot, between us, and he was perfectly aware that I recognized it, though, to enable me to do so, he had no need to look a whit less candid and charming than usual. I could feel in him how he already, from my at first finding nothing to reply, perceived the advantage he had gained. I was so slow to find anything that he had plenty of time, after a minute, to continue with his suggestive but inconclusive smile: "You know, my dear, that for a fellow to be with a lady *always—!*" His "my dear" was constantly on his lips for me, and nothing could have expressed more the exact shade of the sentiment with which I desired to inspire my pupils than its fond familiarity. It was so respectfully easy.

But, oh, how I felt that at present I must pick my own phrases! I remember that, to gain time, I tried to laugh, and I seemed to see in the beautiful face with which he watched me how ugly and queer I looked. "And always with the same lady?" I returned.

He neither blenched nor winked. The whole thing was virtually out between us. "Ah, of course she's a jolly, 'perfect' lady; but, after all, I'm a fellow, don't you see? that's—well, getting on."

I lingered there with him an instant ever so kindly. "Yes, you're getting on." Oh, but I felt helpless!

I have kept to this day the heartbreaking little idea of how he seemed to know that and to play with it. "And you can't say I've not been awfully good, can you?"

I laid my hand on his shoulder, for, though I felt how much better it would have been to walk on, I was not yet quite able. "No, I can't say that, Miles."

"Except just that one night, you know—!"

"That one night?" I couldn't look as straight as he.

"Why, when I went down—went out of the house."

"Oh yes. But I forget what you did it for."

"You forget?"—he spoke with the sweet extravagance of childish reproach. "Why, it was to show you I could!"

"Oh yes, you could."

"And I can again."

I felt that I might, perhaps, after all, succeed in keeping my wits about me. "Certainly. But you won't."

"No, not *that* again. It was nothing."

"It was nothing," I said. "But we must go on."

He resumed our walk with me, passing his hand into my arm. "Then when *am* I going back?"

I wore, in turning it over, my most responsible air. "Were you very happy at school?"

He just considered. "Oh, I'm happy enough anywhere!"

"Well then," I quavered, "if you're just as happy here—!"

"Ah, but that isn't everything! Of course *you* know a lot—"

"But you hint that you know almost as much?" I risked as he paused.

"Not half I want to!" Miles honestly professed. "But it isn't so much that."

"What is it then?"

"Well—I want to see more life."

"I see; I see." We had arrived within sight of the church and of various persons, including several of the household of Bly, on their way to it and clustered about the door to see us go in. I quickened our step; I wanted to get there before the question between us opened up much further; I reflected hungrily that, for more than an hour, he would have to be silent; and I thought with envy of the comparative dusk of the pew and of the almost spiritual help of the hassock on which I might bend my knees. I seemed literally to be running a race with some confusion to which he was about to reduce me, but I felt that he had got in first when, before we had even entered the churchyard, he threw out—"I want my own sort!"

It literally made me bound forward, "There are not many of your own sort, Miles!" I laughed. "Unless perhaps dear little Flora!"

"You really compare me to a baby girl?"

This found me singularly weak. "Don't you, then, *love* our sweet Flora?"

"If I didn't—and you too; if I didn't—!" he repeated as if retreating for a jump, yet leaving his thought so unfinished that, after we had come into the gate, another stop, which he imposed on me by the pressure of his arm, had become inevitable. Mrs. Grose and Flora had passed into the church, the other worshippers had followed, and we were, for the minute, alone among the old, thick graves. We had paused, on the path from the gate, by a low, oblong, tablelike tomb.

"Yes, if you didn't—?"

He looked, while I waited, about at the graves. "Well, you know what!" But he didn't move, and he presently produced something that made me drop straight down on the stone slab, as if suddenly to rest. "Does my uncle think what *you* think?"

I markedly rested. "How do you know what I think?"

"Ah well, of course I don't; for it strikes me you never tell me. But I mean does *he* know?"

"Know what, Miles?"

"Why, the way I'm going on."

I perceived quickly enough that I could make, to this inquiry, no answer that would not involve something of a sacrifice of my employer. Yet it appeared to me that we were all, at Bly, sufficiently sacrificed to make that venial. "I don't think your uncle much cares."

Miles, on this, stood looking at me. "Then don't you think he can be made to?"

"In what way?"

"Why, by his coming down."

"But who'll get him to come down?"

"*I* will!" the boy said with extraordinary brightness and emphasis. He gave me another look charged with that expression and then marched off alone into church.

XV

The business was practically settled from the moment I never followed him. It was a pitiful surrender to agitation, but my being aware of this had somehow no power to restore me. I only sat there on my tomb and read into what my little friend had said to me the fullness of its meaning; by the time I had grasped the whole of which I had also embraced, for absence, the pretext that I was ashamed to offer my pupils and the rest of the congregation such an example of delay. What I said to myself above all was that Miles had got something out of me and that the proof of it, for him, would be just this awkward collapse. He had got out of me that there was something I was much afraid of and that he should probably be able to make use of my fear to gain, for his own purpose, more freedom. My fear was of having to deal with the intolerable question of the grounds of his dismissal from school, for that was really but the question of the horrors gathered behind. That his uncle should arrive to treat with me of these things was a solution that, strictly speaking, I ought now to have desired to bring on; but I could so little face the ugliness and the pain of it that I simply procrastinated and lived from hand to mouth. The boy, to my deep discomposure, was immensely in the right, was in a position to say to me: "Either you clear up with my guardian the mystery of this interruption of my studies, or you cease to expect me to lead with you a life that's so unnatural for a boy." What was so unnatural for the particular boy I was concerned with was this sudden revelation of a consciousness and a plan.

That was what really overcame me, what prevented my going in. I walked round the church, hesitating, hovering; I reflected that I had already, with him, hurt myself beyond repair. Therefore I could patch up nothing, and it was too extreme an effort to squeeze beside him into the pew: he would be so much more sure than ever to pass his arm into mine and make me sit there for an hour in close, silent contact with his commentary on our talk. For the first minute since his arrival I wanted to get away from him. As I paused beneath the high east window and listened to the sounds of worship I was taken with an impulse that might master me, I felt, completely should I give it the least encouragement. I might easily put an end to my predicament by getting away altogether. Here was my chance; there was no one to stop me; I could give the whole thing up—turn my back and retreat. It was only a question of hurrying again, for a few preparations, to the house which the attendance at church of so many of the servants would practically have left unoccupied. No one, in short, could blame me if I should just drive desperately off. What was it to get away if I got away only till dinner? That would be in a couple of hours, at the end of which—I had the acute prevision—my little pupils would play at innocent wonder about my nonappearance in their train. "What *did* you do, you naughty, bad thing? Why in the world, to worry us so—and take our thoughts off too, don't you know?—did you desert us at the very door?" I couldn't meet such questions nor, as they asked them, their false little lovely eyes; yet it was all so exactly what I should have to meet that, as the prospect grew sharp to me, I at last let myself go.

I got, so far as the immediate moment was concerned, away; I came straight out of the churchyard and, thinking hard, retraced my steps through the park. It seemed to me that by the time I reached the house I had made up my mind I would fly. The Sunday stillness both of the approaches and of the interior, in which I met no one, fairly excited me with a sense of opportunity. Were I to get off quickly, this way, I should get off without a scene, without a word. My quickness would have to be remarkable, however, and the question of a conveyance was the great one to settle. Tormented, in the hall, with difficulties and obstacles, I remember sinking down at the foot of the staircase—suddenly collapsing there on the lowest step and then, with a revulsion, recalling that it was exactly where, more than a month before, in the darkness of night and just so bowed with evil things, I had seen the specter of the most horrible of women. At this I was able to straighten myself; I went the rest of the way up; I made, in my bewilderment, for the schoolroom, where there were objects belonging to me that I should have to take. But I opened the door to find again, in a flash, my eyes unsealed. In the presence of what I saw I reeled straight back upon my resistance.

Seated at my own table in the clear noonday light I saw a person whom, without my previous experience, I should have taken at the first blush for some housemaid who might have stayed at home to look after the place and who, availing herself of rare relief from observation and of the schoolroom table and my pens, ink and paper, had applied herself to the considerable effort of a letter to her sweetheart. There was an effort in the way that, while her arms rested on the table, her hands, with evident weariness, supported her head; but at the moment I took this in I had already become aware that, in spite of my entrance, her attitude strangely persisted. Then it was—with the very act of its announcing itself—that her identity flared up in a change of posture. She rose, not as if she had heard me, but with an indescribable grand melancholy of indifference and detachment, and, within a dozen feet of me, stood there as my vile predecessor. Dishonored and tragic, she was all before me; but even as I fixed and, for memory, secured it, the awful image passed away. Dark as midnight in her black dress, her haggard beauty and her unutterable woe, she had looked at me long enough to appear to say that her right to sit at my table was as good as mine to sit at hers. While these instants lasted indeed I had the extraordinary chill of a feeling that it was I who was the intruder. It was as a wild protest against it that, actually addressing her —"You terrible, miserable woman!"—I heard myself break into a sound that, by the open door, rang through the long passage and the empty house. She looked at me as if she heard me, but I had recovered myself and cleared the air. There was nothing in the room the next minute but the sunshine and a sense that I must stay.

XVI

I had so perfectly expected that the return of my pupils would be marked by a demonstration that I was freshly upset at having to take into account that they were dumb about my absence. Instead of gaily denouncing and caressing me they made no allusion to my having failed them, and I was left, for the time, on perceiving that she too said nothing, to study Mrs.

Grose's odd face. I did this to such purpose that I made sure they had in some way bribed her to silence; a silence that, however, I would engage to break down on the first private opportunity. This opportunity came before tea: I secured five minutes with her in the housekeeper's room, where, in the twilight, amid a smell of lately baked bread, but with the place all swept and garnished, I found her sitting in pained placidity before the fire. So I see her still, so I see her best: facing the flame from her straight chair in the dusky, shining room, a large clean image of the "put away"—of drawers closed and locked and rest without a remedy.

"Oh yes, they asked me to say nothing; and to please them—so long as they were there—of course I promised. But what had happened to you?"

"I only went with you for the walk," I said. "I had then to come back to meet a friend."

She showed her surprise. "A friend—*you?*"

"Oh yes, I have a couple!" I laughed. "But did the children give you a reason?"

"For not alluding to your leaving us? Yes; they said you would like it better. Do you like it better?"

My face had made her rueful. "No, I like it worse!" But after an instant I added: "Did they say why I should like it better?"

"No; Master Miles only said 'We must do nothing but what she likes!' "

"I wish indeed he would! And what did Flora say?"

"Miss Flora was too sweet. She said 'Oh, of course, of course!'—and I said the same."

I thought a moment. "You were too sweet too—I can hear you all. But nonetheless, between Miles and me, it's now all out."

"All out?" My companion stared. "But what, miss?"

"Everything. It doesn't matter. I've made up my mind. I came home, my dear," I went on, "for a talk with Miss Jessel."

I had by this time formed the habit of having Mrs. Grose literally well in hand in advance of my sounding that note; so that even now, as she bravely blinked under the signal of my word, I could keep her comparatively firm. "A talk! Do you mean she spoke?"

"It came to that. I found her, on my return, in the schoolroom."

"And what did she say?" I can hear the good woman still, and the candor of her stupefaction.

"That she suffers the torments—!"

It was this, of a truth, that made her, as she filled out my picture, gape. "Do you mean," she faltered, "—of the lost?"

"Of the lost. Of the damned. And that's why, to share them—" I faltered myself with the horror of it.

But my companion, with less imagination, kept me up. "To share them—?"

"She wants Flora." Mrs. Grose might, as I gave it to her, fairly have fallen away from me had I not been prepared. I still held her there, to show I was. "As I've told you, however, it doesn't matter."

"Because you've made up your mind? But to what?"

"To everything."

"And what do you call 'everything'?"

"Why, sending for their uncle."

"Oh miss, in pity do," my friend broke out.

"Ah, but I will, I *will!* I see it's the only way. What's 'out,' as I told you, with Miles is that if he thinks I'm afraid to—and has ideas of what he gains by that—he shall see he's mistaken. Yes, yes; his uncle shall have it here from me on the spot (and before the boy himself if necessary), that if I'm to be reproached with having done nothing again about more school—"

"Yes, miss—" my companion pressed me.

"Well, there's that awful reason."

There were now clearly so many of these for my poor colleague that she was excusable for being vague. "But—a—which?"

"Why, the letter from his old place."

"You'll show it to the master?"

"I ought to have done so on the instant."

"Oh no!" said Mrs. Grose with decision.

"I'll put it before him," I went on inexorably, "that I can't undertake to work the question on behalf of a child who has been expelled—"

"For we've never in the least known what!" Mrs. Grose declared.

"For wickedness. For what else—when he's so clever and beautiful and perfect? Is he stupid? Is he untidy? Is he infirm? Is he ill natured? He's exquisite—so it can be only *that;* and that would open up the whole thing. After all," I said, "it's their uncle's fault. If he left here such people—!"

"He didn't really in the least know them. The fault's mine." She had turned quite pale.

"Well, you shan't suffer," I answered.

"The children shan't!" she emphatically returned.

I was silent awhile; we looked at each other. "Then what am I to tell him?"

"You needn't tell him anything. *I'll* tell him."

I measured this. "Do you mean you'll write—?" Remembering she couldn't, I caught myself up. "How do you communicate?"

"I tell the bailiff. *He* writes."

"And should you like him to write our story?"

My question had a sarcastic force that I had not fully intended, and it made her, after a moment, inconsequently break down. The tears were again in her eyes. "Ah, miss, *you* write!"

"Well—tonight," I at last answered; and on this we separated.

XVII

I went so far, in the evening, as to make a beginning. The weather had changed back, a great wind was abroad, and beneath the lamp, in my room, with Flora at peace beside me, I sat for a long time before a blank sheet of paper and listened to the lash of the rain and the batter of the gusts. Finally I went out, taking a candle; I crossed the passage and listened a minute at Miles's door. What, under my endless obsession, I had been impelled to listen for was some betrayal of his not being at rest, and I presently caught one, but not in the form I had expected. His voice tinkled out. "I say, you there—come in." It was a gaiety in the gloom!

I went in with my light and found him, in bed, very wide awake, but very much at his ease. "Well, what are *you* up to?" he asked with a grace of sociability in which it occurred to me that Mrs. Grose, had she been present, might have looked in vain for proof that anything was "out."

I stood over him with my candle. "How did you know I was there?"

"Why, of course I heard you. Did you fancy you made no noise? You're like a troop of cavalry!" he beautifully laughed.

"Then you weren't asleep?"

"Not much! I lie awake and think."

I had put my candle, designedly, a short way off, and then, as he held out his friendly old hand to me, had sat down on the edge of his bed. "What is it," I asked, "that you think of?"

"What in the world, my dear, but *you?*"

"Ah, the pride I take in your appreciation doesn't insist on that! I had so far rather you slept."

"Well, I think also, you know, of this queer business of ours."

I marked the coolness of his firm little hand. "Of what queer business, Miles?"

"Why, the way you bring me up. And all the rest!"

I fairly held my breath a minute, and even from my glimmering taper there was light enough to show how he smiled up at me from his pillow. "What do you mean by all the rest?"

"Oh, you know, you know!"

I could say nothing for a minute, though I felt, as I held his hand and our eyes continued to meet, that my silence had all the air of admitting his charge and that nothing in the whole world of reality was perhaps at that moment so fabulous as our actual relation. "Certainly you shall go back to school," I said, "if it be that that troubles you. But not to the old place—we must find another, a better. How could I know it did trouble you, this question, when you never told me so, never spoke of it at all?" His clear, listening face, framed in its smooth whiteness, made him for the minute as appealing as some wistful patient in a children's hospital; and I would have given, as the resemblance came to me, all I possessed on earth really to be the nurse or the sister of charity who might have helped to cure him. Well, even as it was, I perhaps might help! "Do you know you've never said a word to me about your school—I mean the old one; never mentioned it in any way?"

He seemed to wonder; he smiled with the same loveliness. But he clearly gained time; he waited, he called for guidance. "Haven't I?" It wasn't for *me* to help him—it was for the thing I had met!

Something in his tone and the expression of his face, as I got this from him, set my heart aching with such a pang as it had never yet known; so unutterably touching was it to see his little brain puzzled and his little resources taxed to play, under the spell laid on him, a part of innocence and consistency. "No, never—from the hour you came back. You've never mentioned to me one of your masters, one of your comrades, nor the least little thing that ever happened to you at school. Never, little Miles—no never—have you given me an inkling of anything that *may* have happened there. Therefore you can fancy how much I'm in the dark. Until you came out, that way, this morning, you had, since the first hour I saw you, scarce even made a reference to anything in your previous life. You seemed so perfectly to accept the present." It was extraordinary how my absolute conviction of his secret precocity (or whatever I might call the poison of an influence that I dared but half to phrase), made him, in spite of the faint breath of his inward trouble, appear as accessible as an older person

—imposed him almost as an intellectual equal. "I thought you wanted to go on as you are."

It struck me that at this he just faintly colored. He gave, at any rate, like a convalescent slightly fatigued, a languid shake of his head. "I don't —I don't. I want to get away."

"You're tired of Bly?"

"Oh no, I like Bly."

"Well, then—?"

"Oh, *you* know what a boy wants!"

I felt that I didn't know so well as Miles, and I took temporary refuge. "You want to go to your uncle?"

Again, at this, with his sweet ironic face, he made a movement on the pillow. "Ah, you can't get off with that!"

I was silent a little, and it was I, now, I think, who changed color. "My dear, I don't want to get off!"

"You can't, even if you do. You can't, you can't!"—he lay beautifully staring. "My uncle must come down, and you must completely settle things."

"If we do," I returned with some spirit, "you may be sure it will be to take you quite away."

"Well, don't you understand that that's exactly what I'm working for? You'll have to tell him—about the way you've let it all drop: you'll have to tell him a tremendous lot!"

The exultation with which he uttered this helped me somehow, for the instant, to meet him rather more. "And how much will *you,* Miles, have to tell him? There are things he'll ask you!"

He turned it over. "Very likely. But what things?"

"The things you've never told me. To make up his mind what to do with you. He can't send you back—"

"Oh, I don't want to go back!" he broke in. "I want a new field."

He said it with admirable serenity, with positive unimpeachable gaiety; and doubtless it was that very note that most evoked for me the poignancy, the unnatural childish tragedy, of his probable reappearance at the end of three months with all this bravado and still more dishonor. It overwhelmed me now that I should never be able to bear that, and it made me let myself go. I threw myself upon him and in the tenderness of my pity I embraced him. "Dear little Miles, dear little Miles—!"

My face was close to his, and he let me kiss him, simply taking it with indulgent good humor. "Well, old lady?"

"Is there nothing—nothing at all that you want to tell me?"

He turned off a little, facing round towards the wall and holding up his hand to look at as one had seen sick children look. "I've told you—I told you this morning."

Oh, I was sorry for him! "That you just want me not to worry you?"

He looked around at me now, as if in recognition of my understanding him; then ever so gently, "To let me alone," he replied.

There was even a singular little dignity in it, something that made me release him, yet, when I had slowly risen, linger beside him. God knows I never wished to harass him, but I felt that merely, at this, to turn my back on him was to abandon or, to put it more truly, to lose him. "I've just begun a letter to your uncle," I said.

"Well then, finish it!"

I waited a minute. "What happened before?"

He gazed up at me again. "Before what?"

"Before you came back. And before you went away."

For some time he was silent, but he continued to meet my eyes. "What happened?"

It made me, the sound of the words, in which it seemed to me that I caught for the very first time a small faint quaver of consenting consciousness—it made me drop on my knees beside the bed and seize once more the chance of possessing him. "Dear little Miles, dear little Miles, if you *knew* how I want to help you! It's only that, it's nothing but that, and I'd rather die than give you a pain or do you a wrong—I'd rather die than hurt a hair of you. Dear little Miles"—oh, I brought it out now even if I *should* go too far—"I just want you to help me to save you!" But I knew in a moment after this that I had gone too far. The answer to my appeal was instantaneous, but it came in the form of an extraordinary blast and chill, a gust of frozen air and a shake of the room as great as if, in the wild wind, the casement had crashed in. The boy gave a loud, high shriek which, lost in the rest of the shock of sound, might have seemed, indistinctly, though I was so close to him, a note either of jubilation or of terror. I jumped to my feet again and was conscious of darkness. So for a moment we remained, while I stared about me and saw that the drawn curtains were unstirred and the window tight. "Why, the candle's out!" I then cried.

"It was I who blew it, dear!" said Miles.

XVIII

The next day, after lessons, Mrs. Grose found a moment to say to me quietly: "Have you written, miss?"

"Yes—I've written." But I didn't add—for the hour—that my letter, sealed and directed, was still in my pocket. There would be time enough to send it before the messenger should go to the village. Meanwhile there had been, on the part of my pupils, no more brilliant, more exemplary morning. It was exactly as if they had both had at heart to gloss over any recent little friction. They performed the dizziest feats of arithmetic, soaring quite out of *my* feeble range, and perpetrated, in higher spirits than ever, geographical and historical jokes. It was conspicuous of course in Miles in particular that he appeared to wish to show how easily he could let me down. This child, to my memory, really lives in a setting of beauty and misery that no words can translate; there was a distinction all his own in every impulse he revealed; never was a small natural creature, to the uninitiated eye all frankness and freedom, a more ingenious, a more extraordinary little gentleman. I had perpetually to guard against the wonder of contemplation into which my initiated view betrayed me; to check the irrelevant gaze and discouraged sigh in which I constantly both attacked and renounced the enigma of what such a little gentleman could have done that deserved a penalty. Say that, by the dark prodigy I knew, the imagination of all evil *had* been opened up to him: all the justice within me ached for the proof that it could ever have flowered into an act.

He had never, at any rate, been such a little gentleman as when, after our early dinner on this dreadful day, he came round to me and asked if I shouldn't like him, for half an hour, to play to me. David playing to Saul could never have shown a finer sense of the occasion. It was literally a charming exhibition of tact, of magnanimity, and quite tantamount to his saying outright: "The true knights we love to read about never push an advantage too far. I know what you mean now: you mean that—to be let alone yourself and not followed up—you'll cease to worry and spy upon me, won't keep me so close to you, will let me go and come. Well, I 'come,' you see—but I don't go! There'll be plenty of time for that. I do really delight in your society, and I only want to show you that I contended for a principle." It may be imagined whether I resisted this appeal or failed to accompany him again, hand in hand, to the schoolroom. He sat down at the old piano and played as he had never played; and if there are those who think he had better have been kicking a football I can only say that I wholly agree with them. For at the end of a time that under his influence I had quite ceased to measure I started up with a strange sense of having literally slept at my post. It was after luncheon, and by the schoolroom fire, and yet I hadn't really, in the least, slept: I had only done something much worse—I had forgotten. Where, all this time, was Flora? When I put the question to Miles he played on a minute before answering, and then could only say: "Why, my dear, how do *I* know?" —breaking moreover into a happy laugh which, immediately after, as if it were a vocal accompaniment, he prolonged into incoherent, extravagant song.

I went straight to my room, but his sister was not there; then, before going downstairs, I looked into several others. As she was nowhere about she would surely be with Mrs. Grose, whom, in the comfort of that theory, I accordingly proceeded in quest of. I found her where I had found her the evening before, but she met my quick challenge with blank, scared ignorance. She had only supposed that, after the repast, I had carried off both the children; as to which she was quite in her right, for it was the very first time I had allowed the little girl out of my sight without some special provision. Of course now indeed she might be with the maids, so that the immediate thing was to look for her without an air of alarm. This we promptly arranged between us; but when, ten minutes later and in pursuance of our arrangement, we met in the hall, it was only to report on either side that after guarded inquiries we had altogether failed to trace her. For a minute there, apart from observation, we exchanged mute alarms, and I could feel with what high interest my friend returned me all those I had from the first given her.

"She'll be above," she presently said—"in one of the rooms you haven't searched."

"No; she's at a distance." I had made up my mind. "She has gone out."

Mrs. Grose stared. "Without a hat?"

I naturally also looked volumes. "Isn't that woman always without one?"

"She's with *her?*"

"She's with *her!*" I declared. "We must find them."

My hand was on my friend's arm, but she failed for the moment, confronted with such an account of the matter, to respond to my pressure. She communed, on the contrary, on the spot, with her uneasiness. "And where's Master Miles?"

"Oh, *he's* with Quint. They're in the schoolroom."

"Lord, miss!" My view, I was myself aware—and therefore I suppose my tone—had never yet reached so calm an assurance.

"The trick's played," I went on; "they've successfully worked their plan. He found the most divine little way to keep me quiet while she went off."

" 'Divine'?" Mrs. Grose bewilderedly echoed.

"Infernal, then!" I almost cheerfully rejoined. "He has provided for himself as well. But come!"

She had helplessly gloomed at the upper regions. "You leave him—?"

"So long with Quint? Yes—I don't mind that now."

She always ended, at these moments, by getting possession of my hand, and in this manner she could at present still stay me. But after gasping an instant at my sudden resignation, "Because of your letter?" she eagerly brought out.

I quickly, by way of answer, felt for my letter, drew it forth, held it up, and then, freeing myself, went and laid it on the great hall table. "Luke will take it," I said as I came back. I reached the house door and opened it; I was already on the steps.

My companion still demurred: the storm of the night and the early morning had dropped, but the afternoon was damp and gray. I came down to the drive while she stood in the doorway. "You go with nothing on?"

"What do I care when the child has nothing? I can't wait to dress," I cried, "and if you must do so I leave you. Try meanwhile, yourself, upstairs."

"With *them?*" Oh, on this, the poor woman promptly joined me!

XIX

We went straight to the lake, as it was called at Bly, and I daresay rightly called, though I reflect that it may in fact have been a sheet of water less remarkable than it appeared to my untraveled eyes. My acquaintance with sheets of water was small, and the pool of Bly, at all events on the few occasions of my consenting, under the protection of my pupils, to affront its surface in the old flat-bottomed boat moored there for our use, had impressed me both with its extent and its agitation. The usual place of embarkation was half a mile from the house, but I had an intimate conviction that, wherever Flora might be, she was not near home. She had not given me the slip for any small adventure, and, since the day of the very great one that I had shared with her by the pond, I had been aware, in our walks, of the quarter to which she most inclined. This was why I had now given to Mrs. Grose's steps so marked a direction—a direction that made her, when she perceived it, oppose a resistance that showed me she was freshly mystified. "You're going to the water, miss?—you think she's *in—?*"

"She may be, though the depth is, I believe, nowhere very great. But what I judge most likely is that she's on the spot from which, the other day, we saw together when I told you."

"When she pretended not to see—?"

"With that astounding self-possession! I've always been sure she wanted to go back alone. And now her brother has managed it for her."

Mrs. Grose still stood where she had stopped. "You suppose they really *talk* of them?"

I could meet this with a confidence! "They say things that, if we heard them, would simply appall us."

"And if she *is* there—?"

"Yes?"

"Then Miss Jessel is?"

"Beyond a doubt. You shall see."

"Oh, thank you!" my friend cried, planted so firm that, taking it in, I went straight on without her. By the time I reached the pool, however, she was close behind me, and I knew that, whatever, to her apprehension, might befall me, the exposure of my society struck her as her least danger. She exhaled a moan of relief as we at last came in sight of the greater part of the water without a sight of the child. There was no trace of Flora on that nearer side of the bank where my observation of her had been most startling, and none on the opposite edge, where, save for a margin of some twenty yards, a thick copse came down to the water. The pond, oblong in shape, had a width so scant compared to its length that, with its ends out of view, it might have been taken for a scant river. We looked at the empty expanse, and then I felt the suggestion of my friend's eyes. I knew what she meant and I replied with a negative headshake.

"No, no; wait! She has taken the boat."

My companion stared at the vacant mooring-place and then again across the lake. "Then where is it?"

"Our not seeing it is the strongest of proofs. She has used it to go over, and then has managed to hide it."

"All alone—that child?"

"She's not alone, and at such times she's not a child: she's an old, old woman." I scanned all the visible shore while Mrs. Grose took again, into the queer element I offered her, one of her plunges of submission; then I pointed out that the boat might perfectly be in a small refuge formed by one of the recesses of the pool, an indentation masked, for the hither side, by a projection of the bank and by a clump of trees growing close to the water.

"But if the boat's there, where on earth's *she?*" my colleague anxiously asked.

"That's exactly what we must learn." And I started to walk further.

"By going all the way round?"

"Certainly, far as it is. It will take us but ten minutes, but it's far enough to have made the child prefer not to walk. She went straight over."

"Laws!" cried my friend again; the chain of my logic was ever too much for her. It dragged her at my heels even now, and when we had got halfway round—a devious, tiresome process, on ground much broken and by a path choked with overgrowth—I paused to give her breath. I sustained her with a grateful arm, assuring her that she might hugely help me; and this started us afresh, so that in the course of but few minutes more we reached a point from which we found the boat to be where I had supposed it. It had been intentionally left as much as possible out of sight and was tied to one of the stakes of a fence that came, just there, down to the brink and that had been an assistance to disembarking. I recognized, as I looked at the pair of short, thick oars, quite safely drawn up, the prodigious character of the feat for a little girl; but I had lived, by this time, too long among wonders and had panted to too many livelier measures. There was a gate in the fence, through which we passed, and that brought us, after a trifling interval, more into the open. Then "There she is!" we both exclaimed at once.

Flora, a short way off, stood before us on the grass and smiled as if her performance was now complete. The next thing she did, however, was to stoop straight down and pluck—quite as if it were all she was there for—a big, ugly spray of withered fern. I instantly became sure she had just come out of the copse. She waited for us, not herself taking a step, and I was conscious of the rare solemnity with which we presently approached her. She smiled and smiled, and we met; but it was all done in a silence by this time flagrantly ominous. Mrs. Grose was the first to break the spell: she threw herself on her knees and, drawing the child to her breast, clasped in a long embrace the little tender, yielding body. While this dumb convulsion lasted I could only watch it—which I did the more intently when I saw Flora's face peep at me over our companion's shoulder. It was serious now—the flicker had left it; but, it strengthened the pang with which I at that moment envied Mrs. Grose the simplicity of *her* relation. Still, all this while, nothing more passed between us save that Flora had let her foolish fern again drop to the ground. What she and I had virtually said to each other was that pretexts were useless now. When Mrs. Grose finally got up she kept the child's hand, so that the two were still before me; and the singular reticence of our communion was even more marked in the frank look she launched me. "I'll be hanged," it said, "if *I'll* speak!"

It was Flora who, gazing all over me in candid wonder, was the first. She was struck with our bareheaded aspect. "Why, where are your things?"

"Where yours are, my dear!" I promptly returned.

She had already got back her gaiety and appeared to take this as an answer quite sufficient. "And where's Miles?" she went on.

There was something in the small valor of it that quite finished me: these three words from her were, in a flash like the glitter of a drawn blade, the jostle of the cup that my hand, for weeks and weeks, had held high and full to the brim and that now, even before speaking, I felt overflow in a deluge. "I'll tell you if you'll tell *me*—" I heard myself say, then heard the tremor in which it broke.

"Well, what?"

Mrs. Grose's suspense blazed at me, but it was too late now, and I brought the thing out handsomely. "Where, my pet, is Miss Jessel?"

XX

Just as in the churchyard with Miles, the whole thing was upon us. Much as I had made of the fact that this name had never once, between us, been sounded, the quick, smitten glare with which the child's face now received it fairly likened my breach of the silence to the smash of a pane of glass. It added to the interposing cry, as if to stay the blow, that Mrs. Grose, at the same instant, uttered over my violence—the shriek of a creature scared, or rather wounded, which, in turn, within a few seconds, was completed by a gasp of my own. I seized my colleague's arm. "She's there, she's there!"

Miss Jessel stood before us on the opposite bank exactly as she had stood the other time, and I remember, strangely, as the first feeling now produced in me, my thrill of joy at having brought on a proof. She was there, and I was justified; she was there, and I was neither cruel nor mad. She was there for poor scared Mrs. Grose, but she was there most for Flora; and no moment of my monstrous time was perhaps so extraordinary as that in which I consciously threw out to her, with the sense that—pale and ravenous demon as she was, she would catch and understand it—an inarticulate message of gratitude. She rose erect on the spot my friend and I had lately quitted, and there was not, in all the long reach of her desire, an inch of her evil that fell short. This first vividness of vision and emotion were things of a few seconds, during which Mrs. Grose's dazed blink across to where pointed struck me as a sovereign sign that she too at last saw, just as it carried my own eyes precipitately to the child. The revelation then of the manner in which Flora was affected startled me, in truth, far more than it would have done to find her also merely agitated, for direct dismay was of course not what I had expected. Prepared and on our guard as our pursuit had actually made her, she would repress every betrayal; and I was therefore shaken, on the spot, by my first glimpse of the particular one for which I had not allowed. To see her, without a convulsion of her small pink face, not even feign to glance in the direction of the prodigy I announced, but only, instead of that, turn at *me* an expression of hard, still gravity, an expression absolutely new and unprecedented and that appeared to read and accuse and judge me—this was a stroke that somehow converted the little girl herself into the very presence that could make me quail. I quailed even though my certitude that she thoroughly saw was never greater than at that instant, and in the immediate need to defend myself I called it passionately to witness. "She's there, you little unhappy thing—there, there, *there,* and you see her as well as you see me!" I had said shortly before to Mrs. Grose that she was not at these times a child, but an old, old woman, and that description of her could not have been more strikingly confirmed than in the way in which, for all answer to this, she simply showed me, without a concession, an admission, of her eyes, a countenance of deeper and deeper, of indeed suddenly quite fixed reprobation. I was by this time—if I can put the whole thing at all together—more appalled at what I may properly call her manner than at anything else, though it was simultaneously with this that I became aware of having Mrs. Grose also, and very formidably, to reckon with. My elder companion, the next moment, at any rate, blotted out everything but her own flushed face and her loud, shocked protest, a burst of high disapproval. "What a dreadful turn, to be sure, miss! Where on earth do you see anything?"

I could only grasp her more quickly yet, for even while she spoke the hideous plain presence stood undimmed and undaunted. It had already lasted a minute, and it lasted while I continued, seizing my colleague, quite thrusting her at it and presenting her to it, to insist with my pointing hand. "You don't see her exactly as *we* see?—you mean to say you don't now—*now?* She's as big as a blazing fire! Only look, dearest woman, *look—!*" She looked, even as I did, and gave me, with her deep groan of negation, repulsion, compassion—the mixture with her pity of her relief at her exemption—a sense, touching to me even then, that she would have backed me up if she could. I might well have needed that, for with this hard blow of the proof that her eyes were hopelessly sealed I felt my own situation horribly crumble, I felt—I saw—my livid predecessor press, from her position, on my defeat, and I was conscious, more than all, of what I should have from this instant to deal with in the astounding little attitude of Flora. Into this attitude Mrs. Grose immediately and violently entered, breaking, even while there pierced through my sense of ruin a prodigious private triumph, into breathless reassurance.

"She isn't there, little lady, and nobody's there—and you never see nothing, my sweet! How can poor Miss Jessel—when poor Miss Jessel's dead and buried? *We* know, don't we, love?"—and she appealed, blundering in, to the child. "It's all a mere mistake and a worry and a joke—and we'll go home as fast as we can!"

Our companion, on this, had responded with a strange, quick primness of propriety, and they were again, with Mrs. Grose on her feet, united, as it were, in pained opposition to me. Flora continued to fix me with her small mask of reprobation, and even at that minute I prayed God to forgive me for seeming to see that, as she stood there holding tight to our friend's dress, her incomparable childish beauty had suddenly failed, had quite vanished. I've said it already—she was literally, she was hideously hard; she had turned common and almost ugly. "I don't know what you mean. I see nobody. I see nothing. I never *have.* I think you're cruel. I don't like you!" Then, after this deliverance, which might have been that of a vulgarly pert little girl in the street, she hugged Mrs. Grose more closely and buried in her skirts the dreadful little face. In this position she produced an almost furious wail. "Take me away, take me away—oh, take me away from *her!*"

"From *me?*" I panted.

"From *you*—from you!" she cried.

Even Mrs. Grose looked across at me dismayed; while I had nothing to do but communicate again with the figure that, on the opposite bank, without a movement, as rigidly still as if catching, beyond the interval, our voices, was as vividly there for my disaster as it was not there for my service. The wretched child had spoken exactly as if she had got from some outside source each of her stabbing little words, and I could therefore, in the full despair of all I had to accept, but sadly shake my head at her. "If I had ever doubted, all my doubt would at present have gone. I've been living with the miserable truth, and now it has only too much closed round me. Of course I've lost you: I've interfered, and you've seen —under *her* dictation"—with which I faced, over the pool again, our infernal witness—"the easy and perfect way to meet it. I've done my best, but I've lost you. Goodbye." For Mrs. Grose I had an imperative, an almost frantic "Go, go!" before which, in infinite distress, but mutely possessed of the little girl and clearly convinced, in spite of her blindness, that something awful had occurred and some collapse engulfed us, she retreated, by the way we had come, as fast as she could move.

Of what first happened when I was felt alone I had no subsequent memory. I only knew that at the end of, I suppose, a quarter of an hour, an odorous dampness and roughness, chilling and piercing my trouble, had made me understand that I must have thrown myself, on my face, on the ground and given way to a wildness of grief. I must have lain there long and cried and sobbed, for when I raised my head the day was almost done. I got up and looked a moment, through the twilight, at the gray pool and its blank, haunted edge, and then I took, back to the house, my dreary and difficult course. When I reached the gate in the fence the boat, to my surprise, was gone, so that I had a fresh reflection to make on Flora's extraordinary command of the situation. She passed that night, by the most tacit, and I should add, were not the word so grotesque a false note, the happiest of arrangements, with Mrs. Grose. I saw neither of them on my return, but, on the other hand, as by an ambiguous compensation, I saw a great deal of Miles. I saw—I can use no other phrase—so much of him that it was as if it were more than it had ever been. No evening I had passed at Bly had the portentous quality of this one; in spite of which —and in spite also of the deeper depths of consternation that had opened beneath my feet—there was literally, in the ebbing actual, an extraordinarily sweet sadness. On reaching the house I had never so much as looked for the boy; I had simply gone straight to my room to change what I was wearing and to take in, at a glance, much material testimony to Flora's rupture. Her little belongings had all been removed. When later, by the schoolroom fire, I was served with tea by the usual maid, I indulged, on the article of my other pupil, in no inquiry whatever. He had his freedom now—he might have it to the end! Well, he did have it; and it consisted—in part at least—of his coming in at about eight o'clock and sitting down with me in silence. On the removal of the tea things I had blown out the candles and drawn my chair closer: I was conscious of a mortal coldness and felt as if I should never again be warm. So, when he appeared, I was sitting in the glow with my thoughts. He paused a moment by the door as if to look at me; then—as if to share them—came to the other side of the hearth and sank into a chair. We sat there in absolute stillness; yet he wanted, I felt, to be with me.

XXI

Before a new day, in my room, had fully broken, my eyes opened to Mrs. Grose, who had come to my bedside with worse news. Flora was so markedly feverish that an illness was perhaps at hand; she had passed a night of extreme unrest, a night agitated above all by fears that had for their subject not in the least her former, but wholly her present governess. It was not against the possible reentrance of Miss Jessel on the scene that she protested—it was conspicuously and passionately against mine. I was promptly on my feet of course, and with an immense deal to ask; the more that my friend had discernibly now girded her loins to meet me once more. This I felt as soon as I had put to her the question of her sense of the child's sincerity as against my own. "She persists in denying to you that she saw, or has ever seen, anything?"

My visitor's trouble, truly, was great. "Ah, miss, it isn't a matter on which I can push her! Yet it isn't either, I must say, as if I much needed to. It has made her, every inch of her, quite old."

"Oh, I see her perfectly from here. She resents, for all the world like some high little personage, the imputation on her truthfulness and, as it were, her respectability. 'Miss Jessel indeed—*she!*' Ah, she's 'respectable,' the chit! The impression she gave me there yesterday was, I assure you, the very strangest of all; it was quite beyond any of the others. I *did* put my foot in it! She'll never speak to me again."

Hideous and obscure as it all was, it held Mrs. Grose briefly silent; then she granted my point with a frankness which, I made sure, had more behind it. "I think indeed, miss, she never will. She do have a grand manner about it!"

"And that manner"—I summed it up—"is practically what's the matter with her now."

Oh, that manner, I could see in my visitor's face, and not a little else besides! "She asks me every three minutes if I think you're coming in."

"I see—I see." I too, on my side, had so much more than worked it out. "Has she said to you since yesterday—except to repudiate her familiarity with anything so dreadful—a single other word about Miss Jessel?"

"Not one, miss. And of course you know," my friend added, "I took it from her, by the lake that, just then and there at least, there *was* nobody."

"Rather! And, naturally, you take it from her still."

"I don't contradict her. What else can I do?"

"Nothing in the world! You've the cleverest little person to deal with. They've made them—their two friends, I mean—still cleverer even than nature did; for it was wondrous material to play on! Flora has now her grievance, and she'll work it to the end."

"Yes, miss; but to *what* end?"

"Why, that of dealing with me to her uncle. She'll make me out to him the lowest creature—!"

I winced at the fair show of the scene in Mrs. Grose's face; she looked for a minute as if she sharply saw them together. "And him who thinks so well of you!"

"He has an odd way—it comes over me now," I laughed, "—of proving it! But that doesn't matter. What Flora wants, of course, is to get rid of me."

My companion bravely concurred. "Never again to so much as look at you."

"So that what you've come to me now for," I asked, "is to speed me on my way?" Before she had time to reply, however, I had her in check. "I've a better idea—the result of my reflections. My going *would* seem the right thing, and on Sunday I was terribly near it. Yet that won't do. It's *you* who must go. You must take Flora."

My visitor, at this, did speculate. "But where in the world—?"

"Away from here. Away from *them.* Away, even most of all, now, from me. Straight to her uncle."

"Only to tell on you—?"

"No, not 'only'! To leave me, in addition, with my remedy."

She was still vague. "And what *is* your remedy?"

"Your loyalty, to begin with. And then Miles's."

She looked at me hard. "Do you think he—?"

"Won't, if he has the chance, turn on me? Yes, I venture still to think it. At all events, I want to try. Get off with his sister as soon as possible and leave me with him alone." I was amazed, myself, at the spirit I had still in reserve, and therefore perhaps a trifle the more disconcerted at the way in which, in spite of this fine example of it, she hesitated. "There's one thing, of course," I went on: "they mustn't, before she goes, see each other for three seconds." Then it came over me that, in spite of Flora's presumable sequestration from the instant of her return from the pool, it might already be too late. "Do you mean," I anxiously asked, "that they *have* met?"

At this she quite flushed. "Ah, miss, I'm not such a fool as that! If I've been obliged to leave her three or four times, it has been each time with one of the maids, and at present, though she's alone, she's locked in safe. And yet—and yet!" There were too many things.

"And yet what?"

"Well, are you so sure of the little gentleman?"

"I'm not sure of anything but *you.* But I have, since last evening, a new hope. I think he wants to give me an opening. I do believe that—poor little exquisite wretch!—he wants to speak. Last evening, in the firelight and the silence, he sat with me for two hours as if it were just coming."

Mrs. Grose looked hard, through the window, at the gray, gathering day. "And did it come?"

"No, though I waited and waited, I confess it didn't, and it was without a breach of the silence or so much as a faint allusion to his sister's condition and absence that we at last kissed for good night. All the same," I continued, "I can't, if her uncle sees her, consent to his seeing her brother without my having given the boy—and most of all because things have got so bad—a little more time."

My friend appeared on this ground more reluctant than I could quite understand. "What do you mean by more time?"

"Well, a day or two—really to bring it out. He'll then be on *my* side—of which you see the importance. If nothing comes, I shall only fail, and you will, at the worst, have helped me by doing, on your arrival in town, whatever you may have found possible." So I put it before her, but she continued for a little so inscrutably embarrassed that I came again to her aid. "Unless indeed," I wound up, "you really want *not* to go."

I could see it, in her face, at last clear itself; she put out her hand to me as a pledge. "I'll go—I'll go. I'll go this morning."

I wanted to be very just. "If you *should* wish still to wait, I would engage she shouldn't see me."

"No, no: it's the place itself. She must leave it." She held me a moment with heavy eyes, then brought out the rest. "Your idea's the right one. I myself, miss—"

"Well?"

"I can't stay."

The look she gave me with it made me jump at possibilities. "You mean that, since yesterday, you *have* seen—?"

She shook her head with dignity. "I've *heard—!*"

"Heard?"

"From that child—horrors! There!" she sighed with tragic relief. "On my honor, miss, she says things—!" But at this evocation she broke down; she dropped, with a sudden sob, upon my sofa and, as I had seen her do before, gave way to all the grief of it.

It was quite in another manner that I, for my part, let myself go. "Oh, thank God!"

She sprang up again at this, drying her eyes with a groan. " 'Thank God?' "

"It so justifies me!"

"It does that, miss!"

I couldn't have desired more emphasis, but I just hesitated. "She's so horrible?"

I saw my colleague scarce knew how to put it. "Really shocking."

"And about me?"

"About you, miss—since you must have it. It's beyond everything, for a young lady; and I can't think wherever she must have picked up—"

"The appalling language she applied to me? I can, then!" I broke in with a laugh that was doubtless significant enough.

It only, in truth, left my friend still more grave. "Well, perhaps I ought to also—since I've heard some of it before! Yet I can't bear it," the poor woman went on while, with the same movement, she glanced, on my dressing table, at the face of my watch. "But I must go back."

I kept her, however. "Ah, if you can't bear it—!"

"How can I stop with her, you mean? Why, just *for* that: to get her away. Far from this," she pursued, "far from *them—*"

"She may be different? she may be free?" I seized her almost with joy. "Then, in spite of yesterday, you *believe—*"

"In such doings?" Her simple description of them required, in the light of her expression, to be carried no further, and she gave me the whole thing as she had never done. "I believe."

Yes, it was a joy, and we were still shoulder to shoulder: if I might continue sure of that I should care but little what else happened. My support in the presence of disaster would be the same as it had been in my early need of confidence, and if my friend would answer for my honesty I would answer for all the rest. On the point of taking leave of her, nonetheless, I was to some extent embarrassed. "There's one thing of course—it occurs to me—to remember. My letter, giving the alarm, will have reached town before you."

I now perceived still more how she had been beating about the bush and how weary at last it had made her. "Your letter won't have got there. Your letter never went."

"What then became of it?"

"Goodness knows! Master Miles—"

"Do you mean *he* took it?" I gasped.

She hung fire, but she overcame her reluctance. "I mean that I saw yesterday, when I came back with Miss Flora, that it wasn't where you had put it. Later in the evening I had the chance to question Luke, and he declared that he had neither noticed nor touched it." We could only exchange, on this, one of our deeper mutual soundings, and it was Mrs. Grose who first brought up the plumb with an almost elate "You see!"

"Yes, I see that if Miles took it instead he probably will have read it and destroyed it."

"And don't you see anything else?"

I faced her a moment with a sad smile. "It strikes me that by this time your eyes are open even wider than mine."

They proved to be so indeed, but she could still blush, almost, to show it. "I make out now what he must have done at school." And she gave, in her simple sharpness, an almost droll disillusioned nod. "He stole!"

I turned it over—I tried to be more judicial. "Well—perhaps."

She looked as if she found me unexpectedly calm. "He stole *letters!*"

She couldn't know my reasons for a calmness after all pretty shallow; so I showed them off as I might. "I hope then it was to more purpose than in this case! The note, at any rate, that I put on the table yesterday," I pursued, "will have given him so scant an advantage—for it contained only the bare demand for an interview—that he is already much ashamed of having gone so far for so little, and that what he had on his mind last evening was precisely the need of confession." I seemed to myself, for the instant, to have mastered it, to see it all. "Leave us, leave us"—I was already, at the door, hurrying her off. "I'll get it out of him. He'll meet me—he'll confess. If he confesses, he's saved. And if he's saved—"

"Then *you* are?" The dear woman kissed me on this, and I took her farewell. "I'll save you without him!" she cried as she went.

XXII

Yet it was when she had got off—and I missed her on the spot—that the great pinch really came. If I had counted on what it would give me to find myself alone with Miles I speedily perceived, at least, that it would give me a measure. No hour of my stay in fact was so assailed with apprehensions as that of my coming down to learn that the carriage containing Mrs. Grose and my younger pupil had already rolled out of the gates. Now I *was,* I said to myself, face to face with the elements, and for much of the rest of the day, while I fought my weakness, I could consider that I had been supremely rash. It was a tighter place still than I had yet turned round in; all the more that, for the first time, I could see in the aspect of others a confused reflection of the crisis. What had happened naturally caused them all to stare; there was too little of the explained, throw out whatever we might, in the suddenness of my colleague's act. The maids and the men looked blank; the effect of which on my nerves was an aggravation until I saw the necessity of making it a positive aid. It was precisely, in short, by just clutching the helm that I avoided total wreck; and I daresay that, to bear up at all, I became, that morning, very grand and very dry. I welcomed the consciousness that I was charged with much to do, and I caused it to be known as well that, left thus to myself, I was quite remarkably firm. I wandered with that manner, for the next hour or two, all over the place and looked, I have no doubt, as if I were ready for any onset. So, for the benefit of whom it might concern, I paraded with a sick heart.

The person it appeared least to concern proved to be, till dinner, little Miles himself. My perambulations had given me, meanwhile, no glimpse of him, but they had tended to make more public the change taking place in our relation as a consequence of his having at the piano, the day before, kept me, in Flora's interest, so beguiled and befooled. The stamp of publicity had of course been fully given by her confinement and departure, and the change itself was now ushered in by our nonobservance of the regular custom of the schoolroom. He had already disappeared when, on my way down, I pushed open his door, and I learned below that he had breakfasted—in the presence of a couple of the maids—with Mrs. Grose and his sister. He had then gone out, as he said, for a stroll; than which nothing, I reflected, could better have expressed his frank view of the abrupt transformation of my office. What he would now permit this office to consist of was yet to be settled: there was a queer relief, at all events—I mean for myself in especial—in the renouncement of one pretension. If so much had sprung to the surface I scarce put it too strongly in saying that what had perhaps sprung highest was the absurdity of our prolonging the fiction that I had anything more to teach him. It sufficiently stuck out that, by tacit little tricks in which even more than myself he carried out the care of my dignity, I had had to appeal to him to let me off straining to meet him on the ground of his true capacity. He had at any rate his freedom now; I was never to touch it again; as I had amply shown, moreover, when, on his joining me in the schoolroom the previous night, I had uttered, on the subject of the interval just concluded, neither challenge nor hint. I had too much, from this moment, my other ideas. Yet when he at last arrived the difficulty of applying them, the accumulations of my problem, were brought straight home to me by the beautiful little presence on which what had occurred had as yet, for the eye, dropped neither stain nor shadow.

To mark, for the house, the high state I cultivated I decreed that my meals with the boy should be served, as we called it, downstairs; so that I had been awaiting him in the ponderous pomp of the room outside of the window of which I had had from Mrs. Grose, that first scared Sunday, my flash of something it would scarce have done to call light. Here at present I felt afresh—for I had felt it again and again—how my equilibrium depended on the success of my rigid will, the will to shut my eyes as tight as possible to the truth that what I had to deal with was, revoltingly, against nature. I could only get on at all by taking "nature" into my confidence and my account, by treating my monstrous ordeal as a push in a direction unusual, of course, and unpleasant, but demanding, after all, for a fair front, only another turn of the screw of ordinary human virtue. No attempt, nonetheless, could well require more tact than just this attempt to supply, one's self, *all* the nature. How could I put even a little of that article into a suppression of reference to what had occurred? How, on the other hand, could I make a reference without a new plunge into the hideous obscure? Well, a sort of answer, after a time, had come to me, and it was so far confirmed as that I was met, incontestably, by the quickened vision of what was rare in my little companion. It was indeed as if he had found even now—as he had so often found at lessons—still some other delicate way to ease me off. Wasn't there light in the fact which, as we shared our solitude, broke out with a specious glitter it had never yet quite worn?—the fact that (opportunity aiding, precious opportunity which had now come), it would be preposterous, with a child so endowed, to forego the help one might wrest from absolute intelligence? What had his intelligence been given him for but to save him?

Mightn't one, to reach his mind, risk the stretch of an angular arm over his character? It was as if, when we were face to face in the dining room, he had literally shown me the way. The roast mutton was on the table, and I had dispensed with attendance. Miles, before he sat down, stood a moment with his hands in his pockets and looked at the joint, on which he seemed on the point of passing some humorous judgment. But what he presently produced was: "I say, my dear, is she really very awfully ill?"

"Little Flora? Not so bad but that she'll presently be better. London will set her up. Bly had ceased to agree with her. Come here and take your mutton."

He alertly obeyed me, carried the plate carefully to his seat and, when he was established, went on. "Did Bly disagree with her so terribly suddenly?"

"Not so suddenly as you might think. One had seen it coming on."

"Then why didn't you get her off before?"

"Before what?"

"Before she became too ill to travel."

I found myself prompt. "She's *not* too ill to travel: she only might have become so if she had stayed. This was just the moment to seize. The journey will dissipate the influence"—oh, I was grand!—"and carry it off."

"I see, I see"—Miles, for that matter, was grand too. He settled to his repast with the charming little "table manner" that, from the day of his arrival, had relieved me of all grossness of admonition. Whatever he had been driven from school for, it was not for ugly feeding. He was irreproachable, as always, today; but he was unmistakably more conscious. He was discernibly trying to take for granted more things than he found, without assistance, quite easy; and he dropped into peaceful silence while he felt his situation. Our meal was of the briefest—mine a vain pretense, and I had the things immediately removed. While this was done Miles stood again with his hands in his little pockets and his back to me—stood and looked out of the wide window through which, that other day, I had seen what pulled me up. We continued silent while the maid was with us—as silent, it whimsically occurred to me, as some young couple who, on their wedding journey, at the inn, feel shy in the presence of the waiter. He turned round only when the waiter had left us. "Well—so we're alone!"

XXIII

"Oh, more or less." I fancy my smile was pale. "Not absolutely. We shouldn't like that!" I went on.

"No—I suppose we shouldn't. Of course we have the others."

"We have the others—we have indeed the others," I concurred.

"Yet even though we have them," he returned, still with his hands in his pockets and planted there in front of me, "they don't much count, do they?"

I made the best of it, but I felt wan. "It depends on what you call 'much'!"

"Yes"—with all accommodation—"everything depends!" On this, however, he faced to the window again and presently reached it with his vague, restless, cogitating step. He remained there awhile, with his forehead against the glass, in contemplation of the stupid shrubs I knew and the dull things of November. I had always my hypocrisy of "work," behind which, now, I gained the sofa. Steadying myself with it there as I had repeatedly done at those moments of torment that I have described as the moments of my knowing the children to be given to something from which I was barred, I sufficiently obeyed my habit of being prepared for the worst. But an extraordinary impression dropped on me as I extracted a meaning from the boy's embarrassed back—none other than the impression that I was not barred now. This inference grew in a few minutes to sharp intensity and seemed bound up with the direct perception that it was positively *he* who was. The frames and squares of the great window were a kind of image, for him, of a kind of failure. I felt that I saw him, at any rate, shut in or shut out. He was admirable, but not comfortable: I took it in with a throb of hope. Wasn't he looking, through the haunted pane, for something he couldn't see?—and wasn't it the first time in the whole business that he had known such a lapse? The first, the very first: I found it a splendid portent. It made him anxious, though he watched himself; he had been anxious all day and, even while in his usual sweet little manner he sat at table, had needed all his small strange genius to give it a gloss. When he at least turned around to meet me it was almost as if this genius had succumbed. "Well, I think I'm glad Bly agrees with *me!*"

"You would certainly seem to have seen, these twenty-four hours, a good deal more of it than for some time before. I hope," I went on bravely, "that you've been enjoying yourself."

"Oh yes, I've been ever so far; all round about—miles and miles away. I've never been so free."

He had really a manner of his own, and I could only try to keep up with him. "Well, do you like it?"

He stood there smiling; then at last he put into two words—"Do *you?*"—more discrimination than I had ever heard two words contain. Before I had time to deal with that, however, he continued as if with the sense that this was an impertinence to be softened. "Nothing could be more charming than the way you take it, for of course if we're alone together now it's you that are alone most. But I hope," he threw in, "you don't particularly mind!"

"Having to do with you?" I asked. "My dear child, how can I help minding? Though I've renounced all claim to your company—you're so beyond me—I at least greatly enjoy it. What else should I stay on for?"

He looked at me more directly, and the expression of his face, graver now, struck me as the most beautiful I had ever found in it. "You stay on just for *that?*"

"Certainly. I stay on as your friend and from the tremendous interest I take in you till something can be done for you that may be more worth your while. That needn't surprise you." My voice trembled so that I felt it impossible to suppress the shake. "Don't you remember how I told you, when I came and sat on your bed the night of the storm, that there was nothing in the world I wouldn't do for you?"

"Yes, yes!" He, on his side, more and more visibly nervous, had a tone to master; but he was so much more successful than I that, laughing out through his gravity, he could pretend we were pleasantly jesting. "Only that, I think, was to get me to do something for *you!*"

"It was partly to get you to do something," I conceded. "But, you know, you didn't do it."

"Oh yes," he said with the brightest superficial eagerness, "you wanted me to tell you something."

"That's it. Out, straight out. What you have on your mind, you know."

"Ah then, is *that* what you've stayed over for?"

He spoke with a gaiety through which I could still catch the finest little quiver of resentful passion; but I can't begin to express the effect upon me of an implication of surrender even so faint. It was as if what I had yearned for had come at last only to astonish me. "Well, yes—I may as well make a clean breast of it. It was precisely for that."

He waited so long that I supposed it for the purpose of repudiating the assumption on which my action had been founded; but what he finally said was: "Do you mean now—here?"

"There couldn't be a better place or time." He looked round him uneasily, and I had the rare—oh, the queer!—impression of the very first symptom I had seen in him of the approach of immediate fear. It was as if he were suddenly afraid of me—which struck me indeed as perhaps the best thing to make him. Yet in the very pang of the effort I felt it vain to try sternness, and I heard myself the next instant so gentle as to be almost grotesque. "You want so to go out again?"

"Awfully!" He smiled at me heroically, and the touching little bravery of it was enhanced by his actually flushing with pain. He had picked up his hat, which he had brought in, and stood twirling it in a way that gave me, even as I was just nearly reaching port, a perverse horror of what I was doing. To do it in *any* way was an act of violence, for what did it consist of but the obtrusion of the idea of grossness and guilt on a small helpless creature who had been for me a revelation of the possibilities of beautiful intercourse? Wasn't it base to create for a being so exquisite a mere alien awkwardness? I suppose I now read into our situation a clearness it couldn't have had at the time, for I seem to see our poor eyes already lighted with some spark of a prevision of the anguish that was to come. So we circled about, with terrors and scruples, like fighters not daring to close. But it was for each other we feared! That kept us a little longer suspended and unbruised. "I'll tell you everything," Miles said—"I mean I'll tell you anything you like. You'll stay on with me, and we shall both be all right and I *will* tell you—I *will*. But not now."

"Why not now?"

My insistence turned him from me and kept him once more at his window in a silence during which, between us, you might have heard a pin drop. Then he was before me again with the air of a person for whom, outside, someone who had frankly to be reckoned with was waiting. "I have to see Luke."

I had not yet reduced him to quite so vulgar a lie, and I felt proportionately ashamed. But, horrible as it was, his lies made up my truth. I achieved thoughtfully a few loops of my knitting. "Well then, go to Luke, and I'll wait for what you promise. Only, in return for that, satisfy, before you leave me, one very much smaller request."

He looked as if he felt he had succeeded enough to be able still a little to bargain. "Very much smaller—?"

"Yes, a mere fraction of the whole. Tell me"—oh, my work preoccupied me, and I was offhand!—"if, yesterday afternoon, from the table in the hall, you took, you know, my letter."

XXIV

My sense of how he received this suffered for a minute from something that I can describe only as a fierce split of my attention—a stroke that at first, as I sprang straight up, reduced me to the mere blind movement of getting hold of him, drawing him close and, while I just fell for support against the nearest piece of furniture, instinctively keeping him with his back to the window. The appearance was full upon us that I had already had to deal with here: Peter Quint had come into view like a sentinel before a prison. The next thing I saw was that, from outside, he had reached the window, and then I knew that, close to the glass and glaring in through it, he offered once more to the room his white face of damnation. It represents but grossly what took place within me at the sight to say that on the second my decision was made; yet I believe that no woman so overwhelmed ever in so short a time recovered her grasp of the *act.* It came to me in the very horror of the immediate presence that the act would be, seeing and facing what I saw and faced, to keep the boy himself unaware. The inspiration—I can call it by no other name—was that I felt how voluntarily, how transcendently, I *might.* It was like fighting with a demon for a human soul, and when I had fairly so appraised it I saw how the human soul—held out, in the tremor of my hands, at arms' length—had a perfect dew of sweat on a lovely childish forehead. The face that was close to mine was as white as the face against the glass, and out of it presently came a sound, not low nor weak, but as if from much farther away, that I drank like a waft of fragrance.

"Yes—I took it."

At this, with a moan of joy, I enfolded, I drew him close; and while I held him to my breast, where I could feel in the sudden fever of his little body the tremendous pulse of his little heart, I kept my eyes on the thing at the window and saw it move and shift its posture. I have likened it to a sentinel, but its slow wheel, for a moment, was rather the prowl of a baffled beast. My present quickened courage, however, was such that, not too much to let it through, I had to shade, as it were, my flame. Meanwhile the glare of the face was again at the window, the scoundrel fixed as if to watch and wait. It was the very confidence that I might now defy him, as well as the positive certitude, by this time, of the child's unconsciousness, that made me go on. "What did you take it for?"

"To see what you said about me."

"You opened the letter?"

"I opened it."

My eyes were now, as I held him off a little again, on Miles's own face, in which the collapse of mockery showed me how complete was the ravage of uneasiness. What was prodigious was that at last, by my success, his sense was sealed and his communication stopped: he knew that he was in presence, but knew not of what, and knew still less that I also was and that I did know. And what did this strain of trouble matter when my eyes went back to the window only to see that the air was clear again and—by my personal triumph—the influence quenched? There was nothing there. I felt that the cause was mine and that I should surely get *all.* "And you found nothing!"—I let my elation out.

He gave the most mournful, thoughtful little headshake. "Nothing."

"Nothing, nothing!" I almost shouted in my joy.

"Nothing, nothing," he sadly repeated.

I kissed his forehead; it was drenched. "So what have you done with it?"

"I've burned it."

"Burned it?" It was now or never. "Is that what you did at school?"

Oh, what this brought up! "At school?"

"Did you take letters?—or other things?"

"Other things?" He appeared now to be thinking of something far off and that reached him only through the pressure of his anxiety. Yet it did reach him. "Did I *steal?*"

I felt myself redden to the roots of my hair as well as wonder if it were more strange to put to a gentleman such a question or to see him take it with allowances that gave the very distance of his fall in the world. "Was it for that you mightn't go back?"

The only thing he felt was rather a dreary little surprise. "Did you know I mightn't go back?"

"I know everything."

He gave me at this the longest and strangest look. "Everything?"

"Everything. Therefore *did* you—?" But I couldn't say it again.

Miles could, very simply. "No. I didn't steal."

My face must have shown him I believed him utterly; yet my hands

—but it was for pure tenderness—shook him as if to ask him why, if it was all for nothing, he had condemned me to months of torment. "What then did you do?"

He looked in vague pain all round the top of the room and drew his breath, two or three times over, as if with difficulty. He might have been standing at the bottom of the sea and raising his eyes to some faint green twilight. "Well—I said things."

"Only that?"

"They thought it was enough!"

"To turn you out for?"

Never, truly, had a person "turned out" shown so little to explain it as this little person! He appeared to weigh my question, but in a manner quite detached and almost helpless. "Well, I suppose I oughtn't."

"But to whom did you say them?"

He evidently tried to remember, but it dropped—he had lost it. "I don't know!"

He almost smiled at me in the desolation of his surrender, which was indeed practically, by this time, so complete that I ought to have left it there. But I was infatuated—I was blind with victory, though even then the very effect that was to have brought him so much nearer was already that of added separation. "Was it to everyone?" I asked.

"No; it was only to—" But he gave a sick little headshake. "I don't remember their names."

"Were they then so many?"

"No—only a few. Those I liked."

Those he liked? I seemed to float not into clearness, but into a darker obscure, and within a minute there had come to me out of my very pity the appalling alarm of his being perhaps innocent. It was for the instant confounding and bottomless, for if he *were* innocent, what then on earth was *I?* Paralyzed, while it lasted, by the mere brush of the question, I let him go a little, so that, with a deep-drawn sigh, he turned away from me again; which, as he faced towards the clear window, I suffered, feeling that I had nothing now there to keep him from. "And did they repeat what you said?" I went on after a moment.

He was soon at some distance from me, still breathing hard and again with the air, though now without anger for it, of being confined against his will. Once more, as he had done before, he looked up at the dim day as if, of what had hitherto sustained him, nothing was left but an unspeakable anxiety. "Oh yes," he nevertheless replied—"they must have repeated them. To those *they* liked," he added.

There was, somehow, less of it than I had expected; but I turned it over. "And these things came round—?"

"To the masters? Oh yes!" he answered very simply. "But I didn't know they'd tell."

"The masters? They didn't—they've never told. That's why I ask you."

He turned to me again his little beautiful fevered face. "Yes, it was too bad."

"Too bad?"

"What I suppose I sometimes said. To write home."

I can't name the exquisite pathos of the contradiction given to such a speech by such a speaker; I only know that the next instant I heard myself throw off with homely force: "Stuff and nonsense!" But the next after that I must have sounded stern enough. "What *were* these things?"

My sternness was all for his judge, his executioner; yet it made him avert himself again, and that movement made *me,* with a single bound and an irrepressible cry, spring straight upon him. For there again, against the glass, as if to blight his confession and stay his answer, was the hideous author of our woe—the white face of damnation. I felt a sick swim at the drop of my victory and all the return of my battle, so that the wildness of my veritable leap only served as a great betrayal. I saw him, from the midst of my act, meet it with a divination, and on the perception that even now he only guessed, and that the window was still to his own eyes free, I let the impulse flame up to convert the climax of his dismay into the very proof of his liberation. "No more, no more, no more!" I shrieked, as I tried to press him against me, to my visitant.

"Is she *here?*" Miles panted as he caught with his sealed eyes the direction of my words. Then as his strange "she" staggered me and, with a gasp, I echoed it, "Miss Jessel, Miss Jessel!" he with a sudden fury gave me back.

I seized, stupefied, his supposition—some sequel to what we had done to Flora, but this made me only want to show him that it was better still than that. "It's not Miss Jessel! But it's at the window—straight before us. It's *there*—the coward horror, there for the last time!"

At this, after a second in which his head made the movement of a baffled dog's on a scent and then gave a frantic little shake for air and light, he was at me in a white rage, bewildered, glaring vainly over the place and missing wholly, though it now, to my sense, filled the room like the taste of poison, the wide, overwhelming presence. "It's *he?*"

I was so determined to have all my proof that I flashed into ice to challenge him. "Whom do you mean by 'he'?"

"Peter Quint—you devil!" His face gave again, round the room, its convulsed supplication. "*Where?*"

They are in my ears still, his supreme surrender of the name and his tribute to my devotion. "What does he matter now, my own?—what will he *ever* matter? *I* have you," I launched at the beast, "but he has lost you forever!" Then, for the demonstration of my work, "There, *there!*" I said to Miles.

But he had already jerked straight round, stared, glared again, and seen but the quiet day. With the stroke of the loss I was so proud of he uttered the cry of a creature hurled over an abyss, and the grasp with which I recovered him might have been that of catching him in his fall. I caught him, yes, I held him—it may be imagined with what a passion; but at the end of a minute I began to feel what it truly was that I held. We were alone with the quiet day, and his little heart, dispossessed, had stopped.

JOYCE CAROL OATES

Joyce Carol Oates mentioned that one of her own stories scares her every time she thinks about it. After you read it, we know you'll agree.

QUEEN OF THE NIGHT

JOYCE CAROL OATES

This is how Claire Falk's marriage of twenty-six years, which accounted for more than half her life, ended one humid Saturday afternoon in June: she blundered into overhearing a conversation.

It was one-sided, only one-half of a conversation, because her husband was on the telephone. And there were no words to it, no distinct recognizable words, because she was nearly out of earshot. She heard only sounds. Her husband's voice, curiously raw and aggrieved, a young man's voice, and yet *his.* She would know it anywhere.

He was arguing with someone. And then begging. His voice rose and dipped and went silent. Then began again: strident, passionate, craven, exasperated, frightened. A harsh, jagged, dissonant music Claire had never known in her own lifetime.

Or, if she had known it—it had been long ago, many years ago.

She shrank back against a wall, listening. Though she did not want, *really,* to eavesdrop. Even in this moment of shock, of sickening apprehension, she did not want to violate another person's privacy. But who was her husband talking with in that angry, intimate tone, why was he so upset, why so suddenly and uncharacteristically abject. . . . Claire half-wanted to go to him, to comfort him. It had been many years since she had had to comfort him.

He was silent awhile. Then began again, this time more evenly. He was trying to convince someone, his manner was more familiar: half-jocular, ironic, bullying. Yet he was still begging. It was the begging that was so ugly, so final: Claire knew what it must mean.

She knew, and retreated.

After all she was a woman of principle. Her instinct turned her away from what she might discover, what she might precisely discover, if she drew nearer, if she pressed her ear against the closed door: it would be *degrading* to eavesdrop now that she knew her husband was quarreling with a woman. She did not at that time think exactly of betrayal, in the sense in which she had been "betrayed," their marriage "betrayed." Her husband's passion excluded her. It had nothing to do with her at all.

She left the house. Retreated. He had not expected her home for another hour, she had made a miscalculation, a fatal blunder. Consequently nothing would be the same again. Now is life very real, is it very convincing?—so Claire Falk queried herself, half-ironically. When she was alone she often spoke to herself in silence and her voice, her tone, at such times was oddly cynical, even impersonal; not exactly a woman's voice. It was frequently reproachful as if it considered her something of a fool, yet it was sympathetic, good-humored, forgiving, if she stayed with it long enough. How much reality can you credit to all this?—so the voice drawled, referring to the street, the busy intersection which she was approaching, a child pedaling energetically on a bicycle, the filmy sky, the day, the world itself. But despite the voice's smug cynicism Claire was trembling, she was really in a state of mild shock, she hardly knew what she was doing. Afterward, when such extreme emotions, centered on her first husband, were to seem merely curious, she was to remember that blind panicked walk that would take her some three miles from home. She did not know what day of the week it was, what time of the day, what she had been doing all afternoon, why she had imagined it important. Her life had come to a stop.

She survived the blow, barely. How must she have looked that afternoon, a woman in her fifties, well dressed, very pale, blind and disheveled and in a great hurry. . . . She must have been a spectacle, people must have stared at her. But she saw nothing. She saw no one. There was a wide street busy with traffic, and the corner of the park, there were a number of people playing tennis, there was the cemetery where for weeks now the groundkeepers had been on strike and weeds grew abundantly. She found herself huddling in the doorway of the little stone chapel in the cemetery.

It was raining, when had it begun to rain? The drops were cool on her overheated face.

You had no idea that your husband was in love with another woman, they would ask, watching her closely.

I had no idea.

There wasn't anything . . . strange . . . ?

I had no idea.

Stubbornly, angrily. But then her jaw would quiver, her voice shake.

In the doorway of the chapel she crouched like an animal, her back against the heavy oak door. Now you can cry if you must, the voice instructed her, impatiently, but nothing happened. Her forehead and cheeks were damp, it was only the rain, which was now being flung against her. An indignity. But somehow consoling.

Such things are blows, after all, people would say. There were many divorced women now. There was a small army of divorced women in this very part of the world, in the wide circle of friends and acquaintances and business associates Claire and her husband knew. A kind of death, people said. Losing a loved one in any way—it's a kind of death. A terrible blow to one's ego, to one's sense of self. So the familiar words went, the litany of clichés. She would hear them all many times, she would not turn away in contempt or anguish or amusement. Chagrined, she would recall that she herself had mouthed such platitudes in the past before she had known what they meant—before she had even guessed at their incontestable truth.

You had no idea, Claire . . . ? Really? So her sister would inquire, staring at her.

I had no idea.

With Ronald it was so obvious, you know, you remember all that year I was calling you late at night, I must have made your life miserable, you must have dreaded picking up the phone. . . . But *you* hadn't any idea, any suspicion?

Nor had she wept. Weeks after that Saturday, months afterward, on the morning of the divorce, on the evening of the divorce, she had been grim and subdued and even a little ravaged but tearless. Not out of defiance or rage but out of a queer impersonal conviction that had come to her . . . that had come to her from nowhere, as she crouched in the stone doorway, her face streaming with rain, her clothes soaking. The conviction had to do with the fact that tears were pointless. What had happened was an event, it was out of her control, in a sense not her responsibility, not her fault. Her husband had evidently fallen in love with another woman. A younger woman, of course. Younger by twenty-five years. *He* had acted, he had turned from her, he had not so much violated their marriage as simply forgotten it. And of course it was not true, as Claire told her friends, that she had "no idea": she had known very well that the two of them were emotionally estranged, no longer really intimate, uninterested in sexual love, uninterested in seeking out the causes of their indifference. She had known very well that they were friends rather than lovers, they were courteous with each other, but not *always* courteous. . . . Yet the marriage had seemed to Claire an absolute unalterable fact, an impersonal condition in which she was to continue to live, neither happy nor unhappy: simply as Claire Falk.

The divorce proceedings were impersonal too. And tedious. Even with the reformed divorce law Claire found the experience tedious, and any emotions she might have felt—after all, the Falks were dissolving not only a marriage but what added up to a small but complicated business partnership involving property, investments, works of art, two cars, a son in his mid-twenties who was studying international law in London—were flattened, drained away. There were too many details, too many fussy points, her husband's attorney and her own were better suited to deal with them, let them deal with such things while she went her own way. She would acquire an apartment, of course the house must be put on the market and sold quickly; though her husband—guilty, embarrassed, proud—had very generously offered it to her, without qualifications. Once she was out of the house and living in an apartment, perhaps one of those large, airy, very modern high-rise apartments along the river . . .

Her son flew home, to comfort her. To accuse his father. But the drama did not really interest her, she found herself embarrassed in her son's presence, as if he were mistaking her for someone else: another, weaker, far less intelligent woman. Has he always thought of me like this, she wondered. His mother. A woman who is his mother, and that only. . . . With him she managed to be "hurt," to express the usual ritual bewilderment. (Why, when things have been going so well, when we've been so happy together, twenty-six years together after all. . . .) He had her long blunt nose and squarish chin and somewhat bold, intimidating stare, and that pronounced widow's peak that had caused her grief as a young girl but which, in later years, she was rather vain about. Unlike her he was tall, and his complexion was coarse. Still he was an attractive young man. Too fussy, too solicitous of her feelings, in a way too inquisitive (for there were private matters Claire would never discuss with anyone, not even members of her family), but an attractive man, a boy who had turned out well.

Could you call him off me? her husband pleaded.

Amused, Claire assured him that their son wouldn't stay long. He had made plans to spend a month with her but of course he would grow restless, he'd soon return to London, they had only to be patient with him. He thinks I am grief-stricken, Claire said with an ironic twist of her mouth. Eventually I will convince him otherwise.

Twenty-six years, now being put behind them. And apart from the burden of the legal problems, and certain flashes of memory that evidently overtook them both (neither Claire nor her husband were sentimental people but they were susceptible, at times, to queer unanticipated painful stabs of nostalgia), the experience of closing off that passage of time, declaring it no longer valid, was not a very difficult one. One lives, after all, day by day; petty problems are more exasperating than large ones; there was no time for Claire's skeptical voice to quiz her about love, the meaning of love, whether it *had* any meaning, when she was arranging with a realtor to put their house on a crowded and grotesquely inflated market.

It *did* hurt, of course, to learn—by way of an acquaintance—that her husband believed he was in love "for the first time in his life." This, at the age of fifty-five. After those twenty-six years. But was the statement, the flamboyant deluded hope, very original . . . ? Claire laughed her infrequent ribald laugh, and said that adultery must have unhinged him. The illicit meetings, the scrambling in corners, the deceit, the silly tiresome guilt. The physical exertion involved in keeping up with a woman that young, and no doubt very experienced.

But even that hurt, that wound, faded. In the judge's chambers she and her husband were polite with each other, they made every effort to smile when smiles were not inappropriate, they were very civilized and responsible adults. Their attorneys, the judge, the recording clerk, the young woman whom Claire's husband was to marry the following week—all must have been impressed with the Falks' behavior.

In truth, Claire had been strangely hopeful about the young woman. Her initial resentment had long since faded, she felt only a curious hope that . . . that her husband would not shame himself, make a fool of himself. For she too was involved. Intimately, and publicly. If the young woman were a disappointment, if everyone talked about them, her husband's new bride, the folly of the alliance, what it must mean about Claire herself as a wife, as a woman . . .

But the girl was not a disappointment. She was not extraordinary, certainly no beauty, Claire could not reasonably feel a tug of envy of her, not even of her youth, which seemed merely shallow; she was attractive, and soft-voiced, and obviously ill at ease, and probably not *very* bright—but she wasn't a disappointment, to Claire's relief. The new Mrs. Falk would not publicly shame her.

And yet—how flattering it would have been, she said, joking, to friends, to her sister, if he had managed to set himself up with a truly beautiful, a truly remarkable woman. A politician friend of theirs had done exceptionally well, though he was in his late fifties. . . . On the other hand, another friend, newly divorced from *his* wife, had made an utter fool of himself by marrying a vulgar simpering divorcée with two small children, who quite clearly wanted only his money. So Claire's husband had not done *too* badly. At least I don't have to feel sorry for him, she said. I can begin the process of forgetting him.

As a young girl Claire had not been especially attractive. The bones of her face were strong, her nostrils flared as if she were impatient, thinking her own rebellious thoughts, cryptically amused, censorious. Her thick dark hair and her deep-set intelligent eyes were her most striking features. As she matured, however, the very uniqueness of her appearance came to have a value; she was set apart from other women, conventionally pretty women, and dependent upon her mood she was sometimes exceptionally beautiful. Who can say, who can judge, she often queried herself, studying that face she was linked to for life, examining it for blemishes or signs of aging, idly, without the anxiety other women commonly feel. By a quirk of fate she was photogenic, and a little vain; but not *really* vain, since she measured such things as a woman's sexual attractiveness against other, more abiding qualities, or were they achievements, or possessions—marriage, family, friends, a home, a fairly busy life, flexible bonds with the community. She did volunteer work for the symphony, for St. Patrick's General Hospital, for the Art Students' Guild; for a while she had been thinking quite seriously of buying into an unusual clothing boutique with the wife of her husband's most frequent golfing companion, but in the end the project had fallen through, no one knew quite why. She handled many of their finances, prepared a good deal of their income tax information for their accountant and tax lawyer, did research on certain investment properties, even wrote, from time to time, free-lance articles for her suburban newspaper. (She had hoped while in college to become a journalist, not knowing at the time how difficult, how exhausting, and how ill paid such jobs were.) Now is all this relevant to your present situation, she quizzed herself, or is it to be brushed away, forgotten with all the rest . . . ? She stared at herself unsmiling. It was remarkable how little the divorce had affected her, how alert, even youthful she still looked. (And another birthday drew near: another!) She had a very pale, opaque skin, a certain heavy and slumberous look, disturbingly erotic; or so someone had told her. Her husband, perhaps. Or a half-drunk admirer. Though she was not overweight there was a solidity, an almost leaden substance to her, as if she were not flesh—not entirely. Something sculpted. Marble. Alabaster.

As a young wife, newly pregnant, she had been eerily lethargic, slow-moving, given to long periods of daydreaming. Her husband would call her back. Sometimes rudely, she thought. Jealously. What are you thinking of, where has your mind gone, he wanted to know. But she could not answer, she could not say. In later years, particularly in the year before the telephone conversation, she had found herself drifting off again. . . . She would stand immobile, as if listening to sounds in the distance, or to a near-inaudible music. Claire, what are you thinking about? her husband would inquire. When you stand like that, staring off like that, what are you thinking of?

Nothing, she said, roused, and a little embarrassed.

But it isn't possible to think of nothing, her husband said.

Now he was good-natured about her moods, her habits. They were harmless, after all. Hardly a threat or a challenge to him. Of course he was in love, and like a young besotted lover he could think of no one else but his love, though he made an attempt to be attentive, even generous; Claire had not understood at the time but she had felt the force of his good-humored, somewhat distracted, curiosity.

My mind just slipped away, she said.

Yes, but where?

An immobile, impassive woman, with a striking profile, a head of thick dark hair wildly streaked with gray. Something glacial about you, something remote and forbidding, the young man who was to be her second husband said, shyly, yet half-mockingly. It was clear that he was in awe of her. Fascinated by her. ". . . Queen of the Night," he whispered.

"What? What did you say?"

He caught his lower lip between his small crowded-together teeth. "Oh nothing. Some nonsense that crossed my mind."

Queen of the Night. She had of course heard him perfectly well. And her heart expanded as though it would burst, flooded with a sudden violent knowledge of her power.

His name was Emil. Which was, or was not, his real name.

On a private stretch of beach in Hollywood, Florida. Between Christmas and New Year's. That busy merciless time of the year that Claire had always disliked, and now positively dreaded. To fill it up, to squander it as brainlessly as possible, she had accepted her sister's invitation to fly south and stay with her. There are some fascinating people here, her sister bragged. Friends of mine. In politics, real estate, show business. And the children too—*their* friends. Wait till you meet them!

Nearly every afternoon there were cocktail parties, nearly every evening beach parties, or parties around lighted pools. Since her divorce Claire's sister had blossomed, but gaudily: a trim nervous woman in her late forties, she had tanned her skin dusky, and bleached her hair, and wore amazing eye makeup—luminous eye shadow, water-repellent mascara. In her flowing robes and ankle-length skirts she *did* look attractive, Claire thought.

"But *you,*" her sister exclaimed, squeezing Claire's face between her hands, studying her almost rudely, "*you* look marvelous. And after all you've gone through. . . . Do you know, Ted dropped me a line when he was back in the States, he said you were in a state of shock, you were very depressed, he was half-tempted to break off his studies. . . . But I didn't *think* so, myself, I mean every time we talked on the phone . . ."

Claire winced, blushing angrily. Her son, gossiping about her with her sister! It was insupportable.

"Ted has always exaggerated things," she said.

"Oh yes—don't they? Children, I mean. And then your Ted is, you know, something of a prig."

She met Emil on the fourth night of her visit though she had seen him, without knowing who he was, or that he was a friend of her niece's, on the very first night. He was "something in the theater." Or was it in music. Mime? Dance? A tall, painfully thin young man, in his late twenties, perhaps, not at all suntanned. He wore snug white trousers and a close-fitting white jersey shirt and a red scarf knotted carelessly about his throat. His blond hair was very pale, almost white, and fell nearly to his shoulders in languid, spent curls. When Claire first happened to see him, quite by accident, he was at the center of a noisy, hilarious group of young people in a sidewalk café near the ocean. Their laughter and outrageous high spirits drew Claire's attention, though she was, at the time, tired from her plane flight, and not terribly interested in her sister's excited chatter. (She was showing Claire around, walking arm in arm with her, pointing out restaurants, nightclubs, Christmas decorations, the high-rise apartments of acquaintances of hers. "This part of the world is so much *alive,*" she kept telling Claire. "It's nothing like—you know—back north.")

If Claire had been a more self-conscious woman she might have imagined that the young people were laughing at her and her sister. But of course they were not. They were interested only in one another. It was the holiday season, they'd been drinking together for some time, they were all young and fairly attractive and . . . One of them drew her eye involuntarily: the willowy young man in the white trousers and jersey, with the bold red scarf about his neck. There was something both mocking and plaintive about him. His eyeglasses caught and reflected light as if he were blinking compulsively. His chin receded delicately, he was far too thin, the laughter that burst from him seemed raw and painful. And his companions: Claire saw with disapproval that they were not really so attractive. One was muscular and very tanned, a good-looking young man, but brash and pushy, with too-red lips. He appeared to have a severe limp. Another, a skinny short-haired girl in a silver halter top and near-transparent black trousers, was giggling shrilly, her eyes shut.

"It's like this every night during the season, isn't it wild?" Claire's sister said, steering her along the crowded sidewalk.

"It's very . . . it's very colorful," Claire said faintly.

Three evenings later she saw the young man again, and it seemed to her that he half-recognized her. We know each other, she thought calmly.

So long as the sun shone one might imagine it was summer, but as soon as the sun dropped away the air became uncomfortably cool. It was winter, after all. It was nearly New Year's. Claire was wise enough to dress prudently, even to wear stockings. She had no intention of catching cold. But the other party guests dressed lightly, the women especially. A number were even barefoot. And the young blond man who watched her so closely, had he kicked off his shoes too? Yes, she saw with a small inexplicable thrill of concern that he was barefoot despite the chill.

His long slender feet danced bluish white in the dusk.

There was a party of "adults" and a party of "young people," some of them very young indeed—fifteen or sixteen. Claire did not approve, really. The two parties overlapped awkwardly, as if by accident. Her sister, vodka

mimicking routines, though it was obvious that he loved Claire very much, and was still somewhat intimidated by her. He liked to attribute to her certain not-quite-natural powers: she could "read" his thoughts, she could pitch him out of a black mood by "focusing" on him, she could draw him to her, to make love to her, by her gaze alone, fixed on the back of his head. On the wide white beach he never tired of oiling her body, or arranging the beach umbrella so that the shadow fell over her face; he never tired of running little errands—getting lemon ices for them at midmorning, and drinks at noon, and beer at odd times. (Claire developed a taste for beer, it must have been because of the sun and the beach, a certain dryness in her mouth, a near-perpetual thirst. They discovered a very interesting Japanese beer, new to them both, which was expensive but well worth the price.)

The only problem was, Emil could not tan: his pale, near-translucent skin simply pinkened and began to smart.

"Just look at you!" he wailed, sitting slump-backed beneath the umbrella. "You're so dark! You're dark as a native! Perfect! You radiate heat and warmth and health and sanity, your body is obviously *wiser* than mine though you don't belong to the daylight any more than I do. . . . Oh God, how I envy you, it just isn't *fair.*"

His nose was burned, and began to peel. Which humiliated him. Which he would not allow her to joke about.

"I feel like a freak. I *am* a freak. Go to the dining room by yourself, you obviously can't want a creature like me to accompany you," he said.

She overheard him speaking in a peremptory way to one of the tennis instructors, a young man his own age, and was startled at first—and then rather thrilled—by the tone of his voice. He could be firm, even somewhat bullying, out of her presence. Though with her, of course, he was always puppyish, boyish, tremulous, uncertain.

"You *do* love me, you *do* love me?" he asked repeatedly.

"I'm your wife now, of course I love you," Claire laughed, stroking his hair, his shoulders, his sides.

"You won't throw me aside someday, the way you snatched me up?"

"Don't be absurd."

"I'm not absurd," he said petulantly. ". . . Am I absurd, Claire?"

"Hush. Why don't you sleep."

"Will you sleep too?"

"Of course."

"You won't stay awake, will you?—and look at me?"

"Hush now. It's very late."

"You *won't* stay awake, will you? After I've gone to sleep?"

"No. Of course not."

"Shall we fall asleep at the very same moment?"

"That's rather difficult, isn't it, Emil?"

"But don't you even want to try!"

Then he would drift off into sleep, his eyelids only partly closed, his pale, almost white eyelashes fluttering with the nervous intensity of unwilled sleep. At such times her heart would expand with love of him—of his awkward, almost crude innocence; and she would kiss his parted lips gently, and murmur a blessing.

"Love, love, love. . . ."

Though her realtor had received an offer of two hundred and seventy-five thousand dollars for her house and the 2.3 acres that went with it Claire decided not to sell after all. Emil saw the house and exclaimed, "Oh Jesus. Is *that . . . ?*" And so she decided not to sell.

Why bother with the fuss of locating an apartment and moving her things and selling much of her lovely furniture? She could not even remember the reason she had wanted to move, had it had something to do with her grief over her first husband's adultery, and her wish to put all memories of him behind . . . ? But now all memories of him *were* behind.

When Emil questioned her about him—lightly, playfully, not at all jealously—Claire had to think before replying. What sort of man was he, this Falk? "Oh, I think basically—basically he was a man of limited imagination," Claire said slowly. "But very solid. Very reliable."

Emil snickered. "He wasn't worthy of you, obviously!" he said.

"He didn't exactly *know* me."

Her husband's closet, empty; and filled now, or partly filled, with Emil's clothes.

"We'll have to buy you some things," Claire said. "You seem to own only summer clothing."

"Yes, it *is* winter up here, isn't it? I'd almost forgotten what winter was."

A houndstooth English jacket, a pale orange blazer, a camel's-hair coat, fur-lined leather gloves made in Hungary, fur-lined leather boots made in Italy, a half-dozen sweaters, a dozen shirts. A smart plaid vest. A suede suit. Trousers of various textures, various hues. A blue terry-cloth bathrobe to slip into when he was still wet from his shower.

Clowning, he went to stand in the plate-glass window of the men's shop in the Fairway Hotel, positioning himself like a mannequin. He was wearing the suede suit, without a shirt. His slightly hollow hairless chest shone.

The salesman managed to laugh but Claire, unamused, spoke sharply.

Whereupon her young husband turned away at once, flushing, hurt, and fled—simply ran out the front door. Claire called after him but he didn't look back.

He was gone, that time, overnight. She stayed up until two and then decided that she would sleep, she wouldn't martyr herself for him; she made herself a rum toddy and fell asleep on her bed, beneath a quilted afghan. Where Emil found her the next morning and awoke her with a wet puppyish kiss.

He crept under the afghan, burrowing into her arms.

"Forgive, forgive. Forgive little Emil."

His breath stank, there was an odor of something dry and harsh in his hair, perhaps smoke; and the stubble on his chin chafed her sensitive breasts. But she held him, and rocked him gently, and forgave him.

There were temper tantrums, there were shouting matches. Claire had never guessed herself so easily enraged. Once she even began to strike Emil's tear-stained face, screaming at him, and he tried to catch her wrists, ducking backward in alarm. He *was* frightened of her, she saw with amusement. But how silly! . . . As if she didn't love him more than life itself.

After the quarrels there were drinking sessions, occasionally. And frequent bouts of lovemaking. And once Emil fished out of a knapsack in his closet something for them to smoke in a pipe—hashish, it was: but Claire demurred. She had read somewhere . . . No, she was afraid.

"But don't you trust me, Claire dear?"

"It isn't that, Emil."

"Yes. But *don't* you trust me?"

"I simply don't want to. I don't want to."

"You hold yourself back from me, judging me. You're always judging. You don't *trust* me."

"Of course I trust you. I love you."

"But you hold yourself off from me, behind a glass case!"

Once, after the most protracted and childishly abusive of their quarrels—he called her a witch, she called him a male slut—they made love on the first-floor landing, gasping and clutching at each other. It was the first time Claire allowed herself to feel passion, to draw the tiny spark of pleasure up, upward, into something resembling a flame, and by the time she came to her climax she was groaning and shouting and tearing at him, her face distorted, her mouth gaping and ugly as a fish's—and still the sensation billowed onward, higher and higher, more and more violent, until she thought she would lose consciousness. *I love you, I love you, I love . . .*

Afterward, dazed, she hardly knew where she was, who this thin shuddering creature was lying on top of her, dripping sweat. Who, why. . . . What had led her to . . .

She began to cry. Her body shook. Everything was naked, exposed: her soul, her brain, her nerves: she had been destroyed, she had been turned inside out: and yet she was living, still, convulsed with sobs of dismay and incredulity and gratitude.

Emil said nothing. He eased himself from her and lay for a while, holding her as she wept and murmured to him, *Love, love, I love.* . . . He held her loosely, one arm beneath her shoulders. Until it became numb. Until the position became distinctly uncomfortable. Then he eased surreptitiously away. She would have called out for him but she was too sleepy, too exhausted. Why was he abandoning her. . . . Why was it so cold. . . .

A long time later she heard, or believed she heard, someone talking. Muttering. She tried to rouse herself but her head ached. There was a person drawing near, there were footsteps, silent, she must have been lying on the floor, on the carpet, but where?—why? Someone laid a blanket atop her, tucking it under her chin.

"Sleep it off, love," came a small cool remote voice.

Afterward, Claire was intensely ashamed of her behavior: that ugly grasping maniacal passion. Her body had gone mad, that was all. And the spell of weeping. . . . She had wept and wept like a giant child though she had sensed, even at the time, in her half-conscious drunken state, her young husband's secret contempt.

She would have liked to vow to him—I will never be that way again. I will never submit the two of us to such an experience again.

She would have liked to beg him—Please forget! *Please forget!*

He hid himself from her, daydreaming. A book in his lap. A notebook opened on the table before him, his pen turning idly between his fingers. And sometimes he sat at the piano, depressing the notes so slowly that they hardly sounded.

There was sheet music in the piano bench—why didn't he play something? Her son Ted had taken lessons at one time, many years ago.

"I can't play with anyone else listening, I'd be too self-conscious," he said.

"But I *won't* listen. I'll be upstairs on the telephone."

He shrugged his shoulders indifferently. In recent weeks his face had become drained of all expression, he no longer clowned and carried on, he never teased her. When he raised his glasses to rub his eyes Claire saw that he looked drawn and tired, much older than his years. There were white crinkles about his eyes like tiny lines etched in the skin.

"You're bored," Claire said recklessly.

"Of course not," he said at once.

He adjusted his glasses and stared at her, blinking. His cheeks colored faintly as if he had been caught out in a lie.

"Of course you *are,*" she said. "And it's quite natural. There isn't enough for you to do here. Wouldn't you like to continue with your theatrical work? There's an experimental theater in the city, I was reading about it in last Sunday's paper, it sounds exactly like something you would . . . But why are you staring at me like that? You *were* interested in the theater when I met you."

"Was I?"

"Well—weren't you?"

"I never liked working with other people. In such close quarters. Subordinating myself to others' ideas. . . . You wouldn't understand," he said, yawning.

"Then what would you like to do?"

"Nothing."

"What?"

"I do what I am doing."

"Yes, but what *are* you doing?"

His pale lips stretched into a wide rapid humorless smile.

"You're too solicitous of me, love," he said softly. "I'm quite all right as I am. I'm perfectly happy. Idyllically happy. . . . I'm waiting."

"Waiting for what?" Claire asked sharply.

He shrugged his shoulders again. Even in his handsome new clothes he looked scrawny and unkempt.

"Would you like to take piano lessons again?—with a good pianist? You could audition at the conservatory."

"Too late. Too old," he said, drawling. He stretched his fingers at her. "Stiff joints."

As the months passed Emil rarely slept with Claire for an entire night: he slipped quietly away as soon as she slept, or as soon as he believed she slept. Once, startled out of a half-sleep, she asked him where he was going and he mumbled guiltily that he couldn't sleep right now—he was too restless. But why can't you sleep? she asked, pulling at his wrist, smiling. Come back to bed, I'll hold you, you'll be asleep in ten minutes.

He hesitated. Then said, "I'm afraid—well—your snoring keeps me awake."

"My snoring!" Claire said, deeply hurt. "But I haven't been asleep. . . . I'm sure I haven't been asleep. . . ."

He shrugged his shoulders and did not contradict her. But he did not return to bed.

Later that night Claire *did* wake herself with a hoarse loud snort. She woke, startled, to find her throat parched and painfully dry. She was grateful, then, that Emil wasn't with her.

He got into the habit of wandering about the house downstairs, late at night. She could not hear his footsteps, exactly—he was barefoot, and of course he moved lightly—but she could feel a subtle, almost imperceptible vibration in the house. He sprawled on the couch in her former husband's study and in the morning she saw the piles of books he had pulled off the shelf and had presumably leafed through. Hawthorne's *Tales, The Iliad, Great Philosophical Ideas of the Western World,* Flaubert's *Bouvard and Pécuchet:* books her husband had acquired over the years, had never read, and hadn't bothered to take along with him. Emil wrote in his notebook, tore the pages out impatiently, discarded them. But when Claire uncrumpled them she saw that he had written only nonsense scrawls, or had covered a page with doodles of misshapen people and animals. In one, a woman with gigantic breasts and a ribald leering smile strode forward, a half-dozen heads hanging from her right fist, held by their hair. In another a man had turned into a phallus—or a phallus had turned into a man—and stared upward with a melancholy expression.

Emil began to sit at the piano for hours, reading music, touching the keys listlessly. Occasionally he struck loud angry chords and the sound was astonishing: though Claire might be far away upstairs the sudden noise would alarm her, her heart would lurch in her chest. Sometimes he played rushed, uneven arpeggios, cursing when he hit a wrong note.

He became obsessed with Chopin, and bought all of Chopin's music. The preludes, the nocturnes, the mazurkas . . . even the polonaises. . . . This is the music in which death speaks secretly, Emil said, but you never know *quite* where. He leafed through the études, he tried to play, attacking the keyboard fiercely, then letting his hands fall on his knees. He couldn't play, he said petulantly, with someone always listening.

Claire returned from shopping late one afternoon to find Emil at the piano, exactly as he had been when she had left hours before. His face was pinched, his mouth puckered. Before him was a Chopin nocturne. In a flat but amused voice he told Claire that he had been trying to play the concluding cadenza, a single cadenza, for an hour and a half. Over and over he played. Each time he made a mistake he forced himself to begin again. It was discipline, it was punishment. He *would not stop* until he played the cadenza perfectly, as Chopin himself must have played it.

"Attention, love!" he said briskly. He flexed his fingers and wriggled them like a clown.

Claire opened her mouth to protest but he cut her short. And began the cadenza again, an octave above high C: his fingers moving so rapidly, so surely, that Claire stared in astonishment. The notes were struck softly, softly, and then gradually harder, building to a delicate crescendo and then almost immediately diminishing. Though Emil's head was tilted back and his eyes were half-closed the tendons in his throat were rigid and Claire could nearly feel his impatience, his terrible rage. She stood waiting helplessly. There was nothing to do but stare at those blurred fingers. He *was* an accomplished pianist, evidently. . . . Then he began a rapid, complex run down the keyboard, and still his fingers moved with an incredible rapid grace, an almost inhuman grace, and Claire held her breath, her own nails dug into her palms, and then—and then of course he struck a wrong note—

He did not scream, he did not bring his fist down on the keyboard. He merely sat there grinning. His breathing was quick and shallow, she could see his thin chest rising and falling, and very nearly feel his murderous heart.

Swaying, she brought her hand to her forehead.

"Oh please don't, please don't. . . ." she whispered.

"Don't *what,* dear Claire?" Emil asked sharply.

"Don't, don't. . . ."

He regarded her with silent contempt, and then laughed shrilly, like a child on the verge of hysteria.

"Don't *what?* Continue to exist?"

He glided, he slid, he plunged into dark moods. Would not sleep, would not eat. Would not leave the house. She came upon him slouched in his underclothes on her husband's old leather couch, staring out the window.

How could he lie there so motionless, what was he brooding about, where was his mind . . .? If she spoke his name he often did not respond at once. If she touched his shoulder he shivered; or, rather, his flesh shivered. Slowly, reluctantly, his spirit eased back into his body and he looked up at her, his eyes narrowed, the white lines edging them pinched and severe.

"Emil? Is something wrong? What are you thinking about?"

"What am I thinking about? . . . Nothing."

She was in danger of bursting into tears. But instead she laughed, a harsh mirthless laugh. And then, flushing deeply, went silent. "But I love you," she said in reproach.

He smiled faintly, quizzically. Love? She loved him? But what was love, where precisely was it? What did it mean?

"Well. I love you too," he said finally.

The moods lightened. He consented to be bathed by her, and to allow her to shampoo his hair. She was gentle, loving, sometimes playful. She stuck her soapy fingers in his ears and wiggled them. She tickled the crisp pale hair beneath his arms. Without his glasses his green-gray eyes were small and close-set and their gaze seemed comfortably blurred.

Now his spirits rose and he was Emil again, the old Emil. But then they sank. Hour by hour, quite perceptibly, they sank. How much can you believe in, Emil said, yawning, indicating with a dismissive wave of his arms the house, the grounds, the sky. How seriously can you take all this? Even when you own it.

Don't, Claire whispered.

She had always thought of depression as a simple pathological state, the consequence of self-indulgence and sluggishness; neither she nor her husband—her former husband—could tolerate it in others. Now, holding and rocking in her arms her stricken young lover, she wondered if it was in some way a sensitive and even intelligent response to certain . . . to certain implacable truths.

Yet she loved him, and she would nurse him back. And so it came about that his spirits *did* rise. . . . He had become interested in real estate, in property investment, and she gave him brochures to read, and articles torn out of *Fortune* and *Business Week;* she loved to answer his questions, which were often naive, but sometimes surprisingly astute. Tax depreciation. . . . Insurance. . . . Tenants' rights. . . . Perhaps they should buy property in the Adirondacks, near Lake Placid? A summer home? A small hotel? A block of shops? A restaurant? Or a small apartment building here in the city, where Emil could oversee the manager at close quarters. . . .

One night when he was especially euphoric he pulled her gently into their bed, and began to make love to her. (In recent months they had stopped making love. For some reason they had stopped. Neither mentioned it, of course, and Claire herself did not really think about it: if she began to think about it her mind simply went blank.) But then he paused. He drew away from her, half-sobbing.

"Emil . . .?"

"I can't."

"Emil, please. It doesn't matter."

He lay very still. He rubbed the back of his forearm against his eyes roughly. "I can't, can't, *can't,*" he whispered.

"It isn't important," Claire said gently.

"Isn't it!"

She could not tell—was his tone sarcastic, was it utterly serious—but when she tried to stroke his face he turned aside and swung his feet over the edge of the bed.

"Emil—"

She grasped his arm but he twisted violently away. "Don't touch!" he said.

He rose naked from the bed and ran from the room. She heard his footsteps on the stairs. . . . For a long time she lay immobile, deeply hurt. She had never been so hurt in her life. We aren't really married, she thought. He isn't really my husband.

She woke before dawn, alone. The bedclothes smelled of sweat and were badly rumpled. When she went downstairs she found him asleep on one of the sofas in the living room, still naked, breathing hoarsely through his mouth. He slept with the single-minded intensity of a small child, his hands curved toward his chest, his chin damp with saliva. So deeply was he plunged into sleep that he fairly quivered with the experience. How profound, how very profound, was the element into which he had fallen. . . . She stood above him, noting his trembling eyelids, the pallor of his hollow, hairless chest, the small pale shrunken penis in the sparse bush of pubic hair. Emil. Her lover Emil. Her husband. He appeared to be dreaming. Certainly he was dreaming. His eyeballs jerked behind his eyelids, his fingers and toes twitched. She gazed upon him calmly. She was not at all jealous. He was dreaming, and she was not jealous: perhaps her shadow fell upon his sleep and it was she of whom he dreamed.

Yet it was unfair, it was unjust, that the man she loved so deeply could slip away from her, and plunge into an element that contained him utterly and set her apart from him. What are the secrets of sleep, who can account for the isolation, the selfishness of that solitude. . . . Odd, she had never cared about her former husband's interior life. She had never thought about it at all. In fact she had often been relieved when in bed he turned from her, overtaken by drowsiness, relinquishing her to her own solitude, her own small universe of dreams. But Emil was different, she would have liked very much to know what he was experiencing, whether indeed she was queen of his sleep or whether there, in that kingdom, he did not know her at all.

She touched his shoulder. But he did not awake: he moaned softly, and tried to burrow into the cushions. His long thin bluish-white feet kicked feebly. So she relented, and went upstairs and came back with an afghan and a pillow to slip beneath his head. Again the sight of him mesmerized her. He slept so hard, so very hard, and he *was* her husband. It crossed her mind that she could smother him, with the pillow. If she chose. She was capable of a single great act of strength and he, surprised, bereft in that other world, would have been powerless to withstand her. . . . But of course she merely slipped the pillow beneath his head, and laid the afghan carefully on top of him so that he would not catch cold. His nakedness was so frail, so vulnerable, except for the premature lines etched rather deeply into his throat, and those small white lines in his face, it was a boy's nakedness, striking in its blunt innocence.

Not long afterward she telephoned her former husband at his office. His voice rose cautiously at first but when he saw that she wanted only to talk, and to talk about casual things—mutual friends, property they had once owned together, finances, city politics—he was cordial, and seemed quite pleased to hear from her. Claire knew that he had received a certain nasty letter from their son because a carbon copy of the letter had been sent to her, in the same envelope with a very nasty letter to *her.* She supposed that her husband had received a carbon copy of her letter; and since both letters questioned their respective characters, what poor furious Ted called their "moral degeneracy," Claire saw no reason to mention them, nor did her husband.

And how is—? her husband asked.

Lovely. Just lovely, Claire said. And you—?

Lovely, he said.

They were silent for a long moment. Then Claire's former husband told her of a new restaurant downtown that *the two of you* might check out sometime: it was overpriced, of course, but charming, with an impressive wine list.

We'll do that, Claire said, delighted.

She had wanted to ask him . . . she had wanted to ask . . .

Well, what *is* marriage, and how does one know when one is married? What *is* love, precisely? The questions were naive and embarrassing, and yet they must be asked. Though Claire herself hadn't the courage.

She *hadn't* the courage, though she was over fifty years old and had lived, had lived, had lived forever.

Then the weather changed, and she and Emil flew to San Francisco for a marvelous two-week vacation—a second honeymoon, of a sort—and there acquired several fascinating jade figures, and looked up old friends of Claire's who were delighted to see them, not at all disapproving of the marriage as Claire had halfway feared. ("But you look radiant, Claire!" they said. "And Emil is so charming—and so deep, so obviously deep. You make a very attractive couple.") And when they returned, the house painters had finished with both the downstairs and upstairs rooms and everything looked lovely, clean and white and blank and new and lovely, and it would be a challenge, they both said, to acquire the right kind of art for the walls. . . . Claire spent much of her time shopping, and at her volunteer organizations; Emil joined an avant-garde theater group in the city. Sometimes they met for a drink downtown, at the Fairway, but often they didn't see each other until dinner, which was eaten late—never before eight o'clock. And there were times, of course, when Emil had rehearsals and wasn't back until one or two in the morning, and Claire, tired from her own activities, did not wait up for him.

It was a new season. A new autumn. Claire was elected first vice-president of the Friends of the Symphony. Emil's theater was to present a play by Lorca, the first of November. When his friends brought him home, when Claire came downstairs to join them for a drink, she saw the surprised, half-reluctant admiration in their faces: for of course they all gossiped about her, they speculated freely about Emil's "older" wife. But she had never looked more regal, more beautiful. Her skin bloomed darkly, her hair was now tinted a rich lustrous brown black, fashioned to rise from her head in a winglike manner, exposing the prominent widow's peak. She wore unusual clothes: black trousers, a coarse-knit white sweater; many-layered muslin skirts in the latest style; simple wraparound housedresses from Saks. She said little, and smiled little. Emil came at once to stand beside her. He was obviously very proud of her. When he introduced her to his friends she shook hands like a man, and fixed her severe dark gaze upon them one by one, and did not allow herself to be too easily won over. For she knew, she knew very well, that young people like these did not value easy conquests.

Sometimes, in the morning, Emil would stroll casually into her dressing room, toweling his hair, or wiping his glasses with a tissue, and he would say, very casually, that he had liked the outfit she'd worn the night before —was it new?—he didn't remember having seen it before. Or he would say with a droll twist of his mouth that one of his friends had fallen in love with her—had begged to be invited back sometime, maybe to dinner —what did Claire think? Yes? No? Occasionally he apologized for their having stayed so late, and having made so much noise. But Claire prudently did not comment. She would *not* comment.

The important thing was—he was busy, he was absorbed in his new life, he was happy. When he forbade her to see the play she was disappointed but did not persist. Your presence in the audience would make me self-conscious, he said. He forbade her also to read any reviews of the opening. She promised that she would not, but sought them out nonetheless in a nearby library: only one review, hardly more than a paragraph, mildly enthusiastic, complimenting the cast on their energy and zeal, and the set designer for his imagination. The names of several actors were mentioned but Emil's was not among them.

After the play's two-week run came to an end Emil often stayed out late, and quite frequently his friends brought him home very early in the morning. Claire came to detest a short burly-chested youth with red curly hair and a thick red beard, whose laughter was always dissolving into coughing fits. He was blatant, he knew himself good-looking, and very young—much younger than Emil. And another creature: tall and thin and delicate-boned as Emil, with a whispery, rather mocking voice, and a bad limp. And there were girls, women, interchangeable, always uncomfortably intense in Claire's presence: to hear them talk they cared about nothing except their "careers," their "work." Claire refrained from questioning them about their plans, their exact plans, for the future. Nor did she comment dryly that so much partying, so much alcohol and marijuana and exhaustion, would hardly help.

But Emil was happy with them, or at any rate diverted from his spells of melancholy. She was not going to judge him, she had come to love him too much, to exalt in him . . . in his mere being, his existence, as one might exalt in the fact of a work of art, or a superbly proportioned animal, or a comely child. She hardly thought of him as her husband. Husband—what did that mean? Its meaning was parochial, claustrophobic. He's like a child of my own, a second son—yet far more interesting than any child of my own, she thought with a curious satisfaction. And anyway one no longer wanted a *husband*, in the old sense. All that was dead, finished.

In mid-December Emil announced his birthday. It was that day, that very day. A small group of his closest friends, his favorite people, were coming that evening to help him celebrate, and he hoped Claire would not mind. They had been somewhat out of touch that week because of their conflicting schedules: for the first time in months Claire had had to attend a dinner, a fund-raising dinner for a local congressional candidate, and she hadn't returned home until well after midnight, and Emil mentioned the fact once or twice, always with a somewhat reproachful air. So they had been out of communication. It was not *his* fault.

"Your birthday . . . ?" Claire said, peering at him over her reading glasses.

"My thirty-fifth. What's wrong? Why stare at me like that? It's rude, it's eccentric. . . . Don't I deserve an occasional birthday, like the rest of you?"

"Your thirty-fifth . . . ?"

"Some of us age quickly," he said with a cheerful smile.

Somehow Claire had known beforehand that the party would be disastrous, and yet she did not forbid it; she felt too weak, too absurdly wounded, to protest. And then Emil did not quarrel fairly: he launched into one of his theatrical tantrums, or delivered a silly insulting speech at the top of his lungs, or threw things—pillows, vases, articles of clothing—onto the floor; or he went utterly cold, utterly silent, and regarded her with a pristine contempt she found terrifying.

Her heart ached, at such times. It was not farfetched to say that her very heart ached in her chest, between her tight constraining ribs. The real, the organic, the pounding heart and not a mere word, not a metaphor. . . . She grew short of breath, her body flushed with an obscure unspeakable shame.

She would stay away from the party. Would go to bed early. No: she would hurry out to the hairdresser's, and perhaps buy herself a new dress, something dramatic, stark, striking. So that he would gaze upon her with love and pride. But no. Perhaps it would be a better strategy to stay away from the party, and deny him the pleasure of seeing her. . . . Where is

Claire, his friends would inquire, why is she keeping herself from us? Is she angry? Is she angry with you?

Even when the first guests began to arrive she could not make up her mind. She regarded herself in the mirror critically. She *was* looking rather tired, and there hadn't been a slot for her at the hairdresser's, and the shortness of breath stayed with her, vexing as an insect buzzing close to her face. "Come on, come on, get a move on, horsey," Emil said gaily, tossing gowns from her closet onto the bed, selecting a pair of high-heeled slippers, but she could not respond to his drollery and in the end sent him away. He made her a double Cuban Manhattan, one of their favorite drinks last summer, and brought it to her as a peace offering. She accepted it but decided against going downstairs. She *would* keep herself away, to punish him.

The party was extraordinarily noisy, and lasted until nearly four in the morning. Claire slept, and woke, and slept again; and still the sounds of gaiety continued.

And then it was silent, and Emil was pawing at her. He half-fell onto the bed, giggling. Before she could push him away he had torn her nightgown and turned her over roughly onto her stomach.

She smelled alcohol on his breath but he did not seem to be drunk: he was too euphoric, too manic. She shouted for him to stop—what on earth was he doing to her—his lean hard thighs gripping her hips, his fingers clenched in her hair. His words were incoherent, interrupted by giggles and brief spasms of coughing. "You like it! You know you like it! Hey, lady, you know you like it! Lovely big soft marvelous thing! A little whale—one of those little ones! They're so lovely! Oh, I love them! One of those—what-do-you-call-them—walruses—a female walrus on the beach! Oh, a cow! A walrus-cow! You know you love it, don't you!"

She forced him off—she *was* stronger than he when it was necessary—and struck him in the face. At once he shrank back. He half-fell out of bed. Holding his mouth in both hands he began to whimper.

"You hurt me. Oh, Claire, you *hurt* me. My lip is cut on the inside, I can taste the . . ."

She pushed at him again and shouted at him to leave her alone, to get out of the room. But still he crouched there, naked, his chest hollow, his shoulders badly hunched. She saw two absurd tears running down his cheeks.

"Don't be ridiculous. Go and rinse your mouth, you aren't hurt, you're drunk and disgusting, you've been taking drugs, haven't you, though you

WALKER PERCY

After mentioning the story you are about to read, Walker Percy discussed his second choice, already included in this volume:

The other is Henry James's "The Turn of the Screw." A really frightening story—because of James's refusal to use the usual Gothic tricks. James knew how good it was and I remember reading James's account of dictating the story to his secretary, watching the man's face for some effect of the sinister goings-on and seeing absolutely nothing. The secretary didn't get it!

But you will—see page 163.

HOW LOVE CAME TO PROFESSOR GUILDEA

ROBERT HICHENS

I

Dull people often wondered how it came about that Father Murchison and Professor Frederic Guildea were intimate friends. The one was all faith, the other all skepticism. The nature of the father was based on love. He viewed the world with an almost childlike tenderness above his long, black cassock; and his mild, yet perfectly fearless, blue eyes seemed always to be watching the goodness that exists in humanity, and rejoicing at what they saw. The professor, on the other hand, had a hard face like a hatchet, tipped with an aggressive black goatee beard. His eyes were quick, piercing and irreverent. The lines about his small, thin-lipped mouth were almost cruel. His voice was harsh and dry, sometimes, when he grew energetic, almost soprano. It fired off words with a sharp and clipping utterance. His habitual manner was one of distrust and investigation. It was impossible to suppose that, in his busy life, he found any time for love, either of humanity in general or of an individual.

Yet his days were spent in scientific investigations which conferred immense benefits upon the world.

Both men were celibates. Father Murchison was a member of an Angelican order which forbade him to marry. Professor Guildea had a poor opinion of most things, but especially of women. He had formerly held a post as lecturer at Birmingham. But when his fame as a discoverer grew, he removed to London. There, at a lecture he gave in the East End, he first met Father Murchison. They spoke a few words. Perhaps the bright intelligence of the priest appealed to the man of science, who was inclined, as a rule, to regard the clergy with some contempt. Perhaps the transparent sincerity of this devotee, full of common sense, attracted him. As he was leaving the hall he abruptly asked the father to call on him at his house in Hyde Park Place. And the father, who seldom went into the West End, except to preach, accepted the invitation.

"When will you come?" said Guildea.

He was folding up the blue paper on which his notes were written in a tiny, clean hand. The leaves rustled dryly in accompaniment to his sharp, dry voice.

"On Sunday week I am preaching in the evening at St. Saviour's, not far off," said the father.

"I don't go to church."

"No," said the father, without any accent of surprise or condemnation.

"Come to supper afterwards?"

"Thank you, I will."

"What time will you come?"

The father smiled.

"As soon as I have finished my sermon. The service is at six-thirty."

"About eight then, I suppose. Don't make the sermon too long. My number in Hyde Park Place is 100. Good night to you."

He snapped an elastic band round his papers and strode off without shaking hands.

On the appointed Sunday, Father Murchison preached to a densely crowded congregation at St. Saviour's. The subject of his sermon was sympathy, and the comparative uselessness of man in the world unless he can learn to love his neighbor as himself. The sermon was rather long, and when the preacher, in his flowing, black cloak, and his hard, round hat, with a straight brim over which hung the ends of a black cord, made his way towards the professor's house, the hands of the illuminated clock disk at the Marble Arch pointed to twenty minutes past eight.

The father hurried on, pushing his way through the crowd of standing soldiers, chattering women, and giggling street boys in their Sunday best. It was a warm April night, and, when he reached number 100, Hyde Park Place, he found the professor bareheaded on his doorstep, gazing out towards the park railings, and enjoying the soft, moist air, in front of his lighted passage.

"Ha, a long sermon!" he exclaimed. "Come in."

"I fear it was," said the father, obeying the invitation. "I am that dangerous thing—an extempore preacher."

"More attractive to speak without notes, if you can do it. Hang your hat and coat—oh, cloak—here. We'll have supper at once. This is the dining room."

He opened a door on the right and they entered a long, narrow room, with a gold paper and a black ceiling, from which hung an electric lamp with a gold-colored shade. In the room stood a small oval table with covers laid for two. The professor rang the bell. Then he said: "People seem to talk better at an oval table than at a square one."

"Really? Is that so?"

"Well, I've had precisely the same party twice, once at a square table, once at an oval table. The first dinner was a dull failure, the second a brilliant success. Sit down, won't you?"

"How d'you account for the difference?" said the father, sitting down, and pulling the tail of his cassock well under him.

"H'm. I know how you'd account for it."

"Indeed. How then?"

"At an oval table, since there are no corners, the chain of human sympathy—the electric current, is much more complete. Eh! Let me give you some soup."

"Thank you."

The father took it, and, as he did so, turned his beaming blue eyes on his host. Then he smiled.

"What!" he said, in his pleasant, light tenor voice. "You do go to church sometimes, then?"

"Tonight is the first time for ages. And, mind you, I was tremendously bored."

The father still smiled, and his blue eyes gently twinkled.

"Dear, dear!" he said, "what a pity!"

"But not by the sermon," Guildea added. "I don't pay a compliment. I state a fact. The sermon didn't bore me. If it had, I should have said so, or said nothing."

"And which would you have done?"

The professor smiled almost genially.

"Don't know," he said. "What wine d'you drink?"

"None, thank you. I'm a teetotaler. In my profession and milieu it is necessary to be one. Yes, I will have some soda water. I think you would have done the first."

"Very likely, and very wrongly. You wouldn't have minded much."

"I don't think I should."

They were intimate already. The father felt most pleasantly at home under the black ceiling. He drank some soda water and seemed to enjoy it more than the professor enjoyed his claret.

"You smile at the theory of the chain of human sympathy, I see," said the father. "Then what is your explanation of the failure of your square party with corners, the success of your oval party without them?"

"Probably on the first occasion the wit of the assembly had a chill on his liver, while on the second he was in perfect health. Yet, you see, I stick to the oval table."

"And that means—"

"Very little. By the way, your omission of any allusion to the notorious part liver plays in love was a serious one tonight."

"Your omission of any desire for close human sympathy in your life is a more serious one."

"How can you be sure I have no such desire?"

"I divine it. Your look, your manner, tell me it is so. You were disagreeing with my sermon all the time I was preaching. Weren't you?"

"Part of the time."

The servant changed the plates. He was a middle-aged, blond, thin man, with a stony white face, pale, prominent eyes, and an accomplished manner of service. When he had left the room the professor continued.

"Your remarks interested me, but I thought them exaggerated."

"For instance?"

"Let me play the egoist for a moment. I spend most of my time in hard work, very hard work. The results of this work, you will allow, benefit humanity."

"Enormously," assented the father, thinking of more than one of Guildea's discoveries.

"And the benefit conferred by this work, undertaken merely for its own sake, is just as great as if it were undertaken because I loved my fellow man, and sentimentally desired to see him more comfortable than he is at present. I'm as useful precisely in my present condition of—in my present nonaffectional condition—as I should be if I were as full of gush as the sentimentalists who want to get murderers out of prison, or to put a premium on tyranny—like Tolstoi—by preventing the punishment of tyrants."

"One may do great harm with affection; great good without it. Yes, that is true. Even *le bon motif* is not everything, I know. Still I contend that, given your powers, you would be far more useful in the world with sympathy, affection for your kind, added to them than as you are. I believe even that you would do still more splendid work."

The professor poured himself another glass of claret.

"You noticed my butler?" he said.

"I did."

"He's a perfect servant. He makes me perfectly comfortable. Yet he has no feeling of liking for me. I treat him civilly. I pay him well. But I never think about him, or concern myself with him as a human being. I know nothing of his character except what I read of it in his last master's letter. There are, you may say, no truly human relations between us. You would affirm that his work woudl be better done if I had made him personally like me as a man—of any class—can like a man—of any other class?"

"I should, decidedly."

"I contend that he couldn't do his work better than he does it at present."

"But if any crisis occurred?"

"What?"

"Any crisis, change in your condition. If you needed his help, not only as a man and a butler, but as a man and a brother? He'd fail you then, probably. You would never get from your servant that finest service which can only be prompted by an honest affection."

"You have finished?"

"Quite."

"Let us go upstairs then. Yes, those are good prints. I picked them up in Birmingham when I was living there. This is my workroom."

They came to a double room lined entirely with books, and brilliantly, rather hardly, lit by electricity. The windows at one end looked on to the park, at the other on to the garden of a neighboring house. The door by which they entered was concealed from the inner and smaller room by the jutting wall of the outer room, in which stood a huge writing table loaded with letters, pamphlets and manuscripts. Between the two windows of the inner room was a cage in which a large, gray parrot was clambering, using both beak and claws to assist him in his slow and meditative peregrinations.

"You have a pet," said the father, surprised.

"I possess a parrot," the professor answered dryly. "I got him for a purpose when I was making a study of the imitative powers of birds, and I have never got rid of him. A cigar?"

"Thank you."

They sat down. Father Murchison glanced at the parrot. It had paused in its journey, and, clinging to the bars of its cage, was regarding them with attentive round eyes that looked deliberately intelligent, but by no means sympathetic. He looked away from it to Guildea, who was smoking, with his head thrown back, his sharp, pointed chin, on which the small black beard bristled, upturned. He was moving his under lip up and down rapidly. This action caused the beard to stir and look peculiarly aggressive. The father suddenly chuckled softly.

"Why's that?" cried Guildea, letting his chin drop down on his breast and looking at his guest sharply.

"I was thinking it would have to be a crisis indeed that could make you cling to your butler's affection for assistance."

Guildea smiled too.

"You're right. It would. Here he comes."

The man entered with coffee. He offered it gently, and retired like a shadow retreating on a wall.

"Splendid, inhuman fellow," remarked Guildea.

"I prefer the East End lad who does my errands in Bird Street," said the father. "I know all his worries. He knows some of mine. We are friends. He's more noisy than your man. He even breathes hard when he is especially solicitous, but he would do more for me than put the coals on my fire, or black my square-toed boots."

"Men are differently made. To me the watchful eye of affection would be abominable."

"What about that bird?"

The father pointed to the parrot. It had got up on its perch and, with one foot uplifted in an impressive, almost benedictory, manner, was gazing steadily at the professor.

"That's the watchful eye of imitation, with a mind at the back of it, desirous of reproducing the peculiarities of others. No, I thought your sermon tonight very fresh, very clever. But I have no wish for affection. Reasonable liking, of course, one desires"—he tugged sharply at his beard, as if to warn himself against sentimentality—"but anything more would be most irksome, and would push me, I feel sure, towards cruelty. It would also hamper one's work."

"I don't think so."

"The sort of work I do, I shall continue to benefit the world without loving it, and it will continue to accept the benefits without loving me. That's all as it should be."

He drank his coffee. Then he added rather aggressively: "I have neither time nor inclination for sentimentality."

When Guildea let Father Murchison out, he followed the father on to the doorstep and stood there for a moment. The father glanced across the damp road into the park.

"I see you've got a gate just opposite you," he said idly.

"Yes. I often slip across for a stroll to clear my brain. Good night to you. Come again some day."

"With pleasure. Good night."

The priest strode away, leaving Guildea standing on the step.

Father Murchison came many times again to number 100, Hyde Park Place. He had a feeling of liking for most men and women whom he knew, and of tenderness for all, whether he knew them or not, but he grew to have a special sentiment towards Guildea. Strangely enough, it was a sentiment of pity. He pitied this hardworking, eminently successful man of big brain and bold heart, who never seemed depressed, who never wanted assistance, who never complained of the twisted skein of life or faltered in his progress along its way. The father pitied Guildea, in fact, because Guildea wanted so little. He had told him so, for the intercourse of the two men, from the beginning, had been singularly frank.

One evening, when they were talking together, the father happened to speak of one of the oddities of life, the fact that those who do not want things often get them, while those who seek them vehemently are disappointed in their search.

"Then I ought to have affection poured upon me," said Guildea, smiling rather grimly. "For I hate it."

"Perhaps some day you will."

"I hope not, most sincerely."

Father Murchison said nothing for a moment. He was drawing together the ends of the broad band round his cassock. When he spoke he seemed to be answering someone.

"Yes," he said slowly, "yes, that *is* my feeling—pity."

"For whom?" said the professor.

Then, suddenly, he understood. He did not say that he understood, but Father Murchison felt, and saw, that it was quite unnecessary to answer his friend's question. So Guildea, strangely enough, found himself closely acquainted with a man—his opposite in all ways—who pitied him.

The fact that he did not mind this, and scarcely ever thought about it, shows perhaps as clearly as anything could, the peculiar indifference of his nature.

II

One autumn evening, a year and a half after Father Murchison and the professor had first met, the father called in Hyde Park Place and inquired of the blond and stony butler—his name was Pitting—whether his master was at home.

"Yes, sir," replied Pitting. "Will you please come this way?"

He moved noiselessly up the rather narrow stairs, followed by the father, tenderly opened the library door, and in his soft, cold voice, announced: "Father Murchison."

Guildea was sitting in an armchair, before a small fire. His thin, long-fingered hands lay outstretched upon his knees, his head was sunk down on his chest. He appeared to be pondering deeply. Pitting very slightly raised his voice.

"Father Murchison to see you, sir," he repeated.

The professor jumped up rather suddenly and turned sharply round as the father came in.

"Oh," he said. "It's you, is it? Glad to see you. Come to the fire."

The father glanced at him and thought him looking unusually fatigued.

"You don't look well tonight," the father said.

"No?"

"You must be working too hard. That lecture you are going to give in Paris is bothering you?"

"Not a bit. It's all arranged. I could deliver it to you at this moment verbatim. Well, sit down."

The father did so, and Guildea sank once more into his chair and stared hard into the fire without another word. He seemed to be thinking profoundly. His friend did not interrupt him, but quietly lit a pipe and began to smoke reflectively. The eyes of Guildea were fixed upon the fire. The father glanced about the room, at the walls of soberly bound books, at the crowded writing table, at the windows, before which hung heavy, dark blue curtains of old brocade, at the cage, which stood between them.

A green baize covering was thrown over it. The father wondered why. He had never seen Napoleon—so the parrot was named—covered up at night before. While he was looking at the baize. Guildea suddenly jerked up his head, and, taking his hands from his knees and clasping them, said abruptly: "D'you think I'm an attractive man?"

Father Murchison jumped. Such a question coming from such a man astounded him.

"Bless me!" he ejaculated. "What makes you ask? Do you mean attractive to the opposite sex?"

"That's what I don't know," said the professor gloomily, and staring again into the fire. "That's what I don't know."

The father grew more astonished.

"Don't know!" he exclaimed.

And he laid down his pipe.

"Let's say—d'you think I'm attractive, that there's anything about me which might draw a—a human being, or an animal irresistibly to me?"

"Whether you desired it or not?"

"Exactly—or—no, let us say definitely—if I did not desire it."

Father Murchison pursed up his rather full, cherubic lips, and little wrinkles appeared about the corners of his blue eyes.

"There might be, of course," he said, after a pause. "Human nature is weak, engagingly weak, Guildea. And you're inclined to flout it. I could understand a certain class of lady—the lion-hunting, the intellectual lady, seeking you. Your reputation, your great name—"

"Yes, yes," Guildea interrupted, rather irritably—"I know all that, I know."

He twisted his long hands together, bending the palms outwards till his thin, pointed fingers cracked. His forehead was wrinkled in a frown.

"I imagine," he said—he stopped and coughed dryly, almost shrilly—"I imagine it would be very disagreeable to be liked, to be run after—that is the usual expression, isn't it—by anything one objected to."

And now he half-turned in his chair, crossed his legs one over the other and looked at his guest with an unusual, almost piercing interrogation.

"Anything?" said the father.

"Well—well, anyone. I imagine nothing could be more unpleasant."

"To you—no," answered the father. "But—forgive me, Guildea, I cannot conceive your permitting such intrusion. You don't encourage adoration."

Guildea nodded his head gloomily.

"I don't," he said, "I don't. That's just it. That's the curious part of it, that I—"

He broke off deliberately, got up and stretched.

"I'll have a pipe, too," he said.

He went over to the mantelpiece, got his pipe, filled it and lighted it. As he held the match to the tobacco, bending forward with an inquiring expression, his eyes fell upon the green baize that covered Napoleon's cage. He threw the match into the grate, and puffed at the pipe as he walked forward to the cage. When he reached it he put out his hand, took hold of the baize and began to pull it away. Then suddenly he pushed it back over the cage.

"No," he said, as if to himself, "no."

He returned rather hastily to the fire and threw himself once more into his armchair.

"You're wondering," he said to Father Murchison. "So am I. I don't know at all what to make of it. I'll just tell you the facts and you must tell me what you think of them. The night before last, after a day of hard work—but no harder than usual—I went to the front door to get a breath of air. You know I often do that."

"Yes, I found you on the doorstep when I first came here."

"Just so. I didn't put on hat or coat. I just stood on the step as I was. My mind, I remember, was still full of my work. It was rather a dark night, not very dark. The hour was about eleven, or a quarter past. I was staring at the park, and presently I found that my eyes were directed towards somebody who was sitting, back to me, on one of the benches. I saw the person—if it was a person—through the railings."

"If it was a person!" said the father. "What do you mean by that?"

"Wait a minute. I say that because it was too dark for me to know. I merely saw some blackish object on the bench, rising into view above the level of the back of the seat. I couldn't say it was man, woman or child. But something there was, and I found that I was looking at it."

"I understand."

"Gradually, I also found that my thoughts were becoming fixed upon this thing or person. I began to wonder, first, what it was doing there; next, what it was thinking; lastly, what it was like."

"Some poor creature without a home, I suppose," said the father.

"I said that to myself. Still, I was taken with an extraordinary interest about this object, so great an interest that I got my hat and crossed the road to go into the park. As you know, there's an entrance almost opposite to my house. Well, Murchison, I crossed the road, passed through the gate in the railings, went up to the seat and found that there was—nothing on it."

"Were you looking at it as you walked?"

"Part of the time. But I removed my eyes from it just as I passed through the gate, because there was a row going on a little way off, and I turned for an instant in that direction. When I saw that the seat was vacant I was seized by a most absurd sensation of disappointment, almost of anger. I stopped and looked about me to see if anything was moving away, but I could see nothing. It was a cold night and misty, and there were few people about. Feeling, as I say, foolishly and unnaturally disappointed, I retraced my steps to this house. When I got here I discovered that during my short absence I had left the hall door open—half-open."

"Rather imprudent in London."

"Yes. I had no idea, of course, that I had done so, till I got back. However, I was only away three minutes or so."

"Yes."

"It was not likely that anybody had gone in."

"I suppose not."

"Was it?"

"Why do you ask me that, Guildea?"

"Well, well!"

"Besides, if anybody had gone in on your return you'd have caught him, surely."

Guildea coughed again. The father, surprised, could not fail to recognize that he was nervous and that his nervousness was affecting him physically.

"I must have caught cold that night," he said, as if he had read his friend's thought and hastened to contradict it. Then he went on: "I entered the hall, or passage, rather."

He paused again. His uneasiness was becoming very apparent.

"And you did catch somebody?" said the father.

Guildea cleared his throat.

"That's just it," he said, "now we come to it. I'm not imaginative, as you know."

"You certainly are not."

"No, but hardly had I stepped into the passage before I felt certain that somebody had got into the house during my absence. I felt convinced of it, and not only that, I also felt convinced that the intruder was the very person I had dimly seen sitting upon the seat in the park. What d'you say to that?"

"I begin to think you are imaginative."

"H'm! It seemed to me that the person—the occupant of the seat—and I had simultaneously formed the project of interviewing each other, had simultaneously set out to put that project into execution. I became so certain of this that I walked hastily upstairs into this room, expecting to find the visitor awaiting me. But there was no one. I then came down again and went into the dining room. No one. I was actually astonished. Isn't that odd?"

"Very," said the father, quite gravely.

The professor's chill and gloomy manner, and uncomfortable, constrained appearance kept away the humor that might well have lurked round the steps of such a discourse.

"I went upstairs again," he continued, "sat down and thought the matter over. I resolved to forget it, and took up a book. I might perhaps have been able to read, but suddenly I thought I noticed—"

He stopped abruptly. Father Murchison observed that he was staring towards the green baize that covered the parrot's cage.

"But that's nothing," he said. "Enough that I couldn't read. I resolved to explore the house. You know how small it is, how easily one can go all over it. I went all over it. I went into every room without exception. To the servants, who were having supper, I made some excuse. They were surprised at my advent, no doubt."

"And Pitting?"

"Oh, he got up politely when I came in, and stood while I was there, but never said a word. I muttered 'don't disturb yourselves,' or something of the sort, and came out. Murchison, I found nobody new in the house—yet I returned to this room entirely convinced that somebody had entered while I was in the park."

"And gone out again before you came back?"

"No, had stayed, and was still in the house."

"But, my dear Guildea," began the father, now in great astonishment. "Surely—"

"I know what you want to say—what I should want to say in your place. Now, do wait. I am also convinced that this visitor has not left the house and is at this moment in it."

He spoke with evident sincerity, with extreme gravity. Father Murchison looked him full in the face, and met his quick, keen eyes.

"No," he said, as if in reply to an uttered question, "I'm perfectly sane, I assure you. The whole matter seems almost as incredible to me as it must to you. But, as you know, I never quarrel with facts, however strange. I merely try to examine into them thoroughly. I have already consulted a doctor and been pronounced in perfect bodily health."

He paused, as if expecting the father to say something.

"Go on, Guildea," he said, "you haven't finished."

"No. I felt that night positive that somebody had entered the house, and remained in it, and my conviction grew. I went to bed as usual, and, contrary to my expectation, slept as well as I generally do. Yet directly I woke up yesterday morning, I knew that my household had been increased by one."

"May I interrupt you for one moment? How did you know it?"

"By my mental sensation. I can only say that I was perfectly conscious of a new presence within my house, close to me."

"How very strange," said the father. "And you feel absolutely certain that you are not overworked? Your brain does not feel tired? Your head is quite clear?"

"Quite. I was never better. When I came down to breakfast that morning I looked sharply into Pitting's face. He was as coldly placid and inexpressive as usual. It was evident to me that his mind was in no way distressed. After breakfast I sat down to work, all the time ceaselessly conscious of the fact of this intruder upon my privacy. Nevertheless, I labored for several hours, waiting for any development that might occur to clear away the mysterious obscurity of this event. I lunched. About half-past two I was obliged to go out to attend a lecture. I therefore took my coat and hat, opened my door, and stepped on to the pavement. I was instantly aware that I was no longer intruded upon, and this although I was now in the street, surrounded by people. Consequently, I felt certain that the thing in my house must be thinking of me, perhaps even spying upon me."

"Wait a moment," interrupted the father. "What was your sensation? Was it one of fear?"

"Oh, dear no. I was entirely puzzled—as I am now—and keenly interested, but not in any way alarmed. I delivered my lecture with my usual ease and returned home in the evening. On entering the house again I was perfectly conscious that the intruder was still there. Last night I dined alone and spent the hours after dinner in reading a scientific work in which I was deeply interested. While I read, however, I never for one moment lost the knowledge that some mind—very attentive to me—was within hail of mine. I will say more than this—the sensation constantly increased, and, by the time I got up to go to bed, I had come to a very strange conclusion."

"What? What was it?"

"That whoever—or whatever—had entered my house during my short absence in the park was more than interested in me."

"More than interested in you?"

"Was fond, or was becoming fond, of me."

"Oh!" exclaimed the father. "Now I understand why you asked me just now whether I thought there was anything about you that might draw a human being or an animal irresistibly to you."

"Precisely. Since I came to this conclusion, Murchison, I will confess that my feeling of strong curiosity has become tinged with another feeling."

"Of fear?"

"No, of dislike, or irritation. No—not fear, not fear."

As Guildea repeated unnecessarily this asseveration he looked again towards the parrot's cage.

"What is there to be afraid of in such a matter?" he added. "I am not a child to tremble before bogies."

In saying the last words he raised his voice sharply; then he walked quickly to the cage, and, with an abrupt movement, pulled the baize covering from it. Napoleon was disclosed, apparently dozing upon his perch with his head held slightly on one side. As the light reached him, he moved, ruffled the feathers about his neck, blinked his eyes, and began slowly to sidle to and fro, thrusting his head forward and drawing it back with an air of complacent, though rather unmeaning, energy. Guildea stood by the cage, looking at him closely, and indeed with an attention that was so intense as to be remarkable, almost unnatural.

"How absurd these birds are!" he said at length, coming back to the fire.

"You have no more to tell me?" asked the father.

"No. I am still aware of the presence of something in my house. I am still conscious of its close attention to me. I am still irritated, seriously annoyed—I confess it—by that attention."

"You say you are aware of the presence of something at this moment?"

"At this moment—yes."

"Do you mean in this room, with us, now?"

"I should say so—at any rate, quite near us."

Again he glanced quickly, almost suspiciously, towards the cage of the parrot. The bird was sitting still on its perch now. Its head was bent down and cocked sideways, and it appeared to be listening attentively to something.

"That bird will have the intonations of my voice more correctly than ever by tomorrow morning," said the father, watching Guildea closely with his mild blue eyes. "And it has always imitated me very cleverly."

The professor started slightly.

"Yes," he said. "Yes, no doubt. Well, what do you make of this affair?"

"Nothing at all. It is absolutely inexplicable. I can speak quite frankly to you, I feel sure."

"Of course. That's why I have told you the whole thing."

"I think you must be overworked, overstrained, without knowing it."

"And that the doctor was mistaken when he said I was all right?"

"Yes."

Guildea knocked his pipe out against the chimney piece.

"It may be so," he said. "I will not be so unreasonable as to deny the possibility, although I feel as well as I ever did in my life. What do you advise then?"

"A week of complete rest away from London, in good air."

"The usual prescription. I'll take it. I'll go tomorrow to Westgate and leave Napoleon to keep house in my absence."

For some reason, which he could not explain to himself, the pleasure which Father Murchison felt in hearing the first part of his friend's final remark was lessened, almost, was almost destroyed, by the last sentence.

He walked towards the city that night, deep in thought, remembering and carefully considering the first interview he had with Guildea in the latter's house a year and a half before.

On the following morning Guildea left London.

III

Father Murchison was so busy a man that he had little time for brooding over the affairs of others. During Guildea's week at the sea, however, the father thought about him a great deal, with much wonder and some dismay. This dismay was soon banished, for the mild-eyed priest was quick to discern weakness in himself, quicker still to drive it forth as a most undesirable inmate of the soul. But the wonder remained. It was destined to a crescendo. Guildea had left London on a Thursday. On a Thursday he returned, having previously sent a note to Father Murchison to mention that he was leaving Westgate at a certain time. When his train ran into Victoria Station, at five o'clock in the evening, he was surprised to see the cloaked figure of his friend standing upon the gray platform behind a line of porters.

"What, Murchison!" he said. "You here! Have you seceded from your order that you are taking this holiday?"

They shook hands.

"No," said the father. "It happened that I had to be in this neighborhood today, visiting a sick person. So I thought I would meet you."

"And see if I were still a sick person, eh?"

The professor glanced at him kindly, but with a dry little laugh.

"Are you?" replied the father gently, looking at him with interest. "No, I think not. You appear very well."

The sea air had, in fact, put some brownish red into Guildea's always thin cheeks. His keen eyes were shining with life and energy, and he walked forward in his loose gray suit and fluttering overcoat with a vigor that was noticeable, carrying easily in his left hand his well-filled gladstone bag.

The father felt completely reassured.

"I never saw you look better," he said.

"I never was better. Have you an hour to spare?"

"Two."

"Good. I'll send my bag up by cab, and we'll walk across the park to my house and have a cup of tea there. What d'you say?"

"I shall enjoy it."

They walked out of the station yard, past the flower girls and newspaper sellers towards Grosvenor Place.

"And you have had a pleasant time?" the father said.

"Pleasant enough, and lonely. I left my companion behind me in the passage at number 100, you know."

"And you'll not find him there now, I feel sure."

"H'm!" ejaculated Guildea. "What a precious weakling you think me, Murchison."

As he spoke he strode forward more quickly, as if moved to emphasize his sensation of bodily vigor.

"A weakling—no. But anyone who uses his brain as persistently as you do yours must require an occasional holiday."

"And I required one very badly, eh?"

"You required one, I believe."

"Well, I've had it. And now we'll see."

The evening was closing in rapidly. They crossed the road at Hyde Park Corner, and entered the park, in which were a number of people going home from work; men in corduroy trousers, caked with dried mud, and carrying tin cans slung over their shoulders, and flat panniers, in which lay their tools. Some of the younger ones talked loudly or whistled shrilly as they walked.

"Until the evening," murmured Father Murchison to himself.

"What?" asked Guildea.

"I was only quoting the last words of the text which seems written upon life, especially upon the life of pleasure: "Man goeth forth to his work, and to his labour.' "

"Ah, those fellows are not half-bad fellows to have in an audience. There were a lot of them at the lecture I gave when I first met you, I remember. One of them tried to heckle me. He had a red beard. Chaps with red beards are always hecklers. I laid him low on that occasion. Well, Murchison, and now we're going to see."

"What?"

"Whether my companion has departed."

"Tell me—do you feel any expectation of—well—of again thinking something is there?"

"How carefully you choose language. No, I merely wonder."

"You have no apprehension?"

"Not a scrap. But I confess to feeling curious."

"Then the sea air hasn't taught you to recognize that the whole thing came from overstrain?"

"No," said Guildea, very dryly.

He walked on in silence for a minute. Then he added: "You thought it would?"

"I certainly thought it might."

"Make me realize that I had a sickly, morbid, rotten imagination—eh? Come now, Murchison, why not say frankly that you packed me off to Westgate to get rid of what you considered an acute form of hysteria?"

The father was quite unmoved by this attack.

"Come now, Guildea," he retorted, "what did you expect me to think? I saw no indication of hysteria in you. I never have. One would suppose you the last man likely to have such a malady. But which is more natural—for me to believe in your hysteria or in the truth of such a story as you told me?"

"You have me there. No, I mustn't complain. Well, there's no hysteria about me now, at any rate."

"And no stranger in your house, I hope."

Father Murchison spoke the last words with earnest gravity, dropping the half-bantering tone—which they had both assumed.

"You take the matter very seriously, I believe," said Guildea, also speaking more gravely.

"How else can I take it? You wouldn't have me laugh at it when you tell it to me seriously?"

"No. If we find my visitor still in the house, I may even call upon you to exorcise it. But first I must do one thing."

"And that is?"

"Prove to you, as well as to myself, that it is still there."

"That might be difficult," said the father, considerably surprised by Guildea's matter-of-fact tone.

"I don't know. If it has remained in my house I think I can find a means. And I shall not be at all surprised if it is still there—despite the Westgate air."

In saying the last words the professor relapsed into his former tone of dry chaff. The father could not quite make up his mind whether Guildea was feeling unusually grave or unusually gay. As the two men drew near to Hyde Park Place their conversation died away and they walked forward silently in the gathering darkness.

"Here we are!" said Guildea at last.

He thrust his key into the door, opened it, and let Father Murchison into the passage, following him closely, and banging the door.

"Here we are!" he repeated in a louder voice.

The electric light was turned on in anticipation of his arrival. He stood still and looked round.

"We'll have some tea at once," he said. "Ah, Pitting!"

The pale butler, who had heard the door bang, moved gently forward from the top of the stairs that led to the kitchen, greeted his master respectfully, took his coat and Father Murchison's cloak, and hung them on two pegs against the wall.

"All's right, Pitting? All's as usual?" said Guildea.

"Quite so, sir."

"Bring us up some tea to the library."

"Yes, sir."

Pitting retreated. Guildea waited till he had disappeared, then opened the dining-room door, put his head into the room and kept it there for a moment, standing perfectly still. Presently he drew back into the passage, shut the door, and said: "Let's go upstairs."

Father Murchison looked at him inquiringly, but made no remark. They ascended the stairs and came into the library. Guildea glanced rather sharply round. A fire was burning on the hearth. The blue curtains were drawn. The bright gleam of the strong electric light fell on the long rows of books, on the writing table—very orderly in consequence of Guildea's holiday—and on the uncovered cage of the parrot. Guildea went up to the cage. Napoleon was sitting humped up on his perch with his feathers ruffled. His long toes, which looked as if they were covered with crocodile skin, clung to the bar. His round and blinking eyes were filmy, like old eyes. Guildea stared at the bird very hard, and then clucked with his tongue against his teeth. Napoleon shook himself, lifted one foot, extended his toes, sidled along the perch to the bars nearest to the professor and thrust his head against them. Guildea scratched it with his forefinger two or three times, still gazing attentively at the parrot; then he returned to the fire just as Pitting entered with the tea-tray.

Father Murchison was already sitting in an armchair on one side of the fire. Guildea took another chair and began to pour out tea, as Pitting left the room, closing the door gently behind him. The father sipped his tea, found it hot, and set the cup down on a little table at his side.

"You're fond of that parrot, aren't you?" he asked his friend.

"Not particularly. It's interesting to study sometimes. The parrot mind and nature are peculiar."

"How long have you had him?"

"About four years. I nearly got rid of him just before I made your acquaintance. I'm very glad now I kept him."

"Are you? Why is that?"

"I shall probably tell you in a day or two."

The father took his cup again. He did not press Guildea for an immediate explanation, but when they had both finished their tea he said: "Well, has the sea air had the desired effect?"

"No," said Guildea.

The father brushed some crumbs from the front of his cassock and sat up higher in his chair.

"Your visitor is still here?" he asked, and his blue eyes became almost ungentle and piercing as he gazed at his friend.

"Yes," answered Guildea, calmly.

"How do you know it, when did you know it—when you looked into the dining room just now?"

"No. Not until I came into this room. It welcomed me here."

"Welcomed you! In what way?"

"Simply by being here, by making me feel that it is here, as I might feel that a man was if I came into the room when it was dark."

He spoke quietly, with perfect composure in his usual dry manner.

"Very well," the father said, "I shall not try to contend against your sensation, or to explain it away. Naturally, I am in amazement."

"So am I. Never has anything in my life surprised me so much. Murchison, of course I cannot expect you to believe more than that I honestly—imagine, if you like—that there is some intruder here, of what kind I am totally unaware. I cannot expect you to believe that there really is anything. If you were in my place, I in yours, I should certainly consider you the victim of some nervous delusion. I could not do otherwise. But—wait. Don't condemn me as a hysteria patient, or as a madman, for two or three days. I feel convinced that—unless I am indeed unwell, a mental invalid, which I don't think is possible—I shall be able very shortly to give you some proof that there is a newcomer in my house."

"You don't tell me what kind of proof?"

"Not yet. Things must go a little farther first. But, perhaps even tomorrow I may be able to explain myself more fully. In the meanwhile, I'll say this, that if, eventually, I can't bring any kind of proof that I'm not dreaming, I'll let you take me to any doctor you like, and I'll resolutely try to adopt your present view—that I'm suffering from an absurd delusion. That is your view, of course?"

Father Murchison was silent for a moment. Then he said, rather doubtfully: "It ought to be."

"But isn't it?" asked Guildea, surprised.

"Well, you know, your manner is enormously convincing. Still, of course, I doubt. How can I do otherwise? The whole thing must be fancy."

The father spoke as if he were trying to recoil from a mental position he was being forced to take up.

"It must be fancy," he repeated.

"I'll convince you by more than my manner, or I'll not try to convince you at all," said Guildea.

When they parted that evening, he said: "I'll write to you in a day or two probably. I think the proof I am going to give you has been accumulating during my absence. But I shall soon know."

Father Murchison was extremely puzzled as he sat on the top of the omnibus going homeward.

IV

In two days' time he received a note from Guildea asking him to call, if possible, the same evening. This he was unable to do as he had an engagement to fulfill at some East End gathering. The following day was Sunday. He wrote saying he would come on the Monday, and got a wire shortly afterward: "Yes Monday come to dinner seven-thirty Guildea." At half-past seven he stood on the doorstep of number 100.

Pitting let him in.

"Is the professor quite well, Pitting?" the father inquired as he took off his cloak.

"I believe so, sir. He has not made any complaint," the butler formally replied. "Will you come upstairs, sir?"

Guildea met them at the door of the library. He was very pale and somber, and shook hands carelessly with his friend.

"Give us dinner," he said to Pitting.

As the butler retired, Guildea shut the door rather cautiously. Father Murchison had never before seen him look so disturbed.

"You're worried, Guildea," the father said. "Seriously worried."

"Yes, I am. This business is beginning to tell on me a good deal."

"Your belief in the presence of something here continues then?"

"Oh, dear, yes. There's no sort of doubt about the matter. The night I went across the road into the park something got into the house, though what the devil it is I can't yet find out. But now, before we go down to dinner, I'll just tell you something about that proof I promised you. You remember?"

"Naturally."

"Can't you imagine what it might be?"

Father Murchison moved his head to express a negative reply.

"Look about the room," said Guildea. "What do you see?"

The father glanced around the room, slowly and carefully.

"Nothing unusual. You do not mean to tell me there is any appearance of—"

"Oh, no, no, there's no conventional, white-robed, cloudlike figure.

Bless my soul, no! I haven't fallen so low as that."

He spoke with considerable irritation.

"Look again."

Father Murchison looked at him, turned in the direction of his fixed eyes and saw the gray parrot clambering in its cage, slowly and persistently.

"What?" he said, quickly. "Will the proof come from there?"

The professor nodded.

"I believe so," he said. "Now let's go down to dinner. I want some food badly."

They descended to the dining room. While they ate and Pitting waited upon them, the professor talked about birds, their habits, their curiosities, their fears and their powers of imitation. He had evidently studied this subject with the thoroughness that was characteristic of him in all that he did.

"Parrots," he said presently, "are extraordinarily observant. It is a pity that their means of reproducing what they see are so limited. If it were not so, I have little doubt that their echo of gesture would be as remarkable as their echo of voice often is."

"But hands are missing."

"Yes. They do many things with their heads, however. I once knew an old woman near Goring on the Thames. She was afflicted with the palsy. She held her head perpetually sideways and it trembled, moving from right to left. Her sailor son brought her home a parrot from one of his voyages. It used to reproduce the old woman's palsied movement of the head exactly. Those gray parrots are always on the watch."

Guildea said the last sentence slowly and deliberately, glancing sharply over his wine at Father Murchison, and, when he had spoken it, a sudden light of comprehension dawned in the priest's mind. He opened his lips to make a swift remark. Guildea turned his bright eyes towards Pitting, who at the moment was tenderly bearing a cheese meringue from the lift that connected the dining room with the lower regions. The father closed his lips again. But presently, when the butler had placed some apples on the table, had meticulously arranged the decanters, brushed away the crumbs and evaporated, he said, quickly: "I ,begin to understand. You think Napoleon is aware of the intruder?"

"I know it. He has been watching my visitant ever since the night of that visitant's arrival."

Another flash of light came to the priest.

"That was why you covered him with green baize one evening?"

"Exactly. An act of cowardice. His behavior was beginning to grate upon my nerves."

Guildea pursed up his thin lips and drew his brows down, giving to his face a look of sudden pain.

"But now I intend to follow his investigations," he added, straightening his features. "The week I wasted at Westgate was not wasted by him in London, I can assure you. Have an apple."

"No, thank you; no, thank you."

The father repeated the words without knowing that he did so. Guildea pushed away his glass.

"Let us come upstairs, then."

"No, thank you," reiterated the father.

"Eh?"

"What am I saying?" exclaimed the father, getting up. "I was thinking over this extraordinary affair."

"Ah, you're beginning to forget the hysteria theory?"

They walked out into the passage.

"Well, you are so very practical about the whole matter."

"Why not? Here's something very strange and abnormal come into my life. What should I do but investigate it closely and calmly?"

"What, indeed?"

The father began to feel rather bewildered, under a sort of compulsion which seemed laid upon him to give earnest attention to a matter that ought to strike him—so he felt—as entirely absurd. When they came into the library his eyes immediately turned, with profound curiosity, towards the parrot's cage. A slight smile curled the professor's lips. He recognized the effect he was producing upon his friend. The father saw the smile.

"Oh, I'm not won over yet," he said in answer to it.

"I know. Perhaps you may be before the evening is over. Here comes the coffee. After we have drunk it we'll proceed to our experiment. Leave the coffee, Pitting, and don't disturb us again."

"No, sir."

"I won't have it black tonight," said the father; "plenty of milk, please. I don't want my nerves played upon."

"Suppose we don't take coffee at all?" said Guildea. "If we do, you may trot out the theory that we are not in a perfectly normal condition. I know you, Murchison, devout priest and devout skeptic."

The father laughed and pushed away his cup.

"Very well, then. No coffee."

"One cigarette, and then to business."

The gray-blue smoke curled up.

"What are we going to do?" said the father.

He was sitting bolt upright as if ready for action. Indeed there was no suggestion of repose in the attitudes of either of the men.

"Hide ourselves, and watch Napoleon. By the way—that reminds me."

He got up, went to a corner of the room, picked up a piece of green baize and threw it over the cage.

"I'll pull that off when we are hidden."

"And tell me first if you have had any manifestation of this supposed presence during the last few days?"

"Merely an increasingly intense sensation of something here, perpetually watching me, perpetually attending to all my doings."

"Do you feel that it follows you about?"

"Not always. It was in this room when you arrived. It is here now—I feel. But, in going down to dinner, we seemed to get away from it. The conclusion is that it remained here. Don't let us talk about it just now."

They spoke of other things till their cigarettes were finished. Then, as they threw away the smoldering ends, Guildea said: "Now, Murchison, for the sake of this experiment, I suggest that we should conceal ourselves behind the curtains on either side of the cage, so that the bird's attention may not be drawn toward us and so distracted from that which we want to know more about. I will pull away the green baize when we are hidden. Keep perfectly still, watch the bird's proceedings, and tell me afterward how you feel about them, how you explain them. Tread softly."

The father obeyed, and they stole towards the curtains that fell before the two windows. The father concealed himself behind those on the left of the cage, the professor behind those on the right. The latter, as soon as they were hidden, stretched out his arm, drew the baize down from the cage, and let it fall on the floor.

The parrot, which had evidently fallen asleep in the warm darkness, moved on its perch as the light shone upon it, ruffled the feathers round its throat, and lifted first one foot and then the other. It turned its head round on its supple, and apparently elastic, neck, and, diving its beak into the down upon its back, made some searching investigations with, as it seemed, a satisfactory result, for it soon lifted its head again, glanced around its cage and began to address itself to a nut which had been fixed between the bars for its refreshment. With its curved beak it felt and tapped the nut, at first gently, then with severity. Finally it plucked the nut from the bars, seized it with its rough, gray toes, and, holding it down firmly on the perch, cracked it and pecked out its contents, scattering some on the floor of the cage and letting the fractured shell fall into the china bath that was fixed against the bars. This accomplished, the bird paused meditatively, extended one leg backward, and went through an elaborate process of wing-stretching that made it look as if it were lopsided and deformed. With its head reversed, it again applied itself to a subtle and exhaustive search among the feathers of its wing. This time its investigation seemed interminable, and Father Murchison had time to realize the absurdity of the whole position, and to wonder why he had lent himself to it. Yet he did not find his sense of humor laughing at it. On the contrary, he was smitten by a sudden gust of horror. When he was talking to his friend and watching him, the professor's manner, generally so calm, even so prosaic, vouched for the truth of his story and the well-adjusted balance of his mind. But when he was hidden this was not so. And Father Murchison, standing behind his curtain, with his eyes upon the unconcerned Napoleon, began to whisper to himself the word—madness, with a quickening sensation of pity and of dread.

The parrot sharply contracted one wing, ruffled the feathers around its throat again, then extended its other leg backward, and proceeded to the cleaning of its other wing. In the still room the dry sound of the feathers being spread was distinctly audible. Father Murchison saw the blue curtains behind which Guildea stood tremble slightly, as if a breath of wind had come through the window they shrouded. The clock in the far room chimed, and a coal dropped into the grate, making a noise like dead leaves stirring abruptly on hard ground. And again a gust of pity and of dread swept over the father. It seemed to him that he had behaved very foolishly, if not wrongly, in encouraging what must surely be the strange dementia of his friend. He ought to have declined to lend himself to a proceeding that, ludicrous, even childish in itself, might well be dangerous in the encouragement it gave to a diseased expectation. Napoleon's protruding leg, extended wing and twisted neck, his busy and unconscious devotion to the arrangement of his person, his evident sensation of complete loneliness and most comfortable solitude, brought home with vehemence to the father the undignified buffoonery of his conduct, the more piteous buffoonery of his friend. He seized the curtains with his hand and was about to thrust them aside and issue forth, when an abrupt movement of the parrot stopped him. The bird, as if sharply attracted by something, paused in its pecking, and, with its head still bent backward and twisted sideways on its neck, seemed to listen intently. Its round eye looked glistening and strained, like the eye of a disturbed pigeon. Contracting its wing, it lifted its head and sat for a moment erect on its perch, shifting its feet mechanically up and down, as if a dawning excitement produced in it an uncontrollable desire of movement. Then it thrust its head forward in the direction of the further room and remained perfectly still. Its attitude so strongly suggested the concentration of its attention on something immediately before it, that Father Murchison instinctively stared about the room, half-expecting to see Pitting advance softly, having entered through the hidden door. He did not come, and there was no sound in the chamber. Nevertheless, the parrot was obviously getting excited and increasingly attentive. It bent its head lower and lower, stretching out its neck until, almost falling from the perch, it half-extended its wings, raising them slightly from its back, as if about to take flight, and fluttering them rapidly up and down. It continued this fluttering movement for what seemed to the father an immense time. At length, raising its wings as far as possible, it dropped them slowly and deliberately down to its back, caught hold of the edge of its bath with its beak, hoisted itself on to the floor of the cage, waddled to the bars, thrust its head against them, and stood quite still in the exact attitude it always assumed when its head was being scratched by the professor. So complete was the suggestion of this delight conveyed by the bird, that Father Murchison felt as if he saw a white finger gently pushed among the soft feathers of its head, and he was seized by a most strong conviction that something, unseen by him but seen and welcomed by Napoleon, stood immediately before the cage.

The parrot presently withdrew its head, as if the coaxing finger had been lifted from it, and its pronounced air of acute physical enjoyment faded into one of marked attention and alert curiosity. Pulling itself up by the bars it climbed again upon its perch, sidled to the left side of the cage, and began apparently to watch something with profound interest. It bowed its head oddly, paused for a moment, then bowed its head again. Father Murchison found himself conceiving—from this elaborate movement of the head—a distinct idea of a personality. The bird's proceedings suggested extreme sentimentality combined with that sort of weak determination which is often the most persistent. Such weak determination is a very common attribute of persons who are partially idiotic. Father Murchison was moved to think of these poor creatures who will often, so strangely and unreasonably, attach themselves with persistence to those who love them least. Like many priests, he had had some experience of them, for the amorous idiot is peculiarly sensitive to the attraction of preachers. This bowing movement of the parrot recalled to his memory a terrible, pale woman who for a time haunted all churches in which he ministered, who was perpetually endeavoring to catch his eye, and who always bent her head with an obsequious and cunningly conscious smile when she did so. The parrot went on bowing, making a short pause between each genuflection, as if it waited for a signal to be given that called into play its imitative faculty.

"Yes, yes, it's imitating an idiot," Father Murchison caught himself saying as he watched.

And he looked again about the room, but saw nothing; except the furniture, the dancing fire, and the serried ranks of the books. Presently the parrot ceased from bowing, and assumed the concentrated and stretched attitude of one listening very keenly. He opened his beak, showing his black tongue, shut it, then opened it again. The father thought he was going to speak, but he remained silent, although it was obvious that he was trying to bring out something. He bowed again two or three times, paused, and then, again opening his beak, made some remark. The father could not distinguish any words, but the voice was sickly and disagreeable, a cooing and, at the same time, querulous voice, like a woman's, he thought. And he put his ear nearer to the curtain, listening with almost feverish attention. The bowing was resumed, but this time Napoleon added to it a sidling movement, affectionate and affected, like the movement of a silly and eager thing, nestling up to someone, or giving someone a gentle and furtive nudge. Again the father thought of that terrible, pale woman who had haunted churches. Several times he had come upon her waiting for him after evening services. Once she had hung her head smiling, and lolled out her tongue and pushed against him sideways in the dark. He remembered how his flesh had shrunk from the poor thing, the sick loathing of her that he could not banish by remembering that her mind was all astray. The parrot paused, listened, opened his beak and again said something in the same dovelike, amorous voice, full of sickly suggestion and yet hard, even dangerous, in its intonation. A loathsome voice, the father thought it. But this time, although he heard the voice more distinctly than before, he could not make up his mind whether it was like a woman's voice or a man's—or perhaps a child's. It seemed to be a human voice, and yet oddly sexless. In order to resolve his doubt he withdrew into the darkness of the curtains, ceased to watch Napoleon and simply listened with keen attention, striving to forget that he was listening to a bird, and to imagine that he was overhearing a human being in conversation. After two or three minutes' silence the voice spoke again, and at some length, apparently repeating several times an affectionate series of ejaculations with a cooing emphasis that was unutterably mawkish and offensive. The sickliness of the voice, its falling intonations and its strange indelicacy, combined with a die-away softness and meretricious refinement, made the father's flesh creep. Yet he could not distinguish any words, nor could he decide on the voice's sex or age. One thing alone he was certain of as he stood still in the darkness—that such a sound could only proceed from something peculiarly loathsome, could only express a personality unendurably abominable to him, if not to everybody. The voice presently failed, in a sort of husky gasp, and there was a prolonged silence. It was broken by the professor, who suddenly pulled away the curtains that hid the father and said to him: "Come out now, and look."

The father came into the light, blinking, glanced toward the cage, and saw Napoleon poised motionless on one foot with his head under his wing. He appeared to be asleep. The professor was pale, and his mobile lips were drawn into an expression of supreme disgust.

"Faugh!" he said.

He walked to the windows of the further room, pulled aside the curtains and pushed the glass up, letting in the air. The bare trees were visible in the gray gloom outside. Guildea leaned out for a minute drawing the night air into his lungs. Presently he turned round to the father, and exclaimed abruptly: "Pestilent! Isn't it?"

"Yes—most pestilent."

"Ever hear anything like it?"

"Not exactly."

"Nor I. It gives me nausea, Murchison, absolute physical nausea."

He closed the window and walked uneasily about the room.

"What d'you make of it?" he asked, over his shoulder.

"How d'you mean exactly?"

"Is it man's, woman's, or child's voice?"

"I can't tell, I can't make up my mind."

"Nor I."

"Have you heard it often?"

"Yes, since I returned from Westgate. There are never any words that I can distinguish. What a voice!"

He spat into the fire.

"Forgive me," he said, throwing himself down in a chair. "It turns my stomach—literally."

"And mine," said the father truly.

"The worst of it is," continued Guildea, with a high, nervous accent, "that there's no brain with it, none at all—only the cunning of idiocy."

The father started at this exact expression of his own conviction by another.

"Why d'you start like that?" said Guildea, with a quick suspicion which showed the unnatural condition of his nerves.

"Well, the very same idea had occurred to me."

"What?"

"That I was listening to the voice of something idiotic."

"Ah! That's the devil of it, you know, to a man like me. I could fight against brain—but this!"

He sprang up again, poked the fire violently, then stood on the hearthrug with his back to it, and his hands thrust into the high pockets of his trousers.

"That's the voice of the thing that's got into my house," he said. "Pleasant, isn't it?"

And now there was really horror in his eyes and his voice.

"I must get it out," he exclaimed. "I must get it out. But how?"

He tugged at his short black beard with a quivering hand.

"How?" he continued. "For what is it? Where is it?"

"You feel it's here—now?"

"Undoubtedly. But I couldn't tell you in what part of the room."

He stared about, glancing rapidly at everything.

"Then you consider yourself haunted?" said Father Murchison. He, too, was much moved and disturbed, although he was not conscious of the presence of anything near them in the room.

"I have never believed in any nonsense of that kind, as you know," Guildea answered. "I simply state a fact, which I cannot understand, and which is beginning to be very painful to me. There is something here. But whereas most so-called hauntings have been described to me as inimical, what I am conscious of is that I am admired, loved, desired. This is distinctly horrible to me, Murchison, distinctly horrible."

Father Murchison suddenly remembered the first evening he had spent with Guildea, and the latter's expression almost of disgust at the idea of receiving warm affection from anyone. In the light of that long-ago conversation, the present event seemed supremely strange, and almost like a punishment for an offense committed by the professor against humanity. But, looking up at his friend's twitching face, the father resolved not to be caught in the net of his hideous belief.

"There can be nothing here," he said. "It's impossible."

"What does that bird imitate, then?"

"The voice of someone who has been here."

"Within the last week then. For it never spoke like that before, and mind, I noticed that it was watching and striving to imitate something before I went away, since the night that I went into the park, only since then."

"Somebody with a voice like that must have been here while you were away," Father Murchison repeated, with a gentle obstinacy.

"I'll soon find out."

Guildea pressed the bell. Pitting stole in almost immediately.

"Pitting," said the professor, speaking in a high, sharp voice, "did anyone come into this room during my absence at the sea?"

"Certainly not, sir, except the maids—and me, sir."

"Not a soul? You are certain?"

"Perfectly certain, sir."

The cold voice of the butler sounded surprised, almost resentful. The professor flung out his hand towards the cage.

"Has the bird been here the whole time?"

"Yes, sir."

"He was not moved, taken elsewhere, even for a moment?"

Pitting's pale face began to look almost expressive, and his lips were pursed.

"Certainly not, sir."

"Thank you. That will do."

The butler retired, moving with a sort of ostentatious rectitude. When he had reached the door, and was just going out, his master called: "Wait a minute, Pitting."

The butler paused. Guildea bit his lips, tugged at his beard uneasily two or three times, and then said: "Have you noticed—er—the parrot talking lately in a—a very peculiar, very disagreeable voice?"

"Yes, sir—a soft voice like, sir."

"Ha! Since when?"

"Since you went away, sir. He's always at it."

"Exactly. Well, and what did you think of it?"

"Beg pardon, sir?"

"What do you think about his talking in this voice?"

"Oh, that it's only his play, sir."

"I see. That's all, Pitting."

The butler disappeared and closed the door noiselessly behind him.

Guildea turned his eyes on his friend.

"There, you see!" he ejaculated.

"It's certainly very odd," said the father. "Very odd indeed. You are certain you have no maid who talks at all like that?"

"My dear Murchison! Would you keep a servant with such a voice about you for two days?"

"No."

"My housemaid has been with me for five years, my cook for seven. You've heard Pitting speak. The three of them make up my entire household. A parrot never speaks in a voice it has not heard. Where has it heard that voice?"

"But we hear nothing?"

"No. Nor do we see anything. But it does. It feels something too. Didn't you observe it presenting its head to be scratched?"

"Certainly it seemed to be doing so."

"It was doing so."

Father Murchison said nothing. He was full of increasing discomfort that almost amounted to apprehension.

"Are you convinced?" said Guildea, rather irritably.

"No. The whole matter is very strange. But till I hear, see or feel—as you do—the presence of something, I cannot believe."

"You mean that you will not?"

"Perhaps. Well, it is time I went."

Guildea did not try to detain him, but said, as he let him out: "Do me a favor, come again tomorrow night."

The father had an engagement. He hesitated, looked into the professor's face and said: "I will. At nine I'll be with you. Good night."

When he was on the pavement he felt relieved. He turned round, saw Guildea stepping into his passage, and shivered.

V

Father Murchison walked all the way home to Bird Street that night. He required exercise after the strange and disagreeable evening he had spent, an evening upon which he looked back already as a man looks back upon a nightmare. In his ears, as he walked, sounded the gentle and intolerable voice. Even the memory of it caused him physical discomfort. He tried to put it from him, and to consider the whole matter calmly. The professor had offered his proof that there was some strange presence in his house. Could any reasonable man accept such proof? Father Murchison told himself that no reasonable man could accept it. The parrot's proceedings were, no doubt, extraordinary. The bird had succeeded in producing an extraordinary illusion of an invisible presence in the room. But that there really was such a presence the father insisted on denying to himself. The devoutly religious, those who believe implicitly in the miracles recorded in the Bible, and who regulate their lives by the messages they suppose themselves to receive directly from the Great Ruler of a hidden world, are seldom inclined to accept any notion of supernatural intrusion into the affairs of daily life. They put it from them with anxious determinatoin. They regard it fixedly as hocus-pocus, childish if not wicked.

Father Murchison inclined to the normal view of the devoted churchman. He was determined to incline to it. He could not—so he now told himself—accept the idea that his friend was being supernaturally punished for his lack of humanity, his deficiency in affection, by being obliged to endure the love of some horrible thing, which could not be seen, heard or handled. Nevertheless, retribution did certainly seem to wait upon Guildea's condition. That which he had unnaturally dreaded and shrunk from in his thought he seemed to be now forced unnaturally to suffer. The father prayed for his friend that night before the little, humble altar in the barely furnished, cell-like chamber where he slept.

On the following evening, when he called in Hyde Park Place, the door was opened by the housemaid, and Father Murchison mounted the stairs, wondering what had become of Pitting. He was met at the library door by Guildea and was painfully struck by the alteration in his appearance. His face was ashen in hue, and there were lines beneath his eyes. The eyes themselves looked excited and horribly forlorn. His hair and dress were disordered and his lips twitched continually, as if he were shaken by some acute nervous apprehension.

"What has become of Pitting?" asked the father, grasping Guildea's hot and feverish hand.

"He has left my service."

"Left your service!" exclaimed the father in utter amazement.

"Yes, this afternoon."

"May one ask why?"

"I'm going to tell you. It's all part and parcel of this—this most odious business. You remember once discussing the relations men ought to have with their servants?"

"Ah!" cried the father, with a flash of inspiration. "The crisis has occurred?"

"Exactly," said the professor, with a bitter smile. "The crisis has occurred. I called upon Pitting to be a man and a brother. He responded by declining the invitation. I upbraided him. He gave me warning. I paid him his wages and told him he could go at once. And he has gone. What are you looking at me like that for?"

"I didn't know," said Father Murchison, hastily dropping his eyes, and looking away. "Why," he added. "Napoleon is gone too."

"I sold him today to one of those shops in Shaftesbury Avenue."

"Why?"

"He sickened me with his abominable imitation of—his intercourse with—well, you know what he was at last night. Besides, I have no further need of his proof to tell me I am not dreaming. And, being convinced as I now am, that all I have thought to have happened has actually happened, I care very little about convincing others. Forgive me for saying so, Murchison, but I am now certain that my anxiety to make you believe in the presence of something here really arose from some faint doubt on that subject—within myself. All doubt has now vanished."

"Tell me why."

"I will."

Both men were standing by the fire. They continued to stand while Guildea went on:

"Last night I felt it."

"What?" cried the father.

"I say that last night, as I was going upstairs to bed, I felt something accompanying me and nestling up against me."

"How horrible!" exclaimed the father, involuntarily.

Guildea smiled drearily.

"I will not deny the horror of it. I cannot, since I was compelled to call on Pitting for assistance."

"But—tell me—what was it, at least what did it seem to be?"

"It seemed to be a human being. It seemed, I say; and what I mean exactly is that the effect upon me was rather that of human contact than of anything else. But I could see nothing, hear nothing. Only, three times, I felt this gentle, but determined, push against me, as if to coax me and to attract my attention. The first time it happened I was on the landing outside this room, with my foot on the first stair. I will confess to you, Murchison, that I bounded upstairs like one pursued. That is the shameful truth. Just as I was about to enter my bedroom, however, I felt the thing

"For what?"

"You hated affection. You put human feeling aside with contempt. You had, you desired to have, no love for anyone. Nor did you desire to receive any love from anything. Perhaps this is a punishment."

Guildea stared into his face.

"D'you believe that?" he cried.

"I don't know," said the father. "But it may be so. Try to endure it, even to welcome it. Possibly then the persecution will cease."

"I know it means me no harm," Guildea exclaimed, "it seeks me out of affection. It was led to me by some amazing attraction which I exercise over it ignorantly. I know that. But to a man of my nature that is the ghastly part of the matter. If it would hate me, I could bear it. If it would attack me, if it would try to do me some dreadful harm, I should become a man again. I should be braced to fight against it. But this gentleness, this abominable solicitude, this brainless worship of an idiot, persistent, sickly, horribly physical, I cannot endure. What does it want of me? What would it demand of me? It nestles to me. It leans against me. I feel its touch, like the touch of a feather, trembling about my heart, as if it sought to number my pulsations, to find out the inmost secrets of my impulses and desires. No privacy is left to me." He sprang up excitedly. "I cannot withdraw," he cried, "I cannot be alone, untouched, unworshipped, unwatched for even one-half second. Murchison, I am dying of this, I am dying."

He sank down again in his chair, staring apprehensively on all sides, with the passion of some blind man, deluded in the belief that by his furious and continued effort he will attain sight. The father knew well that he sought to pierce the veil of the invisible, and have knowledge of the thing that loved him.

"Guildea," the father said, with insistent earnestness, "try to endure this—do more—try to give this thing what it seeks."

"But it seeks my love."

"Learn to give it your love and it may go, having received what it came for."

"T'sh! You talk like a priest. Suffer your persecutors. Do good to them that despitefully use you. You talk as a priest."

"As a friend I spoke naturally, indeed, right out of my heart. The idea suddenly came to me that all this—truth or seeming, it doesn't matter which—may be some strange form of lesson. I have had lessons—painful ones. I shall have many more. If you could welcome—"

"I can't! I can't!" Guildea cried fiercely. "Hatred! I can give it that—always that, nothing but that—hatred, hatred."

He raised his voice, glared into the emptiness of the room, and repeated, "Hatred!"

As he spoke the waxen pallor of his cheeks increased, until he looked like a corpse with living eyes. The father feared that he was going to collapse and faint, but suddenly he raised himself upon his chair and said, in a high and keen voice, full of suppressed excitement: "Murchison, Murchison!"

"Yes. What is it?"

An amazing ecstasy shone in Guildea's eyes.

"It wants to leave me," he cried. "It wants to go! Don't lose a moment! Let it out! The window—the window!"

The father, wondering, went to the near window, drew aside the curtains and pushed it open. The branches of the trees in the garden creaked dryly in the light wind. Guildea leaned forward on the arms of his chair. There was silence for a moment. Then Guildea, speaking in a rapid whisper, said: "No, no. Open this door—open the hall door. I feel—I feel that it will return the way it came. Make haste—ah, go!"

The father obeyed—to soothe him, hurried to the door and opened it wide. Then he glanced back to Guildea. He was standing up, bent forward. His eyes were glaring with eager expectation, and, as the father turned, he made a furious gesture towards the passage with his thin hands.

The father hastened out and down the stairs. As he descended in the twilight he fancied he heard a slight cry from the room behind him, but he did not pause. He flung the hall door open, standing back against the wall. After waiting a moment—to satisfy Guildea, he was about to close the door again, and had his hand on it, when he was attracted irresistibly to look forth towards the park. The night was lit by a young moon, and, gazing through the railings, his eyes fell upon a bench beyond them.

Upon the bench something was sitting, huddled together very strangely.

The father remembered instantly Guildea's description of that former night, that night of Advent, and a sensation of horror-stricken curiosity stole through him.

Was there then really something that had indeed come to the professor? And had it finished its work, fulfilled its desire and gone back to its former existence?

The father hesitated a moment in the doorway. Then he stepped out resolutely and crossed the road, keeping his eyes fixed upon this black or dark object that leaned so strangely upon the bench. He could not tell yet what it was like, but he fancied it was unlike anything with which his eyes were acquainted. He reached the opposite path, and was about to pass through the gate in the railings, when his arm was brusquely grasped. He started, turned round, and saw a policeman eyeing him suspiciously.

"What are you up to?" said the policeman.

The father was suddenly aware that he had no hat upon his head, and that his appearance, as he stole forward in his cassock, with his eyes intently fixed upon the bench in the park, was probably unusual enough to excite suspicion.

"It's all right, policeman," he answered quickly, thrusting some money into the constable's hand.

Then, breaking from him, the father hurried towards the bench, bitterly vexed at the interruption. When he reached it, nothing was there. Guildea's experience had been almost exactly repeated and, filled with unreasonable disappointment, the father returned to the house, entered it, shut the door and hastened up the narrow stairway into the library.

On the hearthrug, close to the fire, he found Guildea lying with his head lolled against the armchair from which he had recently risen. There was a shocking expression of terror on his convulsed face. On examining him the father found that he was dead.

The doctor, who was called in, said that the cause of death was failure of the heart.

When Father Murchison was told this, he murmured: "Failure of the heart! It was that then!"

He turned to the doctor and said: "Could it have been prevented?"

The doctor drew on his gloves and answered: "Possibly, if it had been taken in time. Weakness of the heart requires a great deal of care. The professor was too much absorbed in his work. He should have lived very differently."

The father nodded.

"Yes, yes," he said, sadly.

VINCENT PRICE

Editor's Note:

Vincent Price, one of the great actors of our time, has been closely linked to the horror story from the start of his career (he provided the voice of the Invisible Man in the film *Abbott and Costello Meet Frankenstein*), and from there went on to become the acknowledged "King of the Horrors." His best-known performances were in such masterpieces as *House of Wax, The Fly, The House on Haunted Hill* and *The Abominable Dr. Phibes.*

An important part of his career involved him in the productions of Edgar Allan Poe stories directed by Roger Corman, including "The House of Usher," "The Pit and the Pendulum," "Masque of the Red Death," "Tales of Terror" and "The Tomb of Ligeia." It is particularly fitting that he chose a Poe story for this book, and one of Poe's finest and lesser-known works at that.

THE SPHINX

EDGAR ALLAN POE

During the dread reign of cholera in New York, I had accepted the invitation of a relative to spend a fortnight with him in the retirement of his *cottage ornée* on the banks of the Hudson. We had here around us all the ordinary means of summer amusement; and what with rambling in the woods, sketching, boating, fishing, bathing, music and books, we should have passed the time pleasantly enough, but for the fearful intelligence which reached us every morning from the populous city. Not a day elapsed which did not bring us news of the decease of some acquaintance. Then, as the fatality increased, we learned to expect daily the loss of some friend. At length we trembled at the approach of every messenger. The very air from the South seemed to us redolent with death. That palsying thought, indeed, took entire possession of my soul. I could neither speak, think nor dream of anything else. My host was of a less excitable temperament, and, although greatly depressed in spirits, exerted himself to sustain my own. His richly philosophical intellect was not at any time affected by unrealities. To the substances of terror he was sufficiently alive, but of its shadows he had no apprehension.

His endeavors to arouse me from the condition of abnormal gloom into which I had fallen, were frustrated, in great measure, by certain volumes which I had found in his library. These were of a character to force into germination whatever seeds of hereditary superstition lay latent in my bosom. I had been reading these books without his knowledge, and thus he was often at a loss to account for the forcible impressions which had been made upon my fancy.

A favorite topic with me was the popular belief in omens—a belief which, at this one epoch of my life, I was almost seriously disposed to defend. On this subject we had long and animated discussions; he maintaining the utter groundlessness of faith in such matters, I contending that a popular sentiment arising with absolute spontaneity—that is to say, without apparent traces of suggestion—had in itself the unmistakable elements of truth, and was entitled to much respect.

The fact is that soon after my arrival at the cottage there had occurred to myself an incident so entirely inexplicable, and which had in it so much of the portentous character, that I might well have been excused for regarding it as an omen. It appalled and, at the same time, so confounded and bewildered me, that many days elapsed before I could make up my mind to communicate the circumstance to my friend.

Near the close of an exceedingly warm day, I was sitting, book in hand, at an open window, commanding, through a long vista of the river banks, a view of a distant hill, the face of which nearest my position had been denuded by what is termed a landslide, of the principal portion of its trees. My thoughts had been long wandering from the volume before me to the gloom and desolation of the neighboring city. Uplifting my eyes from the page, they fell upon the naked face of the hill, and upon an object—upon some living monster of hideous conformation, which very rapidly made its way from the summit to the bottom, disappearing finally in the dense forest below. As this creature first came in sight, I doubted my own sanity—or at least the evidence of my own eyes—and many minutes passed before I succeeded in convincing myself that I was neither mad nor in a dream. Yet when I describe the monster (which I distinctly saw, and calmly surveyed through the whole period of its progress), my readers, I fear, will feel more difficulty in being convinced of these points than even I did myself.

Estimating the size of the creature by comparison with the diameter of the large trees near which it passed—the few giants of the forests which had escaped the fury of the landslide—I concluded it to be far larger than any ship of the line in existence. I say ship of the line, because the shape of the monster suggested the idea—the hull of one of our seventy-fours might convey a very tolerable conception of the general outline. The mouth of the animal was situated at the extremity of a proboscis some sixty or seventy feet in length, and about as thick as the body of an ordinary elephant. Near the root of this trunk was an immense quantity of black shaggy hair—more than could have been supplied by the coats of a score of buffaloes; and projecting from this hair downwardly and laterally, sprang two gleaming tusks not unlike those of the wild boar, but of infinitely greater dimension. Extending forward, parallel with the proboscis, and on each side of it, was a gigantic staff, thirty or forty feet in length, formed seemingly of pure crystal, and in shape a perfect prism—it reflected in the most gorgeous manner the rays of the declining sun. The trunk was fashioned like a wedge with the apex to the earth. From it there were outspread two pairs of wings—each wing nearly one hundred yards in length—one pair being placed above the other, and all thickly covered with metal scales; each scale apparently some ten or twelve feet in diameter. I observed that the upper and lower tiers of wings were connected by a strong chain. But the chief peculiarity of this horrible thing was the representation of a death's-head, which covered nearly the whole surface of its breast, and which was as accurately traced in glaring white, upon the dark ground of the body, as if it had been there carefully designed by an artist. While I regarded this terrific animal, and more especially the appearance on its breast, with a feeling of horror and awe—with a sentiment of forthcoming evil, which I found it impossible to quell by any effort of the reason, I perceived the huge jaws at the extremity of the proboscis suddenly expand themselves, and from them there proceeded a sound so loud and so expressive of woe, that it struck upon my nerves like a knell, and as the monster disappeared at the foot of the hill, I fell at once, fainting, to the floor.

Upon recovering, my first impulse, of course, was to inform my friend of what I had seen and heard—and I can scarcely explain what feeling of repugnance it was which, in the end, operated to prevent me.

At length, one evening, some three or four days after the occurrence, we were sitting together in the room in which I had seen the apparition—I occupying the same seat at the same window, and he lounging on a sofa near at hand. The association of the place and time impelled me to give him an account of the phenomenon. He heard me to the end—at first laughed heartily—and then lapsed into an excessively grave demeanor, as if my insanity was a thing beyond suspicion. At this instant I again had a distinct view of the monster—to which, with a shout of absolute terror, I now directed his attention. He looked eagerly—but maintained that he saw nothing—although I designated minutely the course of the creature, as it made its way down the naked face of the hill.

I was now immeasurably alarmed, for I considered the vision either as an omen of my death, or, worse, as the forerunner of an attack of mania. I threw myself passionately back in my chair, and for some moments buried my face in my hands. When I uncovered my eyes, the apparition was no longer visible.

My host, however, had in some degree resumed the calmness of his demeanor, and questioned me very rigorously in respect to the conformation of the visionary creature. When I had fully satisfied him on this head, he sighed deeply, as if relieved of some intolerable burden, and went on to talk, with what I thought a cruel calmness, of various points of speculative philosophy, which had heretofore formed subject of discussion between us. I remember his insisting very especially (among other things) upon the idea that the principal source of error in all human investigations lay in the liability of the understanding to underrate or to overvalue the importance of an object, through mere misadmeasurement of its propinquity. "To estimate property, for example," he said, "the influence to be exercised on mankind at large by the thorough diffusion of democracy, the distance of the epoch at which such diffusion may possibly be accomplished should not fail to form an item in the estimate. Yet can you tell me one writer on the subject of government who has ever thought this particular branch of the subject worthy of discussion at all?"

He here paused for a moment, stepped to a bookcase, and brought forth one of the ordinary synopses of natural history. Requesting me then to exchange seats with him, that he might the better distinguish the fine print of the volume, he took my armchair at the window, and, opening the book, resumed his discourse very much in the same tone as before.

"But for your exceeding minuteness," he said, "in describing the monster, I might never have had it in my power to demonstrate to you what it was. In the first place, let me read to you a schoolboy account of the genus *Sphinx,* of the family *Crepuscularia,* of the order *Lepidoptera,* of the class of *Insecta*—or insects. The account runs thus:

" 'Four membranous wings covered with little colored scales of metallic appearance; mouth forming a rolled proboscis, produced by an elongation of the jaws, upon the sides of which are found the rudiments of manibles and downy palpi; the inferior wings retained to the superior by a stiff hair, antennae in the form of an elongated club, prismatic; abdomen pointed. The death's-headed Sphinx has occasioned much terror among the vulgar, at times, by the melancholy kind of cry which it utters and the insignia of death which it wears upon its corslet.' "

He here closed the book and leaned forward in the chair, placing himself accurately in the position which I had occupied at the moment of beholding "the monster."

"Ah, here it is," he presently exclaimed—"it is reascending the face of the hill, and a very remarkable looking creature I admit it to be. Still, it is by no means so large or so distant as you imagined it; for the fact is that, as it wriggles its way up this thread, which some spider has wrought along the window sash, I find it to be about the sixteenth of an inch in its extreme length, and also about the sixteenth of an inch distant from the pupil of my eye."

IRWIN SHAW

I *haven't been frightened for a long time by anything but real life, but when I was young I came upon the collected works of Edgar Allan Poe, which my parents for some reason had bought. Among them the most frightening for me was "The Narrative of A. Gordon Pym," with its shipwreck, cannibalism and the destruction of the "I" who told the story in the vortex in the South Polar seas. The scenes in which the shipwrecked sailors draw straws still gives me a chill as I remember them. The other stories were also by Poe—"The Pit and the Pendulum" and "The Cask of Amontillado."*
Editors' Note: "The Narrative of A. Gordon Pym" proved too long for inclusion in this anthology, but we're confident you will find Mr. Shaw's second choice, another Poe classic, to be equally chilling . . .

THE PIT AND THE PENDULUM

EDGAR ALLAN POE

I was sick—sick unto death with that long agony; and when they at length unbound me, and I was permitted to sit, I felt that my senses were leaving me. The sentence—the dread sentence of death—was the last of distinct accentuation which reached my ears. After that, the sound of the inquisitorial voices seemed merged in one dreamy indeterminate hum. It conveyed to my soul the idea of *revolution*—perhaps from its association in fancy with the burr of a mill wheel. This only for a brief period, for presently I heard no more. Yet, for a while, I saw—but with how terrible an exaggeration! I saw the lips of the black-robed judges. They appeared to me white—whiter than the sheet upon which I trace these words—and thin even to grotesqueness; thin with the intensity of their expression of firmness—of immovable resolution—of stern contempt of human torture. I saw that the decrees of what to me was fate were still issuing from those lips. I saw them writhe with a deadly locution. I saw them fashion the syllables of my name; and I shuddered because no sound succeeded. I saw, too, for a few moments of delirious horror, the soft and nearly imperceptible waving of the sable draperies which enwrapped the walls of the apartment. And then my vision fell upon the seven tall candles upon the table. At first they wore the aspect of charity, and seemed white slender angels who would save me; but then, all at once, there came a most deadly nausea over my spirit, and I felt every fiber in my frame thrill as if I had touched the wire of

In an instant afterward the fancy was confirmed. Its sweep was brief, and of course slow. I watched it for some minutes somewhat in fear, but more in wonder. Wearied at length with observing its dull movement, I turned my eyes upon the other objects in the cell.

A slight noise attracted my notice, and, looking to the floor, I saw several enormous rats traversing it. They had issued from the well which lay just within view to my right. Even then, while I gazed, they came up in troops, hurriedly, with ravenous eyes, allured by the scent of the meat. From this it required much effort and attention to scare them away.

It might have been half an hour, perhaps even an hour (for I could take but imperfect note of time), before I again cast my eyes upward. What I then saw confounded and amazed me. The sweep of the pendulum had increased in extent by nearly a yard. As a natural consequence its velocity was also much greater. But what mainly disturbed me was the idea that it had perceptibly *descended.* I now observed—with what horror it is needless to say—that its nether extremity was formed of a crescent of glittering steel, about a foot in length from horn to horn; the horns upward, and the under edge evidently as keen as that of a razor. Like a razor also, it seemed massy and heavy, tapering from the edge into a solid and broad structure above. It was appended to a weighty rod of brass, and the whole *hissed* as it swung through the air.

I could no longer doubt the doom prepared for me by monkish ingenuity in torture. My cognizance of the pit had become known to the inquisitorial agents—*the pit,* whose horrors had been destined for so bold a recusant as myself—*the pit,* typical of hell and regarded by rumor as the ultima Thule of all their punishments. The plunge into this pit I had avoided by the merest of accidents, and I knew that surprise, or entrapment into torment, formed an important portion of all the grotesquerie of these dungeon deaths. Having failed to fall, it was no part of the demon plan to hurl me into the abyss, and thus (there being no alternative) a different and a milder destruction awaited me. Milder! I half-smiled in my agony as I thought of such application of such a term.

What boots it to tell of the long, long hours of horror more than mortal, during which I counted the rushing oscillations of the steel! Inch by inch—line by line—with a descent only appreciable at intervals that seemed ages—down and still down it came! Days passed—it might have been that many days passed—ere it swept so closely over me as to fan me with its acrid breath. The odor of the sharp steel forced itself into my nostrils. I prayed—I wearied heaven with my prayer for its more speedy descent. I grew frantically mad, and struggled to force myself upward against the sweep of the fearful scimitar. And then I fell suddenly calm, and lay smiling at the glittering death, as a child at some rare bauble.

There was another interval of utter insensibility; it was brief; for, upon again lapsing into life, there had been no perceptible descent in the pendulum. But it might have been long—for I knew there were demons who took note of my swoon, and who could have arrested the vibration at pleasure. Upon my recovery, too, I felt very—oh! inexpressibly—sick and weak, as if through long inanition. Even amid the agonies of that period, the human nature craved food. With painful effort I outstretched my left arm as far as my bonds permitted, and took possession of the small remnant which had been spared me by the rats. As I put a portion of it within my lips, there rushed to my mind a half-formed thought of joy—of hope. Yet what business had *I* with hope? It was, as I say, a half-formed thought—man has many such, which are never completed. I felt that it was of joy—of hope; but I felt also that it had perished in its formation. In vain I struggled to perfect—to regain it. Long suffering had nearly annihilated all my ordinary powers of mind. I was an imbecile—an idiot.

The vibration of the pendulum was at right angles to my length. I saw that the crescent was designed to cross the region of the heart. It would fray the serge of my robe—it would return and repeat its operations—again—and again. Notwithstanding its terrifically wide sweep (some thirty feet or more), and the hissing vigor of its descent, sufficient to sunder these very walls of iron, still the fraying of my robe would be all that, for several minutes, it would accomplish. And at this thought I paused. I dared not go further than this reflection. I dwelt upon it with a pertinacity of attention—as if, in so dwelling, I could arrest *here* the descent of the steel. I forced myself to ponder upon the sound of the crescent as it should pass across the garment—upon the peculiar thrilling sensation which the friction of cloth produces on the nerves. I pondered upon all this frivolity until my teeth were on edge.

Down—steadily down it crept. I took a frenzied pleasure in contrasting its downward with its lateral velocity. To the right—to the left—far and wide—with the shriek of a damned spirit! to my heart, with the stealthy pace of the tiger! I alternatively laughed and howled, as the one or the other idea grew predominant.

Down—certainly, relentlessly down! It vibrated within three inches of my bosom! I struggled violently—furiously—to free my left arm. This was free only from the elbow to the hand. I could reach the latter, from the

ROBERT SHECKLEY

There are several stories I'd like to mention. I wish I could reread them now, but I'm presently living in a tent in the John Pennekamp State Park in Key Largo, Florida, and research facilities are few and far between.

Abraham Merritt is best known for his fantasy novels. But I remember a short story of his, called "Three Lines of Old French," a chiller that was reprinted in Famous Fantastic Mysteries *many years ago, when I was still in high school. I had a favorite reading routine then. I would take my new science-fiction or fantasy magazines up to my room on the third floor of my family's house. I'd get a big glass of ice cold milk and a sack of my favorite candy from the five-and-ten. Then, curled up in the bay window, mouth full of milk and sugared licorice, I'd trip out into the dream worlds I lived for. The silence of that third-floor room and the creaking of branches outside the window provided a perfect ambiance for imaginative stories, especially strange and eerie ones. It was in this room that I read E. L. White's wonderful "Lukundoo," W. W. Jacobs's "The Monkey's Paw," Oliver Onions's "The Beckoning Fair One," and M. R. James's "Oh, Whistle, and I'll Come to You, My Lad." These well-known stories have probably been chosen by others. If not, I hereby nominate them.*

Another story that stands out for me is Sir Arthur Quiller-Couch's fine tale called "The Seventh Man." A claustrophobic tale of the far North, I read this aboard a sailboat while making a passage from St. Thomas in the Virgin Islands to New York. There were three of us aboard . . . or were there four

THREE LINES OF OLD FRENCH

A. MERRITT

"But rich as was the war for surgical science," ended Hawtry, "opening up through mutilation and torture unexplored regions which the genius of man was quick to enter, and, entering, found ways to checkmate suffering and death—for always, my friends, the distillate from the blood of sacrifice is progress—great as all this was, the world tragedy has opened up still another region wherein even greater knowledge will be found. It was the clinic unsurpassed for the psychologist even more than for the surgeon."

Latour, the great little French doctor, drew himself out of the depths of the big chair; the light from the fireplace fell ruddily upon his keen face.

"That is true," he said. "Yes, that is true. There in the furnace the mind of man opened like a flower beneath a too glowing sun. Beaten about in that colossal tempest of primitive forces, caught in the chaos of energies both physical and psychical—which, although man himself was its creator, made of their maker a moth in a whirlwind—all those obscure, those mysterious factors of mind which men, for lack of knowledge, have named the soul, were stripped of their inhibitions and given power to appear.

"How could it have been otherwise—when men and women, gripped by one shattering sorrow or joy, will manifest the hidden depths of spirit—how could it have been otherwise in that steadily maintained crescendo of emotion?"

McAndrews spoke. "Just which psychological region do you mean, Hawtry?" he asked.

There were four of us in front of the fireplace of the Science Club—Hawtry, who rules the chair of psychology in one of our greatest colleges, and whose name is an honored one throughout the world; Latour, an immortal of France; McAndrews, the famous American surgeon whose work during the war has written a new page in the shining book of science; and myself. These are not the names of the three, but they are as I have described them; and I am pledged to identify them no further.

"I mean the field of suggestion," replied the psychologist. "The mental reactions which reveal themselves as visions—an accidental formation in the clouds that becomes to the overwrought imaginations of the beholders the so-eagerly-prayed-for hosts of Joan of Arc marching out from heaven; moonlight in the cloud rift that becomes to the besieged a fiery cross held by the hands of archangels; the despair and hope that are transformed into such a legend as the bowmen of Mons, ghostly archers who with their phantom shafts overwhelm the conquering enemy; wisps of cloud over no-man's-land that are translated by the tired eyes of those who peer out into the shape of the Son of man himself walking sorrowfully among the dead.

"Signs, portents and miracles; the hosts of premonitions, of apparitions of loved ones—all dwellers in this land of suggestion; all born of the tearing loose of the veils of the subconscious. Here, when even a thousandth part is gathered, will be work for the psychological analyst for twenty years."

"And the boundaries of this region?" asked McAndrews.

"Boundaries?" Hawtry plainly was perplexed.

McAndrews for a moment was silent. Then he drew from his pocket a yellow slip of paper, a cablegram.

"Young Peter Laveller died today," he said, apparently irrelevantly. "Died where he had set forth to pass—in the remnants of the trenches that cut through the ancient domain of the Seigniors of Tocquelain, up near Bethune."

"Died there!" Hawtry's astonishment was profound. "But I read that he had been brought home; that, indeed, he was one of your triumphs, McAndrews!"

"I said that he *went* there to die," repeated the surgeon slowly.

So that explained the curious reticence of the Lavellers as to what had become of their soldier son—a secrecy which had puzzled the press for weeks. For young Peter Laveller was one of the nation's heroes. The only boy of old Peter Laveller—and neither is that the real name of the family —for like the others, I may not reveal it—he was the heir to the grim old coal king's millions, and the secret, best beloved pulse of his heart.

Early in the war he had enlisted with the French. His father's influence might have abrogated the law of the French Army that every man must start from the bottom up—I do not know—but young Peter would have none of it. Steady of purpose, burning with the white fire of the first Crusaders, he took his place in the ranks.

Clean-cut, blue-eyed, standing six feet in his stocking feet, just twenty-five, a bit of a dreamer, perhaps, he was one to strike the imagination of the *poilus,* and they loved him. Twice he was wounded in the perilous days, and when America came into the war he was transferred to our expeditionary forces. It was at the siege of Mount Kemmel that he received the wounds that brought him back to his father and sister. McAndrews had accompanied him overseas, I knew, and had patched him together—or so all thought.

What had happened then—and why had Laveller gone back to France, to die, as McAndrews had put it?

He thrust the cablegram back into his pocket.

"There is a boundary, John," he said to Hawtry. "Laveller's was a borderline case. I'm going to tell it to you." He hesitated. "I ought not to, maybe; and yet I have an idea that Peter would like it told; after all, he believed himself a discoverer." Again he paused, then definitely made up his mind, and turned to me.

"Merritt, you may make use of this if you think it interesting enough. But if you do so decide, then change the names, and be sure to check description short of any possibility of ready identification. After all, it is what happened that is important—if it is important—and those to whom it happened do not matter."

I promised, and I have observed my pledge. I tell the story as he whom I call McAndrews reconstructed it for us there in the shadowed room, while we sat silent until he had entered. . . .

Laveller stood behind the parapet of a first-line trench. It was night—an early April night in northern France—and when that is said, all is said to those who have been there.

Beside him was a trench periscope. His gun lay touching it. The periscope is practically useless at night; so through a slit in the sandbags he peered out over the three-hundred-foot-wide stretch of no-man's-land.

Opposite him he knew that other eyes lay close to similar slits in the

German parapet, watchful as his were for the least movement.

There were grotesque heaps scattered about no-man's-land, and when the star shells burst and flooded it with their glare these heaps seemed to stir, to move—some to raise themselves, some to gesticulate, to protest. And this was very horrible, for those who moved under the lights were the dead—French and English, Prussian and Bavarian—dregs of a score of carryings to the red winepress of war set up in this sector.

There were two Jocks on the entanglements; killed Scots, one colandered by machine-gun hail just as he was breaking through. The shock of the swift, manifold death had hurled his left arm about the neck of the comrade close beside him; and this man had been stricken within the same second. There they leaned, embracing—and as the star shells flared and died, flared and died, they seemed to rock, to try to break from the wire, to dash forward, to return.

Laveller was weary, weary beyond all understanding. The sector was a bad one and nervous. For almost seventy-two hours he had been without sleep—for the few minutes now and then of dead stupor broken by constant alarms was worse than sleep.

The shelling had been well-nigh continuous, and the food scarce and perilous to get; three miles back through the fire they had been forced to go for it; no nearer than that could the ration dumps be brought.

And constantly the parapets had to be rebuilt and the wires repaired—and when this was done the shells destroyed again, and once more the dreary routine had to be gone through; for the orders were to hold this sector at all costs.

All that was left of Laveller's consciousness was concentrated in his eyes; only his seeing faculty lived. And sight, obeying the rigid, inexorable will commanding every reserve of vitality to concentrate on the duty at hand, was blind to everything except the strip before it that Laveller must watch until relieved. His body was numb; he could not feel the ground with his feet, and sometimes he seemed to be floating in air like—like the two Scots upon the wire!

Why couldn't they be still? What right had men whose blood had drained away into the black stain beneath them to dance and pirouette to the rhythm of the flares? Damn them—why couldn't a shell drop down and bury them?

There was a château half a mile up there to the right—at least it had been a château. Under it were deep cellars into which one could creep and sleep. He knew that, because ages ago, when first he had come into this part of the line, he had slept a night there.

It would be like reentering paradise to crawl again into those cellars, out of the pitiless rain; sleep once more with a roof over his head.

"I will sleep and sleep and sleep—and sleep and sleep and sleep," he told himself; then stiffened as at the slumber-compelling repetition of the word darkness began to gather before him.

The star shells flared and died, flared and died; the staccato of a machine gun reached him. He thought that it was his teeth chattering until his groping consciousness made him realize what it really was—some nervous German riddling the interminable movement of the dead.

There was a squidging of feet through the chalky mud. No need to look; they were friends, or they could not have passed the sentries at the angle of the traverse. Nevertheless, involuntarily, his eyes swept toward the sounds, took note of three cloaked figures regarding him.

There were half a dozen of the lights floating overhead now, and by the gleams they cast into the trench he recognized the party.

One of them was that famous surgeon who had come over from the base hospital at Bethune to see made the wounds he healed; the others were his major and his captain—all of them bound for those cellars, no doubt. Well, some had all the luck! Back went his eyes to the slit.

"What's wrong?" It was the voice of his major addressing the visitor.

"What's wrong—what's wrong—what's wrong?" The words repeated themselves swiftly, insistently, within his brain, over and over again, striving to waken it.

Well, what *was* wrong? Nothing was wrong! Wasn't he, Laveller, there and watching? The tormented brain writhed angrily. Nothing was wrong—why didn't they go away and let him watch in peace? He would like it much better.

"Nothing." It was the surgeon—and again the words kept babbling in Laveller's ears, small, whispering, rapidly repeating themselves over and over: "nothing—nothing—nothing—nothing."

But what was this the surgeon was saying? Fragmentarily, only half-understood, the phrases registered: "Perfect cause of what I've been telling you. This lad here—utterly worn, weary—all his consciousness centered upon just one thing—watchfulness . . . consciousness worn to finest point . . . behind it all his subconsciousness crowding to escape . . . consciousness will respond to only one stimulus—movement from without . . . but the subconsciousness, so close to the surface, held so lightly in leash . . . what will it do if that little thread is loosed . . . a perfect case."

What were they talking about? Now they were whispering.

"Then, if I have your permission—" It was the surgeon speaking again. Permission for what? Why didn't they go away and not bother him? Wasn't it hard enough just to watch without having to hear? Something passed before his eyes. He looked at it blindly, unrecognizing. His sight must be clouded.

He raised a hand and brushed at his lids. Yes, it must have been his eyes—for it had gone.

A little circle of light glowed against the parapet near his face. It was cast by a small flash. What were they talking about? What were they looking for? A hand appeared in the circle, a hand with long, flexible fingers which held a piece of paper on which there was writing. Did they want him to read, too? Not only watch and hear—but read! He gathered himself together to protest.

Before he could force his stiffened lips to move he felt the upper button of his greatcoat undone, a hand slipped through the opening and thrust something into his tunic pocket just above the heart.

Someone whispered, "Lucie de Tocquelain."

What did it mean? That was not the password.

There was a great singing in his head—as though he were sinking through water. What was that light that dazzled him even through his closed lids? Painfully he opened his eyes.

Laveller looked straight into the disk of a golden sun setting over a row of noble oaks. Blinded, he dropped his gaze. He was standing ankle-deep in soft, green grass, starred with small clumps of blue flowerets. Bees buzzed about in their chalices. Little yellow-winged butterflies hovered over them. A gentle breeze blew, warm and fragrant.

Oddly he felt no sense of strangeness then—this was a normal home world—a world as it ought to be. But he remembered that he had once been in another world, far, far unlike this one; a place of misery and pain, of bloodstained mud and filth, of cold and wet; a world of cruelty whose nights were tortured hells of glaring lights and fiery, slaying sounds, and tormented men who sought to rest and sleep and found none, and dead who danced. Where was it? Had there ever really been such a world? He was not sleepy now.

He raised his hands and looked at them. They were grimed and cut and stained. He was wearing a greatcoat, wet, mud-spattered, filthy. High boots were on his legs. Beside one dirt-encrusted foot lay a cluster of the blue flowerets, half-crushed. He groaned in pity, and bent, striving to raise the broken blossoms.

"Too many dead now—too many dead," he whispered; then paused.

He *had* come from that nightmare world! How else in this happy, clean one could he be so unclean?

Of course he had—but where was it? How had he made his way from it here? Ah, there had been a password—what had it been?

He had it: "Lucie de Tocquelain!"

Laveller cried it aloud, still kneeling.

A soft little hand touched his cheek. A low, sweet-toned voice caressed his ears.

"I am Lucie de Tocquelain," it said. "And the flowers will grow again—yet it is dear of you to sorrow for them."

He sprang to his feet. Beside him stood a girl, a slender maid of eighteen, whose hair was a dusky cloud upon her proud little head and in whose great, brown eyes, resting upon him, tenderness and a half-amused pity dwelt.

Peter stood silent, drinking her in—the low, broad, white forehead; the curved, red lips; the rounded, white shoulders, shining through the silken web of her scarf; the whole lithe, sweet body of her in the clinging, quality fashioned gown, with its high, clasping girdle.

She was fair enough; but to Peter's starved eyes she was more than that—she was a spring gushing from the arid desert, the first cool breeze of twilight over a heat-drenched isle, the first glimpse of paradise to a soul risen from the centuries of hell. And under the burning worship of his eyes her own dropped; a faint rose stained the white throat, crept to her dark hair.

"I—I am the Demoiselle de Tocquelain, messire," she murmured. "And you—"

"Laveller—Peter Laveller—is my name, mademoiselle," he stammered. "Pardon my rudeness—but how I came here I know not—nor from whence, save that it was—it was a place unlike this. And you—you are beautiful, mademoiselle!"

The clear eyes raised themselves for a moment, a touch of roguishness in their depths, then dropped demurely once more—but the blush deepened.

He watched her, all his awakening heart in his eyes; then perplexity awoke, touched him insistently.

"Will you tell me what place this is, mademoiselle," he faltered, "and how I came here, if you—" he stopped. From far, far away, from league upon league of space, a vast weariness was sweeping down upon him. He sensed it coming—closer, closer; it touched him; it lapped about him; he was sinking under it; being lost—falling—falling—

Two soft, warm hands gripped his. His tired head dropped upon them. Through the little palms that clasped so tightly pulsed rest and strength. The weariness gathered itself, began to withdraw slowly, so slowly—and was gone!

In its wake followed an ineffable, an uncontrollable desire to weep—to weep in relief that the weariness had passed, that the devil world whose shadows still lingered in his mind was behind him, and that he was here with this maid. And his tears fell, bathing the little hands.

Did he feel her head bend to his, her lips touch his hair? Peace came to him. He rose shamefacedly.

"I do not know why I wept, mademoiselle—" he began; and then saw that her white fingers were clasped now in his blackened ones. He released them in sudden panic.

"I am sorry," he stammered. "I ought not touch you—"

She reached out swiftly, took his hands again in hers, patted them half-savagely. Her eyes flashed. "I do not see them as you do, Messire Pierre," she answered. "And if I did, are not their stains to me as the stains from hearts of her brave sons on the gonfalons of France? Think no more of your stains save as decorations, messire."

France—France? Why, that was the name of the world he had left behind; the world where men sought vainly for sleep, and the dead danced.

The dead danced—what did that mean?

He turned wistful eyes to her.

And with a little cry of pity she clung to him for a moment.

"You are so tired—and you are so hungry," she mourned. "And think no more, nor try to remember, messire, till you have eaten and drunk with us and rested for a space."

They had turned. And now Laveller saw not far away a château. It was pinnacled and stately, serene in its gray and lordly with its spires and slender turrets thrust skyward from its crestlike plume flung high from some proud prince's helm. Hand in hand like children the Demoiselle de Tocquelain and Peter Laveller approached it over the greensward.

"It is my home, messire," the girl said. "And there among the roses my mother awaits us. My father is away, and he will be sorrowful that he met you not, but you shall meet him when you return."

He was to *return,* then? That meant he was not to stay. But where was he to go—from whence was he to return? His mind groped blindly; cleared again. He was walking among roses; there were roses everywhere, great, fragrant, opened blooms of scarlets and of saffrons, of shell pinks and white; clusters and banks of them, climbing up the terraces, masking the base of the château with perfumed tide.

And as he and the maid, still hand in hand, passed between them, they came to a table dressed with snowy napery and pale porcelains beneath a bower.

A woman sat there. She was a little past the prime of life, Peter thought. Her hair, he saw, was powdered white, her cheeks as pink and white as a child's, her eyes the sparkling brown of those of the demoiselle—and gracious—gracious, Peter thought, as some grande dame of old France.

The demoiselle dropped her a low curtsy.

"*Ma mére,*" she said, "I bring you the Sieur Pierre la Valliere, a very brave and gallant gentleman who has come to visit us for a while."

The clear eyes of the older woman scanned him, searched him. Then the stately white head bowed, and over the table a delicate hand was stretched toward him.

It was meant for him to kiss, he knew—but he hesitated awkwardly, miserably, looking at his begrimed own.

"The Sieur Pierre will not see himself as we do," the girl said in half-merry reproof; then she laughed, a caressing, golden chiming. "*Ma mère,* shall he see his hands as we do?"

The white-haired woman smiled and nodded, her eyes kindly, and, Laveller noted, with that same pity in them as had been in those of the demoiselle when first he had turned and beheld her.

The girl touched Peter's eyes lightly, held his palms up before him—they were white and fine and clean and in some unfamiliar way beautiful!

Again the indefinable gaze stifled him, but his breeding told. He conquered the sense of strangeness, bowed from the hips, took the dainty fingers of the stately lady in his, and raised them to his lips.

She struck a silver bell. Through the roses came two tall men in livery, who took from Laveller his greatcoat. They were followed by four small black boys in gay scarlet slashed with gold. They bore silver platters on which were meat and fine white bread and cakes, fruit, and wine in tall crystal flagons.

And Laveller remembered how hungry he was. But of that feast he remembered little—up to a certain point. He knows that he sat there filled with a happiness and content that surpassed the sum of happiness of all his twenty-five years.

The mother spoke little, but the Demoiselle Lucie and Peter Laveller chattered and laughed like children—when they were not silent and drinking each other in.

And ever in Laveller's heart an adoration for this maid met so perplexingly grew—grew until it seemed that his heart could not hold his joy. Even the maid's eyes as they rested on his were softer, more tender, filled with promise; and the proud face beneath the snowy hair became, as it watched them, the essence of that infinitely gentle sweetness that is the soul of the madonnas.

At last the Demoiselle de Tocquelain, glancing up and meeting that gaze, blushed, cast down her long lashes, and hung her head; then raised her eyes bravely.

"Are you content, my mother?" she asked gravely.

"My daughter, I am well content," came the smiling answer.

Swiftly followed the incredible, the terrible—in that scene of beauty and peace it was, said Laveller, like the flashing forth of a gorilla's paw upon a virgin's breast, a wail from deepest hell lancing through the song of angels.

At his right, among the roses, a light began to gleam—a fitful, flaring light that glared and died, glared and died. In it were two shapes. One had an arm clasped about the neck of the other; they leaned embracing in the light, and as it waxed and waned they seemed to pirouette, to try to break from it, to dash forward, to return—to dance!

The dead who danced!

A world where men sought rest and sleep and could find neither, and where even the dead could find no rest, but must dance to the rhythm of the star shells!

He groaned; sprang to his feet; watched, quivering in every nerve. Girl and woman followed his rigid gaze; turned to him again and with tear-filled, pitiful eyes.

"It is nothing!" said the maid. "It is nothing! See there is nothing there!"

Once more she touched his lids; and the light and the swaying forms were gone. But now Laveller knew. Back into his consciousness rushed the full tide of memory—memory of the mud and filth, the stenches, and the fiery, slaying sounds, the cruelty, the misery and the hatreds; memory of torn men and tormented dead; memory of whence he had come, the trenches.

The trenches! He had fallen asleep, and all this was but a dream! He was sleeping at his post, while his comrades were trusting him to watch over them. And those two ghastly shapes among the roses—they were the two Scots on the wires summoning him back to his duty; beckoning, beckoning him to return. He must waken! He must waken!

Desperately he strove to drive himself from his garden of illusion; to force himself back to that devil world which during this hour of enchantment had been to his mind only as a fog bank on a far horizon. And as he struggled, the brown-eyed maid and the snowy-tressed woman watched —with ineffable pity, tears falling.

"The trenches!" gasped Laveller. "O God, wake me up! I must get back! O God, make me wake!"

"Am I only a dream, then, *ma mie?*"

It was the Demoiselle Lucie's voice—a bit piteous, the golden tones shaken.

"I must get back," he groaned—although at her question his heart seemed to die within him. "Let me wake!"

"Am *I* a dream?" Now the voice was angry; the demoiselle drew close. "Am I not *real?*"

A little foot stamped furiously on his, a little hand darted out, pinched him viciously close above his elbow. He felt the sting of the pain and rubbed it, gazing at her stupidly.

"Am I a dream, think you?" she murmured, and, raising her palms, set them on his temples, bringing down his head until his eyes looked straight into hers.

Laveller gazed—gazed down, down deep into their depths, lost himself in them. Her warm, sweet breath fanned his cheek; whatever this was, wherever he was—*she* was no dream!

"But I must return—get back to my trench!" The soldier in him clung to the necessity.

"My son"—it was the mother speaking now—"my son, you *are* in your trench."

Laveller gazed at her, bewildered. His eyes swept the lovely scene about him. When he turned to her again it was with the look of a sorely perplexed child. She smiled.

"Have no fear," she said. "Everything is well. You are in your trench —but your trench centuries ago; yes, twice a hundred years ago, counting time as you do—and as once we did."

A chill ran through him. Were they mad? Was he mad? His arm slipped down over a soft shoulder; the touch steadied him, then he was able to go on.

"And you?" he forced himself to ask.

He caught a swift glance between the two, and in answer to some unspoken question the mother nodded. The Demoiselle Lucie pressed soft hands against Peter's face, looked again into his eyes.

"Ma mie," she said gently, "we have been"—she hesitated—"what you call—dead—to your world these two hundred years!"

But before she had spoken the words Laveller, I think, had sensed what was coming. And if for a fleeting instant he had felt a touch of ice in every vein, it vanished beneath the exaltation that raced through him, vanished as frost beneath a mist-scattering sun. For if this were true—why, then there was no such thing as death! And it was true!

It was true! He knew it with a shining certainty that had upon it not the shadow of a shadow—but how much his desire to believe entered into this certainty who can tell?

He looked at the château. Of course! it was that whose ruins loomed out of the darkness when the flares split the night—in whose cellars he had longed to sleep. Death—oh, the foolish, fearful hearts of men!—this death? This glorious place of peace and beauty?

And this wondrous girl whose brown eyes were the keys of heart's desire! Death—he laughed and laughed again.

Another thought struck him, swept through him like a torrent. He must get back to the trenches and tell them this great truth he had found. Why, he was like a traveler from a dying world who unwittingly stumbles upon a secret to turn that world dead to hope into a living heaven!

There was no longer need for men to fear the splintering shell, the fire that seared them, the bullets, or the shining steel. What did they matter when this—*this*—was the truth? He must get back and tell them. Even those two Scots would lie still on the wires when he whispered this to them.

But he forgot—*they* knew now. But they could not return to tell—as he could. He was wild with joy, exultant, lifted up to the skies, a demigod—the bearer of a truth that would free the devil-ridden world from its demons; a new Prometheus who bore back to mankind a more precious flame than had the old.

"I must go!" he cried. "I must tell them! Show me how to return—swiftly!"

A doubt assailed him; he pondered it.

"But they may not believe me," he whispered. "No. I must show them proof. I must carry something back to prove this to them."

The Lady of Tocquelain smiled. She lifted a little knife from the table, and, reaching over to a rose tree, cut from it a cluster of buds; thrust it toward his eager hand.

Before he could grasp it the maid had taken it.

"Wait!" she murmured. "I will give you another message."

There was a quill and ink upon the table, and Peter wondered how they had come; he had not seen them before—but with so many wonders, what was this small one? There was a slip of paper in the Demoiselle Lucie's hand, too. She bent her little, dusky head and wrote; blew upon the paper, waved it in the air to dry it; sighed, smiled at Peter and wrapped it about the stem of the rosebud cluster; placed it on the table, and waved back Peter's questioning hand.

"Your coat," she said. "You will need it, for now you must go back."

She thrust his arms into the garment. She was laughing—but there were tears in the great, brown eyes; the red mouth was very wistful.

Now the older woman arose, stretched out her hand again; Laveller bent over it, kissed it.

"We shall be here waiting for you, my son," she said softly. "When it is time for you to—come back."

He reached for the roses with the paper wrapped about their stems. The maid darted a hand over his, lifted them before he could touch them.

"You must not read it until you have gone," she said—and again the rose flame burned throat and cheeks.

Hand in hand, like children, they sped over the greensward to where Peter had first met her. They stopped there, regarding each other gravely—and then that other miracle which had happened to Laveller and that he had forgotten in the shock of his wider realization called for utterance.

"I love you!" whispered Peter Laveller to this living, long-dead Demoiselle de Tocquelain.

She sighed, and was in his arms.

"Oh, I know you do!" she cried. "I know you do, dear one—but I was so afraid you would go without telling me so."

She raised her sweet lips, pressed them long to his; drew back.

"I loved you from the moment I saw you standing here," she told him, "and I will be here waiting for you when you return. And now you must go, dear love of mine; but wait—"

He felt a hand steal into the pocket of his tunic, press something over his heart.

"The messages," she said. "Take them. And remember—I will wait. I promise, I, Lucie de Tocquelain—"

There was a singing in his head. He opened his eyes. He was back in his trench, and in his ears still rang the name of the demoiselle, and over his heart he felt still the pressure of her hand. His head was half-turned toward three men who were regarding him.

One of them had a watch in his hand; it was the surgeon. Why was he looking at his watch. Had he been gone long? he wondered.

Well, what did it matter, when he was the bearer of such a message? His weariness had gone; he was transformed, jubilant; his soul was shouting paeans. Forgetting discipline, he sprang toward the three.

"There is no such thing as death!" he cried. "We must send this message along the lines—at once! At once, do you understand? Tell it to the world—I have proof—"

He stammered and choked in his eagerness. The three glanced at each other. His major lifted his electric flash, clicked it in Peter's face, started oddly—then quietly walked over and stood between the lad and his rifle.

"Just get your breath a moment, my boy, and then tell us about it," he said.

They were devilishly unconcerned, were they now? Well, wait till they had heard what he *had* to tell them!

And tell them Peter did, leaving out only what had passed between him and the demoiselle—for, after all, wasn't that his own personal affair? And gravely and silently they listened to him. But always the trouble deepened in his major's eyes as Laveller poured forth the story.

"And then—I came back, came back as quickly as I could, to help us all; to lift us out of all this—" his hands swept out in a wide gesture of disgust—"for none of it matters! When we die—we live!" he ended.

Upon the face of the man of science rested profound satisfaction.

"A perfect demonstration; better than I could ever have hoped!" he spoke over Laveller's head to the major. "Great, how great is the imagination of man!"

There was a tinge of awe in his voice.

Imagination? Peter was cut to the sensitive, vibrant soul of him. They didn't believe him! He would show them!

"But I have proof!" he cried.

He threw open his greatcoat, ran his hand into his tunic pocket; his fingers closed over a bit of paper wrapped around a stem. Ah—now he would show them!

He drew it out, thrust it toward them.

"Look!" His voice was like a triumphant trumpet call.

What was the matter with them? Could they not see? Why did their

with books, papers and what seemed to be writing materials—oddly figured jars of a purplish metal, and rods with stained tips. Tall as the pedestals were, I seemed at times able to view them from above. On some of them were great globes of luminous crystal serving as lamps, and inexplicable machines formed of vitreous tubes and metal rods.

The windows were glazed, and latticed with stout-looking bars. Though I dared not approach and peer out them, I could see from where I was the waving tops of singular fernlike growths. The floor was of massive octagonal flagstones, while rugs and hangings were entirely lacking.

Later, I had visions of sweeping through cyclopean corridors of stone, and up and down gigantic inclined planes of the same monstrous masonry. There were no stairs anywhere, nor was any passageway less than thirty feet wide. Some of the structures through which I floated must have towered in the sky for thousands of feet.

There were multiple levels of black vaults below, and never-opened trapdoors, sealed down with metal bands and holding dim suggestions of some special peril.

I seemed to be a prisoner, and horror hung broodingly over everything I saw. I felt that the mocking curvilinear hieroglyphs on the walls would blast my soul with their message were I not guarded by a merciful ignorance.

Still later my dreams included vistas from the great round windows, and from the titanic flat roof, with its curious gardens, wide barren area and high, scalloped parapet of stone, to which the topmost of the inclined planes led.

There were almost endless leagues of giant buildings, each in its garden, and ranged along paved roads fully two hundred feet wide. They differed greatly in aspect, but few were less than five hundred feet square or a thousand feet high. Many seemed so limitless that they must have had a frontage of several thousand feet, while some shot up to mountainous altitudes in the gray, steamy heavens.

They seemed to be mainly of stone or concrete, and most of them embodied the oddly curvilinear type of masonry noticeable in the building that held me. Roofs were flat and garden-covered, and tended to have scalloped parapets. Sometimes there were terraces and higher levels, and wide, cleared spaces amidst the gardens. The great roads held hints of motion, but in the earlier visions I could not resolve this impression into details.

In certain places I beheld enormous dark cylindrical towers which climbed far above any of the other structures. These appeared to be of a totally unique nature and showed signs of prodigious age and dilapidation. They were built of a bizarre type of square-cut basalt masonry, and tapered slightly toward their rounded tops. Nowhere in any of them could the least traces of windows or other apertures save huge doors be found. I noticed also some lower buildings—all crumbling with the weathering of aeons—which resembled these dark, cylindrical towers in basic architecture. Around all these aberrant piles of square-cut masonry there hovered an inexplicable aura of menace and concentrated fear, like that bred by the sealed trapdoors.

The omnipresent gardens were almost terrifying in their strangeness, with bizarre and unfamiliar forms of vegetation nodding over broad paths lined with curiously carven monoliths. Abnormally vast fernlike growths predominated—some green, and some of a ghastly, fungoid pallor.

Among them rose great spectral things resembling calamities, whose bamboolike trunks towered to fabulous heights. Then there were tufted forms like fabulous cycades, and grotesque dark green shrubs and trees of coniferous aspect.

Flowers were small, colorless and unrecognizable, blooming in geometrical beds and at large among the greenery.

In a few of the terrace and rooftop gardens were larger and more vivid blossoms of almost offensive contours and seeming to suggest artificial breeding. Fungi of inconceivable size, outlines and colors speckled the scene in patterns bespeaking some unknown but well-established horticultural tradition. In the larger gardens on the ground there seemed to be some attempt to preserve the irregularities of nature, but on the roofs there was more selectiveness, and more evidences of the topiary art.

The skies were almost always moist and cloudy, and sometimes I would seem to witness tremendous rains. Once in a while, though, there would be glimpses of the sun—which looked abnormally large—and of the moon, whose markings held a touch of difference from the normal that I could never quite fathom. When—very rarely—the night sky was clear to any extent, I beheld constellations which were nearly beyond recognition. Known outlines were sometimes approximated, but seldom duplicated; and from the position of the few groups I could recognize, I felt I must be in the earth's southern hemisphere, near the Tropic of Capricorn.

The far horizon was always steamy and indistinct, but I could see that great jungles of unknown tree ferns, *Calamites, Lepidodendron,* and *Sigillaria* lay outside the city, their fantastic frondage waving mockingly in the shifting vapors. Now and then there would be suggestions of motion in the sky, but these my early visions never resolved.

By the autumn of 1914 I began to have infrequent dreams of strange floatings over the city and through the regions around it. I saw interminable roads through forests of fearsome growths with mottled, fluted and banded trunks, and past other cities as strange as the one which persistently haunted me.

I saw monstrous constructions of black or iridescent stone in glades and clearings where perpetual twilight reigned, and traversed long causeways over swamps so dark that I could tell but little of their moist, towering vegetation.

Once I saw an area of countless miles strewn with age-blasted basaltic ruins whose architecture had been like that of the few windowless, round-topped towers in the haunting city.

And once I saw the sea—a boundless, steamy expanse beyond the colossal stone piers of an enormous town of domes and arches. Great shapeless suggestions of shadow moved over it, and here and there its surface was vexed with anomalous spoutings.

III

As I have said, it was not immediately that these wild visions began to hold their terrifying quality. Certainly, many persons have dreamed intrinsically stranger things—things compounded of unrelated scraps of daily life, pictures and reading, and arranged in fantastically novel forms by the unchecked caprices of sleep.

For some time I accepted the visions as natural, even though I had never before been an extravagant dreamer. Many of the vague anomalies, I argued, must have come from trivial sources too numerous to track down; while others seemed to reflect a common textbook knowledge of the plants and other conditions of the primitive world of a hundred and fifty million years ago—the world of the Permian or Triassic Age.

In the course of some months, however, the element of terror did figure with accumulating force. This was when the dreams began so unfailingly to have the aspect of memories, and when my mind began to link them with my growing abstract disturbances—the feeling of mnemonic restraint, the curious impressions regarding time, the sense of a loathsome exchange with my secondary personality of 1908–13 and, considerably later, the inexplicable loathing of my own person.

As certain definite details began to enter the dreams, their horror increased a thousandfold—until by October 1915 I felt I must do something. It was then that I began an intensive study of other cases of amnesia and visions, feeling that I might thereby objectivize my trouble and shake clear of its emotional grip.

However, as before mentioned, the result was at first almost exactly opposite. It disturbed me vastly to find that my dreams had been so closely duplicated; especially since some of the accounts were too early to admit of any geological knowledge—and therefore of any idea of primitive landscapes—on the subjects' part.

What is more, many of these accounts supplied very horrible details and explanations in connection with the visions of great buildings and jungle gardens—and other things. The actual sights and vague impressions were bad enough, but what was hinted or asserted by some of the other dreamers savored of madness and blasphemy. Worst of all, my own pseudomemory was aroused to wilder dreams and hints of coming revelations. And yet most doctors deemed my course, on the whole, an advisable one.

I studied psychology systematically, and under the prevailing stimulus my son Wingate did the same—his studies leading eventually to his present professorship. In 1917 and 1918 I took special courses at Miskatonic. Meanwhile, my examination of medical, historical and anthropological records became indefatigable, involving travels to distant libraries, and finally including even a reading of the hideous books of forbidden lore in which my secondary personality had been so disturbingly interested.

Some of the latter were the actual copies I had consulted in my altered state, and I was greatly disturbed by certain marginal notations and ostensible *corrections* of the hideous text in a script and idiom which somehow seemed oddly unhuman.

These markings were mostly in the respective languages of the various books, all of which the writer seemed to know with equal, though obviously, academic facility. One note appended to von Junzt's *Unaussprechlichen Kulten,* however, was alarmingly otherwise. It consisted of certain curvilinear hieroglyphs in the same ink as that of the German corrections, but following no recognized human pattern. And these hieroglyphs were closely and unmistakably akin to the characters constantly met with in my dreams—characters whose meaning I would sometimes momentarily fancy I knew, or was just on the brink of recalling.

To complete my black confusion, many librarians assured me that, in view of previous examinations and records of consultation of the volumes in question, all of these notations must have been made by myself in my secondary state. This despite the fact that I was and still am ignorant of three of the languages involved. Piecing together the scattered records, ancient and modern, anthropological and medical, I found a fairly consistent mixture of myth and hallucination whose scope and wildness left me utterly dazed. Only one thing consoled me: the fact that the myths were of such early existence. What lost knowledge could have brought pictures of the Paleozoic or Mesozoic landscape into these primitive fables, I could not even guess; but the pictures had been there. Thus, a basis existed for the formation of a fixed type of delusion.

Cases of amnesia no doubt created the general myth pattern—but afterward the fanciful accretions of the myths must have reacted on amnesia sufferers and colored their pseudomemories. I myself had read and heard all the early tales during my memory lapse—my quest had amply proved that. Was it not natural, then, for my subsequent dreams and emotional impressions to become colored and molded by what my memory subtly held over from my secondary state?

A few of the myths had significant connections with other cloudy legends of the prehuman world, especially those Hindu tales involving stupefying gulfs of time and forming part of the lore of modern theosophists.

Primal myth and modern delusion joined in their assumption that mankind is only one—perhaps the least—of the highly evolved and dominant races of this planet's long and largely unknown career. Things of inconceivable shape, they implied, had reared towers to the sky and delved into every secret of nature before the first amphibian forbear of man had crawled out of the hot sea three hundred million years ago.

Some had come down from the stars; a few were as old as the cosmos itself; others had arisen swiftly from terrane germs as far behind the first germs of our life cycle as those germs are behind ourselves. Spans of thousands of millions of years, and linkages of other galaxies and universes, were spoken of. Indeed, there was no such thing as time in its humanly accepted sense.

But most of the tales and impressions concerned a relatively late race, of a queer and intricate shape, resembling no life form known to science, which had lived till only fifty million years before the advent of man. This, they indicated, was the greatest race of all because it alone had conquered the secret of time.

It had learned all things that ever were known or ever would be known on the earth, through the power of its keener minds to project themselves into the past and future, even through gulfs of millions of years, and study the lore of every age. From the accomplishments of this race arose all legends of prophets, including those in human mythology.

In its vast libraries were volumes of texts and pictures holding the whole of earth's annals—histories and descriptions of every species that had ever been or that ever would be, with full records of their arts, their achievements, their languages and their psychologies.

With this aeon-embracing knowledge, the Great Race chose from every era and life form such thoughts, arts and processes as might suit its own nature and situation. Knowledge of the past, secured through a kind of mind-casting outside the recognized senses, was harder to glean than knowledge of the future.

In the latter case the course was easier and more material. With suitable mechanical aid a mind would project itself forward in time, feeling its dim, extrasensory way till it approached the desired period. Then, after preliminary trials, it would seize on the best discoverable representative of the highest of that period's life forms. It would enter the organism's brain and set up therein its own vibrations, while the displaced mind would strike back to the period of the displacer, remaining in the latter's body till a reverse process was set up.

The projected mind, in the body of the organism of the future, would then pose as a member of the race whose outward form it wore, learning as quickly as possible all that could be learned of the chosen age and its massed information and techniques.

Meanwhile the displaced mind, thrown back to the displacer's age and body, would be carefully guarded. It would be kept from harming the body it occupied, and would be drained of all its knowledge by trained questioners. Often it could be questioned in its own language, when previous quests into the future had brought back records of that language.

If the mind came from a body whose language the Great Race could not physically reproduce, clever machines would be made, on which the alien speech could be played as on a musical instrument.

The Great Race's members were immense rugose cones ten feet high, and with head and other organs attached to foot-thick distensible limbs spreading from the apexes. They spoke by the clicking or scraping of huge paws or claws attached to the end of two of their four limbs, and walked by the expansion and contraction of a viscious layer attached to their vast, ten-foot bases.

When the captive mind's amazement and resentment had worn off, and when—assuming that it came from a body vastly different from the Great Race's—it had lost its horror at its unfamiliar, temporary form, it was permitted to study its new environment and experience a wonder and wisdom approximating that of its displacer.

With suitable precautions, and in exchange for suitable services, it was allowed to rove all over the habitable world in titan airships or on the huge boatlike atomic-engined vehicles which traversed the great roads, and to delve freely into the libraries containing the records of the planet's past and future.

This reconciled many captive minds to their lot; since none were other than keen, and to such minds the unveiling of hidden mysteries of earth—closed chapters of inconceivable pasts and dizzying vortices of future time which include the years ahead of their own natural ages—forms always, despite the abysmal horrors often unveiled, the supreme experience of life.

Now and then certain captives were permitted to meet other captive minds seized from the future—to exchange thoughts with consciousness living a hundred or a thousand or a million years before or after their own ages. And all were urged to write copiously in their own languages of themselves and their respective periods such documents to be filed in the great central archives.

It may be added that there was one special type of captive whose privileges were far greater than those of the majority. These were the dying *permanent* exiles, whose bodies in the future had been seized by keen-minded members of the Great Race who, faced with death, sought to escape mental extinction.

Such melancholy exiles were not as common as might be expected, since the longevity of the Great Race lessened its love of life—especially among those superior minds capable of projection. From cases of the permanent projection of elder minds arose many of those lasting changes of personality noticed in later history—including mankind's.

As for the ordinary cases of exploration—when the displacing mind had learned what it wished in the future, it would build an apparatus like that which had started its flight and reverse the process of projection. Once more it would be in its own body in its own age while the lately captive mind would return to that body of the future to which it properly belonged.

Only when one or the other of the bodies had died during the exchange was this restoration impossible. In such cases, of course, the exploring mind had—like those of the death escapers—to live out an alien-bodied life in the future; or else the captive mind—like the dying permanent exiles—had to end its days in the form and past age of the Great Race.

This fate was less horrible when the captive mind was also of the Great Race—a not infrequent occurrence, since in all its periods that race was intensely concerned with its own future. The number of dying permanent exiles of the Great Race was very slight—largely because of the tremendous penalties attached to displacements of future Great Race minds by the moribund.

Through projection, arrangements were made to inflict these penalties on the offending minds in their new future bodies—and sometimes forced reexchanges were effected.

Complex cases of the displacement of exploring or already captive minds by minds in various regions of the past had been known and carefully rectified. In every age since the discovery of mind projection, a minute but well-recognized element of the population consisted of Great Race minds from past ages, sojourning for a longer or shorter while.

When a captive mind of alien origin was returned to its own body in the future, it was purged by an intricate mechanical hypnosis of all it had learned in the Great Race's age—this because of certain troublesome consequences inherent in the general carrying forward of knowledge in large quantities.

The few existing instances of clear transmission had caused, and would cause at known future times, great disasters. And it was largely in consequence of two cases of the kind—said the old myths—that mankind had learned what it had concerning the Great Race.

Of all things surviving physically and directly from that aeon-distant world, there remained only certain ruins of great stones in far places and under the sea, and parts of the text of the frightful Pnakotic Manuscripts.

Thus the returning mind reached its own age with only the faintest and most fragmentary vision of what it had undergone since its seizure. All memories that could be eradicated were eradicated, so that in most cases only a dream-shadowed blank stretched back to the time of the first exchange. Some minds recalled more than others, and the chance joining of memories had at rare times brought hints of the forbidden past to future ages.

There probably never was a time when groups or cults did not secretly cherish certain of these hints. In the *Necronomicon* the presence of such a cult among human beings was suggested—a cult that sometimes gave aid to minds voyaging down the aeons from the days of the Great Race.

And, meanwhile, the Great Race itself waxed well-nigh omniscient, and turned to the task of setting up exchanges with the minds of other planets, and of exploring their pasts and futures. It sought likewise to fathom the past years and origin of that black, aeon-dead orb in far space whence its own mental heritage had come—for the mind of the Great Race was older than its bodily form.

The beings of a dying elder world, wise with the ultimate secrets, had looked ahead for a new world and species wherein they might have long life, and had sent their minds en masse into that future race best adapted to house them—the cone-shaped beings that peopled our earth a billion years ago.

Thus the Great Race came to be, while the myriad minds sent backward were left to die in the horror of strange shapes. Later the race would again face death, yet would live through another forward migration of its best minds into the bodies of others who had a longer physical span ahead of them.

Such was the background of intertwined legend and hallucination. When, around 1920, I had my researches in coherent shape, I felt a slight lessening of the tension which their earlier stages had increased. After all, and in spite of the fancies prompted by blind emotions, were not most of my phenomena readily explainable? Any chance might have turned my mind to dark studies during the amnesia—and then I read the forbidden legends and met the members of ancient and ill-regarded cults. That, plainly, supplied the material for the dreams and disturbed feelings which came after the return of memory.

As for the marginal notes in dream hieroglyphs and languages unknown to me, but laid at my door by librarians—I might easily have picked up a smattering of the tongues during my secondary state, while the hieroglyphs were doubtless coined by my fancy from descriptions in old legends, and afterward woven into my dreams. I tried to verify certain points through conversations with known cult leaders, but never succeeded in establishing the right connections.

At times the parallelism of so many cases in so many distant ages continued to worry me as it had at first, but on the other hand I reflected that the excitant folklore was undoubtedly more universal in the past than in the present.

Probably all the other victims whose cases were like mine had had a long and familiar knowledge of the tales I had learned only when in my secondary state. When these victims had lost their memory, they had associated themselves with the creatures of their household myths—the fabulous invaders supposed to displace men's minds—and had thus embarked upon quests for knowledge which they thought they could take back to a fancied, nonhuman past.

Then, when their memory returned, they reversed the associative process and thought of themselves as the former captive minds instead of as the displacers. Hence the dreams and pseudomemories following the conventional myth pattern.

Despite the seeming cumbrousness of these explanations, they came finally to supersede all others in my mind—largely because of the greater weakness of any rival theory. And a substantial number of eminent psychologists and anthropologists gradually agreed with me.

The more I reflected, the more convincing did my reasoning seem; till in the end I had a really effective bulwark against the visions and impressions which still assailed me. Suppose I did see strange things at night? These were only what I had heard and read of. Suppose I did have odd loathings and perspectives and pseudomemories? These, too, were only echoes of myths absorbed in my secondary state. Nothing that I might dream, nothing that I might feel, could be of any actual significance.

Fortified by this philosophy, I greatly improved in nervous equilibrium, even though the visions—rather than the abstract impressions—steadily became more frequent and more disturbingly detailed. In 1922 I felt able to undertake regular work again, and put my newly gained knowledge to practical use by accepting an instructorship in psychology at the university.

My old chair of political economy had long been adequately filled—besides which, methods of teaching economics had changed greatly since my heyday. My son was at this time just entering on the postgraduate studies leading to his present professorship, and we worked together a great deal.

IV

I continued however, to keep a careful record of the outré dreams which crowded upon me so thickly and vividly. Such a record, I argued, was of genuine value as a psychological document. The glimpses still seemed damnably like memories, though I fought off this impression with a goodly measure of success.

In writing, I treated the phantasmata as things seen; but at all other times I brushed them aside like any gossamer illusions of the night. I had never mentioned such matters in common conversation; though reports of them, filtering out as such things will, had aroused sundry rumors regarding my mental health. It is amusing to reflect that these rumors were confined wholly to laymen, without a single champion among physicians or psychologists.

Of my visions after 1914 I will here mention only a few, since fuller accounts and records are at the disposal of the serious student. It is evident that with time the curious inhibitions somewhat waned, for the scope of my visions vastly increased. They have never, though, become other than disjointed fragments seemingly without clear motivation.

Within the dreams I seemed gradually to acquire a greater and greater freedom of wandering. I floated through many strange buildings of stone, going from one to the other along mammoth underground passages which seemed to form the common avenues of transit. Sometimes I encountered those gigantic sealed trapdoors in the lowest level, around which such an aura of fear and forbiddenness clung.

I saw tremendous tessellated pools, and rooms of curious and inexplicable utensils of myriad sorts. Then there were colossal caverns of intricate machinery whose outlines and purpose were wholly strange to me, and whose sound manifested itself only after many years of dreaming. I may here remark that sight and sound are the only senses I have ever exercised in the visionary world.

The real horror began in May 1915, when I first saw the living things. This was before my studies had taught me what, in view of the myths and case histories, to expect. As mental barriers wore down, I beheld great masses of thin vapor in various parts of the building and in the streets below.

These steadily grew more solid and distinct, till at last I could trace their monstrous outlines with uncomfortable ease. They seemed to be enormous, iridescent cones, about ten feet high and ten feet wide at the base, and made up of some ridgy, scaly, semielastic matter. From their apexes projected four flexible, cylindrical members, each a foot thick, and of a ridgy substance like that of the cones themselves.

These members were sometimes contracted almost to nothing, and sometimes extended to any distance up to about ten feet. Terminating two of them were enormous claws or nippers. At the end of a third were four red, trumpetlike appendages. The fourth terminated in an irregular yellowish globe some two feet in diameter and having three great dark eyes ranged along its central circumference.

Surmounting this head were four slender gray stalks bearing flowerlike appendages, while from its nether side dangled eight greenish antennae or tentacles. The great base of the central cone was fringed with a rubbery, gray substance which moved the whole entity through expansion and contraction.

Their actions, though harmless, horrified me even more than their appearance—for it is not wholesome to watch monstrous objects doing what one had known only human beings to do. These objects moved intelligently about the great rooms, getting books from the shelves and taking them to the great tables, or vice versa, and sometimes writing diligently with a peculiar rod gripped in the greenish head tentacles. The huge nippers were used in carrying books and in conversation—speech consisting of a kind of clicking.

The objects had no clothing, but wore satchels or knapsacks suspended from the top of the conical trunk. They commonly carried their head and its supporting member at the level of the cone top, though it was frequently raised or lowered.

The other three great members tended to rest downward at the sides of the cone, contracted to above five feet each, when not in use. From their rate of reading, writing and operating their machines—those on the tables seemed somehow connected with thought—I concluded that their intelligence was enormously greater than man's.

Afterward I saw them everywhere; swarming in all the great chambers and corridors, tending monstrous machines in vaulted crypts and racing along the vast roads in gigantic, boat-shaped cars. I ceased to be afraid of them, for they seemed to form supremely natural parts of their environment.

Individual differences amongst them began to be manifest, and a few appeared to be under some kind of restraint. These latter, though showing no physical variation, had a diversity of gestures and habits which marked them off not only from the majority, but very largely from one another.

They wrote a great deal in what seemed to my cloudy vision a vast variety of characters—never the typical curvilinear hieroglyphs of the majority. A few, I fancied, used our own familiar alphabet. Most of them worked much more slowly than the general mass of the entities.

All this time my own part in the dreams seemed to be that of a disembodied consciousness with a range of vision wider than the normal, floating freely about, yet confined to the ordinary avenues and speeds of travel. Not until August 1915 did any suggestions of bodily existence begin to harass me. I say harass, because the first phase was a purely abstract, though infinitely terrible, association of my previously noted body-loathing with the scenes of my visions.

For a while my chief concern during dreams was to avoid looking down at myself, and I recall how grateful I was for the total absence of large mirrors in the strange rooms. I was mightily troubled by the fact that I always saw the great tables—whose height could not be under ten feet—from a level not below that of their surfaces.

And then the morbid temptation to look down at myself became greater and greater, till one night I could not resist it. At first my downward glance revealed nothing whatever. A moment later I perceived that this was because my head lay at the end of a flexible neck of enormous length. Retracting this neck and gazing down very sharply, I saw the scaly, rugose, iridescent bulk of a vast cone ten feet tall and ten feet wide at the base. That was when I waked half of Arkham with my screaming as I plunged madly up from the abyss of sleep.

Only after weeks of hideous repetition did I grow half-reconciled to these visions of myself in monstrous form. In the dreams I now moved bodily among the other unknown entities, reading terrible books from the endless shelves and writing for hours at the great tables with a stylus managed by the green tentacles that hung down from my head.

Snatches of what I read and wrote would linger in my memory. There were horrible annals of other worlds and other universes, and of stirrings of formless life outside of all universes. There were records of strange orders of beings which had peopled the world in forgotten pasts, and frightful chronicles of grotesque-bodied intelligences which would people it millions of years after the death of the last human being.

I learned of chapters in human history whose existence no scholar of today has ever suspected. Most of these writings were in the language of the hieroglyphs; which I studied in a queer way with the aid of droning machines, and which was evidently an agglutinative speech with root systems utterly unlike any found in human languages.

Other volumes were in other unknown tongues learned in the same queer way. A very few were in languages I knew. Extremely clever pictures, both inserted in the records and forming separate collections, aided me immensely. And all the time I seemed to be setting down a history of my own age in English. On waking, I could recall only minute and meaningless scraps of the unknown tongues which my dream self had mastered, though whole phrases of the history stayed with me.

I learned—even before my waking self had studied the parallel cases or the old myths from which the dreams doubtless sprang—that the entities around me were of the world's greatest race, which had conquered time and had sent exploring minds into every age. I knew, too, that I had been snatched from my age, while another used my body in that age, and that a few of the other strange forms housed similarly captured minds. I seemed to talk, in some odd language of claw clicking, with exiled intellects from every corner of the solar system.

There was a mind from the planet we know as Venus, which would live incalculable epochs to come, and one from an outer moon of Jupiter six million years in the past. Of earthly minds there were some from the winged, star-headed, half-vegetable race of paleogean Antarctica; one from the reptile people of fabled Valusia; three from the furry prehuman Hyperborean worshippers of Tsathoggua; one from the wholly abominable Tcho-Tchos; two from the Arachnid denizens of earth's last age; five from the hardy *Coleopterous* species immediately following mankind, to which the Great Race was some day to transfer its keenest minds en masse in the face of horrible peril; and several from different branches of humanity.

I talked with the mind of Yiang-Li, a philosopher from the cruel empire of Tsan-Chan, which is to come in A.D. 5000; with that of a general of the great-headed brown people who held South Africa in 50,000 B.C.; with that of a twelfth-century Florentine monk named Bartolomeo Corsi; with that of a king of Lomar who had ruled that terrible polar land one hundred thousand years before the squat, yellow Inutos came from the west to engulf it.

I talked with the mind of Nug-Soth, a magician of the dark conquerors of A.D. 16,000; with that of a Roman named Titus Sempronius Blaesus, who had been a quaestor in Sulla's time; with that of Khephnes, an Egyptian of the Fourteenth Dynasty, who told me the hideous secret of

Nyarlathotep; with that of a priest of Atlantis's middle kingdom; with that of a Suffolk gentleman of Cromwell's day, James Woodville; with that of a court astronomer of pre-Inca Peru; with that of the Australian physicist Nevel Kingston-Brown, who will die in A.D. 2518; with that of an archimage of vanished Yhe in the Pacific; with that of Theodotides, a Graeco-Bactrian official of 200 B.C.; with that of an aged Frenchman of Louis XIII's time named Pierre-Louis Montagny; with that of Crom-Ya, a Cimmerian chieftain of 15,000 B.C.; and with so many others that my brain can not hold the shocking secrets and dizzying marvels I learned from them.

I awakened each morning in a fever, sometimes frantically trying to verify or discredit such information as fell within the range of modern human knowledge. Traditional facts took on new and doubtful aspects, and I marveled at the dream fancy which could invent such surprising addenda to history and science.

I shivered at the mysteries the past may conceal, and trembled at the menaces the future may bring forth. What was hinted in the speech of posthuman entities of the fate of mankind produced such an effect on me that I will not set it down here.

After man there would be the mighty beetle civilization, the bodies of whose members the cream of the Great Race would seize when the monstrous doom overtook the elder world. Later, as the earth's span closed, the transferred minds would again migrate through time and space —to another stopping place in the bodies of the bulbous vegetable entities of Mercury. But there would be races after them, clinging pathetically to the cold planet and burrowing to its horror-filled core, before the utter end.

Meanwhile, in my dreams, I wrote endlessly in that history of my own age which I was preparing—half voluntarily and half through promises of increased library and travel opportunities—for the Great Race's central archives. The archives were in a colossal subterranean structure near the city's center, which I came to know well through frequent labors and consultations. Meant to last as long as the race, and to withstand the fiercest of earth's convulsions, this titan repository surpassed all other buildings in the massive, mountainlike firmness of its construction.

The records, written or printed on great sheets of a curiously tenacious cellulose fabric, were bound into books that opened from the top, and were kept in individual cases of a strange, extremely light rustless metal of grayish hue, decorated with mathematical designs and bearing the title in the Great Race's curvilinear hieroglyphs.

These cases were stored in tiers of rectangular vaults—like closed, locked shelves—wrought of the same rustless metal and fastened by knobs with intricate turnings. My own history was assigned a specific place in the vaults of the lowest or vertebrate level—the section devoted to the cultures of mankind and of the furry and reptilian races immediately preceding it in terrestrial dominance.

But none of the dreams ever gave me a full picture of daily life. All were the merest misty, disconnected fragments, and it is certain that these fragments were not unfolded in their rightful sequence. I have, for example, a very imperfect idea of my own living arrangements in the dream world; though I seem to have possessed a great stone room of my own. My restrictions as a prisoner gradually disappeared, so that some of the visions included vivid travels over the mighty jungle roads, sojourns in strange cities, and explorations of some of the vast, dark, windowless ruins from which the Great Race shrank in curious fear. There were also long sea voyages in enormous, many-decked boats of incredible swiftness, and trips over wild regions in closed projectilelike airships lifted and moved by electrical repulsion.

Beyond the wide, warm ocean were other cities of the Great Race, and on one far continent I saw the crude villages of the black-snouted, winged creatures who would evolve as a dominant stock after the Great Race had sent its foremost minds into the future to escape the creeping horror. Flatness and exuberant green life were always the keynote of the scene. Hills were low and sparse, and usually displayed signs of volcanic forces.

Of the animals I saw, I could write volumes. All were wild; for the Great Race's mechanized culture had long since done away with domestic beasts, while food was wholly vegetable or synthetic. Clumsy reptiles of great bulk floundered in steaming morasses, fluttered in the heavy air or spouted in the seas and lakes; and among these I fancied I could vaguely recognize lesser, archaic prototypes of many forms—dinosaurs, pterodactyls, ichthyosaurs, labyrinthodonts, plesiosaurs, and the like—made familiar through paleontology. Of birds or mammals there were none that I could discover.

The ground and swamps were constantly alive with snakes, lizards and crocodiles, while insects buzzed incessantly among the lush vegetation. And far out at sea, unspied and unknown monsters spouted mountainous columns of foam into the vaporous sky. Once I was taken under the ocean in a gigantic submarine vessel with searchlights, and glimpsed some living horrors of awesome magnitude. I saw also the ruins of incredible sunken cities, and the wealth of crinoid, brachiopod, coral and ichthyic life which everywhere abounded.

Of the physiology, psychology, folkways and detailed history of the Great Race my visions preserved but little information, and many of the scattered points I here set down were gleaned from my study of old legends and other cases rather than from my own dreaming.

For in time, of course, my reading and research caught up with and passed the dreams in many phases, so that certain dream fragments were explained in advance and formed verifications of what I had learned. This consolingly established my belief that similar reading and research, accomplished by my secondary self, had formed the source of the whole terrible fabric of pseudomemories.

The period of my dreams, apparently, was one somewhat less than one hundred and fifty million years ago, when the Paleozoic Age was giving place to the Mesozoic. The bodies occupied by the Great Race represented no surviving—or even scientifically known—line of terrestrial evolution, but were of a peculiar, closely homogeneous, and highly specialized organic type inclining as much to the vegetable as to the animal state.

Cell action was of an unique sort almost precluding fatigue, and wholly eliminating the need of sleep. Nourishment, assimilated through the red trumpetlike appendages on one of the great flexible limbs, was always semifluid and in many aspects wholly unlike the food of existing animals.

The beings had but two of the senses which we recognize—sight and hearing, the latter accomplished through the flowerlike appendages on the gray stalks above their heads. Of other and incomprehensible senses—not, however, well utilizable by alien captive minds inhabitating their bodies—they possessed many. Their three eyes were so situated as to give them a range of vision wider than the normal. Their blood was a sort of deep greenish ichor of great thickness.

They had no sex, but reproduced through seeds or spores which clustered on their bases and could be developed only under water. Great, shallow tanks were used for the growth of their young—which were, however, reared only in small numbers on account of the longevity of individuals—four or five thousand years being the common life span.

Markedly defective individuals were quickly disposed of as soon as their defects were noticed. Disease and the approach of death were, in the absence of a sense of touch or of physical pain, recognized by purely visual symptoms.

The dead were incinerated with dignified ceremonies. Once in a while, as before mentioned, a keen mind would escape death by forward projection in time; but such cases were not numerous. When one did occur, the exiled mind from the future was treated with the utmost kindness till the dissolution of its unfamiliar tenement.

The Great Race seemed to form a single, loosely knit nation or league, with major institutions in common, though there were four definite divisions. The political and economic system of each unit was a sort of fascistic socialism, with major resources rationally distributed, and power delegated to a small governing board elected by the votes of all able to pass certain educational and psychological tests. Family organization was not overstressed, though ties among persons of common descent were recognized, and the young were generally reared by their parents.

Resemblances to human attitudes and institutions were, of course, most marked in those fields where on the one hand highly abstract elements were concerned, or, where on the other hand there was a dominance of the basic, unspecialized urges common to all organic life. A few added likenesses came through conscious adoption as the Great Race probed the future and copied what it liked.

Industry, highly mechanized, demanded but little time from each citizen; and the abundant leisure was filled with intellectual and aesthetic activities of various sorts.

The sciences were carried to an unbelievable height of development, and art was a vital part of life, though at the period of my dreams it had passed its crest and meridian. Technology was enormously stimulated through the constant struggle to survive, and to keep in existence the physical fabric of great cities, imposed by the prodigious geologic upheavals of those primal days.

Crime was surprisingly scant, and was dealt with through highly efficient policing. Punishments ranged from privilege deprivation and imprisonment to death or major emotion wrenching, and were never administered without a careful study of the criminal's motivations.

Warfare, largely civil for the last few millennia though sometimes waged against the winged, star-headed Old Ones who centered in the Antarctic, was infrequent though infinitely devastating. An enormous army, using cameralike weapons which produced tremendous electrical effects, was kept on hand for purposes seldom mentioned, but obviously connected with the ceaseless fear of the dark, windowless elder ruins and of the great sealed trapdoors in the lowest subterranean levels.

This fear of the basalt ruins and trapdoors was largely a matter of unspoken suggestion—or, at most, of furtive quasi whispers. Everything specific which bore on it was significantly absent from such books as were on the common shelves. It was the one subject lying altogether under a taboo among the Great Race, and seemed to be connected alike with horrible bygone struggles, and with that future peril which would some day force the race to send its keener minds ahead en masse in time.

Imperfect and fragmentary as were the other things presented by dreams and legends, this matter was still more bafflingly shrouded. The vague old myths avoided it—or perhaps all allusions had for some reason been excised. And in the dreams of myself and others, the hints were peculiarly few. Members of the Great Race never intentionally referred to the matter, and what could be gleaned came only from some of the more sharply observant captive minds.

According to these scraps of information, the basis of the fear was a horrible elder race of half-polypous, utterly alien entities which had come through space from immeasurably distant universes and had dominated the earth and three other solar planets about six hundred million years ago. They were only partly material—as we understand matter—and their type of consciousness and media of perception differed widely from those of terrestrial organisms. For example, their senses did not include that of sight; their mental world being a strange, nonvisual pattern of impressions.

They were, however, sufficiently material to use implements of normal matter when in cosmic areas containing it; and they required housing—albeit of a peculiar kind. Though their senses could penetrate all material barriers, their substance could not; and certain forms of electrical energy could wholly destroy them. They had the power of aerial motion, despite the absence of wings or any other visible means of levitation. Their minds were of such texture that no exchange with them could be effected by the Great Race.

When these things had come to the earth they had built mighty basalt cities of windowless towers, and had preyed horribly upon the beings they found. Thus it was when the minds of the Great Race sped across the void from that obscure, transgalactic world known in the disturbing and debatable Eltdown Shards as Yith.

The newcomers, with the instruments they created, had found it easy to subdue the predatory entities and drive them down to those caverns of inner earth which they had already joined to their abodes and begun to inhabit.

Then they had sealed the entrances and left them to their fate, afterward occupying most of their great cities and preserving certain important buildings for reasons connected more with superstition than with indifference, boldness or scientific and historical zeal.

But as the aeons passed, there came vague, evil signs that the elder things were growing strong and numerous in the inner world. There were sporadic irruptions of a particularly hideous character in certain small and remote cities of the Great Race, and in some of the deserted elder cities which the Great Race had not peopled—places where the paths to the gulfs below had not been properly sealed or guarded.

After that greater precautions were taken, and many of the paths were closed forever—though a few were left with sealed trapdoors for strategic use in fighting the elder things if ever they broke forth in unexpected places.

The irruptions of the elder things must have been shocking beyond all description, since they had permanently colored the psychology of the Great Race. Such was the fixed mood of horror that the very aspect of the creatures was left unmentioned. At no time was I able to gain a clear hint of what they looked like.

There were veiled suggestions of a monstrous plasticity, and of temporary lapses of visibility, while other fragmentary whispers referred to their control and military use of great winds. Singular whistling noises, and colossal footprints made up of five circular toe marks, seemed also to be associated with them.

It was evident that the coming doom so desperately feared by the Great Race—the doom that was one day to send millions of keen minds across the chasm of time to strange bodies in the safer future—had to do with a final successful irruption of the elder beings.

Mental projections down the ages had clearly foretold such a horror, and the Great Race had resolved that none who could escape should face it. That the foray would be a matter of vengeance, rather than an attempt to reoccupy the outer world, they knew from the planet's later history—for their projections showed the coming and going of subsequent races untroubled by the monstrous entities.

Perhaps these entities had come to prefer earth's inner abysses to the variable, storm-ravaged surface, since light meant nothing to them. Perhaps, too, they were slowly weakening with the aeons. Indeed, it was known that they would be quite dead in the time of the posthuman beetle race which the fleeing minds would tenant.

Meanwhile, the Great Race maintained its cautious vigilance, with potent weapons ceaselessly ready despite the horrified banishing of the subject from common speech and visible records. And always the shadow of nameless fear hung about the sealed trapdoors and the dark, windowless elder towers.

V

That is the world of which my dreams brought me dim, scattered echoes every night. I cannot hope to give any true idea of the horror and dread contained in such echoes, for it was upon a wholly intangible quality—the sharp sense of pseudomemory—that such feelings mainly depended.

As I have said, my studies gradually gave me a defense against these feelings in the form of rational psychological explanations; and this saving influence was augmented by the subtle touch of accustomedness which comes with the passage of time. Yet in spite of everything the vague, creeping terror would return momentarily now and then. It did not, however, engulf me as it had before; and after 1922 I lived a very normal life of work and recreation.

In the course of years I began to feel that my experience—together with the kindred cases and the related folklore—ought to be definitely summarized and published for the benefit of serious students; hence, I prepared a series of articles briefly covering the whole ground and illustrated with crude sketches of some of the shapes, scenes, decorative motifs, and hieroglyphs remembered from the dreams.

These appeared at various times during 1928 and 1929 in the *Journal of the American Psychological Society,* but did not attract much attention. Meanwhile, I continued to record my dreams with the minutest care, even though the growing stack of reports attained troublesomely vast proportions.

On July 10, 1934, there was forwarded to me by the Psychological Society the letter which opened the culminating and most horrible phase of the whole mad ordeal. It was postmarked Pilbarra, Western Australia, and bore the signature of one whom I found, upon inquiry, to be a mining engineer of considerable prominence. Enclosed were some very curious snapshots. I will reproduce the text in its entirety, and no reader can fail to understand how tremendous an effect it and the photographs had upon me.

I was, for a time, almost stunned and incredulous; for, although I had often thought that some basis of fact must underlie certain phases of the legends which had colored my dreams, I was nonetheless unprepared for anything like a tangible survival from a lost world remote beyond all imagination. Most devastating of all were the photographs—for here, in cold, incontrovertible realism, there stood out against a background of sand certain worn-down, water-ridged, storm-weathered blocks of stone whose slightly convex tops and slightly concave bottoms told their own story.

And when I studied them with a magnifying glass I could see all too plainly, amidst the batterings and pittings, the traces of those vast curvilinear designs and occasional hieroglyphs whose significance had become so hideous to me. But here is the letter, which speaks for itself:

49 Dampier St.,
Pilbarra, W. Australia,
May 18, 1934.

Prof. N. W. Peaslee,
c/o Am. Psychological Society,
30 E. 41st St.,
New York City, U.S.A.

My Dear Sir:

A recent conversation with Dr. E. M. Boyle of Perth, and some papers with your articles which he has just sent me, make it advisable for me to tell you about certain things I have seen in the Great Sandy Desert east of our gold field here. It would seem, in view of the peculiar legends about old cities with huge stonework and strange designs and hieroglyphs which you describe, that I have come upon something very important.

The blackfellows have always been full of talk about "great stones with marks on them," and seem to have a terrible fear of such things. They connect them in some way with their common racial legends about Buddai, the gigantic old man who lies asleep for ages underground with his head on his arm, and who will some day awake and eat up the world.

There are some very old and half-forgotten tales of enormous underground huts of great stones, where passages lead down and down, and where horrible things have happened. The blackfellows claim that once some warriors, fleeing in battle, went down into one and never came back, but that frightful winds began to blow from the place soon after they went down. However, there usually isn't much in what these natives say.

But what I have to tell is more than this. Two years ago, when I was prospecting about five hundred miles east in the desert, I came on a lot of queer pieces of dressed stone perhaps three by two by two feet in size, and weathered and pitted to the very limit.

At first I couldn't find any of the marks the blackfellows told about, but when I looked close enough I could make out some deeply carved lines in spite of the weathering. There were peculiar curves, just like what the blackfellows had tried to describe. I imagine there must have been thirty or forty blocks, some nearly buried in the sand, and all within a circle perhaps a quarter of a mile in diameter.

When I saw some, I looked around closely for more, and made a careful reckoning of the place with my instruments. I also took pictures of ten or twelve of the most typical blocks, and will enclose the prints for you to see.

I turned my information and pictures over to the government at Perth, but they have done nothing about them.

Then I met Dr. Boyle, who had read your articles in the *Journal of the American Psychological Society,* and, in time, happened to mention the stones. He was enormously interested and became quite excited when I showed him my snapshots, saying that the stones and the markings were just like those of the masonry you had dreamed about and seen described in legends.

He meant to write you, but was delayed. Meanwhile, he sent me most of the magazines with your articles and I saw at once, from your drawings and descriptions, that my stones are certainly the kind you mean. You can appreciate this from the enclosed prints. Later on you will hear directly from Dr. Boyle.

Now I can understand how important all this will be to you. Without question we are faced with the remains of an unknown civilization older than any dreamed of before, and forming a basis for your legends.

As a mining engineer I have some knowledge of geology, and can tell you that these blocks are so ancient they frighten me. They are mostly sandstone and granite, though one is almost certainly made of a queer sort of cement or concrete.

They bear evidence of water action, as if this part of the world had been submerged and come up again after long ages—all since those blocks were made and used. It is a matter of hundreds of thousands of years—or heaven knows how much more. I don't like to think about it.

In view of your previous diligent work in tracking down the legends and everything connected with them, I cannot doubt but that you will want to lead an expedition to the desert and make some archaeological excavations. Both Dr. Boyle and I are prepared to cooperate in such work if you—or organizations known to you—can furnish the funds.

I can get together a dozen miners for the heavy digging—the blackfellows would be of no use, for I've found that they have an almost maniacal fear of this particular spot. Boyle and I are saying nothing to others, for you very obviously ought to have precedence in any discoveries or credit.

The place can be reached from Pilbarra in about four days by motor tractor—which we'd need for our apparatus. It is somewhat west and south of Warburton's path of 1873, and one hundred miles southeast of Joanna Spring. We could float things up the De Grey River instead of starting from Pilbarra—but all that can be talked over later.

Roughly the stones lie at a point about 20°3′14″ South latitude, 125°0′39″ East longitude. The climate is tropical, and the desert conditions are trying.

I shall welcome further correspondence upon this subject, and am indeed keenly eager to assist in any plan you may devise. After studying your articles I am deeply impressed with the profound significance of the whole matter. Dr. Boyle will write later. When rapid communication is needed, a cable to Perth can be relayed by wireless.

Hoping profoundly for an early message,

Believe me,
Most faithfully yours,
Robert B. F. Mackenzie

Of the immediate aftermath of this letter, much can be learned from the press. My good fortune in securing the backing of Miskatonic University was great, and both Mr. Mackenzie and Dr. Boyle proved invaluable in arranging matters at the Australian end. We were not too specific with the public about our objects, since the whole matter would have lent itself unpleasantly to sensational and jocose treatment by the cheaper newspapers. As a result, printed reports were sparing; but enough appeared to tell of our quest for reported Australian ruins and to chronicle our various preparatory steps.

Professor William Dyer of the college's geology department—leader of the Miskatonic Antarctic Expedition of 1930–31—Ferdinand C. Ashley of the department of ancient history and Tyler M. Freeborn of the department of anthropology—together with my son Wingate—accompanied me.

My correspondent, Mackenzie, came to Arkham early in 1935 and assisted in our final preparations. He proved to be a tremendously competent and affable man of about fifty, admirably well read, and deeply familiar with all the conditions of Australian travel.

He had tractors waiting at Pilbarra, and we chartered a tramp steamer sufficiently small to get up the river to that point. We were prepared to excavate in the most careful and scientific fashion, sifting every particle of sand, and disturbing nothing which might seem to be in or near its original situation.

Sailing from Boston aboard the wheezy *Lexington* on March 28, 1935, we had a leisurely trip across the Atlantic and Mediterranean, through the Suez Canal, down the Red Sea and across the Indian Ocean to our goal. I need not tell how the sight of the low, sandy West Australian coast depressed me, and how I detested the crude mining town and dreary gold fields where the tractors were given their last loads.

Dr. Boyle, who met us, proved to be elderly, pleasant and intelligent—and his knowledge of psychology led him into many long discussions with my son and me.

Discomfort and expectancy were oddly mingled in most of us when at length our party of eighteen rattled forth over the arid leagues of sand and rock. On Friday, May 31, we forded a branch of the De Grey and entered the realm of utter desolation. A certain positive terror grew on me as we advanced to this actual site of the elder world behind the legends—a terror, of course, abetted by the fact that my disturbing dreams and pseudomemories still beset me with unabated force.

It was on Monday, June 3, that we saw the first of the half-buried blocks. I cannot describe the emotions with which I actually touched—in objective reality—a fragment of cyclopean masonry in every respect like the blocks in the walls of my dream buildings. There was a distinct trace of carving—and my hands trembled as I recognized part of a curvilinear decorative scheme made hellish to me through years of tormenting nightmare and baffling research.

A month of digging brought a total of some twelve hundred and fifty blocks in varying stages of wear and disintegration. Most of these were carven megaliths with curved tops and bottoms. A minority were smaller, flatter, plain-surfaced, and square or octagonally cut—like those of the floors and pavements in my dreams—while a few were singularly massive and curved or slanted in such a manner as to suggest use in vaulting or groining, or as parts of arches or round window casings.

The deeper—and the farther north and east—we dug, the more blocks we found—though we still failed to discover any trace of arrangement among them. Professor Dyer was appalled at the measureless age of the fragments, and Freeborn found traces of symbols which fitted darkly into certain Papuan and Polynesian legends of infinite antiquity. The condition and scattering of the blocks told mutely of vertiginous cycles of time and geologic upheavals of cosmic savagery.

We had an airplane with us, and my son Wingate would often go up to different heights and scan the sand-and-rock waste for signs of dim, large-scale outlines—either differences of level or trails of scattered blocks. His results were virtually negative; for whenever he would one day think he had glimpsed some significant trend, he would on his next trip find the impression replaced by another equally insubstantial—a result of the shifting, windblown sand.

One or two of these ephemeral suggestions, though, affected me queerly and disagreeably. They seemed, after a fashion, to dovetail horribly with something I had dreamed or read, but which I could no longer remember. There was a terrible familiarity about them—which somehow made me look furtively and apprehensively over the abominable, sterile terrain.

Around the first week in July I developed an unaccountable set of mixed emotions about that general northeasterly region. There was horror, and there was curiosity—but more than that, there was a persistent and perplexing illusion of memory.

I tried all sorts of psychological expedients to get these notions out of my head, but met with no success. Sleeplessness also gained upon me, but I almost welcomed this because of the resultant shortening of my dream periods. I acquired the habit of taking long, lone walks in the desert late at night—usually to the north or northeast, whither the sum of my strange new impulses seemed subtly to pull me.

Sometimes, on these walks, I would stumble over nearly buried fragments of the ancient masonry. Though there were fewer visible blocks here than where we had started, I felt sure that there must be a vast abundance beneath the surface. The ground was less level than at our camp, and the prevailing high winds now and then piled the sand into fantastic temporary hillocks—exposing low traces of the elder stones while it covered other traces.

I was queerly anxious to have the excavations extend to this territory, yet at the same time dreaded what might be revealed. Obviously, I was getting into a rather bad state—all the worse because I could not account for it.

An indication of my poor nervous health can be gained from my response to an odd discovery which I made on one of my nocturnal rambles. It was on the evening of July 11, when the moon flooded the mysterious hillocks with a curious pallor.

Wandering somewhat beyond my usual limits, I came upon a great stone which seemed to differ markedly from any we had yet encountered. It was almost wholly covered, but I stooped and cleared away the sand with my hands, later studying the object carefully and supplementing the moonlight with my electric torch.

Unlike the other very large rocks, this one was perfectly square-cut, with no convex or concave surface. It seemed, too, to be of a dark basaltic substance, wholly dissimilar to the granite and sandstone and occasional concrete of the now familiar fragments.

Suddenly I rose, turned, and ran for the camp at top speed. It was a wholly unconscious and irrational flight, and only when I was close to my tent did I fully realize why I had run. Then it came to me. The queer dark stone was something which I had dreamed and read about, and which was linked with the uttermost horrors of the aeon-old legendry.

It was one of the blocks of that basaltic elder masonry which the fabled Great Race held in such fear—the tall, windowless ruins left by those brooding, half-material, alien things that festered in earth's nether abysses and against whose windlike, invisible forces the trapdoors were sealed and the sleepless sentinels posted.

I remained awake all night, but by dawn realized how silly I had been to let the shadow of a myth upset me. Instead of being frightened, I should have had a discoverer's enthusiasm.

The next forenoon I told the others about my find, and Dyer, Freeborn, Boyle, my son and I set out to view the anomalous block. Failure, however, confronted us. I had formed no clear idea of the stone's location and a late wind had wholly altered the hillocks of shifting sand.

VI

I come now to the crucial and most difficult part of my narrative—all the more difficult because I cannot be quite certain of its reality. At times I feel uncomfortably sure that I was not dreaming or deluded; and it is this feeling—in view of the stupendous implications which the objective truth of my experience would raise—which impels me to make this record.

My son—a trained psychologist with the fullest and most sympathetic knowledge of my whole case—shall be the primary judge of what I have to tell.

First let me outline the externals of the matter, as those at the camp know them. On the night of July 17–18, after a windy day, I retired early but could not sleep. Rising shortly before eleven and afflicted as usual with that strange feeling regarding the northeastward terrain, I set out on one of my typical nocturnal walks, seeing and greeting only one person—an Australian miner named Tupper—as I left our precincts.

The moon, slightly past full, shone from a clear sky, and drenched the ancient sands with a white, leprous radiance which seemed to me somehow infinitely evil. There was no longer any wind, nor did any return for nearly five hours, as amply attested by Tupper and others who saw me walking rapidly across the pallid, secret-guarding hillocks toward the northeast.

About 3:30 A.M., a violent wind blew up, waking everyone in camp and felling three of the tents. The sky was unclouded, and the desert still blazed with that leprous moonlight. As the party saw to the tents my absence was noted, but in view of my previous walks this circumstance gave no one alarm. And yet, as many as three men—all Australians—seemed to feel something sinister in the air.

Mackenzie explained to Professor Freeborn that this was a fear picked up from blackfellow folklore—the natives having woven a curious fabric of malignant myth about the high winds which at long intervals sweep across the sands under a clear sky. Such winds, it is whispered, blow out of the great stone huts under the ground, where terrible things have happened—and are never felt except near places where the big marked stones are scattered. Close to four the gale subsided as suddenly as it had begun, leaving the sand hills in new and unfamiliar shapes.

It was just past five, with the bloated, fungoid moon sinking in the west, when I staggered into camp—hatless, tattered, features scratched and ensanguined, and without my electric torch. Most of the men had returned to bed, but Professor Dyer was smoking a pipe in front of his tent.

Seeing my winded and almost frenzied state, he called Dr. Boyle, and the two of them got me on my cot and made me comfortable. My son, roused by the stir, soon joined them, and they all tried to force me to lie still and attempt sleep.

But there was no sleep for me. My psychological state was very extraordinary—different from anything I had previously suffered. After a time I insisted upon talking—nervously and elaborately explaining my condition.

I told them I had become fatigued, and had lain down in the sand for a nap. There had, I said, been dreams even more frightful than usual—and when I was awaked by the sudden high wind my overwrought nerves had snapped. I had fled in panic, frequently falling over half-buried stones and thus gaining my tattered and bedraggled aspect. I must have slept long—hence the hours of my absence.

Of anything strange either seen or experienced I hinted absolutely nothing—exercising the greatest self-control in that respect. But I spoke of a change of mind regarding the whole work of the expedition, and urged a halt in all digging toward the northeast.

My reasoning was patently weak—for I mentioned a dearth of blocks, a wish not to offend the superstitious miners, a possible shortage of funds from the college, and other things either untrue or irrelevant. Naturally, no one paid the least attention to my new wishes—not even my son, whose concern for my health was obvious.

The next day I was up and around the camp, but took no part in the excavations. I decided to return home as soon as possible for the sake of my nerves, and my son promised to fly me in the plane to Perth—a thousand miles to the southwest—as soon as he had surveyed the region I wished let alone.

If, I reflected, the thing I had seen was still visible, I might decide to attempt a specific warning even at the cost of ridicule. It was just conceivable that the miners who knew the local folklore might back me up. Humoring me, my son made the survey that very afternoon, flying over all the terrain my walk could possibly have covered. Yet nothing of what I had found remained in sight.

It was the case of the anomalous basalt block all over again—the shifting sand had wiped out every trace. For an instant I half-regretted having lost a certain awesome object in my stark fright—but now I know that the loss was merciful. I can still believe my whole experience an illusion—especially if, as I devoutly hope, that hellish abyss is never found.

Wingate took me to Perth on July 20, though declining to abandon the expedition and return home. He stayed with me until the twenty-fifth, when the steamer for Liverpool sailed. Now, in the cabin of the *Empress,* I am pondering long and frantically upon the entire matter, and have decided that my son, at least, must be informed. It shall rest with him whether to diffuse the matter more widely.

In order to meet any eventuality I have prepared this summary of my background—as already known in a scattered way to others—and will now tell as briefly as possible what seemed to happen during my absence from the camp that hideous night.

Nerves on edge, and whipped into a kind of perverse eagerness by that inexplicable, dread-mingled, mnemonic urge toward the northeast, I plodded on beneath the evil, burning moon. Here and there I saw, half-shrouded by sand, those primal cyclopean blocks left from nameless and forgotten aeons.

The incalculable age and brooding horror of this monstrous waste began to oppress me as never before, and I could not keep from thinking of my maddening dreams, of the frightful legends which lay behind them and of the present fears of natives and miners concerning the desert and its carven stones.

And yet I plodded on as if to some eldritch rendezvous—more and more assailed by bewildering fancies, compulsions and pseudomemories. I thought of some of the possible contours of the lines of stones as seen by my son from the air, and wondered why they seemed at once so ominous and so familiar. Something was fumbling and rattling at the latch of my recollection, while another unknown force sought to keep the portal barred.

The night was windless, and the pallid sand curved upward and downward like frozen waves of the sea. I had no goal, but somehow plowed along as if with fate-bound assurance. My dreams welled up into the waking world, so that each sand-embedded megalith seemed part of endless rooms and corridors of prehuman masonry, carved and hieroglyphed with symbols that I knew too well from years of custom as a captive mind of the Great Race.

At moments I fancied I saw those omniscient, conical horrors moving about at their accustomed tasks, and I feared to look down lest I find myself one with them in aspect. Yet all the while I saw the sand-covered blocks as well as the rooms and corridors; evil, burning moon as well as the lamps of luminous crystal; the endless desert as well as the waving ferns beyond the windows. I was awake and dreaming at the same time.

I do not know how long or how far—or indeed, in just what direction—I had walked when I first spied the heap of blocks bared by the day's wind. It was the largest group in one place that I had seen so far, and so sharply did it impress me that the visions of fabulous aeons faded suddenly away.

Again there were only the desert and the evil moon and the shards of an unguessed past. I drew close and paused, and cast the added light of my electric torch over the tumbled pile. A hillock had blown away, leaving a low, irregularly round mass of megaliths and smaller fragments some forty feet across and from two to eight feet high.

From the very outset I realized that there was some utterly unprecedented quality about those stones. Not only was the mere number of them quite without parallel, but something in the sandworn traces of design arrested me as I scanned them under the mingled beams of the moon and my torch.

Not that any one differed essentially from the earlier specimens we had found. It was something subtler than that. The impression did not come when I looked at one block alone, but only when I ran my eye over several almost simultaneously.

Then, at last, the truth dawned upon me. The curvilinear patterns on many of those blocks were closely related—parts of one vast decorative conception. For the first time in this aeon-shaking waste I had come upon a mass of masonry in its old position—tumbled and fragmentary, it is true, but nonetheless existing in a very definite sense.

Mounting at a low place, I clambered laboriously over the heap; here and there clearing away the sand with my fingers, and constantly striving to interpret varieties of size, shape, and style and relationships of design.

After a while I could vaguely guess at the nature of the bygone structure, and at the designs which had once stretched over the vast surfaces of the primal masonry. The perfect identity of the whole with some of my dream glimpses appalled and unnerved me.

This was once a cyclopean corridor thirty feet wide and thirty feet tall, paved with octagonal blocks and solidly vaulted overhead. There would have been rooms opening off on the right, and at the farther end one of those strange inclined planes would have wound down to still lower depths.

I started violently as these conceptions occurred to me, for there was more in them than the blocks themselves had supplied. How did I know that this level should have been far underground? How did I know that the plane leading upward should have been behind me? How did I know that the long subterrane passage to the Square of Pillars ought to lie on the left one level above me?

How did I know that the room of machines and the rightward-leading tunnel to the central archives ought to lie two levels below? How did I know that there would be one of those horrible metal-banded trapdoors at the very bottom four levels down? Bewildered by this intrusion from the dream world, I found myself shaking and bathed in a cold perspiration.

Then, as a last, intolerable touch, I felt that faint, insidious stream of cool air trickling upward from a depressed place near the center of the huge heap. Instantly, as once before, my visions faded, and I saw again only the evil moonlight, the brooding desert and the spreading tumulus of paleogean masonry. Something real and tangible, yet fraught with infinite suggestions of nighted mystery, now confronted me. For that stream of air could argue but one thing—a hidden gulf of great size beneath the disordered blocks on the surface.

My first thought was of the sinister blackfellow legends of vast underground huts among the megaliths where horrors happen and great winds are born. Then thoughts of my own dreams came back, and I felt dim pseudomemories tugging at my mind. What manner of place lay below me? What primal, inconceivable source of age-old myth cycles and haunting nightmares might I be on the brink of uncovering?

It was only for a moment that I hesitated, for more than curiosity and scientific zeal was driving me on and working against my growing fear.

I seemed to move almost automatically, as if in the clutch of some compelling fate. Pocketing my torch, and struggling with a strength that I had not thought I possessed, I wrenched aside first one titan fragment of stone and then another, till there welled up a strong draft whose dampness contrasted oddly with the desert's dry air. A black rift began to yawn, and at length—when I had pushed away every fragment small enough to budge—the leprous moonlight blazed on an aperture of ample width to admit me.

I drew out my torch and cast a brilliant beam into the opening. Below me was a chaos of tumbled masonry, sloping roughly down toward the north at an angle of about forty-five degrees, and evidently the result of some bygone collapse from above.

Between its surface and the ground level was a gulf of impenetrable blackness at whose upper edge were signs of gigantic, stress-heaved vaulting. At this point, it appeared, the desert's sands lay directly upon a floor of some titan structure of earth's youth—how preserved through aeons of geologic convulsion I could not then and cannot now even attempt to guess.

In retrospect, the barest idea of a sudden lone descent into such a doubtful abyss—and at a time when one's whereabouts were unknown to any living soul—seems like the utter apex of insanity. Perhaps it was—yet that night I embarked without hesitancy upon such a descent.

Again there was manifest that lure and driving of fatality which had all along seemed to direct my course. With torch flashing intermittently to save the battery, I commenced a mad scramble down the sinister, cyclopean incline below the opening—sometimes facing forward as I found good hand and foot holds, and at other times turning to face the heap of megaliths as I clung and fumbled more precariously.

In two directions beside me, distant walls of carven, crumbling masonry loomed dimly under the direct beams of my torch. Ahead, however, was darkness.

I kept no track of time during my downward scramble. So seething with baffling hints and images was my mind that all objective matters seemed withdrawn to incalculable distances. Physical sensation was dead, and even fear remained as a wraithlike, inactive gargoyle leering impotently at me.

Eventually I reached a level floor strewn with fallen blocks, shapeless fragments of stone, and sand and detritus of every kind. On either side—perhaps thirty feet apart—rose massive walls culminating in huge groinings. That they were carved I could just discern, but the nature of the carvings was beyond my perception.

What held me most was the vaulting overhead. The beam from my torch could not reach the roof, but the lower parts of the monstrous arches stood out distinctly. And so perfect was their identity with what I had seen in countless dreams of the elder world, that I trembled actively for the first time.

Behind and high above, a faint luminous blur told of the distant moonlight world outside. Some vague shred of caution warned me that I should not let it out of my sight, lest I have no guide for my return.

I now advanced toward the wall at my left, where the traces of carving were plainest. The littered floor was nearly as hard to traverse as the downward heap had been, but I managed to pick my difficult way.

At one place I heaved aside some blocks and kicked away the detritus to see what the pavement was like, and shuddered at the utter, fateful familiarity of the great octagonal stones whose buckled surface still held roughly together.

Reaching a convenient distance from the wall, I cast the searchlight slowly and carefully over its worn remnants of carving. Some bygone influx of water seemed to have acted on the sandstone surface, while there were curious incrustations which I could not explain.

In places the masonry was very loose and distorted, and I wondered how many aeons more this primal, hidden edifice could keep its remaining traces of form amidst earth's heavings.

But it was the carvings themselves that excited me most. Despite their time-crumbled state, they were relatively easy to trace at close range; and the complete, intimate familiarity of every detail almost stunned my imagination. That the major attributes of this hoary masonry should be familiar was not beyond normal credibility.

Powerfully impressing the weavers of certain myths, they had become embodied in a stream of cryptic lore which, somehow, coming to my notice during the amnesic period, had evoked vivid images in my subconscious mind.

But how could I explain the exact and minute fashion in which each line and spiral of these strange designs tallied with what I had dreamed for more than a score of years? What obscure, forgotten iconography could have reproduced each subtle shading and *nuance* which so persistently, exactly and unvaryingly besieged my sleeping vision night after night?

For this was no chance or remote resemblance. Definitely and absolutely, the millennially ancient, aeon-hidden corridor in which I stood was the original of something I knew in sleep as intimately as I knew my own house in Crane Street, Arkham. True, my dreams showed the place in its undecayed prime; but the identity was no less real on that account. I was wholly and horribly oriented.

The particular structure I was in was known to me. Known, too, was its place in that terrible elder city of dream. That I could visit unerringly any point in that structure or in that city which had escaped the changes and devastations of uncounted ages, I realized with hideous and instinctive certainty. What in heaven's name could all this mean? How had I come to know what I knew? And what awful reality could lie behind those antique tales of the beings who had dwelt in this labyrinth of primordial stone?

Words can convey only fractionally the welter of dread and bewilderment which ate at my spirit. I knew this place. I knew what lay below me, and what had lain overhead before the myriad towering stories had fallen to dust and debris and the desert. No need now, I thought with a shudder, to keep that faint blur of moonlight in view.

I was torn betwixt a longing to flee and a feverish mixture of burning curiosity and driving fatality. What had happened to this monstrous megalopolis of old in the millions of years since the time of my dreams? Of the subterrane mazes which had underlain the city and linked all the titan towers, how much had still survived the writhings of earth's crust?

Had I come upon a whole buried world of unholy archaism? Could I still find the house of the writing master, and the tower where S'gg'ha, the captive mind from the star-headed vegetable carnivores of Antarctica, had chiseled certain pictures on the blank spaces of the walls?

Would the passage at the second level down to the hall of the alien minds be still unchoked and traversable? In that hall the captive mind of an incredible entity—a half-plastic denizen of the hollow interior of an unknown trans-Plutonian planet eighteen million years in the future—had kept a certain thing which it had modeled from clay.

I shut my eyes and put my hand to my head in a vain, pitiful effort to drive these insane dream fragments from my consciousness. Then, for the first time I felt acutely the coolness, motion and dampness of the surrounding air. Shuddering, I realized that a vast chain of aeon-dead black gulfs must indeed be yawning somewhere beyond and below me.

I thought of the frightful chambers and corridors and inclines as I recalled them from my dreams. Would the way to the central archives still be open? Again that driving fatality tugged insistently at my brain as I recalled the awesome records that once lay cased in those rectangular vaults of rustless metal.

There, said the dreams and legends, had reposed the whole history, past and future, of the cosmic space-time continuum—written by captive minds from every orb and every age in the solar system. Madness, of course—but had I not now stumbled into a nighted world as mad as I?

I thought of the locked metal shelves, and of the curious knob-twistings needed to open each one. My own came vividly into my consciousness. How often had I gone through that intricate routine of varied turns and pressures in the terrestrial vertebrate section on the lowest level! Every detail was fresh and familiar.

If there were such a vault as I had dreamed of, I could open it in a moment. It was then that madness took me utterly. An instant later, and I was leaping and stumbling over the rocky debris toward the well-remembered incline to the depths below.

VII

From that point forward my impressions are scarcely to be relied on—indeed, I still possess a final, desperate hope that they all form parts of some demoniac dream or illusion born of delirium. A fever raged in my brain, and everything came to me through a kind of haze—sometimes only intermittently.

The rays of my torch shot feebly into the engulfing blackness, bringing phantasmal flashes of hideously familiar walls and carvings, all blighted with the decay of ages. In one place a tremendous mass of vaulting had fallen, so that I had to clamber over a mighty mound of stones reaching almost to the ragged, grotesquely stalactited roof.

It was all the ultimate apex of nightmare, made worse by that blasphemous tug of pseudomemory. One thing only was unfamiliar, and that was my own size in relation to the monstrous masonry. I felt oppressed by a sense of unwonted smallness, as if the sight of these towering walls from a mere human body was something wholly new and abnormal. Again and again I looked nervously down at myself, vaguely disturbed by the human form I possessed.

Onward through the blackness of the abyss I leaped, plunged and staggered—often falling and bruising myself, and once nearly shattering my torch. Every stone and corner of that demoniac gulf was known to me, and at many points I stopped to cast beams of light through choked and crumbling, yet familiar, archways.

Some rooms had totally collapsed; others were bare, or debris filled. In a few I saw masses of metal—some fairly intact, some broken, and some crushed or battered—which I recognized as the colossal pedestals or tables of my dreams. What they could in truth have been, I dared not guess.

I found the downward incline and began its descent—though after a time halted by a gaping, ragged chasm whose narrowest point could not be much less than four feet across. Here the stonework had fallen through, revealing incalculable inky depths beneath.

I knew there were two more cellar levels in this titan edifice, and trembled with fresh panic as I recalled the metal-clamped trapdoor on the lowest one. There could be no guards now—for what had lurked beneath had long since done its hideous work and sunk into its long decline. By the time of the posthuman beetle race it would be quite dead. And yet, as I thought of the native legends, I trembled anew.

It cost me a terrible effort to vault that yawning chasm, since the littered floor prevented a running start—but madness drove me on. I chose a place close to the left-hand wall—where the rift was least wide and the landing spot reasonably clear of dangerous debris—and after one frantic moment reached the other side in safety.

At last, gaining the lower level, I stumbled on past the archway of the room of machines, within which were fantastic ruins of metal, half-buried beneath fallen vaulting. Everything was where I knew it would be, and I climbed confidently over the heaps which barred the entrance of a vast transverse corridor. This, I realized, would take me under the city to the central archives.

Endless ages seemed to unroll as I stumbled, leaped and crawled along that debris-cluttered corridor. Now and then I could make out carvings on the age-stained walls—some familiar, others seemingly added since the period of my dreams. Since this was a subterrane house-connecting highway, there were no archways save when the route led through the lower levels of various buildings.

At some of these intersections I turned aside long enough to look down well-remembered rooms. Twice only did I find any radical changes from what I had dreamed of—and in one of these cases I could trace the sealed-up outlines of the archway I remembered.

I shook violently, and felt a curious surge of retarding weakness as I steered a hurried and reluctant course through the crypt of one of those great windowless, ruined towers whose alien, basalt masonry bespoke a whispered and horrible origin.

This primal vault was round and fully two hundred feet across, with nothing carved upon the dark-hued stonework. The floor was here free from anything save dust and sand, and I could see the apertures leading upward and downward. There were no stairs nor inclines—indeed, my dreams had pictured those elder towers as wholly untouched by the fabulous Great Race. Those who had built them had not needed stairs or inclines.

In the dreams, the downward aperture had been tightly sealed and nervously guarded. Now it lay open—black and yawning, and giving forth a current of cool, damp air. Of what limitless caverns of eternal night might brood below, I would not permit myself to think.

Later, clawing my way along a badly heaped section of the corridor, I reached a place where the roof had wholly caved in. The debris rose like a mountain, and I climbed up over it, passing through a vast, empty space where my torchlight could reveal neither walls nor vaulting. This, I reflected, must be the cellar of the house of the metal purveyors, fronting on the third square not far from the archives. What had happened to it I could not conjecture.

I found the corridor again beyond the mountain of detritus and stone, but after a short distance encountered a wholly choked place where the fallen vaulting almost touched the perilously sagging ceiling. How I managed to wrench and tear aside enough blocks to afford a passage, and how I dared disturb the tightly packed fragments when the least shift of equilibrium might have brought down all the tons of superincumbent masonry to crush me to nothingness, I do not know.

It was sheer madness that impelled and guided me—if, indeed, my whole underground adventure was not—as I hope—a hellish delusion or phase of dreaming. But I did make—or dream that I made—a passage that I could squirm through. As I wriggled over the mound of debris—my torch, switched continuously on, thrust deeply in my mouth—I felt myself torn by the fantastic stalactites of the jagged floor above me.

I was now close to the great underground archival structure which seemed to form my goal. Sliding and clambering down the farther side of the barrier, and picking my way along the remaining stretch of corridor with hand-held, intermittently flashing torch, I came at last to a low, circular crypt with arches—still in a marvelous state of preservation—opening off on every side.

The walls, or such parts of them as lay within reach of my torchlight, were densely hieroglyphed and chiseled with typical curvilinear symbols—some added since the period of my dreams.

This, I realized, was my fated destination, and I turned at once through a familiar archway on my left. That I could find a clear passage up and down the incline to all the surviving levels, I had, oddly, little doubt. This vast, earth-protected pile, housing the annals of all the solar system, had been built with supernal skill and strength to last as long as the system itself.

Blocks of stupendous size poised with mathematical genius and bound with cements of incredible toughness had combined to form a mass as firm as the planet's rocky core. Here, after ages more prodigious than I could sanely grasp, its buried bulk stood in all its essential contours, the vast, dust-drifted floors scarce sprinkled with litter elsewhere so dominant.

The relatively easy walking from this point onward went curiously to my head. All the frantic eagerness hitherto frustrated by obstacles now took itself out in a kind of febrile speed, and I literally raced along the low-roofed, monstrously well-remembered aisles beyond the archway.

I was past being astonished by the familiarity of what I saw. On every hand the great hieroglyphed metal shelf doors loomed monstrously; some yet in place, others sprung open, and still others bent and buckled under bygone geological stresses not quite strong enough to shatter the titan masonry.

Here and there a dust-covered heap beneath a gaping, empty shelf seemed to indicate where cases had been shaken down by earth tremors. On occasional pillars were great symbols and letters proclaiming classes and subclasses of volumes.

Once I paused before an open vault where I saw some of the accustomed metal cases still in position amidst the omnipresent gritty dust. Reaching up, I dislodged one of the thinner specimens with some difficulty, and rested it on the floor for inspection. It was titled in the prevailing curvilinear hieroglyphs, though something in the arrangement of the characters seemed subtly unusual.

The odd mechanism of the hooked fastener was perfectly well known to me, and I snapped up the still rustless and workable lid and drew out the book within. The latter, as expected, was some twenty by fifteen inches in area, and two inches thick; the thin metal covers opening at the top.

Its tough cellulose pages seemed unaffected by the myriad cycles of time they had lived through, and I studied the queerly pigmented, brush-drawn letters of the text—symbols unlike either the usual curved hieroglyphs or any alphabet known to human scholarship—with a haunting, half-aroused memory.

It came to me that this was the language used by a captive mind I had known slightly in my dreams—a mind from a large asteroid on which had survived much of the archaic life and lore of the primal planet whereof it formed a fragment. At the same time I recalled that this level of the archives was devoted to volumes dealing with the nonterrestrial planets.

As I ceased poring over this incredible document, I saw that the light of my torch was beginning to fail, hence quickly inserted the extra battery I always had with me. Then, armed with the stronger radiance, I resumed my feverish racing through unending tangles of aisles and corridors—recognizing now and then some familiar shelf, and vaguely annoyed by the acoustic conditions which made my footfalls echo incongruously in these catacombs.

The very prints of my shoes behind me in the millennially untrodden dust made me shudder. Never before, if my mad dreams held anything of truth, had human feet pressed upon those immemorial pavements.

Of the particular goal of my insane racing, my conscious mind held no hint. There was, however, some force of evil potency pulling at my dazed will and buried recollection, so that I vaguely felt I was not running at random.

I came to a downward incline and followed it to profound depths. Floors flashed by me as I raced, but I did not pause to explore them. In my whirling brain there had begun to beat a certain rhythm which set my right hand twitching in unison. I wanted to unlock something, and felt that I knew all the intricate twists and pressures needed to do it. It would be like a modern safe with a combination lock.

Dream or not, I had once known and still knew. How any dream—or any scrap of unconsciously absorbed legend—could have taught me a detail so minute, so intricate and so complex, I did not attempt to explain to myself. I was beyond all coherent thought. For was not this whole experience—this shocking familiarity with a set of unknown ruins, and this monstrously exact identity of everything before me with what only dreams and scraps of myth could have suggested—a horror beyond all reason?

Probably it was my basic conviction then—as it is now during my saner moments—that I was not awake at all, and that the entire buried city was a fragment of febrile hallucination.

Eventually, I reached the lowest level and struck off to the right of the incline. For some shadowy reason I tried to soften my steps, even though I lost speed thereby. There was a space I was afraid to cross on this last, deeply buried floor.

As I drew near it I recalled what thing in that space I feared. It was merely one of the metal-barred and closely guarded trapdoors. There would be no guards now, and on that account I trembled and tiptoed as I had done in passing through that black basalt vault where a similar trapdoor had yawned.

I felt a current of cold damp air, as I had felt there, and wished that my course led in another direction. Why I had to take the particular course I was taking, I did not know.

When I came to the space I saw that the trapdoor yawned wildly open. Ahead, the shelves began again, and I glimpsed on the floor before one of them a heap very thinly covered with dust, where a number of cases had recently fallen. At the same moment a fresh wave of panic clutched me, though for some time I could not discover why.

Heaps of fallen cases were not uncommon, for all through the aeons this lightless labyrinth had been racked by the heavings of earth and had echoed at intervals to the deafening clatter of toppling objects. It was only when I was nearly across the space that I realized why I shook so violently.

Not the heap, but something about the dust of the level floor, was troubling me. In the light of my torch it seemed as if that dust were not as even as it ought to be—there were places where it looked thinner, as if it had been disturbed not many months before. I could not be sure, for even the apparently thinner places were dusty enough; yet a certain suspicion of regularity in the fancied unevenness was highly disquieting.

When I brought the torchlight close to one of the queer places I did not like what I saw—for the illusion of regularity became very great. It was as if there were regular lines of composite impressions—impressions that went in threes, each slightly over a foot square, and consisting of five nearly circular three-inch prints, one in advance of the other four.

These possible lines of foot-square impressions appeared to lead in two directions, as if something had gone somewhere and returned. They were, of course, very faint, and may have been illusions or accidents; but there was an element of dim, fumbling terror about the way I thought they ran. For at one end of them was the heap of cases which must have clattered down not long before, while at the other end was the ominous trapdoor with the cool, damp wind, yawning unguarded down to abysses past imagination.

VIII

That my strange sense of compulsion was deep and overwhelming is shown by its conquest of my fear. No rational motive could have drawn me on after that hideous suspicion of prints and the creeping dream memories it excited. Yet my right hand, even as it shook with fright, still twitched rhythmically in its eagerness to turn a lock it hoped to find. Before I knew it I was past the heap of lately fallen cases and running on tiptoe through aisles of utterly unbroken dust toward a point which I seemed to know morbidly, horribly well.

My mind was asking itself questions whose origin and relevancy I was only beginning to guess. Would the shelf be reachable by a human body? Could my human hand master all the aeon-remembered motions of the lock? Would the lock be undamaged and workable? And what would I do—what dare I do—with what—as I now commenced to realize—I both hoped and feared to find? Would it prove the awesome, brain-shattering truth of something past normal conception, or show only that I was dreaming?

The next I knew I had ceased my tiptoed racing and was standing still, staring at a row of maddeningly familiar hieroglyphed shelves. They were in a state of almost perfect preservation, and only three of the doors in this vicinity had sprung open.

My feelings toward these shelves cannot be described—so utter and insistent was the sense of old acquaintance. I was looking high up at a row near the top and wholly out of my reach, and wondering how I could climb to best advantage. An open door four rows from the bottom would help, and the locks of the closed doors formed possible holds for hands and feet. I would grip the torch between my teeth, as I had in other places where both hands were needed. Above all I must make no noise.

How to get down what I wished to remove would be difficult, but I could probably hook its movable fastener in my coat collar and carry it like a knapsack. Again I wondered whether the lock would be undamaged. That I could repeat each familiar motion I had not the least doubt. But I hoped the thing would not scrape or creak—and that my hand could work it properly.

Even as I thought these things I had taken the torch in my mouth and began to climb. The projecting locks were poor supports; but, as I had expected, the opened shelf helped greatly. I used both the swinging door and the edge of the aperture itself in my ascent, and managed to avoid any loud creaking.

Balanced on the upper edge of the door, and leaning far to my right, I could just reach the lock I sought. My fingers, half-numb from climbing, were very clumsy at first; but I soon saw that they were anatomically adequate. And the memory rhythm was strong in them.

Out of unknown gulfs of time the intricate, secret motions had somehow reached my brain correctly in every detail—for after less than five minutes of trying there came a click whose familiarity was all the more startling because I had not consciously anticipated it. In another instant the metal door was slowly swinging open with only the faintest grating sound.

Dazedly I looked over the row of grayish case ends thus exposed, and felt a tremendous surge of some wholly inexplicable emotion. Just within reach of my right hand was a case whose curving hieroglyphs made me shake with a pang infinitely more complex than one of mere fright. Still shaking, I managed to dislodge it amidst a shower of gritty flakes, and ease it over toward myself without any violent noise.

Like the other case I had handled, it was slightly more than twenty by fifteen inches in size, with curved mathematical designs in low relief. In thickness it just exceeded three inches.

Crudely wedging it between myself and the surface I was climbing, I fumbled with the fastener and finally got the hook free. Lifting the cover, I shifted the heavy object to my back, and let the hook catch hold of my collar. Hands now free, I awkwardly clambered down to the dusty floor and prepared to inspect my prize.

Kneeling in the gritty dust, I swung the case around and rested it in front of me. My hands shook, and I dreaded to draw out the book within almost as much as I longed—and felt compelled—to do so. It had very gradually become clear to me what I ought to find, and this realization nearly paralyzed my faculties.

If the thing were there—and if I were not dreaming—the implications would be quite beyond the power of the human spirit to bear. What tormented me most was my momentary inability to feel that my surroundings were a dream. The sense of reality was hideous—and again becomes so as I recall the scene.

At length I tremblingly pulled the book from its container and stared fascinatedly at the well-known hieroglyphs on the cover. It seemed to be in prime condition, and the curvilinear letters of the title held me in almost as hypnotized a state as if I could read them. Indeed, I cannot swear that I did not actually read them in some transient and terrible access of abnormal memory.

I do not know how long it was before I dared to lift that thin metal cover. I temporized and made excuses to myself. I took the torch from my mouth and shut it off to save the battery. Then, in the dark, I collected my courage—finally lifting the cover without turning on the light. Last of all, I did indeed flash the torch upon the exposed page—steeling myself in advance to suppress any sound no matter what I should find.

I looked for an instant, then collapsed. Clenching my teeth, however, I kept silent. I sank wholly to the floor and put a hand to my forehead amidst the engulfing blackness. What I dreaded and expected was there. Either I was dreaming, or time and space had become a mockery.

I must be dreaming—but I would test the horror by carrying this thing back and showing it to my son if it were indeed a reality. My head swam frightfully, even though there were no visible objects in the unbroken gloom to swirl about me. Ideas and images of the starkest terror—excited by the vistas which my glimpse had opened up—began to throng in upon me and cloud my senses.

I thought of those possible prints in the dust, and trembled at the sound of my own breathing as I did so. Once again I flashed on the light and looked at the page as a serpent's victim may look at his destroyer's eyes and fangs.

Then, with clumsy fingers, in the dark, I closed the book, put it in its container, and snapped the lid and the curious, hooked fastener. This was what I must carry back to the outer world if it truly existed—if the whole abyss truly existed—if I, and the world itself, truly existed.

Just when I tottered to my feet and commenced my return I cannot be certain. It comes to me oddly—as a measure of my sense of separation from the normal world—that I did not even once look at my watch during those hideous hours underground.

Torch in hand, and with the ominous case under one arm, I eventually found myself tiptoeing in a kind of silent panic past the draft-giving abyss and those lurking suggestions of prints. I lessened my precautions as I climbed up the endless inclines, but could not shake off a shadow of apprehension which I had not felt on the downward journey.

I dreaded having to repass through that black basalt crypt that was older than the city itself, where cold drafts welled up from unguarded depths. I thought of that which the Great Race had feared, and of what might still be lurking—be it ever so weak and dying—down there. I thought of those five-circle prints and of what my dreams had told me of such prints —and of strange winds and whistling noises associated with them. And I thought of the tales of the modern blackfellows, wherein the horror of great winds and nameless ruins was dwelt upon.

I knew from a carven wall symbol the right floor to enter, and came at last—after passing that other book I had examined—to the great circular space with the branching archways. On my right, and at once recognizable, was the arch through which I had arrived. This I now entered, conscious that the rest of my course would be harder because of the tumbled state of the masonry outside the archive building. My new metal-cased burden weighed upon me, and I found it harder and harder to be quiet as I stumbled among debris and fragments of every sort.

Then I came to the ceiling-high mound of debris through which I had wrenched a scanty passage. My dread at wriggling through again was infinite, for my first passage had made some noise, and I now—after seeing those possible prints—dreaded sound above all things. The case, too, doubled the problem of traversing the narrow crevice.

But I clambered up the barrier as best I could, and pushed the case through the aperture ahead of me. Then, torch in mouth, I scrambled through myself—my back torn as before by stalactites.

As I tried to grasp the case again, it fell some distance ahead of me down the slope of the debris, making a disturbing clatter and arousing echoes which sent me into a cold perspiration. I lunged for it at once, and regained it without further noise—but a moment afterward the slipping of blocks under my feet raised a sudden and unprecedented din.

That din was my undoing. For, falsely or not, I thought I heard it answered in a terrible way from spaces far behind me. I thought I heard a shrill, whistling sound, like nothing else on earth, and beyond any adequate verbal description. If so, what followed has a grim irony—save for the panic of this thing, the second thing might never have happened.

As it was, my frenzy was absolute and unrelieved. Taking my torch in my hand and clutching feebly at the case, I leaped and bounded wildly ahead with no idea in my brain beyond a mad desire to race out of these nightmare ruins to the waking world of desert and moonlight which lay so far above.

I hardly knew it when I reached the mountain of debris which towered into the vast blackness beyond the caved-in roof, and bruised and cut myself repeatedly in scrambling up its steep slope of jagged blocks and fragments.

Then came the great disaster. Just as I blindly crossed the summit, unprepared for the sudden dip ahead, my feet slipped utterly and I found myself involved in a mangling avalanche of sliding masonry whose cannon-loud uproar split the black, cavern air in a deafening series of earth-shaking reverberations.

I have no recollection of emerging from this chaos, but a momentary fragment of consciousness shows me as plunging and tripping and scrambling along the corridor amidst the clangor—case and torch still with me.

Then, just as I approached that primal basalt crypt I had so dreaded, utter madness came. For as the echoes of the avalanche died down, there became audible a repetition of that frightful alien whistling I thought I had heard before. This time there was no doubt about it—and what was worse, it came from a point not behind but *ahead of me.*

Probably I shrieked aloud then. I have a dim picture of myself as flying through the hellish basalt vault of the elder things, and hearing that damnable alien sound piping up from the open, unguarded door of limitless nether blacknesses. There was a wind, too—not merely a cool, damp draft, but a violent, purposeful blast belching savagely and frigidly from that abominable gulf whence the obscene whistling came.

There are memories of leaping and lurching over obstacles of every sort, with that torrent of wind and shrieking sound growing moment by moment, and seeming to curl and twist purposefully around me as it struck out wickedly from the spaces behind and beneath.

Though in my rear, that wind had the odd effect of hindering instead of aiding my progress; as if it acted like a noose or lasso thrown around me. Heedless of the noise I made, I clattered over a great barrier of blocks and was again in the structure that led to the surface.

I recall glimpsing the archway to the room of machines and almost crying out as I saw the incline leading down to where one of those blasphemous trapdoors must be yawning two levels below. But instead of crying out I muttered over and over to myself that this was all a dream from which I must soon awake. Perhaps I was in camp—perhaps I was at home in Arkham. As these hopes bolstered up my sanity I began to mount the incline to the higher level.

I knew, of course, that I had the four-foot cleft to recross, yet was too wracked by other fears to realize the full horror until I came almost upon it. On my descent, the leap across had been easy—but could I clear the gap as readily when going uphill, and hampered by fright, exhaustion, the weight of the metal case and the anomalous backward tug of that demon wind? I thought of these things at the last moment, and thought also of the nameless entities which might be lurking in the black abysses below the chasm.

My wavering torch was growing feeble, but I could tell by some obscure memory when I neared the cleft. The chill blasts of wind and the nauseous whistling shrieks behind me were for the moment like a merciful opiate, dulling my imagination to the horror of the yawning gulf ahead. And then I became aware of the added blasts and whistling in front of me—tides of abomination surging up through the cleft itself from depths unimagined and unimaginable.

Now, indeed, the essence of pure nightmare was upon me. Sanity departed—and, ignoring everything except the animal impulse of flight, I merely struggled and plunged upward over the incline's debris as if no gulf had existed. Then I saw the chasm's edge, leaped frenziedly with every ounce of strength I possessed and was instantly engulfed in a pandemoniac vortex of loathsome sound and utter, materially tangible blackness.

That is the end of my experience, so far as I can recall. Any further impressions belong wholly to the domain of phantasmagoric delirium. Dream, madness and memory merged wildly together in a series of fantastic, fragmentary delusions which can have no relation to anything real.

There was a hideous fall through incalculable leagues of viscous, sentient darkness, and a babel of noises utterly alien to all that we know of the earth and its organic life. Dormant, rudimentary senses seemed to start into vitality within me, telling of pits and voids peopled by floating horrors and leading to sunless crags and oceans and teeming cities of windowless, basalt towers upon which no light ever shone.

Secrets of the primal planet and its immemorial aeons flashed through my brain without the aid of sight or sound, and there were known to me things which not even the wildest of former dreams had ever suggested. And all the while cold fingers of damp vapor clutched and picked at me, and that eldritch, damnable whistling shrieked fiendishly above all the alternations of babel and silence in the whirlpools of darkness around.

Afterward there were visions of the cyclopean city of my dreams—not in ruins, but just as I had dreamed of it. I was in my conical, nonhuman body again, and mingled with crowds of the Great Race and the captive minds who carried books up and down the lofty corridors and vast inclines.

Then, superimposed upon these pictures, were frightful, momentary flashes of a nonvisual consciousness involving desperate struggles, a writhing free from clutching tentacles of whistling wind, an insane, batlike flight through half-solid air, a feverish burrowing through the cyclone-whipped dark and a wild stumbling and scrambling over fallen masonry.

Once there was a curious, intrusive flash of half-sight—a faint, diffuse suspicion of bluish radiance far overhead. Then there came a dream of wind-pursued climbing and crawling—of wriggling into a blaze of sardonic moonlight through a jumble of debris which slid and collapsed after me amidst a morbid hurricane. It was the evil, monotonous beating of that maddening moonlight which at last told me of the return of what I had once known as the objective, waking world.

I was clawing prone through the sands of the Australian desert, and around me shrieked such a tumult of wind as I had never before known on our planet's surface. My clothing was in rags, and my whole body was a mass of bruises and scratches.

Full consciousness returned very slowly, and at no time could I tell just where delirious dream left off and true memory began. There had seemed to be a mound of titan blocks, an abyss beneath it, a monstrous revelation from the past and a nightmare horror at the end—but how much of this was real?

My flashlight was gone, and likewise my metal case I may have discovered. Had there been such a case—or any abyss—or any mound? Raising my head, I looked behind me, and saw only the sterile, undulant sands of the desert.

The demon wind died down, and the bloated, fungoid moon sank reddeningly in the west. I lurched to my feet and began to stagger southwestward toward the camp. What in truth had happened to me? Had I merely collapsed in the desert and dragged a dream-wracked body over miles of sand and buried blocks? If not, how could I bear to live any longer?

For, in this new doubt, all my faith in the myth-born unreality of my visions dissolved once more into the hellish older doubting. If that abyss was real, then the Great Race was real—and its blasphemous reachings and seizures in the cosmos-wide vortex of time were no myths or nightmares, but a terrible, soul-shattering actuality.

Had I, in full, hideous fact, been drawn back to a prehuman world of a hundred and fifty million years ago in those dark, baffling days of the amnesia? Had my present body been the vehicle of a frightful alien consciousness from paleogean gulfs of time?

Had I, as the captive mind of those shambling horrors, indeed known that accursed city of stone in its primordial heyday, and wriggled down those familiar corridors in the loathsome shape of my captor? Were those tormenting dreams of more than twenty years the offspring of stark, monstrous memories?

Had I once veritably talked with minds from reachless corners of time and space, learned the universe's secrets, past and to come, and written the annals of my own world for the metal cases of those titan archives? And were those others—those shocking elder things of the mad winds and demon pipings—in truth a lingering, lurking menace, waiting and slowly weakening in black abysses while varied shapes of life drag out their multimillennial courses on the planet's age-wracked surface?

I do not know. If that abyss and what it held were real, there is no hope. Then, all too truly, there lies upon this world of man a mocking and incredible shadow out of time. But, mercifully there is no proof that these things are other than fresh phases of my myth-born dreams. I did not bring back the metal case that would have been a proof, and so far those subterrane corridors have not been found.

If the laws of the universe are kind, they will never be found. But I must tell my son what I saw or thought I saw, and let him use his judgment as a psychologist in gauging the reality of my experience, and communicating this account to others.

I have said that the awful truth behind my tortured years of dreaming hinges absolutely upon the actuality of what I thought I saw in those cyclopean, buried ruins. It has been hard for me, literally, to set down that crucial revelation, though no reader can have failed to guess it. Of course, it lay in that book within the metal case—the case which I pried out of its lair amidst the dust of a million centuries.

No eye had seen, no hand had touched that book since the advent of man to this planet. And yet, when I flashed my torch upon it in that frightful abyss, I saw that the queerly pigmented letters on the brittle, aeon-browned cellulose pages were not indeed any nameless hieroglyphs of earth's youth. They were, instead, the letters of our familiar alphabet, spelling out the words of the English language in my own handwriting.

MARGARET TRUMAN

When I was a girl growing up in Missouri, I owned more books than toys. My father was raised on the great classics of literature—as for myself and my mother, mysteries have always been our favorite reading. I cannot recall when in my childhood I first read "The Cask of Amontillado," but the vivid remembrance of the story—and my delicious fright upon reading it—is with me to this day.

THE CASK OF AMONTILLADO

EDGAR ALLAN POE

The thousand injuries of Fortunato I had borne as I best could; but when he ventured upon insult, I vowed revenge. You, who so well know the nature of my soul, will not suppose, however, that I gave utterance to a threat. *At length* I would be avenged; this was a point definitively settled—but the very definitiveness with which it was resolved, precluded the idea of risk. I must not only punish, but punish with impunity. A wrong is unredressed when retribution overtakes its redresser. It is equally unredressed when the avenger fails to make himself felt as such to him who has done the wrong.

It must be understood that neither by word nor deed had I given Fortunato cause to doubt my good will. I continued, as was my wont, to smile in his face, and he did not perceive that my smile *now* was at the thought of his immolation.

He had a weak point—this Fortunato—although in other regards he was a man to be respected and even feared. He prided himself on his connoisseurship in wine. Few Italians have the true virtuoso spirit. For the most part their enthusiasm is adopted to suit the time and opportunity—to practice imposture upon the British and Austrian *millionnaires.* In painting and gemmary Fortunato, like his countrymen, was a quack—but in the matter of old wines he was sincere. In this respect I did not differ from him materially: I was skillful in the Italian vintages myself, and bought largely whenever I could.

It was about dusk, one evening during the supreme madness of the carnival season, that I encountered my friend. He accosted me with excessive warmth, for he had been drinking much. The man wore motley. He had on a tight-fitting parti-striped dress, and his head was surmounted by the conical cap and bells. I was so pleased to see him, that I thought I should never have done wringing his hand.

I said to him: "My dear Fortunato, you are luckily met. How remarkably well you are looking today! But I have received a pipe of what passes for Amontillado, and I have my doubts."

"How?" said he. "Amontillado? A pipe? Impossible! And in the middle of the carnival!"

"I have my doubts," I replied; "and I was silly enough to pay the full Amontillado price without consulting you in the matter. You were not to be found, and I was fearful of losing a bargain."

"Amontillado!"

"I have my doubts."

"Amontillado!"

"And I must satisfy them."

"Amontillado!"

"As you are engaged, I am on my way to Luchesi. If anyone has a critical turn, it is he. He will tell me . . ."

"Luchesi cannot tell Amontillado from sherry."

"And yet some fools will have it that his taste is a match for your own."

"Come, let us go."

"Whither?"

"To your vaults."

"My friend, no; I will not impose upon your good nature. I perceive you have an engagement. Luchesi . . ."

"I have no engagement—come."

"My friend, no. It is not the engagement, but the severe cold with which I perceive you are afflicted. The vaults are insufferably damp. They are encrusted with niter."

"Let us go, nevertheless. The cold is merely nothing. Amontillado! You have been imposed upon. And as for Luchesi, he cannot distinguish sherry from Amontillado."

Thus speaking, Fortunato possessed himself of my arm. Putting on a mask of black silk, and drawing a *roquelaire* closely about my person, I suffered him to hurry me to my palazzo.

There were no attendants at home; they had absconded to make merry in honor of the time. I had told them that I should not return until the morning, and had given them explicit orders not to stir from the house. These orders were sufficient, I well knew, to insure their immediate disappearance, one and all, as soon as my back was turned.

I took from their sconces two flambeaux, and giving one to Fortunato, bowed him through several suites of rooms to the archway that led into the vaults. I passed down a long and winding staircase, requesting him to be cautious as he followed. We came at length to the foot of the descent, and stood together on the damp ground of the catacombs of the Montresors.

The gait of my friend was unsteady, and the bells upon his cap jingled as he strode.

"The pipe?" said he.

"It is farther on," said I; "but observe the white webwork which gleams from these cavern walls."

He turned toward me, and looked into my eyes with two filmy orbs that distilled the rheum of intoxication.

"Niter?" he asked, at length.

"Niter," I replied. "How long have you had that cough?"

"Ugh! ugh! ugh!—ugh! ugh! ugh!—ugh! ugh! ugh!—ugh! ugh! ugh!—ugh! ugh! ugh!"

My poor friend found it impossible to reply for many minutes.

"It is nothing," he said, at last.

"Come," I said, with decision, "we will go back; your health is precious. You are rich, respected, admired, beloved; you are happy, as once I was. You are a man to be missed. For me it is no matter. We will go back; you will be ill, and I cannot be responsible. Besides, there is Luchesi . . ."

"Enough," he said; "the cough is a mere nothing; it will not kill me. I shall not die of a cough."

"True—true," I replied; "and, indeed, I had no intention of alarming you unnecessarily; but you should use all proper caution. A draught of this Médoc will defend us from the damps."

Here I knocked off the neck a bottle which I drew from a long row of its fellows that lay upon the mold.

"Drink," I said, presenting him the wine.

He raised it to his lips with a leer. He paused and nodded to me familiarly, while his bells jingled.

"I drink," he said, "to the buried that repose around us."

"And I to your long life."

He again took my arm, and we proceeded.

"These vaults," he said, "are extensive."

"The Montresors," I replied, "were a great and numerous family."

"I forget your arms."

"A huge human foot d'or, in a field azure; the foot crushes a serpent rampant whose fangs are embedded in the heel."

"And the motto?"

"Nemo me impune lacessit."

"Good!" he said.

The wine sparkled in his eyes and the bells jingled. My own fancy grew warm with the Médoc. We had passed through walls of piled bones, with casks and puncheons intermingling, into the inmost recesses of the catacombs. I paused again, and this time I made bold to seize Fortunato by an arm above the elbow.

"The niter!" I said; "see, it increases. It hangs like moss upon the vaults. We are below the river's bed. The drops of moisture trickle among the bones. Come, we will go back ere it is too late. Your cough . . ."

"It is nothing," he said; "let us go on. But first, another draught of the Médoc."

I broke and reached him a flagon of De Grâve. He emptied it at a breath. His eyes flashed with a fierce light. He laughed and threw the bottle upward with a gesticulation I did not understand.

I looked at him in surprise. He repeated the movement—a grotesque one.

"You do not comprehend?" he said.

"Not I," I replied.

"Then you are not of the brotherhood."

"How?"

"You are not of the masons."

"Yes, yes," I said; "yes, yes."

"You? Impossible! A mason?"

"A mason," I replied.

"A sign," he said.

"It is this," I answered, producing a trowel from beneath the folds of my *roquelaire.*

"You jest," he exclaimed, recoiling a few paces. "But let us proceed to the Amontillado."

"Be it so," I said, replacing the tool beneath the cloak, and again offering him my arm. He leaned upon it heavily. We continued our route in search of the Amontillado. We passed through a range of low arches, descended, passed on, and descending again, arrived at a deep crypt, in which the foulness of the air caused our flambeaux rather to glow than flame.

At the most remote end of the crypt there appeared another less spacious. Its walls had been lined with human remains, piled to the vault overhead, in the fashion of the great catacombs of Paris. Three sides of this interior crypt were still ornamented in this manner. From the fourth the bones had been thrown down, and lay promiscuously upon the earth, forming at one point a mound of some size. Within the wall thus exposed by the displacing of the bones, we perceived a still interior recess, in depth about four feet, in width three, in height six or seven. It seemed to have been constructed for no especial use within itself, but formed merely the interval between two of the colossal supports of the roof of the catacombs, and was backed by one of their circumscribing walls of solid granite.

It was in vain that Fortunato, uplifting his dull torch, endeavored to pry into the depth of the recess. Its termination the feeble light did not enable us to see.

"Proceed," I said, "herein is the Amontillado. As for Luchesi—"

"He is an ignoramus," interrupted my friend, as he stepped unsteadily forward, while I followed immediately at his heels. In an instant he had reached the extremity of the niche, and finding his progress arrested by the rock, stood stupidly bewildered. A moment more and I had fettered him to the granite. In its surface were two iron staples, distant from each other about two feet, horizontally. From one of these depended a short chain, from the other a padlock. Throwing the links about his waist, it was but the work of a few seconds to secure it. He was too much astounded to resist. Withdrawing the key I stepped back from the recess.

"Pass your hand," I said, "over the wall; you cannot help feeling the niter. Indeed it is *very* damp. Once more let me *implore* you to return. No? Then I must positively leave you. But I must first render you all the little attentions in my power."

"The Amontillado!" ejaculated my friend, not yet recovered from his astonishment.

"True," I replied; "the Amontillado."

As I said these words I busied myself among the pile of bones of which I had before spoken. Throwing them aside, I soon uncovered a quantity of building stone and mortar. With these materials and with the aid of my trowel, I began vigorously to wall up the entrance of the niche.

I hard scarcely laid the first tier of the masonry when I discovered that the intoxication of Fortunato had in a great measure worn off. The earliest indication I had of this was a low moaning cry from the depth of the recess. It was *not* the cry of a drunken man. There was then a long and obstinate silence. I laid the second tier, and the third, and the fourth; and then I heard the furious vibrations of the chain. The noise lasted for several minutes, during which, that I might hearken to it with the more satisfaction, I ceased my labors and sat down upon the bones. When at last the clanking subsided, I resumed the trowel, and finished without interruption the fifth, the sixth and the seventh tier. The wall was now nearly upon a level with my breast. I again paused, and holding the flambeaux over the masonwork, threw a few feeble rays upon the figure within.

A succession of loud and shrill screams, bursting suddenly from the throat of the chained form, seemed to thrust me violently back. For a brief moment I hesitated—I trembled. Unsheathing my rapier, I began to grope with it about the recess; but the thought of an instant reassured me. I placed my hand upon the solid fabric of the catacombs, and felt satisfied. I reapproached the wall. I replied to the yells of him who clamored. I reechoed—I aided—I surpassed them in volume and in strength. I did this, and the clamorer grew still.

It was now midnight, and my task was drawing to a close. I had completed the eighth, the ninth and the tenth tier. I had finished a portion of the last and the eleventh; there remained but a single stone to be fitted and plastered in. I struggled with its weight; I placed it partially in its destined position. But now there came from out the niche a low laugh that erected the hairs upon my head. It was succeeded by a sad voice, which I had difficulty in recognizing as that of the noble Fortunato. The voice said—

"Ha! ha! ha!—he! he!—a very good joke indeed—an excellent jest. We will have many a rich laugh about it at the palazzo—he! he! he!—over our wine—he! he! he!"

"The Amontillado!" I said.

"He! he! he!— he! he! he!—yes, the Amontillado. But is it not getting late? Will not they be awaiting us at the palazzo, the Lady Fortunato and the rest? Let us be gone."

"Yes," I said, "let us be gone."

"For the love of God, Montresor!"

"Yes," I said, "for the love of God!"

But to these words I hearkened in vain for a reply. I grew impatient. I called aloud:

"Fortunato!"

No answer. I called again:

"Fortunato!"

No answer still. I thrust a torch through the remaining aperture and let it fall within. There came forth in return only a jingling of the bells. My heart grew sick—on account of the dampness of the catacombs. I hastened to make an end of my labor. I forced the last stone into its position; I plastered it up. Against the new masonry I reerected the old rampart of bones. For the half of a century no mortal has disturbed them. *In pace requiescat!*